Sejanus

SCEPTRE

Sejanus

DAVID WISHART

SCEPTRE

Copyright © 1998 David Wishart

First published in 1998 by Hodder and Stoughton
A division of Hodder Headline PLC
A Sceptre book

The right of David Wishart to be identified as the Author of
the Work has been asserted by him in accordance with the
Copyright, Designs and Patents Act 1988.

10 9 8 7 6 5 4 3 2 1

A CIP catalogue record for this title is available from the British Library

ISBN 0 340 68446 1

Typeset by Palimpsest Book Production Limited,
Polmont, Stirlingshire
Printed and bound in Great Britain by
Clays Ltd, St Ives plc, Bungay, Suffolk

Hodder and Stoughton
A division of Hodder Headline PLC
338 Euston Road
London NW1 3BH

For the McMillans: Kathleen, Derek, Keith and Fiona. Hang on to the cover this time!

Dramatis Personae ∫

The story is set in AD31. Purely fictional characters are given in lower case.

IMPERIALS

AGRIPPINA: widow of Germanicus, and Gaius's mother (she was also the mother of the *other* Agrippina, whose child became the Emperor Nero). Currently in exile on Pandateria, where, two years later, she was to be starved to death.

DRUSUS (1): Tiberius's son and, following the death of Germanicus, his designated successor. He died in AD23, leaving a widow Livilla and a son Gemellus, who was to be one of Caligula's first victims.

DRUSUS (2): the second of Germanicus and Agrippina's sons (with Nero and Gaius). Viewed as a possible successor to Tiberius, but (AD30) arrested and imprisoned. He died in AD33, aged about twenty-six.

GAIUS: the future emperor Caligula (Caligula – Little Army Boot – is a nickname). Youngest son of Germanicus and Agrippina and so Tiberius's (adoptive) grandson. He succeeded Tiberius as emperor on 16 March AD37 and was murdered in a conspiracy four years later, after a reign noted for its arbitrary cruelty.

GERMANICUS: Tiberius's adopted son, husband of Agrippina and father of Gaius (Caligula). Died at Antioch, AD19.

LIVIA: the old empress, now dead; Augustus's widow and Tiberius's mother.

LIVILLA: Drusus (1)'s widow. She committed suicide in AD31.

NERO: the eldest of Germanicus and Agrippina's sons. Seen as a possible successor to Tiberius but died an exile (AD31). The name Nero was traditional to the Claudian family, and very popular. This Nero would have been the emperor Nero's maternal uncle.

SEJANUS, Lucius Aelius: commander of the Praetorian Guard and Tiberius's deputy at Rome.

TIBERIUS ('The Wart'): the emperor, permanently absent from Rome and living in seclusion on Capri.

SENATORS AND EQUESTRIANS

ARRUNTIUS, Lucius: a prominent senator opposed to Sejanus.

CELSUS, Gaius Vibius: Serenus's son. ('Celsus' is an invention: see Author's Note.)

CORDUS, Caesius: former governor of Crete and Cyrene, exiled for treason and extortion.

CORVINUS, Marcus Valerius Messalla: a Roman noble, now living in voluntary exile in Athens.

Cosconia: Corvinus's father's widow.

COTTA: Corvinus's uncle.

Crispus, Caelius: a dealer in rumours, currently employed at the Treasury.

FABATUS, Rubrius: a senator living beyond the Latin Gate.

LACO: overall commander of the City Watch.

LAMIA, Lucius Aelius: former governor of Syria, now a member of the Senate.

LATIARIS, Lucanius: one of the prosecutors in the Sabinus trial.

LENTULUS, Gnaeus Cornelius: an old friend of Tiberius's, accused with Tubero of involvement with Serenus.

MACRO, Sertorius: the commander of Tiberius's guard. As Sejanus's successor as Praetorian commander he was later to be instrumental in ensuring Caligula's election to the throne.

Marcia Fulvina: Perilla's aunt, living in the Alban Hills.

MESSALINUS, Marcus Valerius Messalla: Corvinus's late father.

PERILLA, Rufia: Corvinus's wife; the poet Ovid's stepdaughter.

PISO, Gnaeus Calpurnius: governor of Syria, tried for murder and treason eleven years previously. Now dead.

Priscus, Titus Helvius: Corvinus's mother's husband.

REGULUS, Publius Memmius: currently consul with Trio.

RUFUS, Publius Suillius: Perilla's former husband.

RUSTICUS, Junius: the senatorial archivist.

SABINUS, Titius: equestrian friend of Agrippina's, executed for treason.

SERENUS, Gaius Vibius: former Spanish governor, in exile on Amorgos.

SERVAEUS, Quintus: Germanicus's former lieutenant.

SILANUS, Gaius Junius: former Asian governor, exiled for treason and extortion. His brother Decimus had been exiled by Augustus for adultery with the emperor's granddaughter Julia.

SILANUS, Appius Junius: his son.

SILIUS, Gaius: former military governor of Upper Germany, condemned for treason.

TORQUATA, Junia: Gaius Silanus's sister, and currently chief Vestal.

TRIO, Lucius Fulcinius: current consul and a supporter of Sejanus.

TUBERO, Lucius Seius: Sejanus's stepbrother, accused of involvement with Serenus.

Vipsania: Corvinus's mother.

VITELLIUS, Publius: a prominent senator, and one of Sejanus's principal supporters.

OTHER CHARACTERS

Agron: an Illyrian, Corvinus's client and friend, now married and living in Ostia.

Alexis: one of Corvinus's slaves.

Bathyllus: Corvinus's head slave.

Brito: Marilla's maid.

Crito: a freedman.

Daphnis: a client of Corvinus's, now running Scylax's gymnasium.

EUDEMUS: an imperial doctor.

Felix: a freedman whom Corvinus first encounters on the Janiculan.

Festus: Rubrius Fabatus's gardener.

Lamprus: a very large freedman; Felix's colleague.

Latinius: Lippillus's next-door neighbour.

Lippillus, Decimus Flavonius: a friend of Corvinus's, now a regional Watch commander.

LYGDUS: a cookshop chef.

Marcina Paullina: Lippillus's stepmother.

Marilla: Sextus Marius's daughter (see Author's Note).

MARIUS, Sextus: a rich Spaniard; Marilla's father.

Meton: Corvinus's chef.

MONTANUS, Votienus: a Gaul, condemned for slandering Tiberius.

SACROVIR, Julius: a Gaul, leader (with Julius Florus) of the short-lived Gallic revolt of AD21.

Sarpedon: a Greek doctor.

THRASYLLUS: Tiberius's astrologer; an Alexandrian Greek whose predictions carried a great deal of weight with the emperor. He died in AD36, the year before Gaius's accession.

Valens: Lippillus's deputy.

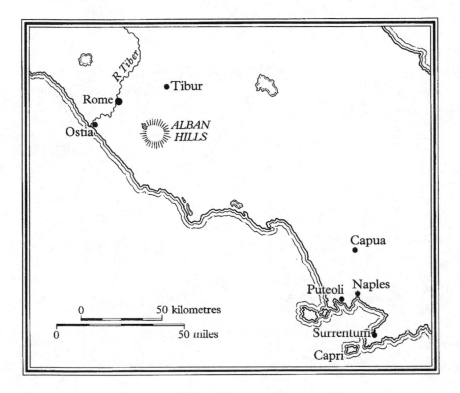

R. Tiber

•Tibur

Rome•

Ostia•

☀ ALBAN
HILLS

Capua
•

Puteoli Naples
•   •

0   50 kilometres

0   50 miles

Surrentum•

Capri

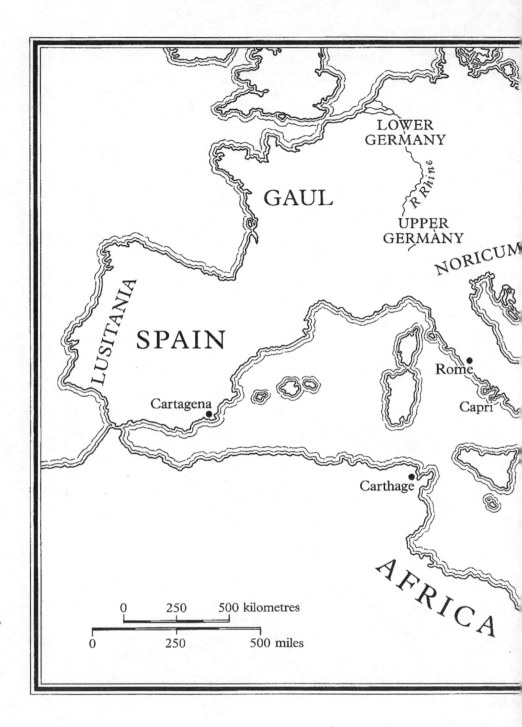

LOWER
GERMANY

R Rhine

GAUL

UPPER
GERMANY

NORICUM

LUSITANIA

SPAIN

Rome

Cartagena

Capri

Carthage

AFRICA

0   250   500 kilometres

0   250   500 miles

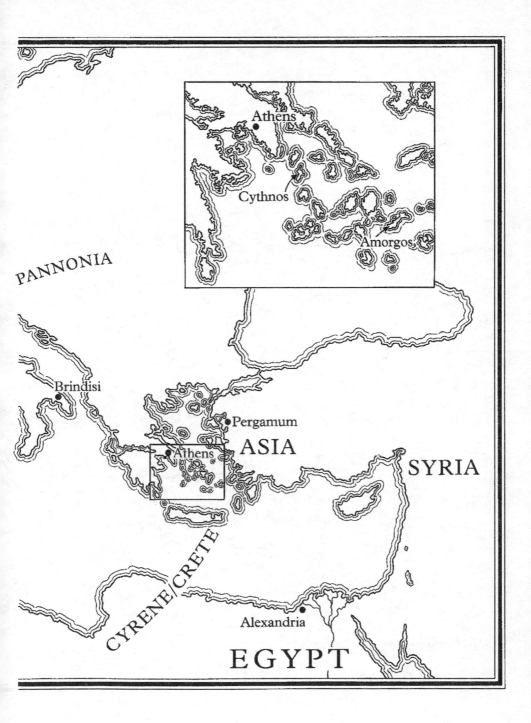

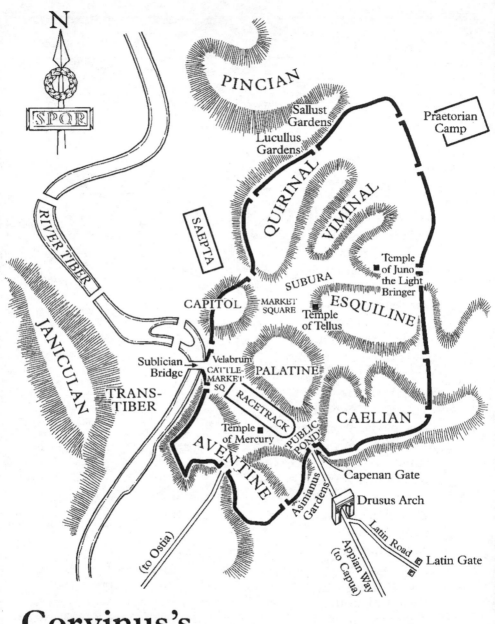

N

SPQR

PINCIAN

Sallust
Gardens

Lucullus
Gardens

QUIRINAL

VIMINAL

Praetorian
Camp

SAEPTA

RIVER TIBER

SUBURA

Temple
of Juno
the Light
Bringer

CAPITOL

MARKET
SQUARE

Temple
of Tellus

ESQUILINE

JANICULAN

Sublician
Bridge

Velabrum
CATTLE-
MARKET
SQ

PALATINE

TRANS-
TIBER

RACETRACK

CAELIAN

Temple
of Mercury

PUBLIC
POND

AVENTINE

Capenan Gate

Asinianus
Gardens

Drusus Arch

(to Ostia)

Latin Road

Latin Gate

Appian Way
(to Capua)

Corvinus's
Rome

I

The smoke from Dad's pyre gusted among the tombs, plain, ordinary woodsmoke, with no spices or perfume to mask the more unpleasant smells. His idea, not mine, and specified in his will: Tiberius disapproved of extravagant funerals, and the old trimmer Messalinus had toed a politically correct line to the last. Specks of soot blew into my eyes, and I wiped them away. After so long in Athens I'd forgotten how windy Rome could be.

Beside me, Perilla touched my hand.

'Marcus?' she said. 'Are you all right?'

'Sure.' I watched as the logs shifted. The fire was at its hottest, and I couldn't see the bier any more; he wouldn't last long at this rate. 'Why shouldn't I be?'

'No reason.' Her fingers wrapped round mine as we watched the flames together. 'I was just checking.'

It had been a good funeral; the old guy would've been pleased that even for a consular he'd rated such a healthy turnout, and I was glad his senatorial cronies had done him proud at the finish. Both consuls had come, Memmius Regulus and Fulcinius Trio. Trio was ignoring me. That came as no surprise. The last time we'd seen each other I'd accused him to his face of treason, and he'd never forgiven me because it had been the truth.

Also conspicuous by his presence was Trio's boss, the imperial rep Aelius Sejanus. An honour, maybe, but one I could do without, and one that Dad, to give him his due, wouldn't have wanted either. When we'd shaken hands and he'd offered his condolences the cold sweat had broken out all down my spine. The last and only time I'd seen Sejanus had been ten years before in Phlebas's curio shop, where I'd been buying an incense burner for Mother's husband Priscus. Ten years may be a long time, but Sejanus was the reason I'd spent them in Greece, and I hadn't forgotten why even if he had. At least I hoped he had. A handshake at a funeral was as much contact with him as I ever wanted, deal with Livia or no deal with Livia.

He was standing now a dozen yards off, his back to the flames, chatting to Trio and my Uncle Cotta. I was surprised he'd stayed so long now he was the Wart's de facto deputy and had an empire to run, but maybe it was business. I didn't want to know about that, either.

'Marcus, dear, I don't think you've met Cosconia.'

I turned. Mother had come up on my blind side. Even in her mourning and without jewellery she still looked good, and twenty years short of her real age. I felt Perilla's fingers tighten on mine as Dad's widow gave me a thin smile. We might not've met formally but I'd seen Cosconia around. Like Mother, she was a looker; if nothing else Dad had had a good eye for women. Cosconia wouldn't stay single for long, that was sure. Female relatives of Sejanus – even distant ones like she was – tended to get snapped up as soon as they hit the market.

'Pleased to meet you, Cosconia.' Perilla's fingers left mine and she held out her hand. Cosconia took it smiling. 'I'm so sorry about Messalinus.'

'He didn't suffer much.' The widow's voice was brisk, and I found myself wondering if she'd started looking round for a replacement already. 'He wasn't conscious towards the end.'

'I wish Marcus and I had got back in time.' Perilla was smiling too. 'But there wasn't a ship.'

'It doesn't matter.' Cosconia gave me a quick glance. 'And I'm glad to have met you both finally after all this time. These family quarrels are such silly things, aren't they, Marcus?'

'Yeah,' I said. 'Yeah, I suppose they are.' I looked away, at the flames. Dad was gone by now, the fire was beginning to die down and the pyre was collapsing in on itself. People would be getting ready to call it a day and head for home and a cup of warm spiced wine. Some of the older ones, like Appianus who'd read the funeral speech, had left already, but there were still a few who looked like hanging on to the very end when the embers were doused and the bones cooled with wine and put in the urn. Sejanus for one, which was bad news. I wanted nothing from that bastard, least of all false sympathy.

Over to my left – and well away from Sejanus – a white-haired old man was deep in conversation with a senator. He saw me looking and raised his hand. I frowned, trying to fit the name to the face. I knew him, sure, but not from Rome. Athens? Alexandria? Pergamum, maybe, or any of a dozen other places; Perilla and I had moved around a lot these past few years. Whoever he was I had the feeling the acquaintance hadn't been all that pleasant.

'Marcus!' Perilla's elbow dug me in the ribs. I turned back. She was looking frosty as hell. Mother, too.

Cosconia's lips had tightened into a line. 'No, don't bother, Perilla,' she said. 'I only wanted to introduce myself properly and welcome you home. Another time, perhaps, if and when Marcus has more liberty for conversation.' She walked off unsmiling before I had a chance to apologise and explain.

'Oh, shit,' I murmured.

'Marcus, I am ashamed of you!' I'd never seen Mother so angry. 'Your behaviour was abominable! And that is no sort of language for a funeral!'

She was right, of course. I knew that without being told, even though I hadn't meant to offend anyone. Still, Mother ought to have known better than spring Dad's second wife on me without warning and expect light social chit-chat.

'Uh, yeah,' I said. The white-haired guy was looking at me again. I still couldn't place him, and it worried me. 'Yeah, I'm sorry. Excuse me, will you?'

'*Marcus!*' Perilla snapped. I ignored her and moved towards him.

Sejanus peeled himself away from Trio and Cotta like bark from an elm branch and stepped into my path.

'Bought any good bronze ducks recently, Corvinus?' he said.

So he did remember. 'It was a goose,' I said. 'Etruscan.'

'Really?' His eyes measured me. 'I thought it was a duck. That's right, Trio, isn't it?'

The consul had joined us, smiling the doughy smile I remembered from other days. Cotta had made himself scarce. That shifty old chancer can scent trouble a mile off.

'A duck it was.' Trio was fingering the broad purple stripe on his expensive mantle. That had come since my day; when I'd seen him last he'd been a lightweight narrow-striper on the make. He'd risen high since then, if you can call it rising. 'A dead one.' He gave me a sour nod. 'How are you these days, Corvinus? Doing well, are we?'

I didn't answer. Sejanus laughed. His eyes hadn't left my face.

'A pity you never took me up on my offer,' he said. 'You'd've done much better working with me than . . .' He paused. 'Just what are you doing at present, exactly?'

'Oh, this and that.' I remembered Dad asking me the same question at Priscus's birthday party. The one I'd brought the Etruscan goose to. I'd given him the same answer, and for the same reasons. 'I'm not a politician, Sejanus. As you know.'

'Who could be, in Athens? It's the world's backside.' He was studying me carefully. 'I'm speaking politically, of course.'

'Yeah. Sure.' I was shaking, and trying hard to hide it. He was being friendly enough once you'd made allowance, but he still made my skin crawl and I had to admit he terrified me. It wasn't the power, although Sejanus had more of that than anyone in Rome, probably more than the Wart himself these days, in real terms; it was just who he was. 'We're happy enough there, Perilla and me.'

'Oh, yes. Your wife. You must introduce us.' He looked across at Perilla, but she was still talking to Mother and Cosconia, who'd rejoined them now the grouchy stepson had made himself scarce. The three of them were probably raking over my roasted giblets. If that isn't an unfortunate phrase at a funeral.

'Yes. I must do that,' I said. 'At some stage.' Whether he had the high on me or not, I wasn't letting the bastard within a mile of Perilla if I could help it, no way. 'Perilla likes the academic atmosphere there. Me, well, the wine's not bad. And as you say it's peaceful.'

'But hardly the place for a Roman.' Sejanus's smile hadn't shifted. 'Or have you decided that being a Roman is outwith your capacities?'

Trio sniggered. I shrugged and turned away. The guy meant to needle me, obviously, but if he thought he could make me lose my temper in public that was one satisfaction I didn't intend giving him.

He laid a hand on my arm and gently pulled me back. 'You're staying here long?' he said.

'No.' I looked past him. The old man with the white hair was still talking to his friend, who I did recognise: Lucius Arruntius, one of the Senate's leading lights. A straight guy, as that mealy-mouthed crew went, but getting on now as were most of the people at Dad's funeral. 'No, not very long. A month or two at most.'

He nodded. 'Good. Rome's no place for slackers.' Another measuring pause. 'Or for fools. Not now.'

'It takes all kinds.' My fist itched to smash itself into his gut. I buried it in the fold of my mantle.

Another nod, a satisfied one this time; whatever I'd said Sejanus seemed to have got what he wanted. I remembered the old empress's words, the last time I'd seen her: *You're beneath his notice, Corvinus. Killing you wouldn't be worth either the trouble or the risk.* Not very flattering, but true enough. I meant to keep it that way.

Sejanus let go of my arm. 'Well, pleasant as this is,' he said, 'I must be off. Affairs of state call, even though I am simply a private citizen nowadays.' He smiled at Trio, who smiled back. Until the beginning of the month Sejanus had been co-consul with the Wart. When Tiberius had given up his consulship he had done the same; a prelude, so rumour went, to even greater honours. 'It's a little late to change your mind, but there might still be something for you. If you ask nicely.'

My fist was clenched so hard now the nails were cutting into my palm. I didn't trust myself enough to say anything, but it seemed an answer wasn't required. Sejanus gave me a bright smile and a wave, then walked with Trio towards the consul's waiting guard of axemen. I was still glaring after them when someone spoke.

'You don't recognise me, Corvinus.' It was the white-haired guy. He put out a trembling hand. 'Aelius Lamia.'

I hesitated, then took the hand and shook it. I remembered him now, sure I did, but remembering I wasn't surprised I hadn't known him. The last time I'd seen Lamia was when he'd thrown me out of Syria for asking too many questions about the Wart's adopted son Germanicus Caesar. Then, he'd been a middle-aged man in his prime. Now something had eaten him up from the inside, and all that was left was the shell.

'How are you, Governor?' I said.

'Well enough.' The skull grinned. 'My condolences. Your father was a splendid man. Splendid.' No reference to Syria, but then I wouldn't've expected it. Even when he was chewing my balls off Lamia had been the perfect diplomat. 'You know Lucius Arruntius?'

'No. At least we've never met formally.' We shook hands. Arruntius would be about Lamia's age, I'd guess, but he looked a dozen years younger and good for a dozen or two more. I'd give Lamia twelve months at the outside.

'You're here for long?' Arruntius asked.

The same question as Sejanus's, and with the same edge. Maybe coincidence, but the hair on my neck still bristled.

'Just a visit,' I said. 'Rome doesn't suit me any more.'

'The place or the climate?'

I was cautious. 'I miss the Subura, sure. And the smell of the Tiber. Other things.'

'But not the politics?'

Sejanus's question again. I was beginning to get bad feelings about this, especially the way they were looking at me. Like lepidopterists deciding where to shove the pin. 'Politics doesn't interest me,' I said. I glanced over to where Dad's pyre was sinking into a pile of glowing ashes. 'I haven't even notched up a junior magistracy.'

'So I hear.' Arruntius dropped his voice. 'Yet you were exiled.'

'I was never exiled. Formally or informally.' This was familiar ground. I'd been over it a dozen times in the last ten years until I had the answer off pat; so pat that I'd begun to believe it myself. 'Choose to live outside Italy if you come from one of the top families and you're automatically in exile, voluntary or otherwise. Finish, end of story. That's the way the Roman mind works; only crooks and disgraced politicians live abroad from choice. I'm no crook, sir, and my reasons had nothing to do with politics.'

Arruntius smiled. Then he said quietly, 'Come now, young man, of course they did. That's why we need to talk.'

Uh-huh. Coincidence nothing; this was a proposition if I'd ever heard one. The old guys were still looking at me like I was some sort of pickled specimen, and I knew I should just walk away from them, collect Perilla and make a run for Puteoli and the first ship out. Wherever it was headed.

Lamia's hand was on my arm, and he moved me further out of earshot. Not that there were many people left to overhear. The crowd was thinning fast.

'Corvinus,' he said, 'matters have reached a crisis. You may or may not know that Tiberius is on the point of naming Aelius Sejanus formally as his successor.'

'Is that right, now?' I tried to keep my voice level. Confidences like this I could do without.

'That is right.' Evidently my tone hadn't fazed him. 'Since you claim to have no interest in politics it may not concern you overmuch. On the other hand, knowing the man as you do you may share our opinion that his nomination would be a disaster for Rome.'

Yeah. No prizes for what was coming next. I could've scripted it myself. And I'd bet good money the 'our' didn't just mean him and Arruntius; it smelled of broad purple stripes.

'Governor,' I said wearily, 'I've met the guy exactly twice, once ten years ago and once today. Neither meeting lasted above five minutes. That's hardly time for a valid assessment. And as far as his being bad for Rome is concerned the emperor obviously thinks otherwise. Or are you calling Tiberius a fool?'

'Personal acquaintance isn't the issue. And as you know, Tiberius is not in full possession of the facts.'

'Oh, really?'

'Corvinus, don't play games!' Lamia snapped. Either he had a lot less patience than when he'd been running one of the empire's top provinces or he was more keyed up than he appeared. 'You're too old for that now, and I certainly am. Ten years ago you were involved in an investigation which it was my duty as the emperor's representative to impede. I wasn't in full possession of the facts then myself, I don't claim to be now and I have no wish to be; however, I suspect they proved that while Sejanus was acting with the emperor's mandate he was also engaged in secret activities of which

Tiberius was unaware, and which he would certainly have viewed as dubious.'

'Dubious', hell: the bastard had been committing treason, only not the kind he could easily be nailed for. Even so, I didn't see why I should make Lamia's job any easier. Let alone agree to what he obviously wanted from me.

'Like you said, Governor, that was ten years ago.' I turned away briefly. Perilla was still talking to Mother and Cosconia, but she shot a glance in my direction. She looked anxious. You and me both, lady, I thought. I turned back to Lamia. 'Maybe you're right, maybe I am too old now to play games. Especially dangerous ones involving Aelius Sejanus.'

Arruntius had been hanging back like a Greek chorus, letting the governor take centre stage. Now he moved closer and took hold of my wrist. He had strong, blunt fingers like a wrestler's.

'We were hoping that you might agree to resume that investigation now, Corvinus,' he said softly, 'so that Tiberius can be apprised of the true situation and change his mind. Before it's too late.'

There it was. Masks down. We stared at one another, and it may've been my imagination but Lamia didn't look any happier than I felt. Well, at least he'd put out the right signals in advance, and Livia had warned me this would happen one day. I'd always wondered, if and when the time came, which way I'd jump.

The snag was that I still didn't know.

'So you want someone to dig the dirt on Aelius Sejanus and hand it over in a nice neat parcel to the Wart?' I said. Neither of them answered. 'Why me?'

'We've been over that,' Lamia grunted. 'You have a head start, Corvinus. And you have the temperament for it. Uniquely so.'

Well, flattery would get him nowhere. If it was flattery.

'I'm still surprised you need me, Lamia,' I said. 'You're the bastard's cousin, after all.'

I regretted the words even before his bony face turned red with anger: I'd never believed even at the time that Lamia was in Sejanus's pay, and I didn't believe it now. But it was a fair point, and it needed making.

'We didn't expect immediate agreement,' Arruntius said quickly. 'Let alone trust. Think it over first before you give us your answer. But remember that in asking for your help we don't ask lightly.'

Yeah. *That* I'd believe. I knew that 'we', I'd heard it all my life from Dad: the patriotic plural comes second nature to broad-stripers, despite the fact that they're the most disunited bunch of self-servers you'd never hope to meet. So. Rome's Senate wanted the upstart Sejanus pegged out for the crows. No surprises there, but I was surprised that Arruntius had agreed to do their asking for them. If he had clout – and he had it in spades – it was because he wasn't one of the gang. Of the three men Augustus once said could run the empire Arruntius was the only one the cunning old bugger had no reservations about. That sort of recommendation doesn't come cheap.

I turned away again; not towards Perilla this time but in the direction of Dad's pyre. It was mostly ash now, with a few glowing embers and a scattering of charred logs at the edges. Time, soon, for the wine and the picking over of the bones. When we burned him, I'd once said, we'd find a poker with the words *Property of the Senate and People of Rome* written on it. I was sorry for that now; he hadn't deserved it, or not in the way I'd meant it at the time. No, there'd be no poker. But a good part of the old guy had been Rome's after all.

'Oh. One more thing, Corvinus.' Arruntius was reaching into the fold of his mantle. He brought out a sealed letter. 'I was instructed to give you this. I don't know the contents, but I suspect they may be relevant, and they may help you decide.'

I took the letter and turned it over in my hands to read the spidery superscription: 'For Marcus Valerius Messalla Corvinus. Personal, to be delivered at the proper time.' No signature, but I recognised the handwriting. Sure I did. I could even smell the camphor.

Livia never let go, did she? Not even when she was two years dead.

2 ∫

We got back late. Bathyllus, as usual, had the door open for us even before we'd stepped out of the litters. If anything, the little guy's psychic powers had improved with age.

I'd kept up the house on the Palatine, partly through sentiment, mostly because to sell it would've been an admission that I was finished with Rome. That I couldn't be, ever. The city was in my bones, and if I'd trusted myself to live there quietly without scratching the dangerous itch of curiosity now and again I'd never have left. Expensive, sure, but we came for visits regularly, and Mother and Priscus had used it for a while after their own place had been gutted in the big Caelian fire.

'Hey, Bathyllus.' I handed him my stripped-off mantle and took the pre-dinner cup of wine he held out. 'Everything okay now?' A genuine question: the caretaker staff we left in Rome didn't come up to the little guy's high standards. The first few days back there was always blood on the walls.

'Yes, sir.' Bathyllus folded the mantle carefully. 'I've cancelled the arrangement with the jobbing gardener and located the missing mushroom dish.'

'Uh, yeah. Great. Good work.' I took a long swallow of the Setinian. Beautiful. You can get it in Athens but somehow it doesn't taste the same. 'That mushroom dish was worrying me.'

Perilla took off her veil while I carried the wine into the living-room and lay down on our usual couch. Bathyllus had brought her a chilled fruit juice. She lay down beside me and sipped at it.

'He'd have been pleased, Marcus,' she said at last. 'Your father. Especially at the funeral speech.'

'Yeah.' I helped myself from the jug on the table. 'Old Appianus did well. If he'd had a few more teeth he would've been almost intelligible.'

'What did Aelius Lamia have to say to you?'

'You recognised him?'

'Oddly enough, I generally do tend to recognise governors who've thrown me out of their provinces. It's one of the skills I had to develop when I married you.'

I grinned and kissed her. How Perilla can be so prickly and yet make a put-down sound like a compliment has always amazed me. She's pretty good at puncturing a black mood, too. 'Nothing much,' I said. 'He and his pal Arruntius want me to put the skids under Sejanus for them, that's all.'

Perilla sat up wide-eyed, spilling her fruit juice over the couch arm.

'Oh, Marcus! *No!*'

'That was my reaction.' I took another swallow of wine; the Special was mellowing nicely now it had a chance to sit in the cellar. Luckily my stepfather Priscus wasn't a drinker. He kept his enthusiasms for important things like tombs and Oscan optatives.

'They're mad!' She was still staring. 'Insane!'

'Sure they are. They're senators. It goes with the stripe.'

'No, but really!'

'Oh, I agree. You want me to give you the arguments against it myself, just to save you time?' I counted them off on my fingers. 'Sejanus is as dangerous as a crocodile in a swimming pool. He's the Wart's ears, eyes and hands in Rome. I don't know the political ropes here any more. I'd get nothing out of it if I won, not even thanks, and a short cut to the death mask if I lost. And it's none of my business anyway. Those do you or should I start on the other hand?'

'Marcus, be serious!'

'I am being serious. Believe it.'

'But why you?'

'No one else is stupid enough.' I didn't tell her about Livia's letter, although it wouldn't've surprised her: Perilla knew as much about the old empress as I did, but I wanted to read that privately first. Or maybe just burn it unopened.

'Corvinus, that is *not* being serious!'

I shrugged. 'They seem to think I'm their best bet. And they're desperate.'

'You turned them down, of course.'

I'd been hoping against hope she wouldn't ask that. 'Uh, not in so many words, Perilla.'

'Oh, Marcus!' She reached for my wine cup and emptied it at a swallow. 'What the *hell* do you think you're playing at?'

'Hey, I didn't actually say I'd do it, lady! I never even said I'd consider it.'

Flannel, flannel. Well, I didn't expect it to work, and it didn't.

'You do realise, don't you,' she said, 'that we left Rome to avoid attracting that man's attention? I would've thought one funeral in the family was enough for a while.'

I shifted uncomfortably. 'It's not that bad. I only—'

'It isn't even as if you have the excuse this time that Livia has forced you into it. And you certainly wouldn't have imperial protection. Quite the reverse.' She filled the cup again, looked at the wine with distaste and set it down. 'Marcus, *why*?'

I put my free arm round her shoulders. She was stiff as a steel rod.

'Because it's something I can do,' I said. 'Instead of making speeches in favour of things I don't believe in, or hammering the hell out of foreigners who'd rather not be blessed with the benefits of Roman civilisation.' I paused. 'Or maybe there's just something wrong with my brain.'

She looked at me for a long time, then smiled gently to herself and kissed me. Her shoulders lost a little of their tenseness.

'Your father understood,' she said. 'He may not have agreed, but he did understand. He never blamed you, not really. Don't forget that.'

'Dad's got nothing to do with this.'

'No. Of course not.' She kissed me again and pressed closer. 'Marcus, I married you because you were different, you didn't fit in. But remember that if you died I'd make a bad and very sad widow. Much worse than Cosconia. Think about that before you do anything silly, won't you? And you don't have to prove anything to me, either.'

*   *   *

After we'd eaten I locked myself in the study and took out
Livia's letter. There was a lamp burning on the desk. I looked
at the clear flame, considering. Then with a twist of my thumb
I broke the seal.

The letter was two years old, dated a month or so before the
empress had died. She'd written it herself – I'd known that from
the superscription – and the writing sprawled across the page like
the tracks of a drunken spider:

> To Marcus Valerius Messalla Corvinus. Livia Julia Augusta
> gives greetings.
>
> Well, young man, I'm dead and burned at last, or you
> wouldn't be reading this. Let me say first that I have no
> regrets, cithcr about being dead or for having removed so
> many of my collateral relatives before their proper hours. I
> acted for the good of Rome; and Rome, although presently
> she believes herself hard done by under Tiberius, will look
> back and thank me for him. She could have done worse;
> she will certainly do worse when my son has gone and she
> discovers the quality of what is left. So no apologies, and no
> justifications.
>
> Which brings me to the point of this letter. Aelius Sejanus.
> We talked a little about him the last time we met. Again the
> fact that you are reading this shows that the time for talk is
> past. The man is a malignant growth, a danger to Rome, and
> he must be removed. No; I dislike metaphorical euphemisms.
> Sejanus must be killed.
>
> I don't suggest you do it yourself. I can't see you knifing him
> in the back or poisoning his porridge, although I could make
> some suggestions there, as you know. That would be far too
> risky, and, besides, overt murder is always a mistake. Consider
> Brutus and Cassius, who performed the very laudable act of
> killing the far-from-divine Julius and got nothing but death
> and infamy for their pains while taking most of Rome's best
> with them. The question mark, Corvinus, must always be
> there, if only for the purposes of insurance. In Sejanus's case
> exposure of his true character in Tiberius's eyes will be quite
> sufficient. Then, assuming my son hasn't lost the wits he was

born with, he can be rendered harmless and those cowardly fools in the Senate relied on to finish the job for you.

So. How is he to be exposed? That, my dear, I leave entirely to you because I have the utmost faith in your expertise. For the same reason (and for the reason which you so astutely divined in our last interview) I am giving you no help whatsoever in the way of inside information. Find things out for yourself, young man. I would, however, suggest that an examination of the records of trials before the Senate over the past eight years will make instructive reading, plus, of course, any others which postdate my own death. I have already approached the Senate's archivist Junius Rusticus in this connection and should he still be alive when you read this he will be happy to give you access. If not you must make your own arrangements.

That is all. I wish you luck, which I am certain you don't need. Oh, one more thing, a personal matter. I called you, at the close of our interview, a 'divine idiot' and compared you to my grandson Claudius. I regret that bitterly: not the term, nor the comparison, but simply that you misunderstood it as an insult. That was most certainly not my meaning, and I apologise sincerely for any hurt caused. Should you ever have the opportunity, talk to my son's astrologer Thrasyllus. Normally, unlike Tiberius and my late husband the god, I have no time for such nonsense, but in Thrasyllus's case I make an exception. He is an honest man by his own lights, and – so far as I can tell – genuinely gifted. Ask him about Claudius; discreetly, please, there are certain understandable rules about these matters. What he tells you – if he tells you anything – will surprise you, and perhaps alter your opinion of my remark.

Again, Corvinus, and for the last time, my thanks. You will be acting, as I have always acted, for the good of Rome. Fools look for public acknowledgment and public honours. You will have neither, ever; and you will not, I think, care too much. We altruistic beings who truly love Rome (don't laugh, young man! I can hear you, but I mean it!) are above such things.

I am entrusting this letter to Lucius Arruntius. He has his faults, but he is, believe me, one of the few true Romans left.

He knows nothing of its contents, and although – because! – he is an honourable man I would hesitate, were I you, to count on his practical assistance. A keen sense of honour is not a quality we require in this business, nor indeed is it a very safe one. Burn this now. You have my prayers.

Yeah. That was Livia, all right. I picked up my cup of Setinian and scattered a few drops to the thrawn, tough-minded old so-and-so's ghost: where she was at the moment I'd bet she needed all the prayers she could get. Then I burned her letter as instructed, in the flame of the lamp, and ground it to ash. There was a lump in my throat as I did it, why I don't know: she'd used me before, she was using me again, and this time she hadn't even had the grace to ask. I owed her nothing; quite the reverse.

I'd go after Sejanus like she wanted me to do; sure I would, I couldn't help myself. Whatever the cost, and however crazy it was. But then Livia, like Lamia, had known that all along.

3

It was good to be walking in Rome again, even if the city had changed. Not physically, or at least not much: buildings had gone up and come down, especially in the Subura where fires and collapsing tenements were a way of life, but the streets themselves were the same. And the smells. I hadn't been kidding when I'd told Arruntius I missed the smell of the Tiber. Athens may have a river of her own, but it's small and reasonably clean, like everything else in the philosophers' city, and that goes a long way towards explaining the Athenian character. A few thousand tons of ripe Tiber mud upwind tend to keep you practical.

But ten years was a long time, and I'd lost friends. Scylax was dead of a stroke five years back. Daphnis ran the gym for me now, and it was just a profitable investment these days: I'd never really hit it off with Daphnis. Agron was still around, but he was in Ostia and married to the daughter of an Alexandrian boat-builder who'd given him three kids and a paunch. The last time I'd seen Agron he had baby puke all down his tunic. He'd been proud of it, too.

Yeah, well. Life moves on, and even Rome can't stay still. I was heading for the Treasury on the Capitol, where the Senate's records are kept, and although the Subura wasn't exactly on my direct route I cut through it for old times' sake. Not that I had much time for sightseeing: Bathyllus had run round – as far as the little guy is capable of running – to make a formal appointment for an hour before noon. After he'd gone I'd wondered whether sending him to Rusticus in advance had been a mistake, but cloak and dagger stuff's never been my bag. It only gets you noticed.

The first person I saw inside the Treasury building was Caelius

Crispus. He'd put on weight and lost hair and teeth, but he still oozed. Good quality mantle, though. Trio wasn't the only slimy bastard who'd gone up in the world since I left.

'Corvinus?' Crispus was looking at me like I'd walked through the wall and rattled my chains at him. 'What the hell are you doing in Rome?'

'Yeah, and I'm glad to see you too, sunshine.' Not true. Given the choice between running into a flea-bitten baboon with halitosis and Crispus I'd've taken the monkey every time. 'You still have your attachments, then.'

'I'm Permanent Under-Secretary of the Military Treasury now, if that's what you mean,' he said with dignity.

'Jupiter! You're saying they let you near the army pay-chest? Do the lads on the Rhine know about this?'

That got me a scowl. Maybe I'd touched a nerve: all sorts of scams go on in the Treasury, even in these rigidly moral days, and Crispus was as straight as an Aventine dice game.

'Look, Corvinus,' he said, 'I haven't got either the time or the inclination for badinage. Just make sure that you and that she-cat wife of yours stay out of my life while you're here, okay?' I grinned: the last time we'd seen Crispus Perilla had almost got him blackballed from his exclusive gentlemen-only club. Evidently he hadn't forgiven or forgotten. 'And you haven't answered my question. What brings you back to Rome?'

I hesitated: information is Crispus's stock-in-trade, the more shop-soiled the better. His next question would be what was I doing up at the Treasury, and that was the one I really didn't want to answer: give Crispus the ball – any ball – and he'd run with it, straight to where he thought he could make most profit. And that could be dangerous.

'I thought you'd know,' I said at last. 'An important guy like you. My father died. I'm here for the funeral.'

'Oh.' He put on his pious expression, the one that made him look like a sick duck. 'Oh, yes, of course, I forgot. The ex-consul Messalinus. My condolences.'

I could see the next question already forming in his eyes so I got in first.

'Dad left some letters in his will to be delivered to the Senate archives. Connected with the Pannonian revolt.'

Without making it obvious I showed Crispus the sheaf of documents I was carrying in my mantle-fold. I wasn't lying. The bit about the will had been true enough; the Pannonian revolt, when Dad had been provincial governor, had been his finest hour, or maybe finest five minutes, and being Dad he didn't want posterity to overlook it.

Crispus grunted, satisfied. He was already moving off. 'Archives is along the west corridor, third on your right,' he said. 'Sorry again about your father, Corvinus. I'll see you around.' He paused. 'Or perhaps not.'

'Yeah. Right.'

The shifty bugger had wilfully misdirected me before. This time I checked with a slave pushing a broom around, but west corridor third on the right it was. Archives was a huge room filled floor to ceiling with creaking bookshelves and smelling of musty paper and old glue, and Rusticus was already there waiting for me.

From Livia's letter I'd been half expecting a little mousy guy of about ninety, with inky fingers and dust in the folds of his mantle, but the Senate's archivist suited his name: a big, beefy countryman in his late fifties, with a florid face and eyebrows like overblown caterpillars. We shook hands over the cramped reading desk.

'My condolences on the death of your father,' he said. 'A fine man. He'll be sorely missed.'

'Yeah. Yeah, he will.' Unlike Crispus, Rusticus sounded like he meant it. Maybe he did. I gave him the Pannonian letters, which he pounced on.

'Excellent,' he said. 'They'll add greatly to our knowledge of the revolt.'

'You're a historian?'

'Not a true one. I have an interest in history, but I don't write. It's why I took this job. Not the most popular senatorial position, even although vital. I'll look after these, don't worry.' He called over one of the clerks and gave the letters to him. 'Now, Corvinus. Everything's ready for you, in accordance with the Augusta's instructions.'

'Uh . . . just what were these, exactly?' I said cautiously. Livia was thorough, I'd give her that. I just hoped she hadn't been too thorough. Rusticus sounded the keen, talkative type, and if he enjoyed his work that much I might be able to cut a few corners.

'That you be shown and given access to the senatorial records from the eighth year of Tiberius's reign up to the present, whenever that was. With no comment and no further guidance on my part.'

Shit. There went that idea. 'Is that so?'

'That is so. "Tell the young puppy to look for himself. It's all there."' He smiled. 'Her words, not mine.'

'Uh-huh.' Bugger the old bitch sideways, she really was determined to make this difficult, wasn't she? 'And you're going to do just exactly what she told you?'

The smile faded. 'I am. Even although I could do more, I won't.'

Well, that was frank enough. 'You mind telling me why?'

'Not at all. I had and have a great deal of respect for Livia. She was a very clever woman, Corvinus, and I know her reasons for making the stipulation, whatever they were, would be good ones. Especially since she insisted I carry it out to the letter.' He looked me square in the eye. 'Don't mistake me, please. I can guess her intentions, and I'd help you gladly if I were free to do so. I've been waiting two years for this, ever since the emperor sent Agrippina and young Nero into exile and confined Drusus to the palace.'

Yeah. That little nugget of information I did have, courtesy of an army pal with a penchant for booze and current affairs who'd stayed with us en route for Asia. As soon as Livia was cold Tiberius had banished his dead adopted son Germanicus's widow and her eldest son. Drusus, the second son, had disappeared from public life shortly afterwards, leaving only the then sixteen-year-old Gaius. Agrippina and Nero had been exiled to separate islands off the Italian coast. Nero, so the official version had it, committed suicide a year later; believe that, as my tribune pal said over the third jug, if you like. Sure, from what I already knew of her Agrippina had deserved all she got; but the Wart's treatment of the old imperial family – or Sejanus's – still left a bad taste. Rusticus obviously agreed, and I'd bet that he was that rare thing now in Rome, a Julian sympathiser. It surprised me that Livia had trusted him enough to count on his help, especially given her own track record where the Julians were concerned; but then maybe an interest in history encourages a certain degree of Olympian objectivity.

'Okay.' I shrugged. 'So give me whatever you can.'

'Willingly.' Rusticus stood up. 'If you'll follow me I'll show you the relevant shelves and leave you to it.'

There were four of them, long ones, crammed solid with papyrus rolls in their heavy protective cylinders. Good sweet Jupiter in a G-string! My jaw dropped and I could almost hear the old harpy chuckling all the way from the shades.

'You're sure that's all there is, pal?' I said at last.

The sarcasm went straight past Rusticus's head; or maybe he just wasn't rising to the bait.

'Yes, that's all,' he said. 'Proceedings of the Senate, Tiberius Eight to current. Ten years' worth. Make all the notes you want, but don't take anything away and put things back as you found them, please, otherwise you'll cause no end of trouble and my clerks will have both our guts for label-ties.'

At which point he shook hands, wished me luck and left. I felt like crying.

Okay. So I had to start somewhere. Wishing I'd had the sense to sneak in a jug of Setinian, I pulled down the nearest roll. Half a dozen others came with it, plus several pounds of dust, a dead mouse and a colony of live spiders. I checked the labels: only four months' worth, September to December, six years back. Shit. This was going to be a long hard slog. A long, hard, *dry* slog.

I took the rolls down and laid them in rows, earliest to latest. Then I started at the beginning and worked my way through, replacing them on the shelves as I went. Trials, Livia had said. There were plenty of these. The trouble was I had to skip through screeds of other stuff to get to them: debates on clearing waterways and repairing roads, appointments to committees, proposals, counter-proposals, counter-counter-proposals. Yard after yard of carefully recorded hot air that no one, ever, would want to read again. Jupiter, how did anyone stand it without dropping dead of boredom ten times over? I felt sorry for the guy who'd taken the minutes, too. It must've been bad enough listening day in day out to this slop without having to write it down as well.

By the time the slaves finally threw me out the lamps were lit. I was just about gibbering, but I'd filled a good few sheets of my own: paper sheets, not tablets, because I would've needed a mule to carry that weight of wood and wax home. As it was, they filled the good-sized bag that I filched from Rusticus's head clerk when his back was turned. The notes weren't all that detailed, but I had the essentials, and that was enough to get me started. Rusticus surely couldn't object if I came back to check finer points where necessary.

Most of the names mentioned had been just that, names: big ones, sure, because not everyone gets the privilege of a trial by the Senate; but they didn't mean a lot at present outside the social register, and anyway I'd tried not to get sidetracked into thinking too much about what I was writing. Nevertheless by the time I'd shoved all the roll-cases back where they belonged, cursed Livia to ten different kinds of hell and staggered out in the direction of the nearest wineshop the hairs on the back of my neck were bristling fit to bust.

Livia had been right: the records had made instructive reading. One word had kept reappearing again and again, so often that it had to be what the empress was pointing me towards.

The word was 'treason'.

4

I wasn't tired when I got back, at least not sleep-tired. I shoved my head round the bedroom door, but Perilla had given up on me hours ago and was flat out, her hair a tawny cloud across the pillow: she never got her maid to bind it up at night, which was okay by me. Bathyllus was still padding around bright-eyed and bushy-tailed, as I knew he would be: Bathyllus takes his responsibilities seriously, and he can always find a table to straighten or a spoon or two to buff up. I sent him for a jug of Setinian and lugged it and my bag of notes into the study. Then I got down to serious work.

There were too many names. That was the problem. In the ten years I'd been away Rome had seen twenty-three trials before the Senate, for everything from treason through adultery to a guy who'd pushed his wife out the window and claimed he'd been sleepwalking at the time. Yeah, well, as a defence I suppose it'd been worth a try, but he must've been desperate, and it didn't say much for his powers of imagination. Some of the names jumped off the page straight at me, as they'd done when I first read them; Suillius Rufus's for one, Perilla's ex who I'd run foul of in Antioch. They'd nailed Rufus seven years back for pocketing bribes as a city judge, and he'd been exiled at the Wart's insistence to a flyspeck off Sicily. Sometimes emperors do get things right, and I raised my cup to the old boil-encrusted bugger's sense of justice. Calpurnius Piso's brother Lucius was there, and Gaius Junius Silanus, whose second brother Decimus had once thrown me out of his urban villa for accusing him of not screwing Augustus's granddaughter. Old friends all. Others I'd never met but were familiar from the social register: the young

Quinctilius Varus's wife Claudia Pulchra (adultery); Gaius Silius and his wife Sosia Galla; Titius Sabinus . . .

The rest were a blur. This needed method. Order. Good old Roman thoroughness. Setinian. I reached for the jug and filled my wine cup.

Taking up my biggest wax tablet I drew my pen down the middle. Dates to the left, names and charges to the right. I started with the big one, the obvious one. Treason.

When I counted down the list four cups later I had seven names in chronological order. Caesius Cordus, senatorial governor of Crete and Cyrene: treason and extortion. Decimus Silanus's brother Gaius, the Asian governor, ditto. According to the charge sheet he'd also been found guilty of 'offences against the divinity of Augustus and the majesty of Tiberius', which reading between the lines meant he'd let his hair down at the wrong party or opened his mouth too wide in the wrong person's hearing. Third, a guy I'd never heard of but who sounded a real peabrain, Lucius Ennius, accused of melting down a statue of the Wart and using the bullion to make dinner plates. Big-league stuff. Tiberius had quashed that one himself.

The fourth name on the list was Gaius Silius. Silius's case had been more serious. Governor of Upper Germany ten years back, he'd been accused of connivance in the Gallic revolt and of profiteering after the event. He'd killed himself before the verdict was given, and his wife Sosia, who was also implicated, had been sent into exile. This one smelled like a month-old anchovy. I'd known Silius vaguely from his visits to Dad about the time he'd got his first Eagle, and although I'd only been a kid at the time frankly I couldn't believe the charge. Sure, he'd had an ego the size of the Capitol – he'd have to, to get where he was – but he hadn't been traitor material. He'd kept his troops loyal to the Wart when the Rhine frontier blew up after old Augustus died, and he was army to the bone. That didn't sit well with the connivance business: for a dyed-in-the-wool army man like Silius consorting with rebels ranks with screwing goats and taking orders from civilians. The profiteering, sure: Silius was as human as the rest of us, and once the Gauls were beaten they were fair game. But not the treason. That stank.

Fifth was Lucius Piso, the Piso of the Germanicus affair; elder brother and one of the defence lawyers at his trial. Charged with treasonable conversation about the Wart, possessing poison and wearing a sword to meetings of the Senate. I discounted the last two items for what they were: malicious ballast, to give the case extra weight. No traitor is that crazy, and whatever else he might be the guy wasn't stupid. The first charge, though, made me think. The case had never come to trial; he'd died a natural death (precise nature unspecified) before the first hearing, which was, if you like, pat. Maybe too pat. Sure, Lucius was no youngster, and he could've eaten a bad oyster or caught something nasty in the woodshed, but I couldn't forget how his brother had gone four years previously. I wondered what the 'treasonable private conversation' was, although I suspected I knew already: 'my' Piso had certainly had secrets to spill that the Wart would give his best boil plaster to keep under wraps. I'd bet good money that Lucius had been another sucker who'd opened his mouth too wide in the wrong company.

Sixth, Votienus Montanus, someone else I didn't know. Not a Roman, with a name like that. Maybe a Gaul, a Spaniard, or a Lusitanian; the records didn't show. In any case Montanus was accused of slandering Tiberius, and condemned to death. That made me pause, too: the Wart may have his faults but he isn't thin-skinned, and simple slander goes straight past him. There'd been instances in the past when he'd been bad-mouthed in private or public, but when a prosecutor tried to get up a case he'd quite rightly laughed it out of court. This time he hadn't laughed. Instead, he'd taken this guy's head. So what made Montanus special? So special that the Wart made sure he was chopped, or at least stood aside and let the Senate chop him?

Last and not least came Titius Sabinus, charged with straight treason. Reading between the lines, it was obvious that he'd been set up six ways from nothing by a gaggle of informers and his hide very carefully nailed to the Senate House floor. We'd never met, but I knew of him. Although he came from a good family, like me he was a political nobody: no consulship, not even a city judgeship. No military command. A narrow-striper, not a senator. Hardly, in other words, the usual traitor material. He wasn't all that rich, either, by aristocratic standards, which, since the successful prosecutor usually gets a large slice of the cake, is a common reason for starting up a case. What did make him stand out was that he'd been a close friend of Germanicus's and – gossip said – an even closer one of Agrippina's after the Caesar's death. Scratch the obvious implication: Agrippina wasn't the type for affairs, casual or otherwise. Also, the records showed that when charges were brought the Wart had written personally to the Senate demanding a conviction; which, for the Wart, was queer as a five-legged cat. Sabinus had been condemned *nem. con.* and strangled the same day.

Interesting, right?

I sat back and took a sip of my wine. At my elbow, the reading lamp guttered. It'd been full when I'd started, and I hadn't realised how long I'd been lying here. It must be almost dawn.

So. Where to now? Sure, there were plenty of other names in my notes, and I wasn't fool enough to believe they weren't important, maybe even more important than the ones I already had. When you get right down to it treason's only a word; the charge itself doesn't matter if the result's the same. As I'd found years back with sweet little Julia, a prosecution for adultery can cover a multitude of sins. Then there were the off-the-wall cases. Like the sleepwalking murder, or the hack poet prosecuted for publishing a premature lament for Tiberius's son Drusus. Bad taste, sure, since Drusus had recovered; but hardly worth garrotting the poor bugger for. Or was it? I could be missing something there or in half a dozen other places. I probably was.

I needed expert help with this. So who could I ask?

I took another mouthful of Setinian and considered the options. A broad-striper like Arruntius or Lamia would've been perfect, but senators were too high-profile to be safe and I doubted anyway if when push came to shove that there was one of them I could trust. Dad might've helped this time; but Dad was dead. Of my other relatives Priscus would be about as much use as a eunuch in a brothel, and I didn't consider Cotta for one second. So who did I know who had both ears to the ground, more inside his skull than feathers, and a low enough profile not to run the risk of going down with me if the shit hit the shovel?

Lippillus, that was who. Flavonius Lippillus.

I'd met him over the Germanicus business, and we'd kept in touch off and on since. When I was back in Rome he and his stepmother had come round for dinner a few times. Forget every stepmother story you've ever heard. Marcina Paullina was a honey: a tall, willowy African with sleepy eyes, not five years older than he was. Yeah. Lippillus would do very well. In fact, he was perfect.

Something was going *squeak squeak* in the lobby outside. Either we'd got a ghost in a new pair of sandals or . . .

I got off the couch and opened the study door. Bathyllus was polishing the bronze statue in the alcove.

'You not in bed yet, little guy?' I said.

'No, sir.' He breathed gently on the dryad's toenails and gave them another rub.

I felt guilty as hell. When I'd taken the jug into the study I should've told him I'd finished for the night. He probably wouldn't've taken any notice, but at least I'd've salved my conscience.

'Then go now,' I said. 'Okay?'

'Yes, sir. In a moment.' He moved on to the left ankle. Ah, well. I'd tried. I paused, my hand on the doorknob.

'Hey, Bathyllus. You happen to know if Flavonius Lippillus is still in town?' One thing I learned early in life: assume your slaves know everything. They usually do, and it saves endless hassle.

The little guy's rag didn't pause. 'Yes, sir,' he said. 'He's a district commander now, I believe. Of the Racetrack and Public Pond regions.'

That made sense. Lippillus had been the best the Aventine Watch could show, and the Watch didn't waste their talent. 'He still live in the same tenement? On the Aventine?'

'That one collapsed a few months ago, sir. During the night, I believe.'

'Jupiter!' Falling tenements are no joke. It isn't so bad during the day when most of the residents are out at work or gossiping in the street, but a collapse at night when everyone's in bed is bad news. 'Is Marcina okay?'

'Oh, yes, sir.' Bathyllus was blushing. He may be getting on a bit and have a scalp as bald as a marble statue's backside, but he'd always had a soft spot for Marcina Paullina. Unrequited, let it be said. Luckily; the little guy wears enough hernia supports to power a catapult. 'She was at her sister's at the time, and Lippillus was on duty. They have a first-floor flat now, near the Temple of Mercury.'

I nodded and yawned. I suddenly felt tired. 'Okay. Bed, Bathyllus. And not too early in the morning, right? We're on holiday, remember.'

As I dragged myself upstairs I thought: Yeah. Some holiday. First a funeral, now an investigation that's practically an act of suicide. Nice one, Corvinus.

Perilla had been right about us being different, anyway. Most people go to Baiae.

5

Next morning I called round at the Watch's regional head-quarters near the Capenan Gate. I'd expected to be told that Lippillus was out, but there he was, bawling at a young squaddie who towered over him by at least a head.

'Hey, Lippillus,' I said.

He looked up, did a double-take and grinned: not so much the twelve-year-old lookalike he'd been when I first met him, more a disreputable dwarf. He jerked his thumb.

'Out!'

The squaddie fled.

'I heard you were back, Corvinus,' he said. The grin had faded. 'And the reason. I'm sorry about your father. And for missing the funeral. A knifing in the Remuria.'

'That's okay.' I watched the squaddie's back as he disappeared. Well, at least if I did nothing else today I'd taken one poor bugger's balls out of the mangle. I could still smell his sweat. 'How are things?'

Lippillus shrugged: he was watching the squaddie as well, but with disapproval. 'A cartload of kitchen ware goes missing and the next day that stupid bastard buys a casserole from a guy in a wineshop and doesn't make the tie-in. Can you believe that?'

'Not easily, no.'

'Fact. The only reason it's come out now is that I overheard him myself telling his mates he knew where they could get a half-set of Samian cost.' He spat on to the floor. 'Jupiter on a bloody tightrope!'

'Yeah. I see what you mean.'

He shook his head. 'They're not a bad lot, the Pisspond lads.

When they get round to telling their arses from their elbows, that is.'

'Better than the Aventine?'

'Rome's Rome, Corvinus. It's the same all over. Just some parts, you get a better class of criminal.'

'Like the Senate House district?'

The grin came back. 'Like the Senate House district.' He paused. 'Split a jug of wine?'

'You twisted my arm.'

'One thing to be said for being the boss,' he said as we left. 'You can slope off for a drink whenever you like and people are glad to see you go.'

The wineshop by the Temple of the Good Goddess was obviously familiar ground: the waiter didn't ask what we wanted and Lippillus didn't tell him. Two minutes later he came back with a jug of white, a charcoal-grilled Lucanian sausage, bread and a saucer of olives in their own oil.

'Cheers. Welcome home.' Lippillus lifted his cup and took a long swallow. I did the same. The wine was a surprise, one you didn't come across very often in Rome: Gauranum, from around Puteoli, cold from the cellar and not at all bad. The sausage wasn't bad, either, heavy with garlic and cumin.

'So. How's life in Athens?'

The way he said the name made it sound like some mud-hut village in the sticks; but then Lippillus didn't have much time for anywhere outside the fifth milestone.

'It's okay, if you happen to like culture and old marble.' I sliced up the sausage. 'I'm learning.'

'How's Perilla? Any kids yet?'

For someone so smart you'd've thought Lippillus would've been more sensitive; but then he wasn't married. Not properly, anyway.

'No,' I said quietly. 'No kids.'

'Shame.'

'Yeah.' I tore off a bit of bread and sopped it in the olive oil. 'Marcina's fine?'

'Putting on weight, but yes, she's fine.' That one I didn't chase; I'd never been exactly sure what Lippillus's relationship with his stepmother was. His father had been dead for years, of course, since long before I knew him, and like I said the lady was no fat-jowled Roman matron. Anyway, it was none of my business.

'Good, good,' I said.

Lippillus laid his knife aside. 'Okay, Corvinus,' he said. 'Don't pussyfoot. Now we've got families out of the way suppose you tell me what I can do for you.'

I grinned. 'It's that obvious?'

'You come all the way down to Pisspond two hours before your normal breakfast time and expect me to think it's a social call? Sure it's obvious.'

'Breakfast, nothing!' I was laughing. 'And I didn't get to bed until five hours ago!'

'So what's unusual?' He bit on a piece of sausage. 'Come on, Marcus, give.'

'Okay.' I nodded. 'I wanted to bounce a few names off you.'

'What kind of names?'

'Big ones. Gaius Junius Silanus. Gaius Silius. Titius Sabinus . . .'

Lippillus had set his wine cup down. He was frowning.

'Corvinus,' he said. 'What is this?'

'They mean anything to you?'

'You're talking old treason, three to ten years old. Silius and Sabinus are dead. Silanus is on Cythnos. So I'll ask you again. What's your interest?'

I couldn't lie to him. Not when I needed him so badly, or considering how much I'd be asking. 'You remember a certain favourite of the emperor we carefully didn't discuss over a drink once upon a time?'

He picked up an olive and chewed carefully before replaying. I could almost hear his brain clicking.

'The Commander of Praetorians.' he said at last. 'Sure I remember. What does Sejanus have to do with this?'

'The Senate want him nailed.'

'*Sejanus?*' Lippillus laughed. 'Corvinus, you're crazy! That's our next emperor you're talking about!'

I kept my voice neutral. 'Maybe. You approve?'

The laughter stopped abruptly. 'Come on, pal! The bastard's a crook, and I don't like crooks, you know that. But like it or not he's still the Wart's successor.'

'Not yet he isn't.'

'Look.' Lippillus pushed the plate of sausage out of the way. 'Approval has nothing to do with it. It's plain fact. Who else is there? The Wart has no natural sons since Drusus died, and as far as Germanicus's boys are concerned Nero's dead, young Drusus is a dangerous maniac and Gaius is still wet behind the ears. Tiberius can't last more than another two or three years at most. Who else has he got but Sejanus? Or do you think he'll hand the empire over to that halfwit Claudius to play with?'

'Hold it.' I'd set my own cup down. 'Young Drusus is mad?'

Lippillus hesitated. 'Yeah. Yeah, so the rumour goes. An inside-edge rumour, Corvinus, so don't spread it around, okay? He wasn't too stable at the best of times, and being locked up has pushed the boy over. The emperor couldn't let him out now even if he wanted to, and as far as making him crown prince is concerned, forget it. The last thing Rome needs is a madman on the throne.'

I took a swallow of the Gauranian. Lippillus was right, of course. Even if Grandson Drusus was family the Wart had his responsibilities, and he knew where they lay, better than anyone. Power was power whichever way you sliced it, and if it came into the wrong hands we were all in trouble. Even Sejanus in charge of the empire would be better than a madman. 'So. What about the names I mentioned?'

Lippillus scowled into his wine cup. 'They're all big Julian supporters, friends of Agrippina. Or they were. If you're looking for a pattern.'

Yeah. I'd thought that might be the answer. It was the only one that made sense. 'You mean we're talking about a political purge,' I said.

Another hesitation. 'You sure you want to discuss this, Corvinus?'

'I'm sure.'

'Okay.' He was still scowling. 'Only be careful how you use it, right? It's not exactly dinnertime conversation, even these days.'

'I'll be careful.'

'There was nothing overt, not at first, but it was a purge right enough. Sejanus knocked them off their perches one by one. Not just them, there were others. Agrippina's cousin Claudia Pulchra. A lady called Aquilia. Gaius Furnius and Varius Ligur.'

I remembered these four from my notes. The women had been exiled for adultery, the two men being named as partners. Four birds with two stones. Not bad going.

'And he finished up with the Julians themselves,' I said. 'Agrippina, Nero and Drusus.' The first two exiled, the third shut away and – as I now knew – a madman. 'Jupiter!'

'Yeah.' Lippillus nodded. 'By that time the Julian party's power was broken and Sejanus could go for the top. Like I said, he's the only one left.'

I pitted an olive. Livia had been right about the Senate's records providing a key to Sejanus. This was what she'd been pointing me at.

'So tell me more,' I said.

'You want a lesson in politics? I'm no political expert, Marcus.'

'Yeah. Sure.' We'd had this conversation before. 'Just give me the basic details, the ones that everybody knows. Pretend I'm an idiot.'

'What's to pretend?' He grinned suddenly and refilled our wine cups. 'Okay. So we'll start from where you left for Greece. You know Tiberius and Drusus – his own son Drusus, not Germanicus's boy – shared the consulship for the next year?'

'Sure.' That had made sense. It had been inevitable, in fact: with Germanicus dead the Wart had had to choose a new crown prince, and Drusus was the obvious choice. Sharing the consulship was the usual way of signalling it; which was why, this year past, the alarm bells had begun ringing with Sejanus.

'Right.' Lippillus broke a piece of bread and dunked it in olive oil. 'Only the Wart had already presented young Nero to the Senate, and married him to his son Drusus's daughter. You with me?'

'You're saying that Tiberius was marking Drusus as his successor, but Nero was next in line.'

'Uh-huh. Then the Wart takes the next step, the big one. He gives Drusus a share of his own tribunician power. But he also makes sure that Nero and his brother, the other Drusus, have their feet on the first rung of the imperial ladder. A working compromise. Drusus is to be the next emperor, but he'll be followed by a Julian.'

There was something wrong here. 'Drusus had a son of his own,' I said. 'What you're saying is that Tiberius's own son agreed to be no more than a stopgap for Agrippina's boys.'

Lippillus shrugged. 'I told you, Corvinus. I'm no politician. Drusus seemed happy enough, in public, anyway. He hadn't been asked to adopt Nero formally, and his own son Gemellus was hardly more than an infant. He couldn't've expected the Wart to do otherwise, not if he had the empire's best interests at heart.'

Yeah, okay, that made sense. Like Lippillus said, it was a working compromise. The empire had an experienced crown prince – Drusus – in the saddle with two up-and-coming Imperials, Agrippina's kids, to back him. And Agrippina couldn't complain that her side of the family was getting a raw deal. 'Only then the situation changed. Drusus died.'

'Drusus died.'

'Uh-huh.' I kept my voice neutral. 'You happen to know how that happened, exactly?'

His eyes held mine. 'Don't jump to conclusions. The death was natural.'

'You're sure?'

'It was a long-standing thing, not sudden. He'd had trouble on and off for years. Some sort of wasting sickness that finally killed him. Sejanus was just lucky, that's all.'

Yeah, okay, maybe; these things happen. But guys like Sejanus make their own luck. I shelved that one for future reference. 'So the game was wide open again. There was a vacancy at the top, for a caretaker.'

'Right. The two young Julians were still in place, but the experienced man was gone.'

'Enter Sejanus.'

Lippillus shook his head. 'No, not yet. He'd've liked the job, sure. Only it wasn't that easy, even if he'd had the Wart's full support.' He chewed on a slice of sausage. 'Court favourite or not, Sejanus is a nobody. We're not talking simple power here, you understand. We're talking family.'

Yeah. That added up. You don't need to tell a Valerius Messalla about family. You either have it or you don't, and if you don't then breaking into the system is as difficult as swimming the Tiber with your hands tied behind you and a brick between your teeth. Sejanus had power, sure, but it came from the Wart and left to itself it would die with the Wart. He may've been fairly well connected on his mother's side, but not well enough to count. There're only two ways to join the inner club at Rome: either you're born into it or you marry into it. Preferably both. Tiberius understood that. He could mark Sejanus as caretaker, sure, but the system would've accepted the guy only as long as the Wart was there to back him; which, when the time came, he naturally wouldn't be. And *that* was no position for a designated successor to be in.

'So Sejanus began to make space for himself by sandbagging the Julians?' I took another swallow of wine.

'Correct. There's the reason for your treason trials, Corvinus.' Lippillus emptied the jug into my cup and signalled the waiter for another. Ah, well. Perilla couldn't blame me this time. 'He had to make himself indispensable by getting rid of the opposition, and he did it by convincing the Wart that the Julians were a danger. Meanwhile he was pestering the emperor over Drusus's widow Livilla. Tiberius turned him down flat, but you see the plan.'

Uh-huh. Sure I did. Like I say, Sejanus's only way into the club was by marriage. As Livilla's husband he'd be the Wart's son-in-law and Gemellus's stepfather. Once the Julians were discredited he'd be sitting pretty. *Was* sitting pretty: to all intents and purposes the Julians were gone, and when the Wart had named Sejanus as his colleague in the consulship he'd also made the betrothal to Livilla official. All he needed now was the tribunician power to mark him indelibly as Rome's future ruler, and that would come because, like Lippillus had said, the emperor had no one else to give it to.

I sat back. 'How much of this is common knowledge?'

Lippillus shrugged. 'All of it, I expect. In the right circles.'

Yeah. That I could understand. It was why Lamia and Arruntius were so desperate to have the guy's plug pulled as of yesterday. 'And to the emperor as well?'

'Naturally. It has to be. Tiberius may've shut himself away in Capri, but he's no fool and most of it happened before he retired.

He's backing Sejanus all the way, Corvinus. He has no choice. And don't you let anyone tell you different.'

Shit. No wonder the Senate were chewing their communal fingernails off at the wrist, or that they'd been desperate enough to ask for my help. If the Wart had decided that Sejanus was going to be the next emperor in full knowledge of what a bastard he was then Livia's plan was stone dead. We could all put the shutters up and go home. Finish, end of story.

There was only one thing that was niggling me, and it had been niggling right from the start of Lippillus's politics lesson. Not a big thing, maybe it meant nothing, but it niggled.

'You said Sejanus began going for the Julians after Drusus died, right?' I said.

'Yeah. So what?'

'One of those guys I mentioned. Junius Silanus. When was he charged exactly?'

Lippillus frowned. 'You want the date? How the hell should I know?'

'Not the exact date. I can check that for myself. Just remind me. Was it before or after Drusus hung up his sandals?'

I'd got him now: I told you, Lippillus was quick. If Sejanus's plan to slug the Julians postdated the death of the Wart's son then Silanus was an anomaly.

'It was before,' he said. 'About a year before.'

'That's what I thought. The next question's obvious. Silanus was charged with treason, and the Wart pressed the case. So what did Silanus do exactly?'

'I don't know.' We were staring at each other now. 'That would be in the senatorial records.'

'It isn't. I've looked. There's just the bare charge and the verdict.'

'Is that so, now?' Lippillus said slowly, and stroked his jaw.

'That's so. But maybe I should have another look at that particular roll.'

'Yeah. I'd do that, too.' He was looking thoughtful. 'Meanwhile I'll tell you something else. Silanus wasn't the first Julian to go. There was a guy a year before him, a Caesius Cordus. He was condemned for treason too.'

Uh-huh. I remembered Cordus from my notes. He'd been

governor of Crete and Cyrene, while Silanus had had Asia. Adjoining provinces, both senatorial and so outwith the emper- or's direct control . . .

Silanus and Cordus. Both Julians, both governors of senatorial provinces. Both condemned for treason and extortion, from adjoining commands . . .

Maybe significant, maybe not, but there was a cold chill at the nape of my neck that told me it mattered.

'Corvinus?' Lippillus was looking at me. 'You okay?'

I brought myself back with a wrench.

'Yeah,' I said. 'Yeah, I'm okay. Thanks, Lippillus. Thanks a lot.'

'Don't mention it.' He emptied his cup and got to his feet. 'Now if you'll excuse me this high-powered stuff's all very well but I've got a salary to earn.'

'We ordered another jug.'

'Have it on me. Grumio'll charge it to my account in any case. You're on holiday, remember?'

'Dinner some time soon? I'll send Bathyllus.'

'Sure.'

'Bring Marcina.'

He flashed me a smile. 'Mother'll look forward to it. I'll see you around, Corvinus.'

I glanced up at the sun. Just after noon. The records office would be open for another three hours at least, a jug was a jug, and, like Lippillus had said, this was supposed to be a holiday . . .

Conscience and duty won. I sighed and rose to go. Perilla would have been proud of me.

6

Rusticus wasn't around, but the slaves knew me and let me pull down the two rolls I needed to check. It fitted. Neither my memory nor my notes were at fault. The main charge was given clearly enough, provincial extortion in both cases. Cordus had been prosecuted by a guy called Ancharius Priscus, who I didn't know, and Silanus by another senator representing the Council of Asian Cities; the treason raps were added riders with no additional explanation or details.

Okay so far. There was one other possibility, that the records had been tampered with physically. Senatorial records, like normal books, are made up of standard-sized sheets glued together top to bottom and wound on to a spindle. If someone wanted to lose a piece of text at the start or finish of a sheet all they'd have to do would be to detach the page, cut it across at the appropriate point and glue it back along the new edge. Taking out a passage in the middle of a page would be more difficult, and so easier to spot; at the very least there'd be traces of rubbing, maybe signs of a different hand or a different colour ink in the necessary filler if the forger wasn't all that competent.

I took the rolls over to the desk by the window and examined them carefully in full daylight. The relevant sheets were numbered and in their proper place in the sequence. So far, so good: no whole pages missing, which had been another possibility. More important, the sheets were the same length and colour as the others either side and several pages back, and the glue between them was the same shade of dirty brown. There was no sign of scraping or rubbing that I could see, and if any part of the text was forged the guy who'd done it must've been a real professional.

So. As far as I could tell, the records themselves hadn't been altered since they'd been written, and what you saw was what you got. Which meant that the treason charges against Cordus and Silanus hadn't been spelled out in open court or an injunction had been put on including them in the formal minutes; either one of which scenarios meant censorship at the imperial level.

So why should the Wart censor the details of a treason charge in the private, official records of the Senate? And did the similarity of treatment mean that the two cases were somehow linked?

I didn't have the answers. Not yet, and maybe I never would. Suddenly, my stomach rumbled. It'd been a long time since Grumio's sausage, and I was starving. Lunch break. I put the records back where they belonged and set off home to the Palatine.

Perilla was reading in the garden. I sneaked up behind her and planted a smacker on the back of her neck, just under the curls.

'Hey, lady,' I said.

She smiled but didn't look round. 'Did you have a good morning, Marcus?'

'Yeah. Yeah, you could say that.' Bathyllus had been following me with a tray. He set the wine jug and cup on the table and I took the chair opposite Perilla's. 'What's for lunch, little guy?'

'Cold braised lung with chickpeas, sir.'

'Great.' At the back of my throat I could still taste the old paper and glue smell of the archives. I took the full cup he was holding out to me and sank it in one. Nectar.

'Uh . . . you hear from Junia Torquata these days, Perilla?' I said.

She set her book down and I took a glance at the label. It was in Greek: Theagenes's *Homeric Allegories*. One of her lighter reads.

'No,' she said. 'I do not hear from Junia Torquata these days, because Junia Torquata as you well know was my mother's friend, not mine, and Mother is dead. However, I assume you have an ulterior motive in asking the question, Marcus, so you may as well tell me what that is now and save yourself the strain of inventing a lie that I won't believe anyway.'

Jupiter! I glanced at Bathyllus, but the little guy had run for cover at the first subordinate clause. 'Uh, yeah. Yeah, I do have a reason for asking, actually. You see . . .'

'It's to do with Sejanus, isn't it?'

Even the frogs in the pool had shut up: one croak out of turn and it might be them next. 'Not directly, no. At least . . .'

'Oh, Marcus!' Perilla sighed. 'Can't you leave this alone? Please?'

That was better. I leaned over and kissed her cheek. 'No,' I said simply. 'I can't.'

Another sigh, but this one had a note of resignation. We were over the hump, and the frogs and I breathed again. I waited.

'So,' Perilla said at last. 'What do you want with Torquata?'

I didn't even try fibbing. It wasn't worth the risk.

'She's Gaius Silanus's sister. Silanus was exiled to Cythnos nine years ago for treason and I want to know why.'

'Do you think Torquata will tell you?'

'There's no reason why she shouldn't, and no harm in asking even if she doesn't. The alternative is to take the case from the other end, through the prosecutor, and I don't want to do that.'

'I see.' Perilla looked at me for a long time, frowning. Then she snapped, '*Bathyllus!*'

The little guy was there almost before she'd got the last syllable out.

'Yes, madam.' Cringe cringe.

'Send someone over to the House of the Vestals to ask if Junia Torquata is free for dinner this evening. Or if not to arrange a suitable date.'

Bathyllus hovered nervously. 'Ah . . . I assume, madam, that you've already mentioned this to the cook?'

Oh, bugger. I saw his point straight off. Meton was touchy as hell at the best of times, and short notice dinner parties always got up his nose. Even the little I knew about Junia Torquata's foibles warned me that he was going to like the idea of this one even less than usual.

Perilla gave Bathyllus a look that would've crisped his hair, if he'd had any.

'Tell Meton I'll discuss the menu with him later,' she said.

'Yes, madam. Certainly, madam.' Bathyllus left, so fast I could hear his truss creak.

'Uh . . . thanks,' I said.

'Don't mention it.' She picked up Theagenes again. 'I don't approve of this, Corvinus, remember that. But I take your point about the prosecutor. Just be careful, please. And don't get Torquata into any trouble, either.'

I had my mouth open to answer, and then I decided not to. In Perilla's present mood any crack about getting a Vestal into trouble would've been as welcome as an owl at a wedding.

Not that anyone had a hope in hell of fooling with Junia Torquata against her will, even if they'd been short-sighted and desperate enough to want to. Given the choice of going two rounds bare-fisted with the lady herself or her complimentary axeman escort I'd've taken the guy with the chopper and rods any day. How a woman can manage to look at the same time completely unworldly and tough as a Suburan bruiser beats me.

On water and vegetables, too. 'I don't eat meat,' she snapped at me that evening as she made her way to the guest couch like a trireme going in for the kill. 'It thickens the blood. And wine enervates. Even the smell is sufficient to cause the greatest bodily harm.' Oh, Jupiter! 'I hope your chef has taken those maxims into account, Caecinus.'

'Uh, yeah.' I glanced at Perilla, who had lain down chastely on a couch of her own three feet from mine: no funny business this evening, not with a Vestal as dinner guest. She'd warned me to watch my language, too. One four-letter word out of place and we'd probably be hit with a curse that'd drive Aeschylus to crochet. 'And it's Corvinus.'

Torquata ignored me. She was prodding the couch's upholstery with a large suspicious forefinger. Maybe she thought it hid our illicit meat-safe.

'Marcus has seen to everything. Haven't you, Marcus?' Perilla gave the old warhorse her best smile.

'Yeah. Yeah, that's right.' I didn't deserve the credit, because Perilla had made all the arrangements, but she obviously wanted me to look good. Jupiter knew what this meal was going to cost us, and I'm not talking cash. I'd been right about Meton. When Perilla had told him she wanted a wholly vegetarian menu he'd thrown, in quick succession, a fit, two saucepans, a skillet and his third-best cleaver. We'd be suffering the after-effects for a month at least.

'Then I hope you double-checked the arrangements yourself, my dear.' Torquata sniffed. 'Men are well enough within their limits but they cannot be totally depended on to remember crucial details.'

Oh, joy. From the sound of things this was going to be a peach of an evening. I wondered what the penalty in the Twelve Tables was for booting a Vestal round your dining-room.

'How do fern roots braised with almonds, lettuce purée, a nut omelette and a milk casserole to finish sound, Junia Torquata?' I said.

'Delicious.' Torquata had finally arranged herself on the couch and was adjusting the woollen girdle that supported her massive breasts. 'The fern roots will not have been braised in wine, I trust? And the milk will be sheep's?'

I counted to ten slowly. Perilla was biting her knuckles.

'The best,' I said. 'And only from contented ewes.' Jupiter's balls on a string! We should've asked Mother round. The pair of them could've swapped idiosyncrasies.

'Oh, how nice.' The Vestal beamed. 'It's almost impossible these days to get really first-rate ewe's milk. You must give me the name of your supplier.'

Perilla gave a choking cough. I turned to Bathyllus who was hovering in the background doing his smarmy butler act. 'Okay, little guy. Wheel it in.'

He signalled to his minions waiting outside. They brought in the appetisers and laid them out.

'Those things look *most* interesting.' Torquata pointed to a plate of green-flecked rissoles. 'What are they?'

'Uh . . . Bathyllus?' I said.

'Pumpkin and buckwheat fritters, madam. With wormwood.'

'Ah.' Torquata nodded. 'Wormwood. Excellent. *So* good for the bowels.'

I'd kill that bastard Meton. Some jokes just aren't funny. 'Just serve the wine, little guy,' I said.

Bathyllus raised an eyebrow at me. 'Wine, sir?'

I stared at him in horror and got a look that was blind and bland as Homer's. Oh, hell. Oh, hell, no! I'd assumed Torquata would miss out on the strong drink, of course, and be given some foul concoction of her own, but not that I'd be expected to join her.

'Whatever we're having, then.' I sighed. 'Just pour.' A peach of an evening was right. I only hoped the mad old biddy was worth the sacrifice.

'We thought you'd enjoy Meton's honey-fruit surprise, Torquata,' Perilla said, smiling at me. 'It really is very refreshing. Marcus absolutely loves it.'

You're next, lady, I thought, as I held my cup up for Bathyllus to pour. It didn't look too bad. I sniffed, then sipped, and the liquid burst into song on my tongue. Shit! Caecuban! And not just any Caecuban but *the* Caecuban – the stuff from the imperial cellars that Livia had sent me. I hadn't known we had any of it left.

Bathyllus gave me the ghost of a wink. What was going on here? The little guy had served Torquata first, and he hadn't switched jugs because I'd been watching all the time. Ergo, our guest was wrapped round a good quarter-pint of prime fermented grape juice, and she must know it. So why was the room still in one piece?

I looked at the Vestal. She was holding out the empty cup for a refill.

'Ah . . . you liked that, Junia Torquata?' I asked carefully.

'Very much.' She must've been working on that strait-laced stare for years. 'It has such a lovely tang of apples.'

'Uh . . . yeah. Yeah, it does, doesn't it?' The refill disappeared. Bacchus, the old girl could pack it away faster than I could. I just hoped we did have another flask in the cellar. Two flasks.

Perilla wasn't drinking much. Not surprising, since she knew what was in the jug: the Caecuban was practically neat, and she genuinely prefers fruit juice.

'We're so glad you could come, Torquata,' she said. 'Marcus has been dying to meet you. He's most interested in the origins of priestly ritual.'

I almost swallowed my wine cup.

'Really?' Torquata smiled at me. 'So nice to find a young man with a taste for tradition. And so rare these days. Which particular aspect of ritual absorbs you most, Caecinus?'

'Ah . . .'

'Don't tell me. I know. The Salian priesthood's. You have the physique of a Salian yourself. Small head, good chest, tight withers. And the right blood, of course. Never forget the blood.' She held out her cup. Bathyllus leaped forwards to fill it. 'Blood always tells.'

Jupiter! She was worse than Priscus on a bad day! It was like having your brain mugged by a theological gorilla. I gritted my teeth and hung on while she drank her way down the jug (without any noticeable effect) and took me through the insanitary personal habits of the Jumping Priests of Mars. By which time we'd gummed the lettuce purée and were squelching our way through the milk casserole.

'And how is your poor brother?' Perilla took advantage of a lull in the conversation.

Torquata frowned. 'Which one, my dear? The goody-goody, the crook, or the fool who got himself involved with Julia?'

Perilla didn't bat a beautiful eyelid.

'The crook,' she said.

'Oh, Gaius is still twiddling his thumbs on that island of his. Silly man. Mind you, he was damned lucky to get off so lightly. He always was too sharp for his own good, even as a child.'

'Extortion is such a sordid crime, I always think.' Perilla scooped the last of the milk and pine nuts from her bowl. 'And so unfortunate for the family.'

Torquata snorted. 'Damn extortion! There's a lot of nonsense talked these days about not exploiting provincials. What did the good gods put provincials out there for if not to be exploited?' She held up her cup for Bathyllus to fill. The little guy was looking punch-drunk; Vestals can be wearing at close quarters. 'There's nothing wrong with a bit of honest extortion, Perilla. Gaius would have been all right if he'd stuck to feathering his own nest decently like a governor should and kept away from You Know Who.'

I sat up. 'Uh . . . "You Know Who"?' I said.

Torquata ignored me. 'Please don't get me wrong, my dear. I

have the utmost respect for her, even if she is a little overbearing.
All the best mothers are. I have no children myself, naturally,
but I do understand the mother's role. You have to dominate
the little vipers from birth. Mould them to shape, for their
own good.'

'Quite right.' Perilla sipped at the half cup of wine she'd
allowed herself.

'Nor did I have anything against the idea as such,' the Vestal
went on. 'I mean, if you're going to do something like that
it's bound to be expensive and the money has to come from
somewhere. And it might well have worked. But it's Gaius's
stupidity that I cannot understand. Did he really imagine for
one moment that the emperor wouldn't *notice*?' She emptied
her cup at a gulp. 'Oh, hell. Let's change the subject. Your poor
hubby's looking bored, and just thinking about that silly man
makes me angry. What sort of fruit have you got? I could just
manage a pineapple or two.'

'Bored' wasn't the word for how I looked, of course; I was
gobsmacked. So gobsmacked that I didn't notice that my mouth
was hanging open until Perilla whispered to me to close it. Maybe
Torquata was short-sighted. Or maybe Meton's honey-fruit surprise had got to her after all. I'd been counting, and I made it two
and a half jugs. One for me and Perilla between us, the rest for
Junia Torquata. Still, I didn't regret them, imperial Caecuban or
not. They'd done their work on the old reprobate, and my brain
was buzzing like a beehive in spring.

It was two in the morning before we finally got rid of her. In the
course of the evening she'd finished off the third jug practically
single-handed and made a fair-sized hole in a jug of the Special,
but she walked out of the front door without either a stumble or
a slur. Impressive stuff. As a drinker I'd've backed her against a
legion's First Spear any day of the month. She certainly had me
beat hands down, no contest.

'Thank you, Perilla,' she said as she eased herself into her litter.
'And you, of course, Caecinus. A marvellous evening. Simply
splendid. We must have a rematch some time soon.' Then, to the
waiting axeman: 'Home, Decimus. "Forth now fare we, forth in
splendour," my dear.'

The litter boys took the strain. Perilla and I looked at each other and tried to keep from laughing until they'd disappeared down Poplicolan Street. We managed, just; but it was a close-run thing.

'And thank you, lady,' I said to Perilla. 'You were brilliant.'

'Oh, it was nothing.'

'Next time we have her we'll invite Uncle Cotta and sell tickets.'

Perilla creased up. I kissed her. 'Bed?'

She kissed me back. 'Bed, Caecinus.'

Vestals are okay in their place, but you wouldn't want to marry one.

7

'Marcus, you're not concentrating.'

'IImm?'

'You do realise that this sleuthing business is simply ruining our love life?'

'Yeah?'

'Yes. I thought we'd done with all of that. And personally I find it very hard to make love with a brain ticking away just above my head.'

I slipped an arm round her shoulders. 'Brains don't tick, lady.'

'Yours does. It's distracting.'

Yeah, well. Maybe I had been putting in a bit of illicit thinking. Thcrc's a timc and a placc for cvcrything, and as far as turning possible political scams over in your head is concerned two in the morning in a beautiful woman's bed isn't either. I pulled her tighter and her chin wedged itself into the hollow of my neck.

'How did you know to pull that stunt with the wine?' I said.

'Mother used to do it. And Aunt Marcia. It's Torquata's one failing.'

'Failing? I'd hate to match that old dear cup for cup in a drinking bout. As a Vestal she's wasted. A shame it had to be the last of the Caecuban, though.'

I felt Perilla grin. 'Nothing else would have done, Marcus. I wanted her in a good mood. She adores wine, but she wouldn't have drunk so much if it hadn't been the best.'

'Oh, I'm not complaining. Not really. The stuff went to a good home, and Livia would've approved. Thanks again, lady.'

She snuggled against me. 'You're welcome.'

'Is that so?' I kissed her ear, then moved on to the cheek. No response. Things should've been warming up by now, but apart from the snuggle they weren't. For a lady who'd just lodged a formal complaint Perilla was being pretty distant. That should've started alarm bells ringing. It didn't.

'You're right about one more thing,' she murmured.

'Yeah?' I carried on westward. 'Namely?'

'Junia Torquata is wasted as a Vestal. Vestals can leave the priesthood and marry after thirty years, when there's still time to have children. One child, at any rate. I'm surprised she didn't do it.'

Uh-oh. There went the bell. I paused, just to the right of her mouth, and tried to keep my voice light. 'You joking, Perilla? After that crack about vipers what kind of a mother do you think she'd make?'

'Torquata isn't as hard-bitten as she likes to appear. And what woman doesn't want children? Even a Vestal?'

There was no answer to that, not one I wanted to make, anyway. And I could feel the spot of dampness on Perilla's cheek under mine. Quietly, I gathered her in and we made love, as we always did, as we'd been doing for the past twelve years or so. In terms of comfort it wasn't much, but it was all I could offer.

Perilla had been right about the brain. I couldn't sleep. Leaving her huddled under the blanket I picked up the nightlight and crept downstairs to the study, via the wine cellar: Bathyllus was in bed long ago and if he'd heard me moving around he would've got up. I'd run the little guy pretty ragged these past few days, and he deserved a break. Bathyllus gets sarky when he doesn't have his eight hours.

I lit the reading lamp next to the couch, pulled out my notes and poured myself a cup of Setinian (no Caecuban left; *really* no Caecuban left, this time. I'd checked). 'You Know Who.' Yeah, well, I did at that. Torquata must've been talking about Agrippina, especially with the bit about the kids: Germanicus's widow was tough as old army boots, and she'd kept both her sons right under her thumb; the third one, too, Gaius, although he was the favourite.

So. Silanus had been mixed up with Agrippina. Sure, I knew

from my talk with Lippillus that he'd been a Julian supporter, but this sounded more specific. And it involved money.

Okay, what had we got? I laid it out. Gaius Silanus had been the governor of the richest province in the empire; better, Asia was *senatorial*, so although Tiberius kept a watching brief, as he did throughout the provinces, he wasn't directly concerned with the admin. Or the taxes. Right. A scenario. Let's say Silanus was creaming a bit off the top, like governors do and have done since we took Sicily from the Greeks and Carthaginians almost three hundred years back; only instead of the money going into his own pocket it went to the Julians. That would fit in with what Torquata had said about her brother not sticking to feathering his own nest. It would explain the treason charge, too, and why the Wart hadn't wanted the details to be made public. He couldn't afford an open breach with Agrippina, and he wouldn't've wanted it, either, not when he was grooming her sons for higher things. So long as the hole was plugged, that was enough. He'd even commuted Silanus's death sentence to exile, as a goodwill gesture.

I took a swallow of wine: the Setinian tasted almost rough after the Caecuban, but like I'd told Perilla Livia's thank-you present had gone to the best home possible. Yeah, that fitted. It fitted with Caesius Cordus, too, the Cyrenean governor who'd also been prosecuted for extortion and treason. Cordus was the other half of the scam. Maybe he'd put in a penny or two himself – Crete/Cyrene wasn't in Asia's league, but it was no pauper – but I suspected his main job had been to launder the cash flow between Silanus and Rome. Whichever way it was, he'd been nailed at the same time; only not jointly, because that would've started people thinking. Or at least made a point that the Wart didn't want made . . .

Asia. There had been something else about Asia, if I could only find it. I shuffled through the notes looking for the reference. There it was, on the top of the third sheet; one of the prosecutions I hadn't included in my shortened treason list. A year after Silanus was exiled to Cythnos a guy named Lucilius Capito had been condemned for – quote – 'usurping the governor's authority and using military force'. And Capito, so my notes said, had been the Wart's Asian factor . . .

Things were falling into place sweet as a nut. I sat back. That made sense, too. As emperor, Tiberius had private estates which he ran through factors: narrow-stripers, plain-mantles, even a few freedmen. Most of the estates were in Italy, but a lot were overseas, and of these Asia was the biggie. Taken together, the revenues from the Wart's Asian properties would've equalled the tax returns of a small province: Noricum, say, or Lusitania. With both the governor and the imperial agent chipping in to the kitty we weren't talking peanuts.

Okay. In Capito's case I was guessing. But let's say he was in on the scam. While Silanus was governor there was no problem; the governor took his cut from the ordinary provincials and Capito milked the private sector for what he could get, with the governor's connivance and support. Only then Silanus gets chopped and Capito is on his own. Sure, the guy could simply have pulled in his horns and crawled back into his shell, but he didn't; maybe he'd just got used to being the big shot and couldn't give it up. Anyway, he carries on the way he's been doing, using the local government troops to provide the muscle, and the new governor, who's Tiberius's man, naturally blows the whistle. Whereupon the Wart hauls Capito back to Rome and has the Senate detach his balls.

It would work. Sure it would, although I'd need to dig if I wanted proof. The important thing was that I had that tingle at the base of my skull that told me I was right. With that amount of cash flowing into Agrippina's secret fund on a regular basis she could really make things happen. Even when the cash flow stopped. A careful Roman housewife like her would know how to make the best use of the pennies.

My jaw muscles tightened and I yawned. Yeah, well, maybe that was enough for one night. If I'd uncovered a major Julian finance scam it wasn't a bad evening's work. A shame to leave the wine, though; I'd hardly touched it. And I knew that as soon as I got upstairs my brain would start buzzing again. Ticking. Whatever.

Okay. One final stretch, and we'd call it a day. What was it for, the Asian money?

I had the answer to that one already. I'd had it ten years back. When Germanicus had been chopped he and Agrippina had been plotting treason. Treason doesn't come cheap, not these days. People have to be bought, and kept bought: I knew a few of them now myself. Oh, sure, there are the altruists who conspire out of principle, but they're pretty thin on the ground. Even the Julians couldn't expect all their supporters to be dewy-eyed devotees willing to give their all for the cause. A Roman doesn't give anything for nothing. He expects something back.

So. Silanus and his pals had been financing a Julian war-chest. The big question was why? The Julian plot was dead; thanks to Sejanus and the Wart it had gone down the tube with Germanicus's own death, a full three years before Silanus had been prosecuted. Yet Torquata had talked about a specific scam, an 'idea', she'd called it, that was linked with Agrippina. When Germanicus had died, he and his wife had had the empire all sewn up, potentially: the Rhine legions, the east, even Italy and Rome itself. The only really important bits left unaccounted for were . . .

Were . . .

I sat up so fast I spilled my wine. Jupiter! Oh, holy Jupiter! Jupiter best and greatest!

The only really important parts left had been Gaul and Spain!

I scrabbled for the notes, ignoring the spilt wine, and fumbled through them. It was all there, starting at the same time as Capito had been prosecuted, four years after Germanicus's death: Vibius Serenus, the Spanish governor, convicted of public violence; Gaius Silius, governor of Upper Germany, convicted of involvement in the Gallic revolt: Silius, whose involvement with rebels I couldn't understand, who commanded half of the biggest army north of the Pyrenees. Shit! And there was more, sure there was! I leafed through the papers frantically. Serenus again, hauled back from exile later in the same year and for the same crime as Silius: involvement with the Gauls. Votienus Montanus, Gaul, condemned for slander . . .

Gaul. Spain. The two major western provinces. The only parts of the empire barring Africa that Agrippina didn't already have her claws into. Or at least at the time I hadn't thought she had. And although Sejanus's uncle Junius Blaesus had held Africa he'd been kept too busy with the rebel Tacfarinas even to scratch himself . . .

The prosecutions all dated to four years after Germanicus's death. Four years after the Julian plot was officially dead and buried. And the year before that . . .

Bull's-eye! I reached out a trembling hand, refilled my empty wine cup and drank the Setinian down.

Sacrovir!

8 ∫

Next morning I went down to Watch headquarters again to see Lippillus. He'd had a late-night mugging and was taking the morning off, but the squaddie I'd caught him bawling out gave me directions to his new flat. I hoped I'd find it. Lippillus was right: the guy was thick as two short planks. Three. Jupiter knew how he'd made it through puberty, let alone been accepted for the Watch.

On the way I turned over in my mind what I already knew about the Sacrovir revolt in Gaul. It wasn't much; I'd been in Athens at the time, and for Athenians Roman politics is a topic of conversation that ranks on a par with bedbugs and the finer points of sewage disposal. For all the Greeks cared, the Germans could've swum the Rhine, taken out all six of our legions and been giving lieder recitals on the Palatine with the Wart singing bass.

It had happened not long after I left Rome. I wasn't sure of the reasons, but they probably involved complaints about taxes. Revolts usually do, when you come right down to it, although you can substitute *tribute* or *reparations* or whatever the appropriate term might be, depending on the status of the areas concerned and what their precise relationship with us is; at least the relationship as we see it. Keeping an empire running doesn't come cheap, and the guys who run it are mostly ordinary human beings with families to feed and expensive tastes to pander to, ready and willing to turn an honest penny when opportunity presents itself. Or even a dishonest penny if they can get away with it. For all Augustus and the Wart's attempted reforms you still get the old republican spiral: high taxes leading to debt leading to profiteering by private loan sharks leading to deeper poverty and discontent. When that gets bad enough – and it happens more quickly in the poorer provinces where hard cash isn't too plentiful and a tax demand means bad news for the goats – there's always trouble. Usually the local rep keeps it in check by knocking heads together, but sometimes things get out of hand and the governor has to send in the heavies.

Which was what had happened in Gaul. The trouble part, anyway. There'd been two revolts, one in the east towards the German border and one in the centre. The eastern rebellion, led by a local chief named Florus, had been put down pretty smartly. The other, which was Sacrovir's, was a tougher proposition altogether. Sure, we broke them, but it took the German governor Silius and a major slice of both Rhine armies to do it; the same Silius, if you remember, who was later prosecuted for helping the rebels . . .

Interesting as far as it went, but not a lot to go on as far as nitty-gritty details were concerned. Which was why I needed to talk to Lippillus again.

I was lucky. Maybe the squaddie had concrete filling between his ears but there was nothing wrong with his directions. I found the tenement without much trouble. It was upmarket for a city island; which meant the graffiti on the stair walls was correctly spelled and passing dogs or local residents who couldn't be bothered to make the trip to the public toilet didn't use the entrance lobby as a latrine. Marcina Paullina answered the door. She was wearing a loose red tunic that made a fantastic threesome with her glossy black hair and olive skin.

'Corvinus!' she said. 'How lovely to see you! Do come in. Decimus is having breakfast.'

'Uh, yeah.' I tried not to look down as I eased past her in the narrow lobby: tenement flats aren't exactly spacious. Jupiter! Stepmothers like that shouldn't be allowed! And if she'd put on weight then she'd done it in all the right places. 'Thanks. I'm sorry to disturb you this early, Marcina.'

'That's all right. Anyway, it's not early. I was just going shopping, in fact.' As I always did, I wondered about Marcina's accent. She was African, sure, but she spoke the kind of pure Roman Latin you don't expect to hear in a city tenement, and I couldn't imagine her haggling for beans in the market.

'Hi, Corvinus.' Lippillus was sitting at the small folding table which was one of the few bits of furniture in the room, working his way through a plate of bread and cheese. 'Pull up a stool. You eaten yet?'

'Yeah.' I sat down. 'Some of that cheese would be good, though.'

'Help yourself.'

Marcina brought a flask of wine and two cups. Sensitive as well as beautiful.

'So how was the mugging?' I said.

'The usual.' He pushed the plate of cheese towards me. 'Smartass Esquiline kid with more money than sense slumming it in Cattlemarket Square. Luckily he had a hard skull. He'll be okay in a month or two, if he lives. So. How's your own investigation going?'

Marcina had taken a red headscarf and a cloak down from a hook behind the door and put them on. 'I'll see you later, Decimus,' she said. 'Sprats for dinner?'

'Fine.' Lippillus grinned at her. 'If I'm back in time. Don't wait up.'

'Do I ever?' She gave me a smile and left. Ah, well. Maybe it was for the best. With Marcina around I'd've found it difficult to keep my mind on business. I turned back to Lippillus.

'What do you know about the Gallic revolt?' I said.

Lippillus poured wine into the two cups. 'Florus and Sacrovir? No more than anyone else.' Yeah. I'd expected that, and I ignored it. The guy was a walking encyclopaedia. 'You think there's a connection with your stuff?'

I told him about the treason trials, the Asian scam, and what Torquata had said. When I'd finished, he nodded slowly.

'It sounds possible. Just. But if you think it was meant to pave the way for a Julian coup in Rome then you're fantasising.'

'Is that right?' I took a sip of the wine. Rough country stuff, but it went well with the goat's cheese.

'That's right. Florus and Sacrovir were amateurs. They caused a stir at the time, but nothing really serious, and nothing long term. Certainly not major enough to threaten the security of the empire.'

Yeah. That was true. If Agrippina had expected the west to rise as one man to the Julian cause she'd been disappointed. 'So you think I'm wrong?'

'No. Not necessarily.' Lippillus cut himself a slice of cheese. 'But you are looking at things from the wrong angle.'

'Okay, Aristotle. Tell me.'

He didn't smile. 'It's obvious. Like I said, Florus and Sacrovir were lightweights, in Roman terms at least. Sure, they had a lot of local support but once the legions were called in they didn't have a chance. The revolt never spread much beyond their own two tribes, let alone to Germany or the Spanish provinces. And if, like you claim, Silius and the Spanish governor were Julian supporters then that's significant, because if they intervened publicly at all it was on the Wart's side.'

True. All of it. Shit.

'So what was going on?'

'You want an educated guess?'

'*Yes*, I want an educated guess!' Jupiter! Getting this clever midget to commit himself was like taking a bone from a seriously disgruntled wolverine.

'All right.' He sipped his wine. 'Let's say the purpose of the rebellion wasn't military at all. It was political; at least as far as the Julians were concerned. Wouldn't that make more sense?'

Uh-huh. It rang a few ten-year-old bells, too, and I wondered why I hadn't thought of it before. 'You mean the Julians were going for the Wart personally? For his political street cred?'

Lippillus nodded. 'Tiberius had his back to the wall at the time. He was in trouble financially, the army was stretched and grousing, and as far as his personal prestige was concerned he'd've had trouble running for office as Caretaker of Weights and Measures if he had to, let alone emperor. Whereas Agrippina and her sons were universally popular.'

Yeah, right. The old story, in other words, only for Germanicus read his wife and kids. And the financial aspect tied in nicely. Wars were expensive. The Treasury was already pretty empty after Pannonia and Germany, and the Wart was scraping in the pennies by cutting public spending to the bone. Logical enough, but your average city punter isn't logical over his Games and corn dole, and even emperors ignore the city punter at their peril. As far as Rome's not so silent majority were concerned Tiberius was a stingy bastard, full stop, end of story. More cuts, to pay for yet another war, might just put the lid on things. This was beginning to sound promising.

I took another swig of wine. 'So anything the Julians could do to mess things up even worse for Tiberius would be a definite plus?'

'Right. The aim was destabilisation, coupled with a smear campaign.' Lippillus pulled off a piece of the loaf. 'I doubt if they planned a formal coup. I'd guess the intention was to weaken him enough to force political concessions, and in those terms I'd say the revolt was pretty successful.'

'Yeah?'

'Yeah. You weren't in Rome at the time, Corvinus. You didn't hear the rumours that were going around. If you'd believed half what was said – and I'm not just talking about wineshop gossip, either – you'd've thought the whole of the west was up in arms, Sacrovir was heading over the Alps like Hannibal with half Gaul, Germany and Spain at his back, and the Wart couldn't care a tuppenny toss.' He bit into the bread and chewed. 'Those rumours weren't accidental. And they did a lot of damage.'

I sat back. It made sense. Sure it did, and if that was where the Asian cash had gone then it'd been money well spent.

'Okay,' I said. 'There's the general theory. Where's the proof?'

'You want me to do all your work for you?' Lippillus's smooth, too-young face split into a grin. 'You're the big political thinker, Corvinus. I'm only an overworked public servant with a nasty mind. And with a nasty mind you can prove anything.'

'True. But you don't get any extra points for modesty.' I took the last bit of cheese from under his knife. 'You've probably got this all worked out already six ways from nothing, Lippillus. Cut the flannel and give.'

The grin changed to a laugh and he ducked his head.

'Okay. So maybe I do have some thoughts. Just don't quote me, right?' He bent down a finger on his left hand. 'One. You know that the family name of both Florus and Sacrovir was Julius?'

'Is that so, now?' No, I hadn't known that, and it was an interesting point. Provincial families given Roman citizenship take the name of the Roman who got it for them, just as a freed slave adds his ex-master's first names to his own. It's not only a compliment, it has a practical and legal purpose as well: out in the sticks, being able to sign three names to a document means you're someone to be reckoned with. 'You think they had Julian connections? Specific Julian connections?'

'It's possible. Sure, every third Gaul who can trace his citizenship back more than two generations is a Julius, but both Florus and Sacrovir were chiefs. Important men from important families whose citizen rights dated back to the early days of the province. Maybe even before that. One gets you ten they had client links with the Julians going back all the way to Caesar.'

'And loyalty's important to a Gaul. Personal loyalty. Florus and Sacrovir *owed*.' I nodded. 'Accepted. Two?'

He bent the second finger down. 'Two is the weapons.'

'Weapons?'

'Sacrovir had an army of forty thousand. Four-fifths of them were armed with knives and hunting spears that they could've brought with them from their villages, but at least six thousand had Roman equipment. Top-notch, state-of-the-art legionary stuff. That doesn't come cheap, it doesn't come easy, and it doesn't come quick. So where did Sacrovir get it from?'

Uh-huh. I hadn't known that either, and the hairs on the back of my neck were beginning to stir. Six thousand sets is more than enough to equip a full-strength legion, and you don't pick up gear like that in the local fleamarket. 'The money came from Asia. And the equipment was Spanish and German, courtesy of the two Julian governors.'

'Right. Who else would have access? It would explain why Silius and Serenus were accused later of helping the rebels. Or partly explain it.'

I nodded. 'The guys had been fiddling their order sheets. And if the scam had been brewing for years Rome wouldn't necessarily have noticed.'

'The arms wouldn't even have had to come through official channels, Corvinus. No local manufacturer is going to query a governorial order. And if the bill's paid cash it's no skin off his nose. It only means a bigger slice of the profit.'

'Yeah,' I said. 'Yeah, I'd swallow that. Three.'

'Three is Montanus.'

I was going to say, 'Who?', but then I remembered. Votienus Montanus was the guy condemned the year after Serenus for bad-mouthing the emperor. I'd wondered about that myself. Like I said, up to that point slander had run off the Wart like water off a duck's back. So why had he been so keen to put Montanus into an urn?

'You think the guy did more than just shoot his mouth off?' I said.

'I don't just think it. I know he did. You've read the account of the trial. Does the name Aemilius mean anything to you?'

'He was one of the prosecution witnesses.'

'Did the records go into any details?'

'No. Just the name, and the fact that he'd given relevant evidence.' Shit! I should've noticed the omission myself, especially after the business with Silanus and Cordus.

'Aemilius was a soldier, one of the Lyons auxiliaries. Also a Gaul. Does that suggest anything?'

I had him now, and if he was right then Tiberius had had good reason to want Montanus dead and buried. 'That it wasn't just a straight case of personal slander. Montanus was inciting the local troops to mutiny.'

'Bull's-eye.'

I stared at him. 'Lippillus, where the hell did you get all of this?'

'I have my sources. Even in the Senate.' He sipped his wine and filled both our cups. 'The reason why there's no exact record of Aemilius's deposition, Corvinus, is that he claimed that Montanus had circulated pamphlets among the troops accusing the Wart of every crime from multiple buggery of children to incest with his mother. Plus, incidentally, the murder of every Julian from Gaius and Lucius Caesar to the Divine Augustus himself.'

Oh, Jupiter! Jupiter best and greatest! I could imagine what Gauls would make of *that* little nugget. The Julian family were like gods in Gaul, had been ever since Old Julius divided the place into three parts and wiped their noses for them. And like I'd said loyalty to family was a point of pride west of the Alps. If the local Gallic troops could be convinced that Tiberius had been responsible for snuffing out the Julians they'd be yelling for his head on a pole. I reached for my wine cup and drained it. My hand was shaking.

'They'd need proof,' I said. 'Rabble-rousing's one thing, but the Gauls aren't fools. And they've been settled for three generations.'

'Montanus gave them it. Circumstantial stuff, naturally, but proof none the less. And Aemilius insisted on repeating it loudly and at length in open court. Names. Dates. Details that fitted so well with what everyone knew already that Tiberius shut the guy up himself.'

'"Shut him up"?'

'I'm putting it mildly. My senatorial informant said he was furious. His friends had to hold him down.'

'The Wart? We're talking about the *Wart*?' Jupiter in a bath-robe! Tiberius never lost control of himself in public! Never!

Lippillus nodded. 'We're talking about the Wart. So where would a hick provincial like Montanus who'd never set foot in Rome get that sort of information from?'

'From the Julians themselves. Where else?' I was still in shock. 'Jupiter!'

'Right. Like I said, a smear campaign. And a pretty effective one at that. You want my fourth point?'

'You mean there's more?'

'This one's more interesting still.' He filled my cup. 'It concerns the guy who might just be your tie-in with Sejanus. The Spanish governor. Vibius Serenus.'

9

Vibius Serenus. Erstwhile Spanish governor, prosecuted after the revolt for fomenting public violence in his province, exiled, then again a few months later for direct involvement with Sacrovir. Yeah. I'd been wondering when we'd get round to him. And uncovering another Julian plot was all very well, but my brief was to nail Aelius Sejanus, not Agrippina. Sure, as the Wart's deputy where the cloak-and-dagger stuff was concerned he must've been involved, but it would be with official blessing. That was no use to me. If I wanted his hide pegged out I needed something more.

'You're saying Serenus was Sejanus's man?' I said.

'Don't rush me.' Lippillus shook his head. 'Maybe. But it's not that simple, at least I don't think it is. He was a real Julian, he had to be. All the same, there's something about him that doesn't square. If you're looking for a starting point then my gut feeling is that Serenus is your best bet.'

'How do you mean, "doesn't square"?'

'Corvinus, I'm not sure I know what I mean myself. Certainly not sure enough to put it into words.'

'You care to try?' I trusted Lippillus's gut feelings more than I would another man's certainties. And it wasn't just because I liked the guy. Plug-ugly dwarfs with no-class names don't make regional Watch commander every day, and if they do it's no accident.

Lippillus's brow creased. 'Think of roles. The Gauls – Florus, Sacrovir, Montanus – were the fall guys, the suckers on the fringes who got chopped. Maybe they were being loyal clients, maybe they were political ingénus who thought they had a genuine chance, I don't know, and it doesn't matter because they died anyway. Silius the German governor was nearer the centre. Sure, if I'm right he helped get things going, but his involvement was never overt and once the rebellion was under way he switched sides. If I'm right and the purpose was to embarrass the Wart politically then that makes sense, because his part was finished and there was no reason for him to stick his neck out further.'

'But Serenus's role was the same, surely?' I objected.

Lippillus hesitated. 'Yes and no.'

'Jupiter! What the hell's that supposed to mean? We've just been saying that—'

'Corvinus, bear with me, will you? I don't have all the answers, and I can't even ask most of the questions. All I'm telling you is that Serenus doesn't fit the pattern. Whether that's significant or not, and if so how, I don't know.'

'Okay.' I took a swallow of wine. 'I'm sorry. Go ahead.'

'When Aelius Sejanus began targeting the main Julian supporters for the Wart he encouraged a lot of the smaller fry to shift their allegiance to him. Right?'

'Right.' That made sense. Politics is a pragmatic business, and based on alliances. The Julians had built up quite a network over the years, and when they were smashed the lesser families who'd been dependent on their patronage were quick to look for a replacement. On Sejanus's side, he might have power through the Wart but he didn't have a party – we'd been through that before – and a leader without a party is nothing. He'd've welcomed the Julian deserters with open arms. Sure he would; he needed them as much as they needed him.

'Okay,' Lippillus said. 'Now we go back a few years. You remember the Libo trial?'

'Sure.' My interest sharpened. Libo had been a rich young smartass framed for treason a couple of years after the Wart came to power. One of the guys behind the framing – and this I did know – had been Sejanus.

'Who were the prosecutors?'

I knew the answer to that one, too, or at least I knew one of them: his involvement in the Libo prosecution had been what put me on to his link with Sejanus in the first place, and incidentally provided the reason why he now hated my guts. 'Fulcinius Trio. Our latest consul.'

'One of the others was Serenus.'

'Is that so?' I sat back. I could see what Lippillus was getting at now, about Serenus being different, and he was right: guys who started out mates of Sejanus's and then switched to the Julian side would be as hard to find as Jews in a pork butcher's. Serenus didn't fit the pattern because he went against the flow. Julian to Sejanian, sure, no problem, that took in half of Rome. But Sejanian to Julian? No way. He was right. Something smelled.

'Axing Libo for Sejanus was what got Serenus his city judge-ship. And, following on that, his Spanish posting. He was a Sejanian from the first, and doing well out of it.' Lippillus was looking at me over his wine cup. 'So why did he switch?'

'The obvious answer is that he didn't. He was a double.'

'Maybe. But if so he went down with the rest. He's in exile now, on Amorgos, and likely to stay there. And if the Senate had had its way he'd be dead.'

Yeah. That, at least, had been in the records. The Senate had voted for death after the second conviction, but Tiberius had vetoed the proposal. If Serenus was a Julian that made sense, like with the Asian governor Silanus: the Wart hadn't wanted to push the Julians too hard. He couldn't afford to. On the other hand, if Serenus had been Sejanus's buddy all along and working for him on the inside then a commuted sentence would still have made sense . . .

Ah, hell. My brain hurt. I was out of my depth here, and I knew it.

'Maybe,' I said slowly, 'a word with the prosecutor in the Serenus trial might clear up a few things.'

Lippillus nodded. 'Exactly. That's what I was thinking, Corvinus. It's not often that a guy's prosecuted for treason by his own son. And if Serenus is on his island, Vibius Celsus is still in Rome. If I were you I'd pay him a visit.'

On the way back home I went over what I remembered from my notes on the Serenus trials, just to make sure I had them straight in my head. They were pretty complicated. The guy had faced prosecution twice in twelve months. The first time the charge was fomenting or failing to discourage public violence in his province, and he'd been convicted and exiled to Amorgos. The second was the occasion we'd been talking about. Serenus had been hauled back from Greece to stand trial before the Senate on the charge – brought by his own son Vibius Celsus – of sending agents to Sacrovir in Gaul. Celsus had cited a collaborator in Rome, one Caecilius Cornutus. Before the case began, Cornutus had committed suicide.

Okay. So far – reading between the lines – so good. Serenus had acted like a pukkah Julian. He'd turned a blind eye to seditious demonstrations, maybe even encouraged them, and established links with the Gallic rebels. Cornutus had been his contact with the Julians themselves back in Rome. He hadn't expected to be implicated, and when it was clear he was under suspicion he'd panicked and taken the quick way out. Or maybe had it taken for him. It wouldn't be the first time that a weak link had been eliminated.

With Cornutus gone Serenus had brazened it out. He'd challenged his son to prove his case by naming other associates. Celsus promptly accused Cornelius Lentulus and Seius Tubero, Lentulus being an old friend of the Wart's and Tubero being Sejanus's elder stepbrother. Naturally the case collapsed. Lentulus and Tubero were discharged by an embarrassed Senate without a hearing, and Celsus quickly left Rome for Ravenna.

Interesting enough, but that wasn't the end of it, because the Wart then proceeded to shove his personal oar in. Despite the fact that Serenus's slaves had given evidence under torture that suggested their master's innocence, Tiberius hauled Celsus back and forced him to carry on with the prosecution. In the teeth of the slaves' evidence Serenus was tried, convicted and sentenced to death. At which point the Wart intervened again, this time on grounds of mercy, and sent the guy back to his original island, where he still was.

Weird, right? And a complete mess into the bargain. However, certain things stuck out like sore thumbs. First, like Lippillus had said, for a son to prosecute his father on a capital charge is practically unheard of even in these degenerate days. Second, why should Celsus have picked on Lentulus and Tubero? Lentulus was a harmless old duffer, practically senile and devoted to the

Wart's interests; Tubero was just as unlikely a crypto-Julian, being one of Sejanus's closest relatives. More, I knew for a fact that ten years ago on Sejanus's instructions he'd used his position as city judge to block a crucial murder investigation. Neither of them, obviously, could be considered a likely supporter of Agrippina's, even given the Senate's overheated imagination. Third, what the hell was the Wart playing at? And fourth, if Celsus had had the nerve to accuse Sejanus's stepbrother of treason in open court then why was he still breathing?

Like I said the whole thing was weird; and as far as plausibility was concerned you could stick it in a pig's ear and drop it down the nearest manhole. Even so, these were the facts. Explaining them was my problem.

By this time I was past Racetrack Corner and on my way to the Publician Incline. It was a beautiful spring day, perfect for walking. Even the tenements looked good in the sunshine, splashed with colour where housewives had planted bulbs outside the doors in tubs. Sure, the streets stank; but the stink was friendly, and the noise was friendly, too.

Hell, what I really needed was a holiday. This was Rome, after all, and I hadn't been back for years; not properly back, anyway. I carefully put politics out of my head as I walked through the huge open market of the Velabrum and Cattlemarket Square that spills southwards past the Temple of Hercules and covers the triangle between Racetrack, Aventine and river: past the stalls with vegetables and herbs, butchers' tables, racks of cheap ready-made tunics and headscarves, cheesemongers, knife-sellers, all one glorious muddle as if the bits and pieces left over from the city's separate trading areas had been bundled together and dropped down at random. Like always, it was crowded and I had to shove in places; ordinary Romans pay no attention to a striped mantle, unless it has a few slaves with heavy sticks in front of it. The sun had brought out the hucksters with their trays of roasted pumpkin seeds, hot sausages and doughnuts in honey. Whores, too. A couple of them in red mantles glittering with tin and glass jewellery waved to me and I flung them a silver piece each for the hell of it, just because they looked like they were enjoying life.

Maybe Livia had been right about me and Rome after all. Certainly I was enjoying myself, really enjoying myself, for the first time in ten years, and Rome was the reason. Not the Rome that belonged to the hypocrites in the Senate who'd sell their grandmothers for a four-month consulship, but the filthy, sprawling, gutsy city itself, that never left you feeling empty, like Athens did or any other of the dozen cities Perilla and I had stayed in since we'd moved abroad. And if that was what the old sinner had meant by altruism then I agreed with her, one hundred per cent.

Maybe Serenus was just a guy on the make, Celsus no better, and neither of them had had any more dealings with Sejanus than an oyster knows Greek. Maybe the whole thing was one great mare's nest. At that moment I didn't particularly care. It was too good a day to waste thinking, and in a hundred years' time we'd all be dead together, Sejanus, the Wart and Agrippina included. The hell with it.

Well, if that was my holiday I'd had it. I bought a nut-stuffed pastry for Perilla, watched a group of jugglers and a guy sucking flames from a lighted torch, then headed back towards the Palatine and home.

10

Scratch the idyllic atmosphere of a spring day in Rome; when I arrived back I found myself in the middle of a grade one domestic crisis. Meton the chef had been sulking in his kitchen like a culinary Achilles since the Torquata affair two days before. Now the bastard had hit the cooking wine and barricaded himself in. He wasn't coming out for no one.

'You talk to him, Marcus.' Perilla was standing outside the kitchen door with Bathyllus and a couple of gawping kitchen skivvies. She looked flushed and angry. 'I've tried, but he won't pay any attention.'

Jupiter! The guy must be far gone if Perilla couldn't get through to him. Still, as head of the household I owed it to the good old Roman ethos to give it a go, at least.

'Hey, Meton!' I banged on the wooden panelling. 'Cut that out right now and open the door!'

No answer, bar a snatch of an Alexandrian love song. He could cook better than he could sing, that was for sure. And from the sound of him he was pissed as a newt. I turned to Bathyllus.

'You've tried forcing the door?'

'He has the chopping table wedged against the other side.'

'Shit. How about the outside window? Any chance of taking him from behind?'

'We've tried that too, sir, but it's too high and narrow. Also, he throws things.'

'Onions?'

'Knives.' The little guy was bristling with disapproval. Bathyllus always had thought Meton was too anarchic to live, and his musical appreciation was zilch.

'Uh-huh. Knives, eh? *Kitchen* knives?'

'Yes, sir.'

This was a bad one. Meton normally looked after his kitchen knives as carefully as if they were new-born babies. No one was allowed even to breathe on them in case they lost their edge. And the last time he'd gone on a bender it had lasted three days. I'd've recycled the bugger for scratchings long since if he hadn't been the best cook we'd ever had.

I banged on the door with my fist. 'Meton! I know you're listening! Open up this minute! That's an order!'

The singing stopped momentarily in favour of a loud raspberry. One of the skivvies sniggered and Bathyllus shot him a look that would've curdled milk.

I turned away from the door and shrugged. 'Okay, guys, that's it, show's over. We leave him to it. He'll come out eventually.'

'Oh, marvellous!' Perilla snapped. 'And what do we do for meals in the meantime?'

Yeah. She had a point there. The larder was on Meton's side of the door as well as the cooking facilities. Still, the problem wasn't insuperable.

'We live on take-away sausages and meatballs,' I said. 'I know a cookshop off Tuscan Street where they don't use rats. Or not many, anyway. Unless you'd prefer to sponge off Mother and Priscus.'

'And have your stepfather throw sauce over every good mantle I've got? No, thank you, Corvinus. Not until I'm desperate.'

'Okay, lady, it's your decision.' I held out the pastry that I'd bought her on the way home. 'Here. Make it last.'

She looked at it and her mouth trembled. A moment later and we were hugging each other and laughing helplessly while Bathyllus glared. That little guy has no sense of the ridiculous. Left to himself, he'd probably have called in the City Guard to evict Meton with a battering ram, and told them not to take prisoners.

'I'll get back to polishing the silverware, then, sir, shall I?' he said finally. If I didn't know better I'd've guessed he'd just swallowed a neat pint of vinegar.

I nodded while I tried to get myself under control. Perilla was leaning against the wall hugging her ribs.

'Yeah. Yeah, you do that, little guy,' I said at last. 'And keep me informed. When that bastard in there sobers up enough to move the table I want to see him.'

'Certainly, sir,' Bathyllus said primly, and turned to go. 'It will be a positive pleasure.'

A thought struck me. 'Hey, Bathyllus. One more thing. Where does Vibius Celsus hang out, do you know?'

'No, sir.' A sniff. 'I've no idea.'

Sure he knew; Bathyllus knew everything. He just wasn't co-operating. Jupiter! Slaves! There must be a better way to run a household. 'So find out, sunshine. Ask around when you go for the sausages.'

'I'll try my best, sir.'

'You do that. And take something for that cold.'

'Yes, sir.'

'Who's this Celsus, Marcus?' Perilla was her normal cool self by now, except for a certain raggedness round the edges that I found sexy as hell.

'Just someone I want to talk to.' I put my arm round her waist. 'Come into the living-room and I'll tell you about it. Hey, and Bathyllus?'

'Yes, sir. At your orders, sir.'

'Cut the sarcasm. And bring us a jug.' That was one thing saved. After the first time Meton threw an alcoholic wobbler I'd made damn sure we had a separate wine cellar with a solid lock.

Bathyllus sidled in with the address an hour or so later, like I knew he would: one thing Bathyllus can't stand is to smudge his reputation with me for omniscience.

With the first premonitory rumbles in my stomach I set out for the Esquiline.

Celsus lived in a modest house just off Patrician Street near the Temple of Juno the Light-Bringer. Not a particularly good neighbourhood, and the outside walls were pretty tatty, with the brick showing in places through the cement facing. The mosaic in the entrance lobby was patched as well, and it hadn't been all that impressive to begin with. The Venus had a distinct squint and there was something wrong with her legs.

I gave my name to the door slave. Luckily the master was at home.

He was a thin, weak-chinned man of about my own age, maybe a bit older, and going bald on top. The minute I saw his eyes I knew I wouldn't trust him further than I could throw him.

'Valerius Corvinus?' We shook hands and he showed me to the guest couch. 'What can I do for you?'

I ignored the question. No point in coming on heavy until I had to, and the situation was pretty delicate.

'You're a relation of Vibius Marsus?' I said. 'We met in Syria ten years back, when he was deputy governor.'

'He's a distant cousin.' Like I'd hoped he would, Celsus relaxed slightly. There're rules to these things. Establish a connection with the family and you're halfway there. You've shown your credentials, even if they're bogus as hell, like mine were. I was glad, though, that Marsus wasn't a close relative because I'd liked the guy, even though he had been on the other side. Celsus I didn't like at all. 'You were in Syria, you say?'

'Antioch. I spent some time there just after Germanicus died.'

Did his eyes flicker? I couldn't be sure, because he was turning to his own couch. A slave brought wine in plain silver cups. Not much, and no jug. I drank. Massic, and not the best vintage either. That fitted with everything else I'd seen so far. Money was tight in the Vibius household; and that told me something in itself.

'I've never been to Syria.' Celsus was sipping his own wine. 'A charming province, they say. My own service was in the west.'

'With your father in Spain.'

'That's right.' His voice was neutral. 'I was on his staff. A junior tribune.'

'That'd be when he was prosecuted the first time, for maladministration.'

Celsus gave me a long, slow look. Finally he said, 'Corvinus, what exactly do you want with me?'

I shrugged. 'Just making conversation.'

'Is that what it is?' The carefully brushed eyebrows dropped. 'Curious. You're from a good family, I know that from your name. And of course although we haven't met I've heard of your father and uncle.'

'So?'

'So didn't anyone ever tell you that to begin a conversation with a reference to the other person's criminal antecedents is terribly bad form?'

I grinned and took another sip of the wine. What there was of it. Two more decent swallows and it'd be gone.

'Yeah. Yeah, they told me that,' I said.

'Why do it, then?' His mouth pouted like a puzzled child's. 'I assume it wasn't accidental.'

'I shouldn't've thought you'd've been too sensitive on the topic. Considering the second time you blew the whistle on Serenus yourself.'

I was still getting that long, puzzled look. I wondered if Celsus was altogether sane, and a small cold finger touched my spine.

'My father was a traitor,' he said slowly, 'and treachery supersedes family loyalties. What I did, Corvinus, was unpleasant but necessary. And the fact is that we were never very close.'

'Close enough for him to want you on his staff.'

Celsus drew his mouth into a thin line, like a child who's decided it isn't going to play any longer.

'I'm sorry, Valerius Corvinus,' he said. 'I'm trying hard to be polite, but you really are making it very difficult. Father has been in exile for over six years now, deservedly so. I rarely even think of him, let alone talk about him, certainly not with a total stranger. So would you mind either changing the subject or telling me straight out what you want from me?'

'Let's just say I'm curious. I was wondering why a son would accuse his own father of treason.'

'And I've answered your question, to my own satisfaction if not to yours. I did what I considered and still consider was my duty.' Celsus got up and set his wine cup on a small side table. 'Now if your curiosity is satisfied then perhaps we can end this ridiculous conversation and part in reasonable amity.'

I hadn't moved. 'So you were working for Aelius Sejanus.'

'What?' He turned quickly. The puzzled look had gone. If he was a child now, he wasn't a very pleasant one.

'Your father was mixed up in a Julian plot against the emperor. Sejanus used you to nail him.'

'My father was certainly plotting against Tiberius. But my accusations had nothing to do with Sejanus. I told you, I was motivated by duty. And now, Corvinus – he cleared his throat – 'I really do think you ought to leave.'

I ignored him. 'The thing I don't understand, pal, is why you should accuse Lentulus and Tubero. If you were working for Sejanus then that wouldn't make sense. It's almost as if you wanted . . .' I stopped as the answer hit me. Fool!

'Wanted what?' He'd been plucking up the nerve to call the slaves. Now he shot me a look like I'd caught him with his hand in the biscuit jar.

Duty. Oh, Jupiter! Yeah, yeah, sure it was. That was it exactly. But not duty to the emperor. There were other varieties. I'd done the man an injustice.

'Celsus,' I said, 'I apologise. You weren't working for Sejanus at all, were you? Or for Tiberius.'

He stared at me, and said nothing.

'You were working for your father.'

Smack on the button. His face turned chalk white and very slowly he walked back to the table, picked up the wine cup and took a swallow. I felt almost sorry for him. For all his bluster and man-of-the-world polish he hadn't the guts of a frog, and he'd reached his limit.

'That's nonsense,' he said at last. I doubt if he sounded convincing even to himself. 'Absolute nonsense. It doesn't even make a modicum of sense.'

'Doesn't it?' I could almost hear the clicks as the bits of the puzzle fell into place. 'The whole thing was a set-up from start to finish. A piece of pure theatre. Your father knew he was blown, so instead of waiting for Sejanus to bring the charge through one of his chums he had you do it. He even fed you your line by challenging you to name his accomplices so that by citing Lentulus and Tubero you could destroy your own credibility as a prosecutor. He hoped that once that happened the case against him would collapse because our lickspittle Senate wouldn't touch these guys with a bargepole.'

'But my father was exiled none the less.' Celsus's voice was the barest whisper.

'Sure he was, because the Wart knew he was guilty, whatever his slaves said. Which was why he brought you back to finish what you'd started.' I took a full swallow of wine. The taste didn't improve with further acquaintance. 'It was a good plan, Celsus. The gamble just didn't come off. Anyway, why should you be ashamed? Filial duty's as good as any other, and better than some.' He didn't answer. 'Hey, come on. I'm right, and you know it. I've got no quarrel with you, quite the reverse. So sit down and let's talk.'

He collapsed on to the couch like a string puppet, still holding the wine cup like it was his lifeline. If I hadn't been there I suspect the poor little bugger would've been sobbing his heart out. I was almost sorry I'd come now, but I had to see this thing through.

'All right, Corvinus,' he said. 'What do you want? Money? I haven't got any, not any more.'

'No,' I said. 'I can see that. It's one reason why I didn't really believe you were one of Sejanus's cronies.'

'So if not that then what?' He was shaking so hard I could hear his teeth rattle. I doubt if I'd ever met a more complete coward. Sure, I knew what he was worried about: his father had only escaped the public executioner himself by a whisker, and if it got out now that Celsus had been involved in the conspiracy then old history or not his neck was legally forfeit. The fact that the Wart probably couldn't've cared a bust boil plaster after all this time wouldn't enter his head.

'I want information,' I said. 'Just that. Nothing more.'

He took a deep breath and emptied his wine cup at a gulp. 'Very well. What do you know already?'

'That Serenus was part of a major Julian scam to discredit Tiberius in the west. That it involved Silius the German governor, the rebels Florus and Sacrovir, and the governors of Asia and Cyrene who provided most of the cash.'

'Yes.' He looked down into his empty cup. 'Yes. Very thorough, and quite correct. In fact I doubt if I can add much more. I wasn't really all that important, you see.'

Surprise, surprise. 'Never mind. At least you can answer a few straight questions.'

'Of course. If I can.'

'Okay. First question. Your father supported Sejanus originally. Why did he switch sides?'

'Money.' Celsus gave a pale smile. 'Oh, I know, Corvinus, I told you I hadn't got any and I wasn't lying. It's spent long ago, and it wasn't all that much to begin with. Perhaps because even more than he liked money Father enjoyed the excitement of plotting for its own sake.'

Yeah, I'd believe that. Serenus was obviously a different character to his son, a much harder case altogether. Not that that would be difficult. He'd prosecuted Libo for what he could make on the deal, and like I'd said his attempt to four-flush the Wart had been a pure gambler's trick that could well have come off. And if he'd managed to persuade or bully this sad streak of dripping into joining in the gamble then he'd been a man to be reckoned with. 'Okay. Second question. Cornutus. The accomplice at Rome who committed suicide before the trial. How did he fit in?'

'He channelled the cash from the Asian end. I only knew that and his name. I never met him, even when we were back in Rome.'

'Did he kill himself, or was he helped?'

'I'm not a murderer, Corvinus.' Yeah, that I'd believe too. The poor sap wouldn't have the nerve, even at second hand. 'I can't answer for anyone else because I don't know.'

'How did you manage to accuse Lentulus and Sejanus's stepbrother and come out the other side in one piece?'

'I don't know.' I opened my mouth to protest but he spread his hands. 'That's the truth. Honestly, I don't know! Perhaps because the accusations were so ridiculous that the Senate threw them out at once. They were Father's idea, in any case, not mine.'

And maybe Sejanus just didn't think he was worth the effort; but I didn't say that. I'd been on the receiving end of that particular comment once myself, and I knew how it felt.

'Okay,' I said. 'Last question, and then I'll go. What else have you got for me in your locker?'

His eyes glinted from under lowered lashes. 'Such as what?'

'Don't play games, Celsus! You know what I mean. Names. Details. Facts and dates.'

'Connected with the Julian plot?'

He was giving me the run-around here, and I knew it. 'To hell with the Julian plot,' I said. 'I'm after Sejanus.'

His jaw dropped. He lifted the wine cup to his lips then set it down again when he realised that it was empty. It rattled against the marble table-top and overbalanced.

'He'll kill you,' he whispered.

'Yeah, maybe, but that's my problem. So give, or your name'll be splashed all over the next edition of the Senate's *Daily Register*. In the Forthcoming Executions column.'

'I can't, Corvinus!' He was almost crying again. 'Really, I can't! I don't know any more!'

'Fine.' I got up myself. 'I'll see you around. Maybe.'

I was heading for the front door when he called me back.

'Corvinus!'

I turned. 'Yeah?'

Celsus hesitated. 'Marius. Sextus Marius.'

'That all? Just the name?'

'I swear!' He was quivering like a dish of aspic prawns. 'I told you! I don't know any more!'

'So why give me that much? Who's this Marius?'

'My father mentioned him once or twice. He was one of his associates, but Father never trusted him.'

'Where was he based? Rome? Spain?'

'I don't know! I never even saw the man!' He was actually wringing his hands. 'Corvinus, I swear! I've told you all I know!'

I sighed. Yeah, he probably had, at that.

'Thanks, Celsus,' I said. 'Thanks a lot. And don't worry any more. You're safe.'

I didn't wait for his answer.

Sextus Marius. I turned the name over in my mind as I left. It wasn't one I recognised, from my general knowledge or from the Senate's records. Not a purple-striper, that was clear, not with that name. Maybe not even a Roman. Yet Celsus had used the word 'associate', which implied that the guy had been important, his father's equal.

So who the hell was he?

11

I called in at Lippillus's flat on the way back to tell him how the talk with Celsus had gone, but there was no one in. He wasn't at Watch headquarters either, so I left a message there and went home.

We were still in the midst of the crisis: Meton hadn't emerged, and he had enough cooking wine squirrelled away to last him a month, even at the rate he was getting through it. Worse, he'd moved on from Alexandrian love songs to wineshop *café chantant*, and after hearing a sample couple of verses I forbade Perilla to go anywhere near the kitchen on pain of divorce.

She was in the study, making a list of friends we could sponge off until the siege was raised.

'Marcus, this is silly,' she said when she'd kissed me. 'Can't we just break the door down and haul him out?'

'It isn't worth the hassle. He'll give up eventually. Cooking just for himself is a chef's idea of hell.' I lay down on the reading couch and cradled a cup of Setinian. 'Especially when he has to do it out of jars.'

'But Bathyllus says it would be easy to . . .'

'Don't listen to Bathyllus, lady. That guy has delusions of military grandeur that'd make Alexander look like a pacifist. Besides, we'd need a catapult to get through that door and it'd play hell with the paintwork.'

Perilla sighed. 'Very well.'

'Who've you got down so far?'

She consulted her notes. 'Not all that many, I'm afraid. It comes of being so out of touch. Plancus and Gemella owe us a meal. I suppose we could invite ourselves there if they're free.'

'They're in Tibur.'

'Ah.' She drew a line. 'Uncle Cotta?'

'Jupiter, Perilla! Be serious!'

'I agree. Lepida and Barbatus?'

I sat up. 'No way!' Barbatus was a cousin of mine. He and Lepida were okay, just, but their kid Messallina was a real hell-cat. On the one occasion they'd been round they'd sent her to play in the garden, and in the space of an hour she'd set fire to a peacock, broken a vital part off my marble Poseidon and tried to seduce the gardener. Almost succeeded, too. Not bad going for a ten-year-old. She must be rising thirteen now; an awkward age. That girl had a future, if someone didn't have the sense to strangle her first.

'No,' Perilla said slowly. 'No, I suppose not.'

'Fine. Who else have you got?'

'That seems to cover it, I'm afraid.' She paused. 'Apart from your mother and Priscus, of course.'

We looked at each other. I took a morose swallow of wine.

'Oh, yeah,' I said at last. 'Mother and Priscus. Let's hear it for desperation.'

Unfortunately Mother and Priscus were dining in that evening and would be delighted to feed us. Perilla put on the mantle she least minded getting gravy stains all over and we whistled up the litter for the Caelian.

'Uh, as a matter of interest, little guy,' I said to Bathyllus as we prepared to set off, 'what are your plans for dinner tonight?'

'The kitchen staff at the neighbour's have rallied round, sir.' Bathyllus straightened our cushions. 'Their master is having a birthday banquet, and the leftovers should be sufficient for both households.'

'Is that right?' I kept my voice neutral. 'A birthday banquet, eh? You, uh, happen to know what's on the menu?'

'Sturgeon was mentioned, sir. Roast sucking pig stuffed with dates and pastry. And, I think, a sweetbread fricassee with forcemeat dumplings. Plus the sundries, of course.'

'The sundries. Great. Great.' Jupiter! 'Sounds nice. Well, enjoy yourselves.'

'You too, sir. Have a very pleasant evening.'

Bastard. Still, it was Mother's or starve, if you can call that a choice. Off we went.

'Marcus! Perilla! Do come in, we were just going to start without you.' Mother kissed the air beside my right cheek. 'Something to drink?'

Uh-uh. I'd been caught out on that one before. 'Some plain ordinary wine'd be nice, Mother,' I said. 'If you've got it.'

'Nonsense, dear!' Mother looked shocked. 'You must try Phormio's spiced wine surprise. He made it specially for this evening from his own recipe.'

'Uh, in that case no. No thanks.' Phormio was Mother's chef, and he was even crazier than she was. One day he'd finally manage to poison someone, and I didn't want it to be me, whether it meant offending his professional susceptibilities or not. 'I'll pass. Perilla?'

'Just a fruit juice, please, Vipsania,' Perilla said firmly.

'Very well.' Mother frowned. 'Suit yourselves.'

We went through to the dining-room. Priscus was on the host's couch. He hadn't changed since I'd seen him last. He still looked like a cross between a sheep and a dried prune.

'Mmmmaaa!' he bleated. 'Good to see you both. Perilla, you're beside me as usual, my dear.' Well, she'd got her sauceproof mantle on this time, anyway.

'Hi, Stepfather,' I said, taking the last couch. 'How are the joints now?' They were the reason he'd missed the funeral: a bout of galloping arthritis caught in a damp Caerean tomb.

'I can't complain. I can't complain. Lartia Tarchna was worth a few twinges. A lovely woman in her day, Marcus, lovely.' Yeah, if you like five-hundred-year-old funerary statues. 'Beautiful breasts. And we're having celery soup with watercress tonight. That should help.'

Jupiter, that sturgeon! Those suckling pigs! Bathyllus would be tucking in to them even now. Never let anyone tell you that a slave's life is the pits.

'Celery soup with watercress, eh?' I said. 'Yum. Delicious. I can't wait.'

The spiced wine surprise arrived. I was glad I'd passed it up: from the smell and the colour it seemed that the surprise was that it wasn't wine at all; but then I hadn't ever thought it would be, and faking things was part of Phormio's bag. I could still remember how, the last time we'd eaten at Mother's, he'd served up a dish of pickled anchovies that had turned out to be caramelised radishes. I'd swallowed one before I realised and been off fish for a month.

The soup came next, together with a plate heaped high with what looked like green worms. I goggled.

'Hey, great!' I said. 'Baby eels with fennel!' This was more like it: good plain Roman cooking for a change. Maybe we were going to be lucky after all.

Mother gave me a brittle smile. 'No, dear. Not eels. Not even close.'

Hell. This sounded bad, even by Mother's standards. 'You want to tell us what they are?'

'Not until after you've had a taste and told me what you think.'

'Ah.' Bad was right.

'A trader I met told me about them and I had Phormio recreate the recipe with my own adaptations.' Mother held out a spoon. 'Go on, Marcus. They won't bite you.'

From the look of the things I wouldn't've bet on it. Still, it looked like the worms were all we were getting. Dubiously, I let her spoon some on to my plate. They slithered off again.

'Uh . . . a trader from where, exactly?' I asked. Britain. It had to be Britain.

'Syria, dear. But the recipe itself came from much further away. Somewhere along the silk route, I think.'

Perilla was already digging in. 'They're lovely. Most unusual. Go on, Marcus, try them.'

With some difficulty I picked up two or three of the worms on my spoon and bit.

'*Jupiter!*'

'Interesting, aren't they?' Mother said. 'Thin strands of flour and egg paste, dried and then boiled, with a sauce of oil, pounded cheese, garlic, pine nuts and rue. I'm not sure about the rue. Perhaps something else might give a less astringent flavour.'

'Yeah. Yeah, I'd go along with that.' Jupiter in a bucket! It was like having your mouth scraped out with a gorse bush. I turned to the slave behind me. 'You got any common-or-garden fish sauce there, pal?'

With a barely concealed sniff – Mother's got her whole staff brainwashed – he passed me the small jug. I poured it on lavishly. Thank the gods for plain fermented anchovies.

I didn't even touch the soup.

Priscus was tucking in to both like there was no tomorrow. Well, maybe there was something to be said for a diet of boiled celery and rue-worms, because dried prune or not the guy was wiry. And he had to be seventy, at least.

'You're enjoying your holiday, Marcus?' He sucked up a recalcitrant worm. A droplet of sauce flew off the end and landed on Perilla's tunic. She sighed and dabbed at it with her napkin.

'*Titus!*' Mother snapped.

Priscus gave her a look of mild-eyed surprise. 'Mmmaa. You know what I mean, my dear. I've already extended my condolences.'

Yeah, well. I didn't blame the old bugger. He had one foot in the grave himself, or he ought to have by his time of life, and he'd raked around cemeteries for so long he must've looked on death as the only worthwhile reason for existence.

'It's okay,' I said, surreptitiously pushing my plate aside. 'I keep myself busy.'

'Doing what?' Mother asked. She'd noticed the plate. Mother never misses anything.

'This and that. Looking up old friends. Passing on messages.' There were some plain ordinary bread rolls on the table; at least they looked plain and ordinary. I broke one and tasted it carefully. It was edible, if you ignored the green bits. 'Speaking of which, you don't know of a guy called Sextus Marius, do you by any chance?'

I was looking at Mother; I doubted if the offhand tone would fool her for a minute, but she was my best bet because Priscus never knew anybody.

'Ah, yes,' Priscus said. 'The Carthage man.'

I choked on a crumb. 'You know him?'

'Of course. Not that he actually comes from Carthage, mind. He's Spanish.' Priscus spooned up more worms. Sauce flew. 'And he has a lovely daughter, I understand.'

Spanish fitted, anyway. But I couldn't see anyone who was a mate of Priscus's being involved in a treason scam. Most of that crew only got worked up about issues like an aberrant use of the genitive in early Oscan. As for politics three of them out of every five might know who Tiberius was, but beyond that was stretching things.

'Uh . . . the Carthage man?' I said cautiously.

Priscus nodded, chewed and swallowed, while Mother looked on fondly. I was grateful: she'd obviously never heard of Marius herself, and if Priscus knew him then ipso facto my question couldn't be all that out of line.

'Yes, Marcus,' he said. 'His special area of interest is Carthaginian seal-rings. Marius is quite a collector. We often meet in Phlebas's.'

Oh, Jupiter! Jupiter best and greatest! 'He's here in Rome?'

Priscus stared at me like it was the stupidest question he'd ever heard. 'But of course he is! He has been for several years. The Carthaginians have never been favourites of mine. A crude race, but artistic in their way. Take their sculpture . . .'

Oh, shit! No, no digressions, not now! I had to head the old guy off before he went chasing after one of his esoteric rabbits.

'You happen to know where I can find him?' I said quickly.

'Marius?' Priscus looked surprised at the name, as if we'd been discussing someone completely different. 'He has a villa on the Janiculan, if I remember rightly. Quite a nice one. I've never been there myself, but Phlebas would know, if you think it's really important.'

'Yeah, I do.' I glanced at Mother. She was beginning to look suspicious. 'You . . . ah . . . know anything more about him?'

'Not a great deal, no. Apart from his antiquarian interests he isn't really my type. Not a true . . . mmmaaa! . . . *afictionado*.'

'I see.' I took a gamble. 'Priscus, didn't he, uh, get into a bit of trouble at one time?'

'Marcus . . .' Mother began. Perilla glared at me.

Priscus was beaming, and blossoming like a shrivelled rose: it wasn't often he could keep his end up in a man-of-the-world conversation and he was obviously enjoying himself. 'Oh, yes! Yes, indeed! Something to do with Gaul, wasn't it?'

'Uh, yeah. Yeah, that's right.'

'Marcus,' Mother interrupted firmly, 'I don't know what

you're after here, but this is all horribly familiar and I want you to stop it now.'

'I agree,' Perilla snapped. 'Marcus, behave!'

'Oh, tush, tush, my dears!' Priscus waved a hand and shifted on his couch. I'd never actually seen a louche sheep before, but he must've come pretty close. 'It was during the Latin Festival. Tiberius was away and Drusus was standing in. Marius was accused of treason or some such nonsense.'

'Yeah? Who by?'

'I really can't recall, my dear fellow. In any case, the charge wasn't even . . . countenanced? Is that the word?'

'It'll do.' That would explain why there'd been no mention of Marius in the Senate records: the accusation hadn't got that length, or it had been deliberately struck out. 'So what—?'

'*Marcus!*' Mother's eyes flashed. 'That's all! I forbid you to continue with this! And Titus, you've indulged the boy quite enough for one evening!'

There was no arguing with Mother in this mood. I held my hands up.

'Okay, okay!' I said. 'So what's for dessert?'

It was puréed plums with an elderberry and mint sauce. Mother made me eat two helpings as a punishment.

We left shortly afterwards, in frigid silence. I felt sorry for Priscus: he was obviously in for it as soon as the door closed behind us, and it hadn't been his fault.

Perilla wasn't too pleased with me either.

'You . . . ah . . . want to stop in at that cookshop on Tuscan Street?' I said finally, when the silence had dragged on just that bit too long. 'The one with no rats?'

'If you must, Corvinus.' Shirty as hell. 'It's out of our way, of course. And personally after that meal I'm feeling quite full enough already.'

Yeah, well, Perilla might classify what we'd just had as a meal, but I didn't. My stomach needed an honest sausage and half a dozen meatballs. Even if they did turn out to be dog they'd at least be recognisable. I opened the litter curtains and got the leading litter slaves' attention.

'Hey, guys, take us home by Gratus's place in the Meat Market, okay?'

'Okay, boss.'

A good idea, but it came to nothing. When we got there there was a note on the door that said: *'Closed due to family illness'*. Clearly it just wasn't my night.

12

When we pulled up outside Bathyllus had the door open for us as usual. The little guy was grinning like a drain, he looked well fed, and I could swear there was a streak of lovage and cumin sauce on his chin.

'How was your meal, sir?' he asked.

'Don't talk about it.' I started to strip off my mantle. 'Just don't talk about it. Ever.'

'Very well, sir.' He took Perilla's cloak.

'How's the Meton situation?' I said. 'Any change?'

'He's out, sir.'

I stared. The mantle slipped to the floor. 'Out?'

'Out of the kitchen. Since shortly after you left, sir.'

'Since shortly after we left.' My empty stomach rumbled. I pushed past him. 'Just let me get my hands on the bastard!'

'Certainly, sir. But perhaps you should see your visitor first.'

I stopped. 'Visitor?'

'Flavonius Lippillus. He's in the dining-room.'

Lippillus was on the guest couch with a jug of Setinian beside him. And on the table – spread across the whole length and width of the dining table – was . . .

'Jupiter! Food! Real food!' My jaw dropped.

'Hi, Corvinus.' Lippillus waved a canapé. 'You don't mind, do you? I'm sorry, I got tired waiting.'

'Yeah. I mean, no.' I was heaping a plate. Jupiter in spangles! Roast stuffed guinea-fowl! Snails! Mushrooms in wine! 'Did Meton make all this?'

'Sure. He's been slaving away like a demon for hours.' He looked up. 'Hi, Perilla.'

'Good evening, Lippillus.' Perilla had followed me in. She was staring at the table too. 'Marcus, what is going on here?'

'I don't know, lady.' I bit into a leg of guinea-fowl: marinated, if I didn't miss my guess, in cherry juice and juniper. Delicious! 'And frankly at the moment I don't care.'

Lippillus poured me a cup of wine. 'I think it's a peace offering,' he said.

'Meton's wasting his time. When I get my strength back I'll beat him to death with his own omelette pan.' Gods, though, that guinea-fowl was good! I chased it down with a throatful of Setinian and reached for the mushrooms. 'What happened? He come out voluntarily?'

'Oh, he was no trouble. Not after I pitched in the smoke bomb.'

'The *which*?'

'Smoke bomb. A little something I learned once from a Greek army engineer.' Lippillus scooped olive pâté on to a crust. 'I borrowed the ingredients from your neighbour, mixed the thing up, lit it and chucked it through the outside window. Bathyllus and his lads were waiting to grab Meton at the other end. Don't worry, there's no damage.'

'Screw the damage.' If Lippillus had managed to winkle Meton out without calling in the City Guard he'd performed a minor miracle. Even for him it was impressive. 'Brilliant. Absolutely brilliant.'

'If you'll excuse me I'll just go and change into something that doesn't smell of rue sauce,' Perilla said. She disappeared upstairs.

'Rue sauce?' Lippillus stared after her. '*Rue* sauce?'

'Believe it.' I de-shelled a snail.

'Bathyllus said you were out to dinner at your mother's.'

'Out, yes.' Gods, the snails were even better than the guinea-fowl: boiled in wine must with the barest touch of caraway. 'Dinner . . .'

Lippillus looked at me, then shrugged and poured us another cup of wine. 'So. Business. You left a message to say you wanted to see me. Or was it just that you needed help with your domestic problems?'

My stomach was quieter now. The rumbles had settled to a

contented purring. 'You know anything about a man called Sextus Marius? Reported to Drusus for treason?'

Lippillus frowned. 'A Spaniard?'

'Yeah. That's him.' I evicted a second snail.

'Accuser Calpurnius Salvianus. The case was thrown out unheard and Salvianus was exiled.'

I nearly choked. 'He was *what*?'

'Exiled. Tiberius gave him a public reprimand and packed him off east.' Lippillus was still watching me closely. 'I'd forgotten about Marius. Where did you dig him up?'

I told him what Celsus had told me. He nodded.

'That would fit. Salvianus was none too bright by all reports. Sejanus used him to kill the two birds with the one stone.'

He was ahead of me. 'Hold on. I understand why the Wart threw the case out, sure; as Sejanus's agent against the Julians Marius would have his protection. But who's your other bird?'

'Drusus himself, of course. Who else would it be?'

'Yeah?' I took a swallow of wine. 'You mind explaining why the Wart's accredited deputy should get himself into trouble by sitting in for his dad on the first stages of a treason trial?'

'Corvinus.' Lippillus sighed. 'You've got hold of the wrong end of the stick somewhere. We're not talking about Tiberius's son. This only happened five years ago. It was the other Drusus. Agrippina's boy.'

I sat back. Jupiter! My own fault, of course; Priscus hadn't given an exact date, and I'd assumed when he told me the story he'd meant the Wart's Drusus. Five years ago, *that* Drusus had been dead. If the judge concerned had been the Julian kid then that was a different thing entirely, and what Lippillus was saying made sense. A lot of sense.

'Sejanus used the same scam as Serenus did,' I said slowly. 'Only he was more successful. He had Marius accused on his own terms, and the case collapsed. Better, it never got started.'

'Right.' Lippillus nodded. 'Marius was charged during the Latin Festival, when Tiberius and the senior magistrates were out of Rome. Leaving the boy as a very junior City Prefect.'

'And if Salvianus was no mental heavyweight he wouldn't realise he was being used as a political cat's-paw until it was too late.' I pulled off another guinea-fowl leg and chewed on it while I thought over the implications. Yeah. Clever. Real clever. Sharp-as-a-brick Salvianus must've thought he was on to a sure thing, especially if he knew nothing about the Julians' involvement with the Gallic revolt: he was lodging a public-spirited accusation, and as a judge the inexperienced Drusus would be a walkover. Drusus was just as culpable, but in his case, like I said, it would've been through inexperience, not stupidity. During the Latin Festival no important business is conducted because none of those authorised to conduct it are in the city; so by agreeing to preside over a case of treason he was inadvertently laying public claim to the full powers of an imperial deputy. Given the Wart's fear of the Julians, it was no wonder he'd reacted as he did and thrown the case out the window. As a piece of slick political manoeuvring on Sejanus's part it was beautiful: his agent got off, the Julian faction lost another brownie point with the Wart and Tiberius's own popularity slipped a further notch because rapping squeaky-clean young Drusus across the knuckles wouldn't go down well with the Roman public.

'So Marius is our man,' I said.

'It seems that way. He's not a straight Julian, that's for sure. Like Serenus. Only Sextus Marius was protected.'

Protected. Right. Protected was the word. Marius was someone I just had to see.

Just then Perilla came in wearing a clean mantle. I shifted over on my couch to give her room.

'You want to join us now you're sauce-free and respectable, lady?' I said.

She settled down beside me. 'Marcus, this is lovely. A banquet. What on earth happened?'

'Ask our resident military genius.'

'Bathyllus?'

'*Not* Bathyllus. The real military genius sitting over there looking smug and hogging the larks'-tongue pastries.'

'Cut it out, Corvinus.' Lippillus blandly reached for another canapé. 'It was simple. I'd've come round before if I'd known you were having problems.'

'Tell her about the smoke bomb.'

Lippillus explained while Perilla shelled a quail's egg and dipped it in fish pickle.

'You must give us the recipe,' she said. 'We may need it again some time.'

'I doubt it. Your husband here intends effecting a few domestic changes with an omelette pan.'

'Oh, he didn't mean that.' She leaned over and kissed my cheek. 'Did you, Marcus?'

'Yeah, well . . .'

'Pity.' Lippillus took a swallow of wine. 'You can send Meton to us any time. We could use a good chef, and Mother could keep him in the cupboard.'

I grinned. Yeah, as an experiment that might just work. Not that I intended making it, even on a temporary basis. Living in close proximity to Marcina Paullina might have its compensations. The guy might not want to come back.

'This is lovely, anyway.' Perilla popped in the quail's egg and licked the sauce from her fingertips. 'Absolutely delicious. Marcus, the mushrooms, please.'

'I thought you weren't hungry.'

'What on earth gave you that idea? I'm starving.'

'But in the litter you said . . .'

'Yes, I know.' She spooned mushrooms on to her plate. 'But then I can *pretend* to eat the nonsense Vipsania serves, even while I'm being splattered by her husband, whereas you can't. Besides, I doubt if her silk-route food will ever catch on. You feel hungry again too soon afterwards. Oh, incidentally' – she reached into a fold of her mantle and took out a pendant – 'I brought this down for you. It belonged to my mother. A present from Sidon.'

I picked the thing up and examined it. It was a small jet cylinder with tiny stick figures cut into the surface. Obviously some sort of primitive seal. And from Sidon, Phoenicia. Phoenicia as in Carthage . . .

Hey! I kissed her while Lippillus looked on smiling.

'I love you sometimes,' I said. 'You know that?'

'Yes, Marcus. Just be careful, won't you? And I don't mean with that.' She indicated the seal.

'Aren't I always?'

'Not especially. Are those meatballs over there beside your left elbow, by the way?'

I passed her the meatballs, plus the rest of the snails and what was left of the guinea-fowl. It was the least I could do when she'd given me the key to Marius.

13 ∫

Next morning I called in at Phlebas's in the Saepta to get Marius's address, then crossed the Tiber to the Janiculan. Not my usual stamping ground, in fact I hadn't been in this part of the city for years; not since I'd interviewed Torquata's brother Decimus Silanus about what he didn't do to Augustus's granddaughter Julia. Silanus was still around, and rich as ever, as far as I knew. Not that I cared: him I didn't want to see again, ever. I just hoped this visit wouldn't have the same sort of ending.

Marius was out riding, and his head slave showed me into the garden. It may not've been quite as grand as Silanus's but you could still have squeezed my modest patch of the Palatine into the bit where they kept the compost.

'Perhaps you'd care to wait for the master in the summer-house, sir,' the slave said.

'Sure. Wherever.'

He took me there. It was fitted out as a small dining-room overlooking the villa itself, and open on three sides. Very nice, and very pricey.

'Some wine, sir?'

'Yeah. Yeah, that'd be great.' I lay down on one of the couches and looked around while he went to get it. The garden was neat as a new mantle. Marius obviously had money, but there were signs of taste here too, which you don't always get on the Janiculan: old money tends to prefer the east side of the river where the family has lived for generations, even if the houses are smaller and if the wind's in the right direction you can spit into your neighbour's fish-pond. There were the usual bits and pieces: rose garden, formal hedges, a few bronze and marble statues. Not too many of these, either, and that impressed me too: the recently wealthy tend to crowd them in like they were a job lot up for public auction. Also I might not be an expert but Marius's selection looked like good copies of good originals. Not provincial taste, either. If he didn't have style himself (and there was no reason why he shouldn't) he knew how to buy it.

The wine came – Setinian, and good as mine – and the slave left me alone. I looked up at the house. It was big, but not showy. A balcony ran the length of the first floor, and I was calculating the number of rooms that led off it when a girl walked out of one of them holding a birdcage. She saw me watching and went back inside.

She was a stunner: glossy black hair, ivory skin, big eyes. I remembered what Priscus had said about a daughter. Yeah, well, I doubted if we'd be introduced. Spaniards, even Romanised ones, keep their female relations on a tight lead. A pity. Those eyes were something.

I was halfway down the second cup when Marius got back. Knowing Priscus, and despite what he'd said about the man not being his type, I'd expected a dried-up academic prune. Marius was a fit forty, built like a wrestler, with a Spanish nose you could've used to fell trees bisecting a face that wouldn't've been out of place on the First Spear of a crack legion. Heavily muscled, too. Not a man to cross, I suspected, and a long way from Vibius Celsus.

'No, don't get up, Valerius Corvinus,' he said. His accent had the Hispanic twang, but the vowels were good. He gripped my hand and almost crushed the fingers. 'I'm sorry to keep you waiting. It was such a pleasant morning that I made the most of it. You like riding?'

'It's okay,' I said.

He turned away and signalled to the slave. I had the feeling I'd lost a point, and I suspected I knew where: when you're talking to a Spaniard, to be less than wildly enthusiastic about horses is almost as bad as telling a Greek you don't like arguing. The slave came over with a fresh wine cup – the set was silver, like Celsus's, but beautifully decorated – and poured for both of us.

Marius put his cup down on the summerhouse table and

reclined on the other couch. 'You don't mind if we stay out here?' he said.

'Uh . . . no. Not at all.' He'd surprised me again. Obviously Marius was that rarity in Rome, a fresh-air freak. Still, if you lived on the Janiculan it made sense to get your money's worth. Besides, from my point of view there was always the chance that the girl with the eyes would come back out.

He had manners, too. We'd chatted about this and that for a good ten minutes before he finally asked politely what the hell I wanted.

'Just some information, sir,' I said. 'My wife and I were round at my stepfather Helvius Priscus's for dinner last night and he happened to mention you were an expert on Carthaginian curios.'

'Hardly an expert, Corvinus, certainly not in Priscus's terms.' Marius smiled. 'But I do have an interest. My family are from Cartagena. We have Carthaginian blood.'

Uh-huh. That would explain the money. Cartagena's silver mines supply a pretty sizeable chunk of Rome's coinage, and although they're owned by the state the old local families still get their cut one way or another. It explained how Marius fitted into the scheme of things, too. If he had traditional connections with the Cartagenan mines then he was Rich with a capital R. Silius and company would've welcomed him with open arms. They wouldn't've asked too many questions, either.

'Priscus would disagree,' I said. 'He was pretty impressed with your qualifications.' No harm in buttering him up a little. 'Anyway, I was wondering if maybe you could tell me something about this.' I brought out Perilla's pendant and handed it over. 'It belonged to my wife's mother.'

He took the thing from me like it was made of cobwebs and examined it carefully. Then he looked up.

'It's a cylinder seal. Phoenician, not Carthaginian. Although Carthage was a Phoenician colony the art was quite different.'

'Yeah. My wife said it came from Sidon.'

'Not originally, I think.' He held it out to me. 'You see the central figure?' It was a seated woman in a wig, her head surmounted by a disc between two tall horns. 'Ba'alat. The

Lady Goddess. There were other Ba'alats but this one ruled Byblos. And she's very old, Corvinus. Very old indeed.'

'Yeah? How old exactly?'

'Much older than Carthage. Older even than Sidon.' He shrugged. 'Perhaps three thousand years.'

I whistled. I was genuinely impressed. 'Jupiter! Is that so?'

'That's so. If the Egyptians have their dates right. It's a beautiful piece, in excellent condition, perhaps unique. Were you considering selling?'

'No. Perilla – my wife – was just curious about it.' I held out my hand and he passed the pendant back reluctantly. 'Three thousand years, right?'

'At least.'

The skin on my palm prickled where the stone touched it; when that thing was carved Homer hadn't been born; in fact, Troy hadn't been built, let alone taken. And Rome wasn't even a twinkle in Jupiter's eye. For the first time I had an inkling of the feeling that drove Priscus. It was eerie.

Marius leaned over and filled our cups from the jug the slave had left on the table.

'You're sure you won't sell, Corvinus?' he said. 'I'd give you a good price.' Casually, he named a figure that had me staring. Forget Phlebas. I didn't know that numbers as big as that existed outside property registers. Rich was right.

'Uh, no,' I said eventually. 'No thanks. Like I say, it has sentimental value.'

'A pity. If you change your mind just let me know.' He stood up suddenly. 'Perhaps you'd like to see my own collection? I have nothing nearly so old, nor so fine, but it would put your piece in context. And perhaps you would . . . appreciate it more.'

'Yeah. Yeah, that would be great.' I meant it: I needed the time and the excuse to stay. Marius was no Celsus, I'd known that as soon as I saw him, and there was no way I was going to mention the Julian scam straight out, let alone ask him what part he'd played in it; no way at all. However, maybe I could pick something up indirectly.

'We'll go in, then,' he said. 'More wine?'

'Sure.' I emptied my cup.

'Good. I like a guest who appreciates wine. And riding always gives me a thirst. Simo!' he called to the slave hovering in the portico. 'Another jug, please. We'll be in the Carthage room.'

'Collection' wasn't the word; maybe 'hoard' comes nearer. The room was stacked thick as a magpie's nest. Jupiter knew where all the stuff had come from, or how much it had cost to put together. I wouldn't've thought there were that many bits of Old Carthage in existence.

'Impressive,' I said. It was. Not just the amount or the cost, but the single-mindedness of it.

'Rome tends to dismiss Carthage.' Marius was frowning. 'Jealousy, of course. And fear. Naturally there's the arch-bugbear Hannibal, who almost destroyed your empire before it was properly started. I understand your mothers still use the name to frighten recalcitrant children, even after two hundred years.'

'Yeah.' I remembered once after I'd raided the pantry three nights in a row my old nurse had scared me half to death by saying that next time old Hannibal would jump out from behind the door and cut my little wollocks off. The name still made me shudder. It would any Roman, whatever their age. 'Yeah, they do.'

'The culture was alien, you see. You Romans have never been able to tolerate alien cultures. Not on equal terms, and not when they pose a threat to your own interests.'

You Romans. Well, fair enough. I suppose the guy was Spanish, but there was an edge to the words that I didn't quite like. We moved along a row of fragmented slabs and stopped in front of the carving of a horned god flanked by two rams.

'Ba'al Hammon,' Marius said. His hand went out briefly, palm first.

'Uh-huh. That the one they burned children to?'

He glanced back at me. 'Rome practised human sacrifice within living memory, Corvinus. Captured enemy leaders are still strangled in honour of Jupiter Capitolinus. And what are your gladiatorial games if not a survival of the Etruscan bloodletting ceremony at funerals? Don't accuse the Carthaginians of barbarity, please.'

Uh-oh. The guy was serious, too serious to contradict, and his eyes glittered. For the first time I wondered if he might even be mad. Oh, shit, I thought. First Celsus, now Marius. Two in a row. Maybe I should make my excuses and go before he started biting chunks out of the furniture.

He moved on to another slab. This one showed a series of figures.

'The myth of Keret.' His finger touched a helmeted figure in a kilt, clutching a knife. 'A Phoenician folk-hero. He was defeated in battle by enemies invading his country. The Supreme God arranged for him to have a magical son who drove out the invaders.' He smiled. 'This was long before the Romans came, naturally.'

'Is that so?' I said. Just then there were footsteps on the wooden floor of the corridor outside. I looked up expecting the wine slave, but it was the girl with the beautiful eyes. She was even more of a looker than I'd thought. She paused when she saw me, then came in.

'I'm sorry, Father.' The eyes were lowered; she could've been fifteen, certainly no older. 'I thought you were alone.'

'That's all right, my dear.' Marius opened his arms and she moved into them like a fish drawn in by a line. He kissed her forehead, and I thought she shuddered. 'This is my daughter, Corvinus. My Ta'anit.'

'Yeah?' Something was wrong somewhere, although I couldn't quite put my finger on it. 'Unusual name.'

'Oh, officially she's Marilla.' His lips brushed her hair. 'A good solid Latin name. But to me she is Ta'anit-pene-Ba'al, the Face of the Lord. Isn't she beautiful? Quite perfect. And she will breed perfect sons. Marvellous sons.' He paused. 'Magical sons.'

The girl looked up at me with scared, ashamed eyes, and I knew.

'Yeah,' I said softly. Oh, Jupiter! Jupiter best and greatest! Madness was only the half of it. 'Yeah, she is beautiful.'

Someone coughed: the wine slave this time, for sure. He'd come too late for me. My skin was crawling, and my belly churning. All I wanted now was to get out.

'Master, Crito is downstairs,' he murmured.

'Tell him to wait.' With his free hand Marius held out his cup for the slave to fill. 'I have a guest.'

'Uh, no,' I said. 'That's okay. I'd best be getting back.'

'Really? But you've only just arrived.'

'Yeah. Well.' I tried a shrug. 'You know how it is. Thanks for the information. And for the tour.'

'You're welcome, Corvinus.' His fingers were absently teasing open the neck of the girl's tunic. 'And if you do decide to sell that cylinder seal then let me know first, won't you?'

'Sure.' I handed the slave my empty wine cup. 'Thanks again. Don't worry, I can find my own way out.'

I was glad to get into the fresh air of the Janiculan; but then after Marius's house even a walk along the Tiber would've smelled good.

14

I was almost clear of the Janiculan and heading along the path towards Trans-Tiber when the guy stepped out in front of me from behind a rock. I was lucky; I had a moment to duck, and the iron bar just brushed the top of my hair and clipped my left shoulder. As I drew my knife I was thinking, *Oh, shit, not again!* This was my second visit to the Janiculum in ten years and I'd been mugged both times. It seemed I'd only to set foot across the Sublician for the word to go out to the local yobbos that Corvinus was out to play.

At least this time I'd give myself better odds. Ten years back there'd been three of them, all professionals, and although this guy was big he was no Suburan hard-man. Most of him was flab, and he was breathing heavily already. He'd hesitated when he saw the knife, losing the advantage, and now we were standing staring at each other like actors who've forgotten their lines.

'Boo,' I said at last.

He scowled – no sense of humour, these amateurs – and swung the iron bar on a collision course with my left temple: predictable as hell, and years too late. I ducked into the swing and took him in his exposed side, but the jerkin he was wearing turned the knife and it only cut leather. We grappled, and I straightened up and drove the top of my head hard into his chin. His head snapped back and he let go, falling away from me and lashing out with the bar as he went. The tip caught the blade of my knife and sent it clattering out of sight among the stones somewhere to the left.

Bugger! I backed off quickly. It had been a fluke, sure – Ganymede was looking as surprised as I was – but it left me knifeless and facing three feet of iron thicker than my thumb. Not the best of scenarios, and it served me right for being cocky. Ten years ago I could still've taken him without breaking sweat. Now I wouldn't've liked to bet any more which of us would come out the other end. He moved forward, grinning now and breathing hard, while I started thinking about which way to dive and whether or not I could kick his kneecap loose when I did . . .

'Hey! You stop that!' The shout came from behind me. I wasn't fool enough to look round, but Ganymede's head went up and his grin slid away like oil off a hot griddle. Then he turned and ran. Fast: he may not've been able to fight for nuts but where running was concerned he could've given a hare lessons. I stopped for a rock and flung it at his head, but it fell miles short.

'After him, Lamprus!'

I turned round finally just as something that was just arguably human hurtled past me and threw itself along the path. Jupiter! If that was Lamprus then I wished the other guy luck, iron bar or not. Then I saw who'd been doing all the shouting. A prim little man in a neat lemon tunic was picking his way carefully across the open ground towards me. If this was what I had to thank for saving my life, I thought, then it was positively embarrassing.

'You're hurt, sir?' he said when he reached me.

'No.' I massaged my shoulder where Ganymede's first attempt at taking my head off had caught it. 'No. I'm okay.'

'Isis be praised! What a brute!' He was sweating worse than I was; I could see the beads of moisture glistening among the thin strands of hair combed carefully across his bald scalp. 'A dreadful experience. Simply dreadful.'

'I've had worse.' I was looking around for my knife. I found it eventually wedged between two stones, far enough away and invisible enough to have ruled it out if I'd really needed it. 'Thanks, friend. He'd've had me cold if you hadn't come along.'

'Don't mention it, sir. We're only too glad to have been of service.' He took a napkin out of his tunic and mopped his forehead. 'The authorities really ought to do something about these footpads. Nights are bad enough, but when a gentleman can't walk the public streets in daylight without being set upon there's something sadly wrong with the world.'

'The Janiculan's hardly the Market Square,' I said. I could've added, *And that guy was hardly an ordinary footpad*, but I didn't; it would only have led to questions. I wiped the knife and slipped it back into its sheath.

'No, that's true, sir. Even so . . .' He looked beyond me. 'Ah. Here's Lamprus back. I don't think he caught your friend. Did you, Lamprus?' The man-mountain gave a negative grunt and came over to stand beside him. It was like watching a warship docking. 'A shame. He's willing, sir, but he's no Pheidippides. Still, we'd better see you safely through Trans-Tiber just in case.'

'Thanks, but there's no need for that. I'm fine now.' I frowned; something smelled fishy here, although I couldn't quite say what. 'Uh, by the way, I didn't catch your name.'

He paused and smiled. 'Felix.'

'A freedman?'

'Yes, sir.' He ducked his head.

'Whose?'

'I used to belong to Sextus Titius Sabinus, sir.'

Uh-huh. The smell of rotten fish was getting stronger. I knew the name, sure I did. Sabinus was one of the men on my original shortlist, the close friend of Agrippina set up by a crowd of informers and executed for treason three years back. Now here was one of his freedmen jumping up out of nowhere with a tame gorilla in tow, just in time to save my neck for me. Neat; too neat. Coincidences like that happen, but I'd bet a year's income to a pitted olive that this wasn't the time. Felix and his big pet had been shadowing me.

'Titius Sabinus?' I said. 'Is that so?'

'Yes, sir. That is so.' His eyes met mine. They were grey and candid; and very, very smart.

'Sabinus is dead,' I said. 'Who do you work for now?'

'Myself, mostly. Although I still have connections with the family, of course.'

I folded my arms and grinned. 'Nuts. I don't believe you, pal. Not about working for yourself, anyway. You want to try again?'

There was a long silence while we stared at each other. I had the impression he was laughing, although his face was perfectly serious. Finally he took a deep breath and said, very slowly and carefully, 'No. Not really, Valerius Corvinus.'

Uh-huh. So he knew my name, and he'd used it quite deliberately. Scrap coincidence, he'd been tailing me right enough. The only surprising thing was that he should give the game away straight off and so easily; and in that case maybe he could tell me a bit more. I uncrossed my arms and took a step forward.

Lamprus growled deep in his throat.

'I don't think, sir,' Felix said quietly, 'that that is a terribly good idea.'

My spine went cold and I backed off quickly. The rumbling subsided. Yeah, well, perhaps the guy had a point.

'You sure you don't want a second shot at telling me who your current boss is?' I said.

'Quite sure.' A half-smile. 'I'm sorry.'

'That's okay. Just checking.' I glanced at Lamprus. 'Uh . . . is that thing safe?'

'Reasonably. Although he does tend to get overexcited.' He paused. 'What I will say, sir, is that I work for someone who has an interest in your continued survival.'

Yeah. That much I'd worked out for myself. 'That's nice to know, pal, but I like to know my friends' names. Are we talking about one of the Julians? Or maybe Arruntius or Lamia? Or someone else altogether?'

'Perhaps.'

Jupiter! I'd met looser clams. 'You care to tell me which?'

'That, unfortunately, I'm not at liberty to say.' His mouth drew itself into a prim line. 'Honestly, sir, I hate prevarication as much as you do and I really didn't envisage this conversation taking place at all. I find this whole affair most embarrassing.'

'You and me both, sunshine,' I said. Personally, I was finding it totally weird, and my head was beginning to spin. Maybe Ganymede had clipped me with his iron bar after all, and somehow I'd missed it.

'Also,' the little guy continued, 'I've been given very strict instructions which it's more than my life's worth to disobey. And I don't mean that figuratively. Isn't that so, Lamprus?'

The seven-foot gorilla grunted. Maybe it was a reply, but it could've been wind. I hadn't heard him speak yet, and I doubted if he included it in his repertoire of talents. Maybe he'd never learned, or lost the knack somehow.

'So your being Sabinus's freedman was a lie as well?' I said.

Felix looked shocked. 'Oh, no, sir! Most certainly not! I was his slave for many years. Lamprus also. In fact . . .' Felix stopped. 'No, perhaps I shouldn't say any more.'

'Hey, don't mind me, pal! Talk away! Feel free!'

'I'm sorry, Valerius Corvinus,' he said firmly. 'I've talked quite enough already. My fault entirely. Lamprus, I think we should leave the gentleman before I exceed my brief totally. You agree?' The giant grunted again and Felix turned back to me, looking prim as hell. 'My apologies, sir. I'm simply not used to secrecy, you see, and I find it very uncongenial. I'm an open person normally, as I hope you appreciate, and I've been as frank with you as my instructions permit, but anything further would not be in anyone's interest, least of all my own. I'm pleased to have been of service, and happy that you escaped relatively unscathed. If you don't mind, we'll leave it at that.'

Jupiter! I didn't believe this! In a way, I was glad Lamprus was there to stop me shaking more out of him. Not that I kidded myself it would've been easy. Soft as Felix seemed, if push came to shove I suspected he'd simply refuse to talk altogether and I'd've felt guilty as hell putting the squeeze on him, whatever the result.

'Yeah. Yeah, okay.' I took a gold piece from my purse and held it out. 'Forget it. Here, friend. With my thanks.'

Felix looked shocked. 'Oh, we really couldn't take that, sir, could we, Lamprus?' A negative grunt. 'We will, however, see you back safely to the Sublician as per our instructions. From a suitable distance, of course. Good luck, sir, with your investigation. A pleasure to have met you, even under these unfortunate circumstances.'

'Wait!' I laid a hand on his arm. Lamprus growled, and I dropped it. 'One more thing. You know who that guy was? The one who attacked me?'

'No, sir.' I got a look that was completely bland. 'I've no idea.'

'Uh-huh.' Like hell he didn't. 'Yeah, well, forget that too.' I turned away, then back as a thought struck me. 'Oh, by the way and just out of interest. Your name isn't really Felix, is it? And when he's not running down muggers the Last of the Titans here doesn't answer to Lamprus, either?'

I knew as soon as I'd said the words that I'd hit the bull. Not that he seemed put out at all. In fact his face lit up in a huge smile.

'No, sir,' he said. 'Oh, well done! You're quite correct, these are not our proper names. Could I ask how you knew?'

I couldn't help smiling back. 'Just a hunch.'

'A very perspicacious one, then. Although it was lucky for you that I came along, wasn't it? And although Lamprus isn't exactly bright he really is rather splendid.'

I laughed. Puns, now. I was beginning to like Felix, or whoever the hell he really was: Lamprus is Greek for 'bright' or 'splendid', just as Felix means lucky. So much for putting Bathyllus on a name hunt along the slave grapevine, which I would've done as soon as I got back.

'Thanks again,' I said. 'This time for saving me some effort.'

He nodded. 'Don't mention it, sir. A pleasure.'

I moved off down the path towards the road and the river. I was sorry I probably wouldn't be seeing this little guy again. He was smart, and he had a sense of humour. He'd shown himself a pretty good tail, too: Jupiter knew how long he and his pal had been following me, but I'd never even suspected they were there, and if it hadn't been for the attack I still wouldn't know. Also, for someone who'd claimed to be totally wet behind the ears in the sneaky tricks department he'd done all right; better than all right. Forget the wide-eyed innocent pose, he'd told me just exactly as much as he'd wanted to, truth or lies, whichever, without making me feel he was holding anything back. That had taken real brains, and more than a pinch of downright sneakiness.

In which case before I was much older I'd make a point of finding out more about Titius Sabinus. Whether Felix had told the truth there or not, I'd bet a jug of Caecuban to a week-old mussel that handing me the name had been no accident.

I got home an hour later. There was a note waiting for me from Lippillus asking me to meet him on the Esquiline.

Someone had smashed in Vibius Celsus's skull.

15

It was quite definitely murder: the back of Celsus's head had been smashed like an eggshell. Shit. This I felt really bad about; when I'd left him I'd told the poor bugger he was safe. Sure, I'd meant 'safe' as far as I was concerned, but it still left a bad taste, like any broken promise.

We were in the garden of the house. I hadn't been out here when I'd visited, of course. Although it was bigger than I'd thought it would be it was seriously run down and there were no statues worth talking about. If Celsus had been lying when he claimed he was broke then he certainly hadn't spent any ill-gotten Spanish gains on impressing the neighbours.

'When was it done?' I asked Lippillus's opposite number, the head of the Third Region Watch; the Third handled the Isis and Serapis and Temple of Peace districts, which took in both the Esquiline and the Caelian.

'Some time between mid-morning and noon.' Libanius Clemens indicated the stone bench and the blood-soaked book beside it: although the body itself had been removed for tidying up no one had touched the book-roll. 'He liked a quiet read in the mornings, seemingly. His chef found him when he came for the dinner instructions.'

I glanced at the book's title, miraculously unsplashed with bits of Celsus's brain: *The Pirates' Prisoner*, one of the more lurid Alexandrian romances and not exactly adult reading. The poor guy should've stuck to getting all his thrills second-hand. Mid-morning was right. It would've left plenty of time for Ganymede to have got over from the Esquiline to the Janiculan and have a go at parting my own hair for me. And he would've succeeded if it hadn't been for the pseudo-Felix and his tame mountain.

'Celsus was a bachelor,' Clemens said, 'so there was no one else in the house, barring slaves. We'll have them tortured, naturally.' He glanced at Lippillus, who was frowning. 'They must've seen or heard something. It may even have been one of them who did it.'

'The killer came over the back wall and left the same way, Clemens.' Lippillus's voice was level. 'You can see where the ivy's been pulled down in that far corner. And the flowers in the flower-bed have been trampled. We're out of sight of the house. If any of the slaves saw anything it had to be the gardener, and that poor bastard's lying in the slave quarters with a poisoned foot. Torturing slaves isn't going to get anyone anywhere.'

'Is that so, now?' Clemens picked the book-roll up and set it carefully on the bench. 'Lippillus, let's just get one thing clear from the start. A narrow-striper's been murdered, this is my ward, and I'll do things my way, okay? I may stretch the rules and allow you and your nosey aristocratic friend here in as a favour, but that doesn't mean I want your advice.'

Hey! I was beginning to take a positive dislike to this arm of the law.

'Not even if we can give you a description of the guy responsible, pal?' I said.

Clemens looked up sharply. *'What?'*

'The man you want is just short of six foot, late twenties, heavily built but running to fat. Close-cropped straight dark hair, thick nose and lips.' Clemens was staring at me. 'Probably Asiatic Greek. And he has severe problems with body odour. Is that enough for you, or do you want me to draw you a picture?'

I must've sounded pretty pissed off because the stare had turned into a scowl. 'How do you know all this, Corvinus?' he said.

'Because he nearly put me underground a couple of hours later on the Janiculan. With an iron bar. Identical weapon, identical method. Or maybe you think that's coincidence.'

'Maybe. That depends if you can prove a definite connection.'

'Jupiter best and greatest!' I turned away, furious: it was guilt, sure; if he hadn't talked to me Celsus would still be alive, and the poor sap hadn't been a real villain, just a weak character caught up in something too big for him. 'No, I can't prove it. But there would be reasons.'

'Reasons,' Clemens said slowly. 'Okay. I'm ready to listen if you'd care to spell them out.'

'No.' I shook my head. 'I can't do that.'

A shrug. He turned away. 'Then we go by the book and torture the slaves.'

Lippillus looked at us, from one to the other. 'Clemens,' he said, 'This is high-level stuff. Political. Believe me, the slaves had nothing to do with it.'

'Sure I'll believe you. Once you give me the evidence.'

'For the gods' sakes!' Lippillus turned away in disgust.

I'd had enough of this. I grabbed at Clemens's throat. 'Okay, pal. You want to know who killed Celsus? Who *really* killed him? The real murderer's name is Aelius Sejanus, Commander of Praetorians and the Wart's best buddy. Now go ahead and torture your slaves and if you're very unlucky, *friend*, you might just get that nugget of information out of one of them yourself. In which case then pity help you when he finds out you've got it!'

'Marcus, this isn't helping,' Lippillus muttered. I ignored him.

Clemens's eyes had widened, and his face had gone the colour of milk. Not just because I had a fistful of his mantle, either. Sejanus's name tended to have that effect on people.

Lippillus leaned forward and laid a quiet hand on my arm.

'That's enough,' he said. 'Now put him down or I'll have to arrest you for obstruction.'

He would, at that. Yeah, well, maybe I shouldn't've lost my temper. It wasn't Clemens's fault, he was only doing his job as he saw it. I relaxed my grip, and the guy sat down hard on the blood-soaked bench. His laundress wasn't going to like that, not one little bit.

'Sejanus?' His voice was a sick whisper.

'Sejanus. You still want me to give you reasons?'

'No. No.' He passed a hand over his mouth. 'We'll take them as read. Jupiter, Corvinus! You're sure?'

'Sure I'm sure.'

'Oh, gods! Oh, Jupiter!' He licked his lips. 'So what should I do?'

'What Laco tells you,' Lippillus said. Laco was the overall Watch Commander for the city; an okay guy in his way, but definitely a political appointment with his own fish to fry. 'And, believe me, that will be to drop this case down the nearest sewer and put the lid back on fast.'

Clemens nodded. He was shaking, and his face was a sickly grey now. I could smell the fear.

'One more thing,' I said. 'Find me Ganymede.'

The Watch head simply stared.

'Clemens is okay.' Lippillus walked with me as far as the front door. 'He just plays by the rules. And he's right about the slaves. Celsus was a purple-striper. These things you don't skimp.'

'Yeah, I know.' The door slave opened up for me. He was only a kid, and he looked scared to death, as well he might. He knew the laws governing murder investigations as well as I did, and with his dead master being a knight there wasn't any leeway. 'I know. I just don't like waste, that's all.'

'Nor do I. So we'd best find your friend quickly, just in case Laco isn't as sensible as I think he is.' Lippillus paused. 'By the way, what colour tunic was your Janiculan pal wearing when he hit you?'

'Ganymede? Blue. A dirty blue, pretty much patched, under a leather jerkin.'

'He'll need another patch, then, when he gets home.' Lippillus held up a scrap of torn material he'd been holding in his hand. 'I found it caught on one of the rose bushes in the bed near the wall.'

'Uh-huh.' It was dark blue wool, about an inch square. 'You didn't think of passing that over to Clemens, I suppose?'

'I wouldn't rely on any help from Clemens, Corvinus. Like I said, if he's got the slightest inkling of the truth Laco'll shut this investigation down so fast it'd make your head spin. I'll do the digging myself.'

'You think that's wise?'

'Not really. But that's how it has to be. Now he knows Sejanus is involved, investigating officer or not, Laco or not, Clemens won't touch the case with a forty-foot pole. I won't be stepping on any sensitive toes.'

'That wasn't what I meant. At least, not in that sense.'

'Yeah.' He shrugged. 'Still, it has to be done and someone's got to do it.'

'But . . .'

'Corvinus.' He looked me in the eye, as far as a five-foot dwarf can manage something like that. 'Understand this. I don't like murder in cold blood, and I like still less the thought of covering it up, whoever's patch it's on. Besides, it's my job. With the description you gave I should be able to lay my hands on the killer without too much trouble.' He stood with one hand on the door jamb. 'I'll keep in touch. Stay safe, right?'

'Yeah. You, too, pal.'

He went back inside. It was building up for rain as I rejoined Patrician Street and headed for the eastern end of the Subura and home. *Stay safe.* I didn't like the way things were going; I didn't like it above half. Celsus's death and the attack on the Janiculan showed that however careful I'd thought I was being I'd been noticed, and Aelius Sejanus wasn't one to let the grass grow under his feet. This investigation could turn very nasty, very quickly, and not just for me. Clemen's attitude may've verged on the spineless, but I couldn't fault his caution. Maybe I should've told Lippillus to leave things alone too. After all, it wasn't his fight, slaves or no slaves. Maybe I should still tell him . . .

I almost turned round and went back to Celsus's house, but I didn't. I should've done; but by the time I realised that it was too late.

16

At least I knew where to go for information on Titius Sabinus. His nephew Columella was a regular customer at Scyllax's gym – what I still thought of as Scyllax's gym – over by the Racetrack, and he'd be there for sure the next day. There wasn't any point in going early, though. Columella held down a junior finance officer's job in the Department of Water and Roads, and he'd be busy in the mornings. Mid-afternoon I could be sure of catching him.

Besides, the next morning turned out too beautiful for work, and while we were back in Rome I owed Perilla some sort of holiday. I broached the idea over breakfast. Sallust Gardens.

She smiled over her cup of fruit juice. 'Separate litters, Corvinus?' she said.

Yeah. She'd got the reference, and the reason for the choice. Sallust Gardens in spring had special memories for us, especially one grotto in particular. It'd be nice to see that again, maybe even visit and press a few ferns. You never knew, something might catch.

'*Not* separate litters, lady.' I was grinning. 'Not this time. And wear your oldest mantle.'

'Marcus, I am *not* going to be seen in Sallust Gardens wearing an old mantle. Besides, I'm too old to go rolling about on the grass playing games. If that's what you had in mind.'

'So what's wrong with games suddenly?'

'Very well.' She stood up. 'But if we go we walk. *Just* walk. Along the paths, like any other respectably married couple, enjoying the scenery.' I winced. Jupiter! 'And definitely no grottoes.'

'You sure about that?'

'I'm sure.'

'Hundred per cent, cast-iron sure?'

'Yes.'

'Spoilsport.' Ah, well. Maybe she'd change her mind when we got there. I kissed her and went to tell Bathyllus to order up the litter.

Sallust Gardens are in the north of the city, between the Pincian and the Quirinal. They were beautiful at this time of year, and like I say they had memories. The good weather had pulled out a lot of punters, even more than usual, and the place was crowded. We walked around a bit like Perilla wanted. Then I bought some toasted melon seeds from one of the snack-sellers by the Faunus statue and we sat down on the grass to eat them.

'You remember what we talked about, Marcus?' Perilla licked the salt from her fingers. 'The last time we were here?'

'It's not the talking I remember,' I said.

'No.' She smiled and lowered her eyes. 'I do, though.'

'So tell me.'

'We talked about how this park happened. And about your father.'

'Ah. Yeah.' I remembered now; also that I'd been pretty concerned to get her off both subjects. Some things don't change.

'I think that was when I finally fell in love with you.'

'Is that right?' Jupiter! I shifted uncomfortably and looked up at the sun. Maybe we should be getting on.

'You were so angry over things I took for granted because I'd never really thought about them. I'd never met that before. Someone who didn't fit and was ready to say so.'

'Yeah. Well.' I cleared my throat. 'Maybe I've grown up a bit since then.'

'Marcus, you'll never grow up.'

'Hey, thanks! Thanks a bunch!'

She took my hand and put it round her shoulder. From a nearby bench a dowager with the face of a constipated camel glared at us. Perilla gave her her best smile and she turned away.

'That was an observation,' she said, 'not a criticism. Most

certainly not a criticism. In fact if you ever did grow up – at least in the way I mean – I'd probably divorce you or take a lover out of boredom.'

'Uh . . . yeah.' Jupiter on wheels with a squeaker! What had brought this on? Was this Perilla? The trouble was I could see she was serious. Or half serious. 'Lady, it's getting late. I've got to be over at the Racetrack. You feel like calling it a day?'

'In a moment. I may not ever have the nerve to say this again.' She leaned her head against my shoulder. 'I just wanted you to know, Marcus, that however much I complain I wouldn't really have you any different. Remember that, won't you? Oh, yes, it would be nice to have children' – she put her finger against my opening mouth—' but they're not everything. Lots of couples are a lot less lucky than we are, and I can stand a little disappointment.'

I didn't say anything. There wasn't anything to say. Suddenly she shook herself and stood up.

'I'm sorry. This, to use one of your phrases, is getting heavy. Let's see if we can find our grotto, shall we?'

I couldn't swear to it, but I was almost sure she put out her tongue at old camel-face as we passed.

Daphnis had a sleek and prosperous look about him these days, but I didn't grudge him it: the erstwhile sand-pushing duckling had turned out to be a financial swan, and the gym was coining money for me hand over fist. I'd got someone else in on the practical side, of course – an ex-legionary with a limp and a whole sheaf of good-conduct certificates – but he was just another client, like anyone else's. There wasn't the rapport I'd had with Scylax, and there never would be.

'Hey, Daphnis,' I said, clapping him on the shoulder. 'How are things?'

I got the familiar long slow stare. Some things don't change. I doubt if he'd even noticed I'd been away.

'Not bad, Corvinus,' he said. 'You want to see Publius? He isn't in yet.'

Publius was the retired soldier, and his only vice was drink: now he'd got shot of army discipline he was making up for lost time. No doubt his long-suffering daughter would be walking him up and down the living-room floor to sober him up after last night's binge with the boys. He was a good trainer, though.

'Not particularly.' I sat on the corner of the desk. Daphnis sniffed and pointedly moved the half a dozen wax tablets he was working on out of the way. 'You know anything about a guy called Marius? Sextus Marius?'

That got me the stare again. 'Never heard of him,' Daphnis said at last, and picked up his pen. 'Now if you've quite finished messing up my desk . . .'

Jupiter! The same old Daphnis, friendly and helpful to a fault. I got up again quickly before he accidentally-on-purpose prodded me in the leg with the pen. Well, it'd been worth a try: Daphnis was Spanish himself, and they're a clannish lot. But then there are Spaniards and Spaniards, and Marius hadn't struck me as the sort to mix with ex-skivvies like the world's most cheerful freedman here.

'Columella around this afternoon?' I said after a pause.

'Sergius Columella?' Daphnis grunted with supreme disinterest. 'Sure. He came early. He's in the bath-house.'

Yeah. That'd explain why I hadn't seen him outside, banging away with the wooden foils and working up a sweat along with the other punters.

'The bath-house,' I said. 'Right.'

'You know your way, don't you?'

Without waiting for an answer he turned back to his wax tablets. That, it would seem, was all I was getting of the great man's valuable time. I know when I'm not wanted. I gave him the finger and walked over to the bath-house.

I collected a towel from the slave at the door, checked my mantle and tunic in the changing rooms and went straight through to the cold room. A bath would've been great, but this was business and I couldn't afford to miss Sabinus's nephew. He was stretched out by the side of the cold plunge, having his post-bathing rub-down.

'Corvinus!' He sat up. 'You back in Rome?'

'Yeah. So it would seem.' I sat down beside him with my back to the wall. Columella was okay, but he was an acquaintance rather than a friend. And fortunately for my purposes what there was between his ears was solid bone. Jupiter knew how the Water and Roads Department functioned at all if they had any more like him on the payroll. We were lucky we weren't all dead of thirst.

'So how's it going?' Columella sent the slave away and sat back. 'I hear your father died.'

'Yeah. Perilla and I came home for the funeral.'

'What was it? Do you know?'

'One of these sudden winter fevers. At least it was quick.' I paused. 'Your family all okay?'

'Mother died last September.'

'I'm sorry to hear that.' I was: I'd never met Titia Plautina, but she was a decent old stick, a perpetual invalid who'd been confined to her bed for years.

'Yeah. She was glad to go, though. She never really got over Uncle Sextus's death.'

Plautina, of course, had been Sabinus's sister. Now Columella had raised the subject himself this was going to be easier than I'd thought.

'Uh, I heard something about that in Athens,' I said carefully. 'There was some sort of scandal, wasn't there?'

Columella glared at me. 'Not on my uncle's side, Corvinus. Whatever people said. The bastards set him up.'

'So I heard.' I kept my voice neutral. 'There were four of them, weren't there?'

'That's right.' The glare didn't slacken. 'Latiaris, Cato, Rufus and Opsius. If you want the names.'

Sure I did; but none of them rang any bells. Nevertheless I filed them away for future reference. 'So what happened?'

He scratched absently at a raw patch where the slave had caught him with the scraper. 'The usual.'

'The usual?'

'The usual farce of a trial. You weren't in Rome then, Corvinus. You don't know what it was like.'

'No, that's true.' I paused. 'He was set up, you say?'

'Six ways from nothing. You know he was friendly with Agrippina?'

'Yeah,' I said. 'Yeah, I'd heard that.'

'Friendly, mind. Nothing more.' Columella scowled. 'We may

not've got on especially, but Uncle Sextus wasn't the type for affairs. Not with someone like Agrippina, anyway.'

'I've heard that as well.'

'Good. Believe it.' He shifted against the wall. Luckily we were on our own: it was still early, and the other gym regulars were either thrashing around outside trying to carve bits off each other or sweating next door in the hot room. I doubt if there'd been anyone else around he would've told me even this much. Politics – even stale politics – wasn't a safe topic of conversation at Rome these days.

'So,' I said. 'How did they do it?'

Anyone else would've been getting slightly suspicious about my motives by this time, but like I say Columella was solid bone from the neck up. He never blinked.

'They sweet-talked him. Got him seriously to bad-mouth Aelius Sejanus and the emperor in what he thought was private. Only they'd got round Uncle's slaves beforehand and arranged for witnesses to be smuggled into his own house and hidden in the attic directly above the study. They bored holes through the ceiling panels. After that it was an open and shut case.'

There was anger in Columella's voice, and I didn't blame him. Anyone who was fool enough to slander Tiberius or Sejanus in public deserved all they got, sure, but what you said among friends – or those who professed themselves to be friends – in the privacy of your own home was something else. Sabinus had been set up with a vengeance, and 'sneaky' didn't do the thing justice. I had to hand it to Sejanus, though, and Sejanus had to be behind this. It'd been slick, very slick indeed.

'So the four reported what your uncle had said directly to the emperor,' I said. 'With the witnesses' backing.'

'Yeah.' Columella made to spit. 'The poor sod never had a chance. The Senate convicted him as they'd have to do on the strength of the evidence and he was dead before the month was out.'

'Uh-huh,' I said. This needed thinking about, and maybe I'd have that bath after all, when I'd left Columella. Sure, what had happened to Sabinus was interesting, but it didn't add much to what I knew already: that Sejanus had been going out of his way to target the leading Julians. So why had Felix and his sidekick been so keen to make sure I checked the story up? Which reminded me . . .

'Columella, you happen to know if your uncle had a couple of weird slaves? A fussy little guy going bald on top and a man-mountain that grunted?'

'Not that I know of.' Columella looked suspicious for the first time; well, I suppose that had been pushing it. 'Although like I say we didn't get on all that well, and I wasn't really on visiting terms. He might have done. You got a reason for asking?'

'No, just passing curiosity.'

'Mmm.' I could see him putting it out of what served him for a mind, and I blessed the patron god of idiots, whoever that was. 'So. Tell me about Athens. I'm thinking of going out there this summer, when Rome hots up a bit. You know any good brothels?'

I sighed. Columella always had been direct and to the point. I gave the guy a few addresses and left him to his thoughts. Such as they were.

17

I had the bath, although it didn't get me any further forward with the Sabinus puzzle. Ah, well. At least it meant that when I got back home I was clean.

We'd just started dinner when Bathyllus brought a little fat guy into the dining-room. I knew at once that something was wrong. Badly wrong. Both of them had that serious look that signals bad news.

'This is Latinius, sir,' Bathyllus said quietly. 'Flavonius Lippillus's next-door neighbour. He has a message from Marcina Paullina.'

Perilla glanced over at me, her face ashen. The fat guy was shifting his weight nervously from foot to foot. Even at this distance he smelled of fish. A stallholder in the market, maybe.

'Marcina asks if you'd call in at the flat as soon as you can, sir,' he said. 'Her stepson's had an accident.'

I was on my feet by now. 'He's dead?'

'No. At least not when I left.' Jupiter! 'They found him near the Latin Gate, sir. He'd been attacked.' His hand gestured towards his head. 'The poor lad's in a bit of a mess.'

Oh, Jupiter! Jupiter best and greatest, no! First Celsus, then Lippillus. I should've gone back and warned him off, I'd known that at the time.

'Is he at home?'

'Yes, sir.' Latinius nodded. 'The men who found him took him straight round. Marcina's doing her best, but . . .' His voice tailed off and he shrugged.

Oh, hell! And there'd be no doctors in a city tenement.

'Bathyllus,' I snapped. 'Send for Sarpedon. Tell him to meet me at Lippillus's flat. You know where that is?'

'Yes, sir.' Sarpedon was my father's doctor, one of the best in Rome. Dad had freed him five years back, and he had a lucrative practice now near the Market Square. I just hoped he wasn't out to dinner, or on call to some society lady with a fit of the vapours.

'Thanks for coming round, pal,' I said to Latinius. 'I appreciate it.'

'That's nothing. Whatever I can do.'

'I'll fetch your mantle, sir.' That was Bathyllus.

'Bathyllus!' I was tying on my sandals. Or trying to. 'Forget the sodding mantle, just get Sarpedon! Send your fastest runner. If he's not at home then find him.'

Bathyllus left. I turned back to Latinius. 'What happened? Exactly?'

Another shrug. 'No idea, sir. Not exactly. I'd only just got back from work myself when they brought him in. But Marcina'll tell you.'

Oh, shit! Marcina! How was I going to face Marcina? The laces of the second sandal snagged. I jerked them free and tied a rough knot. 'Okay, let's go. Perilla, don't wait up.'

'Nonsense, Marcus.' She was putting her own sandals on. 'Give me a moment to get my mantle and cloak. I'm going with you.'

'Like hell you are!'

'Don't argue,' she snapped. I couldn't if I'd tried, because she was heading for the stairs. 'And don't bother with a litter, either.'

'I wasn't going to, lady,' I said to myself. Under different circumstances, I might've smiled, but now wasn't the time.

The news had spread, and we had to push our way through a crowd of locals who filled the stairwell and the first-floor landing. Maybe Lippillus was popular, but I suspected most of them were the ghouls you always get when there's an accident or a killing. In any case I wasn't too gentle. Latinius disappeared without another word through the door of his own flat opposite, but I knew he'd be keeping his eyes and ears open. Marcina was lucky. Neighbours like Latinius are good to have.

The door wasn't locked, and I didn't knock: she'd have other things to worry about than the conventional niceties. She was in the bedroom, sitting beside the still figure on the double bed.

'Hello, Corvinus,' she said. She didn't look up and I couldn't see her face clearly in the light of the single lamp, but she sounded pretty washed out. When Perilla put her hands on her shoulders she never moved. 'Perilla. Good of you to come.'

'How's he doing?' I said.

'He's alive.' She shook her head. 'Otherwise I don't know. He's been like this since they found him.'

She'd cleaned his face up, that was all; his hair was caked with blood and the blanket under his head was damp and stained a dark red. His eyes were shut and his breathing was very shallow. Every so often it stopped altogether for a few seconds before restarting. Worrying as hell. Even with my slim knowledge of medicine I could see the poor guy was in deep trouble.

'I've sent for a doctor,' I said. 'He should be here soon.'

'That's nice.' Marcina still hadn't moved.

Keep safe . . . I winced. Lippillus was lying there with his head bashed in because of me, and we all knew it. If I could've gone back a day and changed things I would've done, gladly, but there was nothing now anyone could do. And from the looks of Lippillus that included Sarpedon.

'You know anything about how it happened?' I said quietly.

'He left this morning for headquarters as usual.' Marcina was still speaking in that terrible, level voice. She hadn't looked at either of us since we'd arrived. 'I wasn't worried when he didn't come home for dinner. That happens more often than not, although usually he sends a message. Then – I don't know when, maybe an hour ago, maybe two, maybe three – his deputy Valens came round to say he'd been picked up by two carters near the Latin Gate. He'd had them bring him straight here on a blanket.'

'Did the carters see the attack?'

Her shoulders lifted. 'Maybe. I don't know. I didn't ask. It wasn't all that important at the time. It still isn't.'

'Marcus.' Perilla's fingers touched my arm. 'Go downstairs and wait for Sarpedon. Please.'

'Uh, yeah. Yeah, okay.' Perhaps that was best. I wasn't doing any good here, anyway. I paused at the door.

'Marcina, I'm sorry,' I said. 'Terribly, terribly sorry.'

Her head didn't turn. Her voice was quite calm. 'If he dies, Corvinus,' she said, 'I'll never forgive you. Never ever. Do you understand?'

'Yeah. I understand,' I said; and left.

Sarpedon arrived half an hour later, in a litter that put mine to shame, looking every inch the society doctor in a Greek cloak and mantle that must've cost an arm and a leg. Probably someone else's. The crowd parted to let him through, which was superstition, not respect; in the tenements, doctors and undertakers are given plenty of space, and for the same reasons. Most of the time there isn't much difference between them anyway. I just hoped Sarpedon would prove the ghoulish bastards wrong, despite the snazzy turnout.

'Where's the patient, sir?' he said when he saw me. Old habits die hard; I was still the master's son, even if Sarpedon had come a long way since he patched me up the time of my last visit to the Janiculan.

'One floor up. I'll take you.'

'Fine.' He signalled to his slave, another Greek, but thirty years younger. 'Mnester, bring the bag.'

The man pulled a leather bag out of the litter and followed us up the steps.

Marcina and Perilla were where I'd left them, Marcina sitting on the bed beside Lippillus and Perilla in the room's only chair. They got up as we came in. Lippillus was still breathing, and I murmured a quick prayer of thanks to whatever god happened to be on duty. Sarpedon took off his cloak and bent over to examine him, his long fingers moving lightly and methodically over the blood-crusted scalp. Finally he straightened, frowning.

'How long has he been like this?' he asked.

I looked at Marcina, but she'd turned away. 'Two hours,' I said. 'Three. Maybe longer.'

Sarpedon grunted, and his frown deepened. 'I need more light. Fetch as many lamps as you can find. A basin of hot water. And some clean cloths.'

'We'll see to it, Marcus,' Perilla said quietly. 'Marcina, come with me. I don't know where things are.'

They left. Sarpedon turned to the slave.

'The bag, please, Mnester.'

The slave pulled over a small table, set the bag on it and began unpacking a collection of instruments: bronze forceps, a razor, a small saw . . .

'You think he'll live?' I asked.

Sarpedon hesitated before answering. 'I'll do what I can, of course,' he said, 'but I doubt it. I doubt it very much. The blow has broken the side of the skull and there's a collection of bruised blood pressing on the brain. If I can trephine the skull without killing him in the process and relieve the pressure then he has a chance. A very poor one.'

'How poor?'

A pause. 'I'm not a gambler, sir. But if I were I would not like the odds.'

Jupiter! Still, it was as well to know. 'Is there anything I can do?'

'Yes. Two things. Keep out of my way, and offer a prayer to Asclepius.'

'You think that'll do any good?'

He smiled softly. 'No, sir. Not much. And I'm very much afraid that the Lord Asclepius would agree with me. However, it will keep you busy.'

Perilla came back with four oil lamps on a pedestal hanger.

'These were all I could find,' she said. 'Marcina's borrowing more from Latinius.'

'Twist the arms of a few of these ghouls outside and see what they can come up with,' I said sourly. 'Let them make themselves useful for once. What about the water?'

'Latinius's wife had a brazier already lit. It's coming.'

'Hermes be praised for a sensible woman.' Sarpedon stripped off his mantle and rolled up the sleeves of his long-sleeved tunic. 'Your pardon, sir. Madam. Mnester can do everything needful for me now, and I'm afraid the next part is not going to be pleasant. Could I ask you to leave, please? I'll call when it's over.'

'Uh, yeah. Sure.' I edged towards the door. 'Come on, Perilla.'

Then I paused, and spoke softly to the figure on the bed. 'Good luck, pal.'

We sat round the table in the other room, staring into the darkness and listening for sounds. Asclepius had had his prayers. They weren't much in my line, but the old guy couldn't complain that I didn't mean them. Finally the bedroom door opened and Sarpedon came out drying his hands on a towel.

No one asked the question. None of us dared. Sarpedon answered it anyway.

'Perhaps,' he said. 'He's still alive, at any rate. And the operation, I think, was successful.'

Marcina buried her face in her hands. She hadn't cried; all evening, she hadn't cried. Now she did. I felt like joining her, but she was doing fine on her own.

'Can we see him?' she said at last.

'If you like, madam. He's still not awake, of course. That's the next hurdle.' Sarpedon hesitated, and cleared his throat. 'You do understand, don't you, that he may not live even yet? I've done my best, but from now on the matter is out of my hands. My dear, your husband may simply . . . not wake up. I've seen it before, many times, with head injuries. The patient goes deeper and deeper into sleep, and no amount of stimulation will rouse them.'

Cheerful bastard; but then he was quite right to warn her. I didn't correct the assumption that they were man and wife, either.

'We'll just have to hope your Asclepius was listening, then,' I said.

'Indeed, sir.'

We hesitated at the door. 'Go on, Marcina,' Perilla said.

Marcina Paullina blew her nose on a napkin and stood up.

'We'll all go,' she said.

The bedroom seemed very bright after the darkness of the other room: Perilla and Marcina had managed a good dozen lamps eventually, plus the oil to fill them, and over half were still lit. Mnester was packing away Sarpedon's surgical tools. On the floor, the basin of what had been warm water was filmed with a scum of blood and hair. I gave it one quick look and decided my stomach wouldn't take another. On the bed, Lippillus looked like death. His eyes were still closed and his face was grey beneath the turban of bandages, but at least he was breathing normally now.

'Hey, pal,' I said quietly.

Marcina picked up his hand and laid it against her cheek.

'Try calling him, madam,' Sarpedon said. 'A familiar voice sometimes brings them back.'

'Decimus?' Marcina whispered. Then louder: 'Decimus!'

The breathing didn't alter. Marcina tried again; and again. Finally Sarpedon shrugged.

'Never mind,' he said. 'It's early days yet. Keep trying. And don't be afraid to touch him. Gently, and not his head, of course.' He reached out for the mantle which Mnester put into his hand. 'I'll call back tomorrow to see if there's any change.'

I saw him out and followed him to his litter. The vultures had gone elsewhere now. I hoped it was a good sign.

'You think he'll pull through?' I said.

Sarpedon paused; even in the light of the torches that the litter slaves held I could see how tired he looked. I wasn't feeling too bright myself, but the numbness had worn off.

'Perhaps,' he said at last. 'If he wakes quickly. Otherwise no. We can only hope.'

'Yeah.' I swallowed. 'Yeah. Thanks anyway. Whatever happens.'

'Oh, I'll send you my bill, sir.' He gave me a fleeting smile and signalled to Mnester who'd followed us downstairs with the bag. 'It won't be a small one, either. And you owe something to my Lord Asclepius too. If I were you I'd keep him sweet, because your friend is going to need all the help he can get.'

I waved them off and turned back to the tenement entrance. No, I wouldn't forget Asclepius. I wouldn't forget the bastard with the iron bar, either. Whether he had Sejanus's protection or not, if I found him – and I'd find him, sure I would – he was dead meat. That was one debt I intended to pay in full, personally.

18

There was still no news from Marcina next morning. I gave breakfast a miss and went over to Watch headquarters first thing in the hope of catching Lippillus's deputy Valens. I was lucky: he was just going through the previous night's reports at his boss's desk.

'Corvinus.' We shook hands. 'Pleased to meet you. Have a seat.'

'Thanks.' I pulled up a bench and looked around. Lippillus's office was pretty stark. Its only decoration – if you could call it that – was a plan of the First and Second Regions stuck up on the wall.

'How's Lippillus?' Valens said.

'No change. The doctor says if he comes round he has a chance, but he's still unconscious.'

'Mm.' Valens grunted. 'We'll get the man who did it. Don't you worry.'

'What exactly happened?' I said. 'Do you know?'

The deputy stood up. He'd've towered head and shoulders over Lippillus, and he looked like he had German blood somewhere. 'No more than you do yourself by now, I suppose. Did Marcina tell you about the carters?' I nodded. 'They found him here' – he pointed to the city plan – 'tucked behind the Liber shrine just this side of the Latin Gate, an hour before sunset. It was lucky they recognised him and gave themselves the trouble to bring him back. Carters aren't usually so co-operative.'

'So they didn't see the attack?'

'No.' Valens smiled sourly. 'Or if they did they're not saying. Their story is they went for a quiet piss, which is likely because the shrine's hidden from the main road and there're bushes behind it. The boss was lucky they came along.'

I looked at the plan. The Latin Gate was at the very edge of the First Region, where Latin Road leaves the city boundaries. Pretty far out, in other words, right on the border of Lippillus's patch and well away from the more thickly populated urban area that was the Watch's usual stamping ground. Yeah. Lucky was right. Off the main drag, he could've lain unnoticed for days.

'Any idea what he could've been doing over there?' I said.

'None. We'd no reports of any trouble around that area. He may've been following up something that happened elsewhere, connected to another case.'

Yeah. Or maybe it had been unofficial; and if so I'd be prepared to lay bets on the subject matter.

'You get the names of the two who found him?'

'Naturally.' Valens consulted one of the wax tablets on his desk. 'A pair of brothers, Hasta and Pertinax. Local lads. Not that they'll be any more help. Like I say, carters tend to avoid official questions, and I've sweated them already. Personally and very thoroughly. They don't know anything more than they've already told us.'

'You're sure about that?'

'As sure as I can be.'

Uh-huh. Well, maybe, but it was still worth checking, and a few silver pieces might jog a memory or loosen a tongue where an official sweating gets you nowhere. I shelved that idea until later: carters work nights, because wheeled traffic is banned within the boundaries any other time. My best chance of catching Hasta and Pertinax would be at the cart station outside the gate just before sunset.

'Lippillus didn't say anything to you about his plans?' I said. 'Nothing at all?'

Valens shook his head. 'No. Mind you, that doesn't necessarily mean anything. We work overlapping shifts, and if a problem or a lead had just come up he'd've told me about it at the changeover or left a message, and he was hit before he could do either. He didn't say anything to any of the lads on his own shift, either, not the ones I've talked to, anyway, which is most of them by now. And the rest've just come on.' He paused. 'Corvinus, what is this? I know you're a close friend of his, but this is Watch business.'

'Meaning the Watch can handle it on their own and nosey half-arsed purple-stripers can butt out?'

I was grinning while I said it, and he grinned back and ducked his head.

'Something along these lines,' he said. 'I wouldn't put it so politely myself.'

'Fair enough. Let's just say I have a vested interest. And like you said Lippillus is a friend. You object all that much?'

'No.' Valens's grin faded. 'No, Valerius Corvinus, I don't object at all. Lippillus is well liked in the Watch, and if you can nail the bastard who hit him for us you can drink free for a month, no questions asked. And any squaddie on the station will say the same.'

Well, you couldn't say fairer than that. Information goes both ways, though. Without mentioning the Celsus tie-in I gave him the description of Ganymede that I'd given to Lippillus and Clemens. The hell with caution now; I wanted the guy cold. I wanted it so much I could taste it.

When I'd finished, Valens nodded. If he thought I was holding something back – and he probably did, because he was no fool – then he was polite enough not to say so.

'Thanks,' he said. 'That helps a lot. I'll spread the word to the other regions, too. Someone must know the man, and if Lippillus was looking for him then what happened to him makes sense.'

'Maybe you should concentrate on the area round the Latin Gate,' I said.

'Good idea.' *Don't teach your grandmother to suck eggs*, his tone said; but he was too polite to say so out loud. 'I'll spread the word, Corvinus, don't you worry. Like I said, we'll get him. Even if it takes a year.'

'Yeah, sure.' I stood up. 'Just give me first refusal when you do, okay?'

'Stand in line, boy.' Valens didn't smile. 'Stand in line.'

I called in at Lippillus's flat on my way back home. There was still no change. His face was a better colour, but his eyes were still closed and the lids didn't even flicker.

'Has Sarpedon been?' I asked Marcina.

'Yes.' At least she was talking to me now. 'He came first thing.'

'He say anything?'

'No. Except to tell me to keep trying to rouse him. I said I'd understood his instructions perfectly well the first time round.'

Ouch. I'd bet she hadn't stopped trying, either, since we'd left the night before. 'You had any sleep yourself, Marcina?'

'I'm not tired.' A lie: she was dead on her feet, and there were heavy bags under her eyes. 'Thank you for sending your slaves, by the way, but they're not necessary. Latinius next door is quite willing to run any errands that are needed.'

Jupiter! 'Marcina, you know how sorry I am,' I said. 'Let me help, okay? I'd change things if I could, but I can't.'

'No. Of course you can't.' She turned away, and looked down at Lippillus. 'His job was bad enough at the best of times. I'm just angry that you had to make it worse. Now go, please. I'll let you know if and when he wakes up.'

'Uh, yeah. Yeah, okay.' That was some bitter lady, but I couldn't blame her. I could only blame myself. *Keep safe* . . . I left without touching Lippillus, and feeling sick as hell. My two lads were next door. I told them to hang around in the street outside in case they were wanted, and set off for home.

For the first time since the attack I found myself turning round to look for Felix and his mate the jolly Titan. I couldn't see any sign of them, naturally, but I knew they'd be around somewhere. That was another unsolved mystery, although one I didn't have the leisure just now to chase up. Who the hell were those two working for? And what was this Titius Sabinus stuff Felix had pointed me so carefully towards? Sure, Sejanus had framed the guy, but I knew that anyway: Sabinus had only been one of several Julians he'd stitched up in the killing years. There was the scam over the Sacrovir revolt, of course, but again I couldn't see that it mattered even if Sabinus had been directly involved at the Rome end. So what the hell was so special about Sabinus?

I cudgelled my brains, but nothing came. Somehow no doubt it all made sense, but I couldn't for the life of me see how.

Well, there was nothing else I could do for the moment, not until sundown when I could talk to Valens's carters. I went back to the Palatine, to sit and worry and feel like ten different kinds of rat, and wait for the message from Marcina that didn't come.

The sun was just above the horizon when I got to the Latin Gate. That part of the city is pretty sparsely populated. There're a few big houses on the slopes leading up to Asinianus Gardens, but the tenement blocks stop short of the beginning of Latin Road, and the Appian fork beyond Drusus Arch only has a scattering of cheap properties before the Tomb of the Scipios and the Appian Gate itself. After which there're lots of tombs but precious few houses. I was more sure than ever that Lippillus had been after Ganymede. He'd known where to lay his hands on the guy, sure he had: he was out there somewhere, on the edge of Lippillus's patch or beyond it. Only Ganymede had found Lippillus first.

Carters are a breed to themselves: night-owls who live a life separate from your ordinary city punter. Each gate has its quota, and the quota is self-limiting. All the carts along a given stretch are run by just a few families who've been there for generations, and they don't take kindly to strangers muscling in on the available trade. Like the aristocracy, if you want to join the club you either have to get yourself born into it or marry into it. There ain't no other way.

When I reached the gate the line of carts was getting ready to move out. In. Whatever. The loads were anything and everything that had come up Latin Road the day before: marble blocks, drainpipes, vegetables, chickens, scrap metal, sawn timber. All Italy's bounty. I picked on a big red-haired guy at the front whose cart was loaded with enough furniture to equip half a tenement.

'Hey, pal,' I shouted. 'Someone moving house?'

He looked down at me. I thought for a moment he'd tell me to piss off – carters aren't the friendliest of Rome's citizen body – but the sight of my mantle must've changed his mind. You don't turn your nose up at possible business if you're on the carts, especially purple-striper business.

'Nah,' he said. 'Special delivery for Zosimus's shop in the Velabrum. The brother's an auctioneer in Tusculum. You want anything carried, sir? I'm fixed but my cousin's free. Special rates.'

I took out a silver piece and held it up. 'Not today, friend. But I am after information. You know Hasta and Pertinax?'

'Latro's boys?' He frowned. 'This about the Watch commander that was hit two nights ago?'

I nodded. 'No hassle. I just want to talk to them.'

The frown lifted. 'Okay. They're not here yet, sir. Had a cousin married this morning, and they'll still be sleeping it off.'

'Uh-huh.' Carter weddings, unlike the usual variety, happen early in the day; that way the celebrations don't cut into work time. 'You think they'll be along later?'

The man shrugged. 'Could be, but they were both pissed as newts when I saw them last. It depends if they've a load waiting.'

'How can I find that out?'

'Ask Surdus.' He jerked his thumb towards an old man with a wax tablet who was walking down the length of the line. 'He keeps the lists.'

'Right. Thanks a lot, pal.' I tossed him the coin. He grabbed it, spat on it for luck and tucked it into his tunic.

Surdus fitted his name: he was deaf as a post. I had to shout into his good ear for five minutes solid before the message got through.

'Hasta and Pertinax?' he said. 'They've a load of charcoal for the Aventine. Should be along any minute now, with the cart. They needed it for the wedding.'

'Yeah? What did they need a cart for?'

'What's that?' He held his hand to his ear.

'I said: WHAT DID THEY NEED A CART FOR?'

'Who told you they needed an apartment? It's good of you to offer, sir, but they live with their father. He has . . .'

'CART, for Jupiter's sake! *CART!* WHY DID THEY NEED A . . !'

'Pardon?'

Jupiter with bells on! 'Okay. Okay, Granddad,' I muttered, turning away. 'Forget it. I wasn't really interested anyway. Just curiosity.'

'What's that?'

'I SAID FORGET IT, I WASN'T . . . Hell, never mind.' I was looking down Latin Road towards the gate. Suddenly I froze.

Someone was coming through: a big guy in a dark tunic. He

caught sight of me, did a double-take, turned and ran back the way he'd come.

Shit! Ganymede! I pushed old Surdus aside and dodged round the line of wagons, with a sick feeling in my stomach. I'd seen the guy run before, and I knew I didn't have a hope in hell of catching him, not with that much of a start. However, I had to try. I couldn't let him get away this time . . .

I'd almost reached the gate when someone shouted beyond it. Then there was a scream and a horrible crunching noise, like a bundle of sticks breaking slowly. Uh-oh. I'd been through this before, ten years back. That time it'd been messy: a scythe. It just went to show that sometimes history does repeat itself; or maybe it was just a warning that you should always think twice before running blind round corners. I slowed to a walk, knowing there wasn't any reason now to hurry.

He'd been looking over his shoulder, obviously, and the incoming cart had knocked him down and rolled over his back before they could stop it. It may've been empty, but the iron wheel had done a thorough job. He lay half underneath, pinned down and still twitching. The two youngsters on the box were staring at what was left of him in horror. The cart oxen, on the other hand, didn't look too concerned. My sympathies were with them: the bastard had deserved all he got. I was just sorry I hadn't been the one to give it to him.

I bent down to inspect the body: Ganymede, right enough. His back was broken, and his ribs. He'd stopped twitching now, and you didn't get deader. Then I looked up.

'He ran straight out in front of us, sir!' the first lad – the driver – said. He was shaking. His mate had leaned to one side and was being quietly sick on to the ground. 'We couldn't do nothing about it! Honest!'

Yeah, well, there was a certain poetic justice here. Sophocles would've approved.

'Hasta and Pertinax?' I said.

The kid swallowed, and nodded.

'You recognise him?' We'd got Ganymede out from underneath the wheel and laid him beside the gate.

Hasta and Pertinax looked at each other, then shook their

heads. I felt sorry for them: they were just kids, no more than sixteen, and without enough whiskers between them for one decent shave.

'I've seen him around, sir, sure.' That was Pertinax, the one who'd lost his dinner over the side of the cart. He was still looking pretty pale. So was his brother, although some of it could've been the hangover. 'But I don't know who he is.' He swallowed, with a sidelong look at Ganymede's remains. 'Was.'

'Never mind, son,' I said. 'Don't let it worry you.' Ah, well. Maybe one of the other carters could help. Problem was, the sun was down by now and most of them had left. Delivery schedules don't wait for corpses, seemingly, and like Valens had said carters don't hang around when they scent trouble. At least Ganymede wouldn't be parting any more scalps this side of the Styx.

Just then Surdus came up with his wax tablet. He'd been checking the carts out of the gate. Now, it seemed, his work was over for the night and he had time to indulge a little personal curiosity. I stepped aside and he looked down at what the two youngsters had left of our killer.

'What about you, Granddad?' I asked him. 'You any ideas?'

'What's that?'

Jupiter! It had to be Surdus, didn't it? I put my hand to his good ear and yelled, 'DO . . . YOU . . . KNOW . . . WHO . . . ?'

He stopped me with a beautiful smile.

'I can't hear you, sonny,' he said. 'I'm a bit deaf. But if you want to know who this is his name's Crito. Rubrius Fabatus's head slave, from the villa up the road.'

Rubrius Fabatus I didn't know at all; but Crito, now. Crito was different. That name rang a faint bell.

Who the hell had mentioned a Crito?

19

By the time I got back home Marcina had been in touch. Lippillus had woken up.

'Thank the gods!' I said when Bathyllus told me. 'First thing tomorrow morning you buy the biggest ram you can find and send it round to the Temple of Asclepius with my compliments. Okay, little guy?' Junia Torquata would've been proud of me. Instant conversion. But if Asclepius had swung this then he deserved more than just a thank you.

'Yes, sir.' Bathyllus was beaming all over his face. 'Although I don't think Asclepius is fond of rams.'

'Yeah? What, then?'

'Cocks, sir.'

Ah, well. To each his own. 'Whatever. A pair. Five. Do it, little guy, but make sure they're the best you can get.'

'Isn't it marvellous news, Marcus?' Perilla appeared from the direction of the dining-room. She was radiant.

'Yeah, the old guy certainly worked his fillet off for us.' I hugged her and planted a smacker dead centre between nose and chin. 'When did it happen?'

'About an hour after you left. Latinius came round to tell us.'

'He . . . uh . . . he say what he was doing at the time? Lippillus, I mean?' It didn't much matter now, of course, with Ganymede – Crito – part of history's glowing pageant, but I was curious.

'No, he didn't.' Perilla had turned icy. 'And Marcus, if you even *think* of bothering either him or Marcina with . . .'

'Okay. Okay.' I held up my hands, one of which was occupied

with the cup of Setinian Bathyllus had poured for me. 'Just a thought. Forget it.'

'Damn right I'll forget it!' Jupiter, but the lady was peeved! 'If it wasn't that he'd asked for you specially I'd . . .'

'He asked for me? Really?'

'Marcina did mention it. But she also said that although you'll be welcome in the morning one word out of place and she will personally murder you. And frankly, Corvinus, if she doesn't then I will.'

Ouch. I swallowed. 'Point taken, lady. No crime, not a whisper. You have my solemn pledge.'

'Good.' Her voice thawed. 'Sarpedon is delighted. He says the chances for recovery now are much better.'

Hey, great! If the old misery guts was actually showing a bit of optimism then Lippillus was really out of the woods. I drained the cup and got Bathyllus to pour me another.

'So.' Perilla straightened her mantle. 'How did you get on at the Latin Gate?'

'I found the guy who did it. He's dead.'

Her eyes widened. 'Oh, Marcus!'

'Nothing to do with me. Or not much, anyway. It was an accident.' I told her the story. 'So now I've got two more names to add to the list. Rubrius Fabatus and Crito.' There was that itch again. Who the hell had I been talking to recently who'd mentioned a Crito?

'Do they mean anything to you?' Perilla made room for me on the couch. I lay down and put my free arm round her shoulders.

'Uh-uh. Fabatus is obviously rich enough to have a villa outside the city boundaries, but he's just a name. At the moment, anyway. Crito, now . . .' Shit, where had I heard that name? Or was I imagining things? I shrugged. 'Ah, forget it. It doesn't matter. I'm just glad Lippillus is going to be okay.'

'He isn't, yet.' She snuggled against me.

'Oh yes, he is. Asclepius has got his cocks, or he will have tomorrow. He wouldn't back out of the deal now.'

'Marcus, I'm not sure you should be flippant about these things.'

'Who's being flippant? It's good old Roman practice. Contract fulfilled, both sides. Even a Greek god like Asclepius has to understand basic business etiquette if he wants to stay solvent this side of Corinth. Speaking of which' – I kissed her – 'bed. I've had a long day.'

'What has bed got to do with contracts?'

'Nothing, so far as I know. It's what's called an anacoluthon.'

Perilla was laughing. 'Corvinus, that's nonsense! That isn't an anacoluthon! An anacoluthon is . . .'

I never did find out what an anacoluthon was; but by the time we'd come up for air it didn't seem all that important.

Lippillus still looked like death warmed up, but at least he was awake and sensible.

'Hey, Corvinus!' he said as I edged cautiously round the bedroom door. His voice was barely a whisper. 'Thanks for coming.'

The room was pretty crowded already. Sarpedon was there, but he'd finished doing whatever doctors do for recovering patients; I could see he'd left some evil-looking mixture in a cup by the bed. And Marcina, of course, had followed me in. No sharp instrument at the ready, as far as I could tell, but if I broke my promise she'd probably use her bare hands.

At least she looked like she'd had a night's sleep, and if she hadn't been exactly friendly when she answered the door the temperature was a whisker or two above freezing. Maybe I'd come through this after all. If so, then it was more than I deserved.

'How's things, pal?' I eased myself on to the stool next to the bed.

Lippillus gripped my arm. 'Marcus, listen! The man you're after is called Crito. He's head slave to Rubrius Fabatus, who's got a suburban villa down the Latin Road just before the Asinaria crossroads.'

'There.' That was Marcina, and sounding jaundiced as hell; but she wasn't talking to me. 'Are you happy now?'

'Yeah. Yeah, I'm happy.' Lippillus's lips barely moved. That long speech must've taken a lot of his energy. 'You got all that, Marcus?'

'Sure,' I said softly. 'Don't worry, pal. I already found him.

The bastard won't be swinging iron bars around any more, ever.'

'He's dead?'

I nodded. 'Came off second best in an argument with a cart.'

Lippillus's lips twitched. 'That's that, then,' he whispered. 'One more thing. Fabatus is a friend of Sejanus's. Minor league, but maybe . . .'

'Decimus, that's enough!' Marcina snapped. 'You are *not* going to tire yourself out over nothing! And Corvinus, I want you to leave, please. Now.'

'I agree, sir.' Sarpedon had been watching us, frowning slightly. His tone might be more polite than Marcina's, but he wasn't taking any prisoners either. 'I recommended that you be sent for because the patient was fretting. Now I think it would be advisable for you to go. In fact, I insist on it.'

'Okay.' I stood up. 'No arguments. And I'm sorry, Marcina. This wasn't my idea.'

She didn't answer. I turned back to Lippillus.

'Take it easy, right, pal?' I said. 'And don't worry, everything's under control.'

His hand lifted, but his eyes were already closing. I slipped out.

Sarpedon came with me. And Marcina, which was more of a surprise. She shut the door quietly behind her.

'Corvinus, wait a moment, please.' She laid a hand on my arm. 'I've got something more to say to you.'

Uh-oh. I waited while she saw Sarpedon out. Then she turned to face me.

'I want to apologise,' she said.

'Uh . . . pardon?'

She took a deep breath and let it out slowly. 'I know that Decimus was hurt directly because of you. But I also know how . . . single-minded he can be at times when he thinks he ought to get involved in something. And you've helped a great deal, especially with Sarpedon. Decimus would have died if it hadn't been for him.'

'Marcina, it was the least I could do. It's nothing, believe me.'

'No.' She shook her head sharply. 'It is *not* nothing! I hate to think what all this cost . . .'

'Jupiter, Marcina!'

'. . . but the least *I* can do is be grateful. I am, Marcus. Very.'

'Yeah, well.' I shrugged. 'You don't have to be. Like you said, it was my fault.'

'You would've done the same if he'd been hurt on a Watch case, wouldn't you?'

This was getting embarrassing. I wished now I'd left with Sarpedon. 'Yeah, but—'

She cut me short. 'That's my reason for apologising. I was angry, naturally. I'm still angry, with both you and Decimus. But that's not to say I can't see things in perspective. Decimus is very lucky to have you as a friend, Marcus. As am I.' She tried a smile, the first one I'd seen on her face since the attack. 'There, now. That's over, and I'm glad.'

I smiled back. 'You and me both.'

The smile widened. She even laughed. 'Quite. But do leave Decimus alone, please. For a few days, anyway. Although you may be able to keep off touchy subjects I doubt if he can.'

I felt the black mood that had been pressing down on me for days lift. Not altogether, but enough.

'Don't worry, lady,' I said. 'You'll get no hassle from me.'

I left, whistling.

So. Crito's master Rubrius Fabatus was a friend of Sejanus's. Well, that didn't come as a surprise, but it was nice to know it for certain. I walked along Racetrack Road towards the Publician Incline. Another glorious day: spring was definitely in the air, and it looked like being a good Spring Festival. I turned round, but there was still no sign of Felix and Lamprus. Maybe their boss, whoever he was, had called them off, but I doubted it.

Lippillus had said that Fabatus was minor league, and that made sense. Sejanus wouldn't've risked a direct connection, not in the strong-arm department. But it meant that I had to prove another link in the chain if I wanted to tie him in with what was going on, and I had to go carefully while I did it. There wasn't much point in barging in on Fabatus and accusing him to his face, because with Crito safely dead he'd simply deny everything and run straight back to tell tales to his boss. Which wouldn't do me much good at all. There had to be a better way.

Okay. So just exactly what was I after here? I'd got a long-dead Julian plot involving laundered money from the east being used to finance a smear campaign against the Wart at home. Sejanus had been party to that as the Wart's agent, first setting the Julians up and then knocking them down in the Wart's interests. Also – and crucially for me – in his own, because with the top Julians gone or discredited he was a prime contender for the immediate succession and he could use his growing prestige to build up the political support he needed. Even where that support worked against the emperor's – and the empire's – best interests. It was this second side that I had to concentrate on, because I'd bet a gold piece to a poke in the eye that it was the side the Wart didn't know about. If I could get enough evidence to show Tiberius where his deputy's true loyalties lay, and that they posed a threat to Rome, then I had a fighting chance of toppling the guy. The problem would be separating that off from the legitimate stuff.

I wasn't just whistling at the wind, I knew that. There was the Germanicus case, for a start. The Wart hadn't known the whole story there, that I knew for certain. And since I'd been back in Rome Sejanus had done his best to make sure I didn't dig any deeper into his affairs than I had already. Celsus had known something, sure. He'd pointed me at Marius, who hadn't figured at all in the Julian scam up to now except for that double-finesse with the botched treason charge; and Celsus had died as a direct result. Then there was Felix and his pet hulk, and the business with Sabinus. That angle I still had to work out, but it was important. Sure it was.

The dirt was there waiting to be dug, just under the surface. All I had to do was recognise it for what it was.

There was a hot-pie-seller on Racetrack Corner. I bought a meat pasty from him and bit on it as I turned up the Incline for home.

Fabatus. How the hell was I to handle Fabatus?

20

I was in my study the next day working through my accounts when Bathyllus knocked on the door.

'Yeah? What is it?' I said, grumpy as hell; arithmetic has never been my strong point, and this visit to Rome was costing us an arm and a leg.

'I'm sorry to disturb you, sir.' Bathyllus had on his prim disapproving expression. 'There's a man outside who wishes to see you.'

Man, not gentleman. But it must be urgent for the little guy to break in on the accounts. Disturbing the master when he's beating his head against an abacus is a hanging offence in the Corvinus household.

'This man got a name?' I said.

'He wouldn't give it, sir. Or tell me his business.' A sniff. Bathyllus was seriously peeved; and no one, but no one, ranking below a consul seriously peeves Bathyllus and lives. Whoever he was, the visitor had guts. He was lucky still to be breathing.

'Is that so?' I said.

'That's so, sir.' He paused. 'If it's of any relevance he told me to tell you that Felix had sent him.'

I almost dropped the pen I'd been chewing the end off.

'*He told you what?*'

'I didn't recognise the name either, sir, but I thought . . .'

I was stuffing the accounts books into the bureau drawer. 'Wheel him in,' I said. 'Do it now.' Jupiter! What the hell was this?

I saw what Bathyllus had meant as soon as he appeared. Our surprise visitor was no gentleman. A slave, probably; not even a freedman. He was so filthy I could've planted carrots all over him; got a good crop, too.

'Okay, Bathyllus, you can go,' I said. The little guy gave another sniff – justified this time, the atmosphere had turned pretty heavy all of a sudden – and left.

'You Marcus Valerius Messalla Corvinus?' The guy was confident enough, I'd give him that.

'Yeah.' I wondered whether I should've taken out the dagger I keep with the family strongbox, but apart from posing a general risk to health he looked harmless. Weedy, if that isn't a bad pun. 'That puts you one up on me, pal. You didn't give my slave your name.'

'Festus.' Uninvited, he pulled up a chair and sat on it. I said nothing, but I could imagine Bathyllus throwing five different kinds of fit at once. 'The little bald guy with the sniff tell you Felix sent me?'

'Uh-huh. He also said you'd refused to state your business.'

'I'm Rubrius Fabatus's head gardener. Was, anyway, as of three days ago.'

Jupiter!

'Is that right, now?' I said slowly, my brain buzzing. It explained his loamy aftershave, anyway. And other scents. Some really keen gardeners have a private arrangement with the slaves who muck out the public privies, and Festus smelled like one of the keenest. But it didn't explain how he came to be here. I'd just made the Rubrius connection myself. 'Fabatus's gardener, eh?'

'Ex-gardener.'

'Whatever. Before we start splitting hairs you care to tell me: one, what your connection with Felix is and two, why the hell you think I might be interested?'

He grinned. I'd seen more teeth on a garden fork. In better condition, too. 'Yeah. I can manage that. Your answers are one: None whatsoever – up to three days ago, that is – and two: Because I can give you a cast-iron link between my fucking ex-master and Aelius Sejanus. That do you?'

Jupiter best and greatest! Forget the buzzing; my brain had gone numb. I got up and poured myself a cup of wine from the jug on the table beside him.

'Thanks. Don't mind if I do.' Festus leaned over, took the cup from me and sank it in one. 'Good stuff. Pity about the water.'

Silently I filled another cup, topped his up again and took mine back to the couch where I'd been sitting. This Festus was definitely getting up my nose. Literally and metaphorically.

'The price is five gold pieces,' he said.

I nearly dropped the cup. Shit! I could've bought the guy himself for that, easy!

'One,' I said. 'If you're lucky.'

'Five. Or there's no deal. I'm laying my neck on the line here.'

Yeah, well, I supposed he had a point. Although why anyone would touch his neck with anything shorter than a ten-foot pole I couldn't imagine.

'This had better be good, chum,' I said. 'Especially with the damage you're doing to my wine cellar.' He didn't say anything; just grinned. 'Okay. Five. If and provided that I decide the information is worth it.'

'Oh, it's worth it.' He downed the second cup and poured himself another. 'You mind?'

'Go ahead.' I could see now how he'd managed to bull-doze Bathyllus. By comparison, rhinos were thin-skinned. 'Feel free.'

He sipped at this one. Not a fool, then: he wanted to keep sober, which was wise. 'To answer your first question first,' he said. 'This weird guy in a lemon tunic—'

'Felix.'

'Right. Felix comes up to me three days ago when I'm out seeing to the manure. He says how would I like to make a lot of money and get my freedom into the bargain – *guaranteed* freedom – for coming round here and telling you what I know.'

'"Guaranteed" freedom? Guaranteed by who?' And why the hell should Felix bother? I thought, but I didn't say it out loud. It might've confused the issue.

'That I'm not telling, but believe me you don't get better. I'm no cabbage, Corvinus. He gave me proof; real proof. But the deal's off if I snitch so don't waste your breath asking.'

'Okay. Forget it.' Well, it would've been nice to know, but I could live with that. For the moment. 'Carry on.'

'How he knew *I* knew anything I don't know, and I don't care.' He sipped the wine. 'That's some smart little bugger, your pal. Maybe he reads minds. But he was right, I did have something to sell. Only I couldn't do anything with the information myself. Get me?'

'I get you.' I sipped my own wine. 'So after talking with Felix and with his guarantee in your pocket you went over Fabatus's wall. Did a runner.' Jupiter! Whatever Felix's guarantee was backed by, like Festus said, it had to be one hundred per cent, cast-iron genuine: we both knew what the chances of a slave escaping successfully were, and what would happen if the poor bastard got caught. That wasn't pleasant, not pleasant at all.

'I did a runner.' Festus took a swallow of Setinian. 'Felix gave me somewhere to go, somewhere safe where the food's good and the drink's better. I'm not complaining, and I'm not greedy. You get a decent crack at freedom, you take it, whether it pays or not.' He shifted on his chair. 'And if you can have money as well then you're laughing. Right?'

'Right.' Yeah, well, at least he had realistic priorities. And garden slaves were the bottom of the domestic ladder, one step higher than the chickens and one under the pet monkey. Who was I to sneer?

'Now your second question,' Festus said. 'The link with Sejanus. For that we've got to go back a couple more days. I've got this hide I built myself at the bottom of the garden. Doesn't look like much even close up, just a pile of rotten branches and garden shit, which is the idea. I go there for some peace and quiet, or when I'm wanted real bad. You know?'

'Yeah. I get the picture.' The way he described it I wouldn't've been too anxious to dig him out myself, even if I knew he was in there. Not without gloves and a good set of nose plugs.

'Okay, so this day I was in the hide when I hear the master coming. He's got that bastard Crito with him, the head slave, and somebody else.' He paused. 'Hey, I hear that Crito got his finally. You responsible for that?'

'No, it was an accident.'

'Pity. Crito was a sod. If you'd asked anyone in the household to put him under we'd've done it gladly. Congratulations, anyway.'

'You care to get back to your story, Festus?' I knew what was coming. Sure I did. 'Tell me about this "somebody else". He got a name?'

'Wait. That's your answer, Corvinus. The five gold pieces' worth. Be patient, okay?'

'Okay.' I settled back. I could wait. It looked like Felix had done my job for me, and five gold pieces was cheap at the price. 'They were discussing a murder, right?'

'Two murders. Guy named Vibius Celsus and yourself. I sat tight because I knew if I stuck my nose out it'd be bye-bye Festus, but I could hear everything clear. See it as well, because there're chinks in the hide I made specially for that sort of thing. The – someone else – says you both have to go, Celsus because he knows too much and he's soft as butter, you because you're too nosey by half and a real pain in the arse.' He paused and grinned. 'His words, not mine.'

'Sure. No offence, I've been called worse. Go on.'

'He doesn't want to deal with things himself, right, because he's too big a wheel and if things go wrong he's in the shit up to his eyeballs with no way to go but down. He wants to borrow Crito, because he's used him before. And the master owes. You still with me?'

'I'm with you. Fabatus agreed?'

'Yeah.' Festus spat on the floor: Bathyllus would have a fit. 'The master's got no balls. Never has had, and he'd lick any arse in range to make consul. Even city judge. Sure he agreed. Fell over himself. Crito wasn't too happy, but with the pressure these two were putting on him he didn't have much option.'

That was something I hadn't thought of. Maybe I ought to feel a bit of sympathy for Crito. Not that I could manage it, mind.

'And?'

'That was it. They went back to the house. I gave them a good hour then slipped round to the rose garden to do a bit of mulching. Two days later your pal Felix turns up.' He was watching me closely. I got up, refilled my cup, and sat back down again. 'So, Valerius Corvinus, what do you reckon? A good five gold pieces' worth?'

'Yeah, I suppose so. Only you haven't given me the important name yet, your "someone else". Maybe I can do it for you. The someone else was Sejanus, right?'

Festus spat again, scornfully. 'No, it wasn't him. Aelius Sejanus wouldn't do his own dirty work, even I know that. And if it had been I'd've asked you for more than five measly gold pieces. But the guy was the next best thing. I told you, he's a cast-iron link.'

'Okay. So tell me his name.'

'The third guy was Sejanus's stepbrother. Seius Tubero.'

21

Tubero!

I sat back. I'd dismissed Seius Tubero, or rather I hadn't even considered him in the first place. Not because he wasn't a double-dyed crook, or prime treason material: I'd known he'd been working for Sejanus ten years back when as a city judge he'd quashed the investigation into Regulus's murder. No, I'd ignored Tubero because Celsus had cited him along with old Cornelius Lentulus as his father's collaborator in the Sacrovir scam and I'd bracketed the two together. Which was exactly what Serenus had intended people should do.

It made sense. Now I was starting at the other end, with Tubero's involvement in the Gallic scam proven fact, it made a lot of sense. Celsus had said that the choice of Lentulus and Tubero had been his father's, not his, although he'd gone along with it. I'd assumed that the idea behind choosing them was to destroy Celsus's credibility as a prosecutor; which was true enough. But that was only half the story, seemingly. The scam had another purpose as well, and with that Serenus had been more successful than I'd given him credit for.

It was slick as virgin oil, for a start. To have accused Tubero alone of involvement with the Sacrovir revolt would've been disastrous for everyone concerned. If Serenus had turned state's evidence and gone for the guy properly he might've succeeded in taking Tubero down with him, but he wouldn't've lived much past the trial. The consequences for Tubero were equally obvious: no one knew he'd been involved, not even Celsus; he'd kept his nose clean and covered his tracks well. A direct accusation from a confessed traitor backed – as it would be backed – with hard evidence would undo all that careful planning. For Sejanus's part, the last thing he'd've wanted was for one of his shady operations to be brought out into the open, when even the Wart might start to think about treason in more general terms.

Messy, right? And in no one's interests.

So Serenus hadn't accused just Tubero. What he'd done was to have his son name Lentulus as well; and that made all the difference because the poor old duffer was patently – even blatantly – innocent: by all accounts he hadn't had marbles enough left to spearhead a trip to the bathroom, let alone a full-scale conspiracy. It was a beautiful double-double bluff. Serenus had saved his neck with the Senate and with Sejanus at the same time by saying to him in effect: 'I've got the goods on you, but I'm not going to use them because I'm not stupid. It's a standoff. Let's agree to leave each other alone.' He'd succeeded as far as he could realistically have expected to; Sejanus hadn't put any pressure on the Wart to have him chopped, as he could well've been for a second treason offence; in fact, he'd persuaded the emperor to intervene on the side of clemency. Even so, Tiberius had smelled a rat and at least made sure he was convicted. And that was how matters stood until I'd gone barging in to Celsus's life and forced him to break the bargain . . .

Yeah. I regretted that now; or at least I regretted that it'd been necessary. I'd killed Celsus just as surely as if I'd smashed his silly head in with the iron bar myself. I just hoped that in the end his death wouldn't be wasted.

Festus was looking at me, a half-smile on his face.

'Okay, Corvinus,' he said. 'Contract fulfilled. So hand over the cash and I'll be on my way.'

I took the key of the strongbox I kept by the shrine of the household gods out of the bureau, unlocked it and gave the guy his five gold pieces. He grinned, spat on them for luck and turned to go.

'Wait a minute, pal,' I said. 'We haven't finished yet. I may need you later.'

'Yeah?' He slipped the money into his breech clout. 'What for?'

'That's a valuable chunk of evidence you have tucked away

in your skull. If this ever comes to a trial you'll need to repeat it to the proper authorities.'

'You kidding, Corvinus? You know how they take statements from slaves.' He made a stretching movement with his two hands. 'And on a runaway they wouldn't even call time when they had what they wanted.'

'If your guarantee of freedom is as good as you say it is, pal, torture wouldn't be an issue. You'd be a free man, and it'd act retrospectively.'

I could see him considering: he may've been just a garden slave but he was honest by his lights. He'd made a reasonable point, too: in a court of law a slave's evidence against his master is inadmissible unless it's given under torture.

'Yeah. Yeah, I suppose that's right,' he said at last. 'Okay, you've got it.'

Jupiter! I thought, That must be some guarantee, if the guy's that ready to bet his life on it holding! 'So. How do I contact you?' I said. 'If and when?'

'Felix knows. But remember, I'm only willing to talk if I don't suffer for it.'

Well, I couldn't expect more. Of course it begged the question of whether I could find my friend in the lemon tunic when I wanted him.

'Another five gold pieces,' I said. 'If and when it happens. Deal?'

He grinned again: he hadn't expected that, which was why I'd made the offer.

'Deal,' he said; and left.

When I came out of the study Perilla was in the atrium. She had a letter in her hand, and she could've modelled for Athene just before she zapped Arachne into a spider.

'Just who exactly is Marilla, Marcus?' she said. 'And why is she making assignations?'

I stared at her, eyes popping and jaw sagging. 'What?'

'Here. Read it for yourself.' She passed the letter over.

Jupiter! Someone was crazy here, and it wasn't me. 'Lady, I don't even *know* anyone called Marilla, let alone . . .'

'Read.'

It was a note rather than a letter. Three lines:

Valerius Corvinus, I have to get away. Father will be in Tibur for a few days, and it may be my only chance. The south-west corner of the garden wall, this evening at sunset. Please come. Marilla.

The 'Please come' had been underlined twice.

'Perilla, I swear . . .' I began. Then I remembered. Marilla. The beautiful Spaniard with the frightened eyes. Sextus Marius's daughter. 'Lady, where did you get this?'

'Her maid brought it a few minutes ago. Bathyllus gave it to me because you were busy.' She sniffed. 'He didn't know the contents, of course.'

'Uh-huh. Where's the maid now?'

'I sent her down to the kitchen.' Jupiter! The house was filling up like Market Square on election day! 'Corvinus, I'm waiting for an explanation.'

If it hadn't been so serious I would've laughed, because I'd never ever seen Perilla jealous before and she was greener than a ripe fig. However, this was no time for playing around. I explained to her just exactly who Marilla was. And what I suspected the sleeping arrangements were in the Janiculan villa.

'Oh, Marcus!' She sat down on the couch. 'The poor child!'

'Yeah.' I read the note again. Melodramatic stuff, the kind of thing a teenage girl might've written. Sure, it could be genuine. And if I was right about her relationship with her father she could well be desperate enough to catch at any chance of escape that offered. Maybe that was why she'd come down to Marius's Carthage room that day, to check me out.

There again, the girl might not have written the note at all. And the Janiculan at sunset would be the perfect place for a murder.

'We'd better talk to the maid,' I said.

She was no chicken, that was for sure: sixty if she was a day, and the motherly type. Her name was Brito.

'It was on my advice, sir,' she said firmly. 'Completely. She's only thirteen.' Jupiter! Was that all? She'd looked older than that: mid teens, anyway. 'I've been terrified for months now since the first time it happened that the poor thing would do away with herself when I wasn't there to stop her. She may yet.'

'But why me?' I said. 'I never even spoke to the girl.'

'We don't often get visitors, sir. And she told me you had a kind face.' Jupiter! I didn't dare look at Perilla. 'Will you help? Please?'

She sounded genuine, I'd give her that. But even if she was . . .

'Look, let's be sensible about this,' I said. 'Marius may be a bastard, but he's the girl's father. Her legal guardian. If I help her to escape it's tantamount to kidnapping a minor. You know what the penalty is for that?'

'Why can't she just report him to the city judge?' Perilla said. 'Or have a member of her family do it for her?'

'Because there isn't anyone, madam.' Brito was outwardly calm, but her hands twisted together in her lap. 'The master's a widower, she's an only child, and the rest of the family's in Spain. Besides, she's frightened. Ashamed, too.'

'Shit, it's not her fault.' I stood up. 'I'll bring the charge myself. Once the authorities know what he's been up to the guy'll get a one-way trip off the Tarpeian Rock with plenty of hands willing to do the shoving.'

'Will he?' Brito said quietly. 'Are you sure, sir?'

I sat down again. Yeah. She was right. Marius had everything going for him. He was socially respected, from a good provincial family, and a big wheel financially, not just in Spain but at Rome as well. Probably all over. And, most important of all, he was a pal of Sejanus's: *protected* – I'd used the word myself. Try to charge a guy like that with incest on a teenage girl's say-so and it wouldn't even make the courts. Worse, for the prosecutor it would be a direct ticket to an island.

'Marcus, we have to help,' Perilla said. 'She's just a child.'

'Yeah, I know.' I sighed. 'But it isn't as simple as that. You say the family's in Spain?' Brito nodded. 'So she'd be our responsibility, at least for the time being. And like I say, it's kidnapping.'

'Marcia Fulvina would take her.' Marcia Fulvina was the

eighty-year-old sister of Perilla's courtesy aunt, the one who'd been married to old Fabius Maximus. That Marcia was long dead now, but her sister lived in retirement up in the Alban Hills near Caba. You didn't even see many goats that far out.

'Uh-uh,' I said. 'It's too risky.'

'Marcus, *please*!'

I'd never seen Perilla so upset. Shit! I swallowed.

'Yeah, okay,' I said. 'We'll give it a try.'

Perilla hugged me. Brito was beaming.

'You won't regret it, sir,' she said. 'I promise.'

Yeah. Well, maybe. But I wasn't taking any bets.

22

I wasn't taking any chances, either. This could still be a set-up. I rounded up four of my beefiest slaves (shades of the Sunshine Boys, but they'd long gone to flab) and made sure they each had a knife and a nice heavy stick with enough lead in the end to make a serious impression on anybody who got in its way. Then I stuck my own knife into its wrist-sheath and took my cavalry-length sword from its oilskin wrappings. All strictly illegal, of course, inside the city boundaries; but what we were planning was no evening stroll along the Saepta. And if Brito turned out not to be the kind-eyed old biddy she seemed and I got jumped – still a distinct possibility – then I wanted to be ready for the bastards.

Which brought us to the next problem.

'Marcus, I'm coming with you,' she said.

'Like hell you are!' Jupiter! Here we go again, I thought. I knew I'd lose in the end, but it was the principle of the thing.

'Corvinus.' Perilla's voice changed to pure ice. 'You are *not* going on some nocturnal slash-and-bash this time.' Gods! Where did she pick up that language? Not from me, that was sure. 'The poor child will be nervous enough already, and to be lugged through the middle of Rome at night by four hulking Gauls and a stand-in for Spartacus won't help matters.'

Yeah, well, she had a point. About the Gauls, anyway. 'Brito'll be with her, Perilla. And she said I had a kind face.'

'Hah!'

'Don't "hah!" me, lady! I know what I'm talking about here. This thing may be on the level, but if not you're a liability. I can't watch you and my back at the same time.'

She sighed. 'Corvinus, don't argue, please. And don't be ridiculous. We'll be taking a small army with us. Plus enough weapons to hold off every footpad in Rome. And I have infinite confidence in your abilities to maim in my defence should the occasion arise.'

'Uh, yeah.' I wasn't quite sure how to take that last one. 'Still . . .'

'Good. Then that's settled. We'll need both litters. And wrap up well, we don't want you clanking.'

We left the litters on the path and stole across the rough ground to the corner of Marius's wall, both muffled to the eyeballs in heavy cloaks for extra secrecy. Personally I'd've thought two mysterious hooded figures crawling about the Janiculan in the dark with a ladder and four seriously weaponed gorillas in tow would've looked suspicious enough for anyone, but then I felt pretty silly about this whole business. If you listened hard enough you could just about hear the squeak of the Alexandrian bodice-ripperist's stylus. It wasn't a full moon, anyway. That was a plus. Alexandrian novelists love full moons, but when you're being sneaky they can be embarrassing.

When we got closer I could see why Marilla had specified the south-west corner of the garden. We wouldn't need the ladder. A fresh-fallen tree had knocked a major chunk of masonry down from the garden side, and what was left of the wall couldn't've been any more than six feet high, tops. Also, because the tree was still in place there were branches to clamber up on the other side.

I motioned the Gauls to wait. 'Okay,' I murmured to Perilla. 'You want to go for it while I keep watch?'

She nodded and put her mouth to the crack in the broken brickwork under the trunk. 'Marilla?' she whispered. 'Are you there?'

There was a movement beyond the wall, and Brito's voice said, 'We're here, madam, and ready. I'll help her up.'

The tree branches rustled and the girl's face appeared through them. She looked like I'd imagine a dryad might: a lovely, dark-eyed dryad who was scared half to death and trying not to show it.

'Valerius Corvinus?' she whispered.

'Yeah, that's me, princess. Jump and I'll catch you.'

'Let me just get Diana first.'

'Who the hell's Diana?'

'My sparrow.'

Oh, yeah. The birdcage she'd been carrying when I first saw her on the balcony.

'Jupiter! You got a menagerie waiting behind that wall, bright-eyes?'

'Marcus!' Perilla snapped.

'Yeah, okay.' I sighed. 'Go ahead, princess, let's have the sparrow. But just leave the pony behind, right?'

The face disappeared and the branches rustled again. A moment later she was back with the wicker cage.

'Can you reach if I hand her down to you?'

'Sure.' I stretched up and took the cage. The bird fluttered. 'Okay. Now you.'

She was feather-light, no heavier than a bird herself. Good bones. And she was trembling.

'Don't worry, princess,' I said gently. 'That's you out for keeps now. Go with Perilla to the litter.'

She went, and I handed Brito down with her bundle. It was comfortably small. At least she'd been sensible over the packing.

'No problems?' I said.

'No problems, sir. And the Three-Faced-Mother bless you.'

'Sure.' I picked up the birdcage and gave it to one of the Gauls. 'Here, sunshine. You're in charge of pets. Guard it with your life.'

We lit the torches when we were well clear of the Marius place and headed for the Sublician and home: a litter without torchbearers stands out like a sore thumb on the night streets, and I didn't want to attract any attention either from would-be freelance entrepreneurs or the local Watch squaddies. Bathyllus had performed his usual psychic trick and was waiting for us at the door. I sent the Gauls off minus the birdcage to play with their marbles while Perilla sneaked Marilla inside suitably wrapped: Poplicolan Street was deserted, like it usually was at this hour, but there was no point in taking chances.

When I came into the living-room myself, Marilla had just taken off her cloak.

'I want to thank you, Valerius Corvinus,' she said in a precise voice. The scared look had gone, but she still looked pale. Beautiful, sure, but every inch a thirteen-year-old trying to act grown up. 'You too, Perilla. You could get into terrible trouble over this, I know.'

'That's okay, princess,' I said. 'Our pleasure. Don't give it another thought.'

'Sit down and drink this, dear.' Perilla took the cup of hot honeyed wine from the tray Bathyllus was holding and gave her it. 'You're safe now.'

Marilla sat down on the couch and cradled the cup in both hands, taking little sips. The grown-up image was evaporating fast, but she seemed more comfortable without it. Like it was something she was glad to be rid of.

Suddenly she looked up.

'Where's Diana?' she said.

'Here.' Perilla set the cage on the table beside her. 'Safe as well. Brito, perhaps you'd like to go with Bathyllus to see about a bedroom.'

'Everything's ready, madam.' The little guy was smiling; we'd told him the whole story before we left, and got his gracious approval. 'I've put our guest in the west wing. And the bed's been aired. Would you like some dinner?'

'Marilla?' Perilla asked.

'No. No, I'm not hungry.' The wine was doing its work and there was more colour in her face. 'Or tired. If I could just sit a while, perhaps?'

She was like a kid asking for permission to stay up late. Perilla smiled.

'Yes, of course, dear,' she said. 'As long as you like.'

'I'll take your things upstairs anyway, mistress,' Brito said. 'You'll be all right while I'm gone?'

'Oh, yes.' For the first time the girl tried a smile. 'Yes. Perfectly. Thank you.'

The maid left with Bathyllus. I poured myself a cup of Setinian from the jug he'd brought with the honeyed wine and sat down on my usual couch. Perilla took the chair next to me.

'How long have you had Diana?' she asked.

'Only about two months. My last sparrow died – that was Sophocles, he was a male and I'd had him almost a year. Brito gave me Diana. She bought her in the market.' The girl paused. 'Perilla, what arc you and Valerius Corvinus going to do with me?'

The words had come out in a rush. Perilla waited a moment and then said, 'There's a sister of my aunt. A very nice old lady called Marcia Fulvina. She has a villa in the hills, and she's very fond of birds and children. She would be very glad to have you, for as long as you wanted to stay with her.'

'She wouldn't mind that I've . . .' She made a slight movement with her hand. 'I mean that I'm not . . .'

'No, dear,' Perilla said gently. 'She wouldn't mind that at all.'

Jupiter, I'd get that bastard the Rock if it was the last thing I did! 'Uh . . . you have any family in Spain, Marilla?' I said. 'Someone we could get in touch with?'

She hesitated. 'An uncle. Father's brother. I don't like him much.'

'Anyone else?'

'No. There's no one else.'

Uh-huh. Well, scratch that one. I took a swallow of wine. We couldn't've risked contacting the uncle straight away in any case, but it would've been nice to know he was waiting in the wings. As it was, this looked like being a tough one. 'Never mind, princess,' I said. 'It doesn't matter. And don't worry, we're not going to hand you over anywhere you don't want to go.'

I could feel the tension go out of her, but she said nothing and sipped her hot drink. Then, suddenly, she yawned and covered her mouth, almost spilling the wine. Perilla reached forward and gently took the cup from her.

'I'm sorry,' Marilla said. 'I think I may be tired after all. Do you think I could go to bed now?'

'Of course.' Perilla was smiling. 'I'll show you where it is.'

Marilla stood up to follow her, swaying slightly. Yeah, well, the poor kid had had an exciting evening, and the hot wine on top of it had obviously finished her off.

'Sleep tight, princess,' I said.

'Thank you, Valerius Corvinus.' She smiled. 'I was right, wasn't I? Despite what Perilla said in the litter?'

'Yeah? Right about what?'

'You do have a nice face.'

Perilla snorted, and I grinned. 'The best,' I said. 'I'll see you in the morning.'

'Mmm.' She paused, her hand on the banister. 'Oh, I almost forgot, and it's important. Very important. I promised myself I'd tell you if I got the chance, because you looked like you'd care.'

'Care about what, bright-eyes?'

'It's my father. He's planning to murder the emperor.'

23 ∫

Jupiter! That was an exit line, if I'd ever heard one; but the kid was dead on her feet and it could wait till morning. I didn't sleep much that night, though. Nor did Perilla, although for different reasons. I felt her getting up two or three times – quietly, so as not to disturb me – and heard her padding off along the corridor towards the west wing: there's a squeaky board that way, and you can always tell. Marilla must've been tidily asleep, because she came straight back.

I didn't raise the subject over breakfast, either, because the lady would've had my head. Marilla would tell me in her own time, no doubt, and then we'd decide what to do about it. The kid was looking a lot better this morning, anyway; brighter, and a more healthy colour. She could pack it away, too; I had to send Bathyllus off for a second cheese omelette and more bread rolls.

I'd left the two of them alone and gone out to sit in the garden. It was an hour later when she finally came through, and she'd got her grown-up face on.

'Valerius Corvinus?' she said.

'Hi, princess. Everything okay?'

'Yes. Yes, thank you.' She lowered her eyes. 'But I'd like to talk to you, please. About my father. And about what I said last night.'

'Sure. Pull up a chair.' It was another beautiful spring day, and the flowers were out. Marcia Fulvina's garden in the Alban Hills would be nice, now, as well.

She sat down. 'Do you mind if I start at the beginning?'

'Start any place you like, princess. But don't feel you have to tell me everything, okay?'

'No, that's all right.' Her eyes were still lowered. 'It doesn't only concern me.'

I waited.

Finally, she said, 'My father's mad. You know that, don't you?'

'Uh, yeah . . . well . . .' That was putting it mildly, but I couldn't exactly say so.

'He hates Rome. He hates Romans. Everything you've done, everything you are, everything you stand for. He told you, that day you came, that he had Carthaginian blood?'

'Yeah.'

'He's very proud of that. In fact, it's more important to him than anything else.' She paused. 'Except for me, of course. I was his Ta'anit-pene-Ba'al, his Face of the Lord. But you know that already, don't you?'

I said nothing. She'd taken on that peaky, inward, too-old-for-her-years look she'd had the night before.

'Did he tell you the myth of Keret?' She still wasn't looking at me.

'Uh, yeah. He mentioned it, anyway.' I remembered the slab we'd been discussing when she'd come in: the old Phoenician carving showing a guy in a kilt carrying a knife.

'Do you remember it?'

'No. Not the details.'

'Keret was the king of Sidon, the mortal son of the Great God El. His kingdom was attacked by the forces of the moon god Terah. Keret tried to resist, but the moon god's forces were too powerful for him, and he was defeated and his kingdom occupied. On El's orders he took a wife. He had a son by her: a magical son who sprang from her womb crying, 'I hate the enemy!' And the son drove the moon god's forces from the kingdom.'

She'd recited it like she'd learned the thing by heart. Probably she had. A magical son, to drive the enemy from the kingdom. Sure. That made sense. And I could hear Marius now, talking about his daughter: 'She will breed perfect sons. Marvellous sons. Magical sons . . .'

'Uh-huh,' I said slowly. 'I understand, Marilla. You don't have to say any more.'

'It's all right.' Her fingers were picking at a stray thread in her tunic, and I noticed that the nails were bitten to the quick. 'There's a special magical potency about a child got in incest, Valerius Corvinus. Or so Father thinks.' She finally looked up, and her eyes weren't those of a child now. 'He had his reasons, you see.'

'Yeah. I see.' I did: Jupiter, the poor kid! She was right, the bastard was mad. Barking mad. He'd wanted to breed the Messiah from his own daughter in the belief that by doing it he'd throw us out of Spain. Africa. Wherever.

Marilla was still picking at the thread. 'That was for the future,' she said. 'In the meantime he worked against Rome in any way he could. I don't know the details but he used to tell me bits of it. He wanted me to be proud, you see.' Her voice was bitter, and not young at all. 'He said he'd make you tear yourselves apart.'

Yeah. And that's what we'd done. That's what we were still doing. We'd been doing it for years.

'You have any names, Marilla?' I asked gently. 'Names or faces? Of people your father's involved with?'

'No.' She shook her head. 'Not many, anyway. In Spain there was a man called Seius Quadratus. An ex-slave, I think. He used to visit my father quite often. I called him Uncle Seius because he asked me to, but I didn't like him. He touched me.'

I whistled silently. I'd never heard of the guy himself, but with that name he'd be a freedman of Tubero's. So. I'd got my link at the Spanish end. 'Anyone else?'

'Not in Spain. There were others but I can't remember them. I was too young.'

'Okay. How about here in Rome?'

'We didn't have many visitors. There was Crito, of course, the man who came the same day you did. He came quite regularly, two or three times a month.'

As soon as she said it I remembered. That was where I'd heard the name before. Just before I'd left, Marius's slave had told him that Crito was waiting to see him downstairs. He must've come straight round after murdering Celsus, and then gone out after me. And Festus had said that Tubero had used Crito in the past. Uh-huh. So. Another link in the chain. I sat back.

'Anything else you can tell me, princess?'

Her brow furrowed. 'There was a soldier five years ago. A Gaul. Father gave him money, a lot of money. I don't know his name, but I think it was for giving evidence in one of the trials. I was only small at the time, but I remember because Father said the emperor was furious about it. He was so pleased that he bought me my first pony.'

Aemilius. The guy who Lippillus had told me had insisted on repeating the slanders that had made the Wart lose his rag so spectacularly at the Montanus trial. Shit! I'd got Sejanus cold! At least as far as his involvement in the western scam went. And when Tiberius found out his buddy had been behind *that* bit of bad-mouthing he'd feed him to the lampreys personally.

Marilla was looking at me anxiously: a child with too-old eyes, desperate for praise. 'Does this help?' she said. 'I'm sorry, I can't tell you much more.'

'Yeah, princess. It helps. It helps a lot. Thanks. Now what's this about your father planning to kill the emperor?'

She squirmed in her chair. 'I don't know much about that, just the plain fact. He isn't going to do it himself, but he's in touch with the people who are.'

'Tiberius is on Capri. He has been for years.'

'Yes. I know. But I don't think that matters.'

Jupiter! I stared at her. Capri was like a fortress, naturally defended, with just one possible landing place. Nobody got in or out without Tiberius knowing about it, and with his permission. And of course everyone who was there already had been carefully vetted six ways from nothing; the paranoid old bugger made sure of that. So if it didn't matter that the Wart was squirrelled away in his self-constructed bastion then Marius – Sejanus – must have someone in place on the inside. And in that case we were looking at a whole new can of worms.

'You . . . uh . . . know when this is supposed to happen, princess?' I asked casually.

'Yes. July 28th.'

I goggled. '*July 28th?* Jupiter, you know the *date?*'

She nodded. 'Father said it was a lucky omen. July 28th was the day the Romans were beaten at Amtorgis.'

'You don't say?' Yeah, well, history never was my strong point. 'Remind me about that, will you?

'Amtorgis is a place in the Baetis valley,' she said carefully, like a schoolgirl repeating a history lesson of her own. 'The battle happened in Carthage's second war with Rome after the Spanish troops in the Roman army went over to the Carthaginians. Your general Publius Scipio was killed, his army was destroyed, and you lost all of Spain south of the Ebro.'

Uh-huh. I could see how the symbolism of *that* little anniversary would appeal to a nationalistic screwball like Marius. I'd noticed the 'you' from Marilla, too. Well, it was how the kid had been brought up, I supposed. If you can call what she'd been through bringing up. July 28th was a whole three months away, sure, but that didn't necessarily make things any easier.

'Marilla,—' I began. Then I looked up. Perilla was coming towards us through the portico. She looked frightened. Badly frightened.

'Marcus,' she said quietly, 'I think you'd better come. It's your Uncle Cotta.'

Cotta was standing in the atrium.

'Hey, Cotta, how're things?' I said; and then I saw what Perilla had meant. His thin, weaselly face was pale. Either with fright, or fury, or possibly both.

It was both.

'Marcus,' he said, 'what the *hell* have you been doing?'

I temporised. 'Uh . . . how do you mean?' Shit! We'd been rumbled! I'd known this would happen. I just hoped there were enough honest men left at the top to give me a fair hearing, because if I couldn't successfully plead extenuating circumstances for kidnapping Marius's daughter then I was dead. Maybe literally.

'Don't give me that, boy!' Cotta snapped. 'The rumour's all over the city, and I've just had it confirmed by Pomponius Secundus.' I knew Secundus: a close friend of Sejanus's, but not a bad guy in his way, just careful.

'What rumour's this, Uncle?' Hell, I hoped Perilla had had the sense to tell our house guest to keep out of sight. Brito too.

Cotta obviously wasn't listening. I'd never seen him so angry, or so frightened: trouble in a family had a habit of rubbing off on all its members. 'How could you be so stupid, Marcus? How could you be so bloody stupid? I thought you kept your nose out of politics. And you've only been back in Rome for a few days.'

There was something screwy here. He'd said politics, not kidnapping. Maybe this had nothing to do with Marilla after all.

'Uncle,' I said, 'I haven't the least idea what you're talking about here. You want to sit down and tell me calmly, or what?'

'Fuck calmly! What was it, a letter? Or did you just shoot your silly mouth off in the wrong direction once too often?'

'Neither, as far as I know.' I'd had enough of this. 'Now what exactly has Secundus been telling you?'

Cotta stared at me. 'You mean you don't know? You honestly don't know?'

'Look, just . . .'

'Aelius Sejanus is getting ready to arrest you for treason!'

24

Oh, Jupiter! Jupiter best and greatest!

I sat down. My brain had gone numb.

'Just what am I supposed to have done?' I said.

'How the hell do I know? That's what I was asking you!' Cotta picked up the wine jug on the table, splashed some wine into a cup and drank it down. 'You must've done something to get Sejanus's back up.'

Sure I had. Quite a lot. But nothing against the Wart. And nothing, barring last night's little episode, that he could legitimately charge me with.

'It's a set-up,' I said. 'It has to be.'

'Set-up or not, boy, as of now you're up shit creek without a paddle.' Cotta poured himself another cup of wine and sat down with it. 'And it serves you bloody right, what's more.'

'How do you mean?'

'You think I don't know what Arruntius and Lamia talked to you about the day of your father's funeral? You shove your nose into Aelius Sejanus's business and you can expect it to be cut off.'

I got up, poured myself a bumper of Setinian and took it back to the couch just as Perilla came back in. She'd been seeing, I knew, to Marilla. I also knew from her face that Cotta had already told her about the treason rap. Without a word she sat down beside me and gripped my hand.

'Hey, Cotta,' I said. 'Thanks for the show of solidarity, pal.'

'It's not a question of solidarity.' Cotta was scowling. 'You're my nephew and I'll defend you to the hilt. In court and out of it.'

'Is that right, now?' Yeah. Sure. I'd believe that last bit when I saw it. If Cotta agreed to be my lawyer it'd only be because society expected it of him, and he wouldn't bust a gut over the case in public or private.

'Of course I will.' He put on an injured expression. 'Now your father's gone it's my simple duty. However, we've got to be realistic here, Marcus. If you've any sense you won't let it come to a trial at all.'

A cold finger touched the back of my neck. 'You mean I should kill myself now?' I said calmly. Perilla's hand stiffened in mine.

'Jupiter, no, boy!' Cotta waved the words away. 'We aren't at that stage yet.' I noticed the *yet*, and it chilled me. 'Secundus more or less told me straight that Sejanus expects you to get on the first boat east and stay the hell away from Rome for the foreseeable future.'

Yeah. That made sense, and it explained the leak and why he hadn't sent his Praetorians round already to drag me to the Mamertine. All Sejanus wanted was to get me off his back. Sure, I could stay in Rome and dare him to prove a charge that both of us knew would be phoney as a landlord's tears, but I'd be a fool to try. And as for going direct to the Wart with what I'd got and expecting him to believe me, with a treason rap pending I might as well start looking out for flying pigs. No, it looked like I'd have to cut my losses and run back to Athens.

'Fine, Uncle.' I closed my eyes wearily. 'You've delivered your message and made your recommendation. I'll think about it. Now leave me the hell alone, okay?'

'Marcus, boy . . .'

'I said I'd think about it!' I snapped.

I could hear him getting to his feet. I opened my eyes again. He was standing looking down at me, and he wasn't too happy.

'Okay, Marcus,' he said. 'It's your life. But don't think too long. Secundus mentioned two days.'

'Is that so? Two whole days, eh? I'll see you around, Uncle.'

'Not if you're sensible, you won't!'

'Cotta.' My temper broke. 'Just do yourself a favour and piss off, okay?'

He left. Perilla put her arms round me and hugged me, very tightly. Neither of us said anything.

*   *   *

So it looked like we'd be saying goodbye to Marilla even sooner than we'd expected. I was sorry for Perilla, because she was fond of the kid. Well, I suppose we both were. Still, it had to be done. I sent a rider to Marcia Fulvina's place in the Alban Hills asking her if she'd give the girl a home for the time being, and explaining the circumstances. That last part was only fair because if this ever came out she'd be charged as an accessory, but I knew it'd also make the asking a formality. Fulvina was one of the old school, tough as a leather bootsole, and she'd've taken on the whole Praetorian Guard before she let the kid go back to Marius.

The slave had just gone when a message from Mother arrived. Not a dinner invitation this time; she wanted to see me urgently.

Uh-huh. I wasn't really surprised. Bad news travels fast, and the family were standing in line to tell Corvinus what a bloody fool he'd been and help him decide to give up and leave gracefully. Not that I needed telling, if you discounted the 'gracefully'. Forget 'decide', too, because there wasn't a decision involved. If Sejanus wanted me gone it'd be suicide to stay in Rome and fight it out. Literally; either that or the public executioner's noose. And if by some miracle the Senate decreed the lesser penalty or the Wart intervened then it'd still mean exile. At least Athens was home.

There was no point putting it off. I went round to the Caelian straight away.

Priscus wasn't in evidence, but Mother was waiting for me in the atrium. She was looking suitably serious.

'Hi,' I said.

She took my head between her palms and kissed my forehead. 'Marcus,' she said softly, 'what on earth *have* you been doing?'

The same question as Cotta's. Ah, well, I supposed it was inevitable under the circumstances.

'Would you believe nothing, Mother?' I said.

'Quite frankly no, dear.'

'Nothing deserving prosecution on a treason rap, anyway.' I sat down on the couch by the pool. 'Where's Priscus?'

'Tomb-bashing in Veii. I don't expect him back until tomorrow. Or for several days, if he forgets to come home, as usually happens.' She lay down on the other couch facing me. 'So. What are your plans?'

I shrugged. 'Back to Athens, I suppose. You know Sejanus is letting me go?'

'Horrible man.' Mother frowned. 'A pusher. And so terribly hairy in the hoof.' She paused. 'Marcus, I promised myself that I wouldn't ask you about your dealings with him, but I have to know. This thing is an attempt to remove you from Rome, isn't it? Because you're causing Sejanus some sort of bother?'

'Uh, yeah. Yeah, you could say that.'

She nodded, her lips pressed together. 'Yes, I thought so. How typically underhand of him. I'm not really surprised: Aelius Sejanus was one of the few subjects your father and I agreed on. Oh, Marcus had to be polite to him, of course, but he saw through the man from the start. He was quite proud of you, you know, over that Germanicus business, even if it didn't lead anywhere much.'

'Is that right?' I was cautious. I never did trust Mother when her conversation rambled. It might sound disconnected but when you untangled the various strands later you found they'd all led to the same important place. Direct, too, only from half a dozen different angles. Mother was a sharp cookie, and I never forgot it either.

'Yes. Very proud,' she said absently. 'In fact I suppose that's why he made the arrangement.'

'What arrangement?' I'd had enough of this pussyfooting around. I'd got other things to do. Like packing. 'Mother, I'm sorry, but will you get to the point, please? You asked me round here for a reason. So spit it out, okay?'

'But I didn't want to see you, Marcus!' she said. 'Or at least only to offer my commiserations.'

Shit! One of us was crazy, and I was pretty sure it wasn't me. 'Yeah? So what am I doing here, then?'

'Why don't you go along to the study and find out, dear.'

The study door was closed. I opened it carefully. There was a guy sitting at Priscus's desk, a big guy who would've made two of Priscus, easy. He turned round . . .

'*Agron!*'

'Hi, Corvinus.' He grinned. 'Good to see you.'

The big Illyrian had aged and got himself a paunch since I'd seen him last: marriage and good living evidently agreed with him. His grip was as hard as ever, though.

'Yeah.' I was staring at him. 'But what the hell are you doing here?'

'Your mother sent for me when she heard about the treason rap.' He paused. 'As per the arrangement.'

That was the second time I'd heard that word. 'What arrangement?'

'The one we – your mother and I – had with your father.' His face clouded. 'I'm sorry I didn't get to the funeral, by the way. I was out of Rome. My condolences.'

'Yeah. Thanks.' My head was spinning, and I sat down on the reading couch. 'Now will you just tell me what all this is about?'

'Here.' He handed me a sealed packet. 'This'll explain for me.'

I took the packet. It was addressed to me in my father's neat, precise handwriting. 'What's this?'

'Open it.'

I broke the seal with my thumb. There were two enclosures: a thick document and a thinner one. The thick document was the title deeds to a property in the Subura. The thinner one was a letter from my father.

I looked at Agron.

'Go ahead,' he said. 'Read.'

I lay back on the couch and read.

Marcus Valerius Messalla Messalinus to his son Marcus. Greetings.

I sincerely hope, my boy, that you will never read this. If you do it means that you are in trouble; very deep and possibly fatal trouble. Knowing you, and knowing the direction in which political events are taking us, I suspect that the hope is a false one; however, that is not important. Let it go.

I have felt for some years that Aelius Sejanus is a danger to the state; perhaps its greatest danger. We have only ourselves to blame, of course (we being the Senate) in that we have systematically alienated the emperor; not by anything we have done, particularly, but by being the servile crew that we are. This is no one's fault, although I include myself in the charge and am making no excuses: you cannot reverse four generations of subservience overnight, although Tiberius has tried. It is one of the reasons why I admire him.

Sejanus is dangerous because he is what we are not: a strong-willed, capable, organised and directed force. Which is, of course, why the emperor likes him. Were he directed to the state's good I would have nothing but praise for the man, but his interests are purely selfish. To get what he wants he is prepared to pull Rome apart and throw the good out with the bad. In consequence, he must be stopped.

Marcus, I am mediocre in every sphere: a mediocre speaker, a mediocre politician, a mediocre general. A mediocre husband and father. I attract no superlatives, either good or bad. That is how I am made, and it lies at the root of our disagreements over the years. However – and I stress this – I am first and foremost a Roman, and I will not willingly see Rome go down into the dark, even although I am too cowardly to do anything to prevent it myself. Hence this letter, and its enclosure.

I know, from past events, that you have some sort of private commission regarding Sejanus from the Empress Livia, and that this commission is open-ended. The time must come (has come now, indeed, since you are reading this) when you are forced to choose between leaving Rome with your task uncompleted or staying to risk Sejanus's malice. For me the choice would, unfortunately, be easy. For you it will be more difficult, and what you decide may affect the fate of Rome. Should you decide as I think you will, the enclosed title deed will perhaps help in some small way. Agron will explain how.

The gods bless you, my boy. You have, as always, my love and my respect. Kiss Perilla and my grandchildren for me.

Farewell.

My eyes were smarting when I finished.

'Arrangement' was right. Jupiter! The devious old bugger!

25

'So what is this property exactly?' I said. I was still trying to take this on board. Owning a secret bolthole in Rome – so secret I didn't even know about it myself, for Jupiter's sake! – meant that I didn't have to leave after all. Sure, it was a gamble. If I was caught it'd mean the noose for certain, or a politely worded order from Tiberius to slit my wrists; but on the plus side it'd wrong-foot Sejanus completely. Accused of treason, your normal purple-striper's reaction is to fight or to run. Straight disappearance isn't an option. Maybe I could shake the bastard's complacency enough to force a few mistakes.

'A tenement off Cyprian Street, behind the Temple of Tellus,' Agron said. 'The rents are paid into an account in Ostia, with me as the factor.'

'Neat.' Agron would be known in Ostia, but not Dad, and not me; like all the old families we did business through our own bankers in Rome. And when the big guy had moved from the Subura he'd've left his city connections behind. 'How long's this been going on?'

'Almost ten years now. So your balance is pretty healthy.' Agron was grinning. 'Some of it's gone on renovations and repairs, of course. Your dad and I didn't cut any corners. Neither of us wanted the place falling down before you needed it.'

Yeah. Still, the money was good news, too, almost as good as having the place itself, and tenements were real money-spinners. If – when – I did a runner the authorities would freeze my bank accounts, probably sequestrate them altogether, and confiscate my property. Even if I had somewhere to stay I'd still have to eat.

'Dad set this up ten years ago?' I said. I still couldn't believe it. '*Dad* did?'

'Just after you left Rome. He bought the property under a false name. I only handled the finances and the everyday running arrangements.'

'Part of the block's unlet?'

'The first-floor flat. There's a caretaker, but he'll be no problem. The agreement was the flat would be kept ready at any time if and when the owner wanted it.'

I looked at the title deed again. The owner's name was given as Marcus Ufulanius, address (smudged) Pergamum.

'Who's Ufulanius?' I said. 'He exist at all?'

'No. But he's real enough to his banker and the tenants, I've made sure of that. He's an Oscan from Capua, a small-time wine-shipper who wants to keep a toehold in the old country.' Agron was still grinning. 'Just another money-grubbing absentee landlord, in other words.'

Neat again. Even the Oscan bit fitted. That'd be Dad's work: my old nurse had been Capuan, and I'd picked up the accent and a lot of the language while I was still in leading-strings. I knew Pergamum well, too, and it was a smart choice. Having Ufulanius live in Athens would've been pushing things.

'I like the wine-shipper, too,' I said. 'Talking wine I can manage.'

'Really?' Agron's grin broadened. 'You don't say?'

'So when Ufulanius suddenly decides to come back to Rome and move into his flat in the Subura then no one's going to think twice about it, right?'

'That's the idea. You approve?'

'Sure I do. It's beautiful.' I had to hand it to Dad, he'd not only carved out a badly needed bit of space for me, he'd given me a new face as well. 'There's only one flaw.'

'Yeah?' The grin slipped. 'What's that?'

'I hate to sound snobbish about this, pal, but certain things are still going to get noticed. Like my clean-cut patrician features and the way I pronounce my diphthongs, for example.'

Agron shrugged. 'No problem,' he said. 'Ufulanius catches a disease on the ship over. Something very nasty that keeps him out of circulation for two months. Time enough for him to grow a beard and learn to murder his vowels.'

I stared at him. 'Two *months*? I can't wall myself up in a tenement for two months!'

'Marcus, listen to me.' Agron wasn't smiling now. 'Two months is the minimum. You need time to get yourself forgotten about. Tenements're little worlds of their own, and as the new guy on the block you're going to stand out like an elephant in a bathtub. You skip bail one day as Marcus Valerius Corvinus and turn up the next as Marcus Ufulanius from the sticks with a sharp Market Square haircut and polished patrician vowels and you'll have the Praetorians beating your door down before you can say "fraud". Take two months to let things settle, grow your hair and beard, dye them maybe, and you might have a chance.'

Yeah, he was right. I couldn't rush this, I didn't dare. Shit, though! Two months shut up in a tenement flat and they'd be peeling me off the walls! And then there was the date Marilla had given me: July 28th. Suddenly that didn't seem so far off after all.

Well, there was nothing I could do. At least Perilla would be out of this. She could go back to Athens with Bathyllus and wait for results. If any.

'Okay,' I said. 'So my name's Marcus Ufulanius. Let's go for it.'

'Corvinus, I am *not* going to leave you alone in Rome!'

I sighed. Well, I should've known better than to expect Perilla to agree straight off when I told her the plan, but then I've always been an optimist.

'Look, lady,' I said, 'we don't have any choice. This is going to be dangerous, it's going to be uncomfortable, and the first part's going to be plain and simple boring. Don't make things any more difficult than they are already, okay?'

'I don't get bored easily, I can stand being uncomfortable in a good cause, and as far as the danger is concerned if you are willing to risk it then so am I. Besides, Athens is impossible.'

'Yeah? And why is that, now?'

She sighed. 'Marcus, if you disappear people are going to ask questions. The first person they are going to ask them of is your wife, and whether she is in Athens or Rome it is not going to matter much. When she refuses to answer, as she will, they are going to turn nasty, very nasty indeed. Sejanus might not risk accusing me of treason as such, but I wouldn't be the first to face a trumped-up charge of adultery.' Shit. I hadn't thought of that. It was obvious when you came to think of it, sure, but then even I couldn't think of everything. Sejanus would do it, too, if only to smoke me out. 'Besides, what would I live on?'

'You'd have . . .' I stopped. She was right again, and for the same reasons. The bar on my income and property wouldn't only be valid at Rome, it would hold throughout the empire. And of course it would extend to her. 'Yeah, okay, maybe holing up in the Subura wasn't such a good idea in the first place. Let's forget it.'

'We certainly will not forget it! Not after your father and Agron have gone to so much trouble for you!' She was really angry now. 'Besides, Marcus, if we go back to Athens now it'll kill you, just as surely as Sejanus would, only much more slowly and painfully. I don't want that, and I won't be the reason for it happening. I'd sooner kill myself and solve the problem that way, and believe me if I have to I will. Is that perfectly clear?'

I looked at her, shaken. There were tears in her eyes but her mouth was set in that hard line that I knew meant she was serious. Deadly serious.

'Yeah,' I said. 'Yeah, that's clear.'

'Good.' She stood up, and tried a smile. 'In any case, it might be fun. I've only been inside a Suburan flat once, and that was just the cupboard.'

'Think of it as practice, lady.' My throat was still dry. I swallowed. 'These places are pretty pokey.'

'Then I'd better think about what to pack, hadn't I?'

Someone coughed. I turned round. Bathyllus was standing by the door, shifting from foot to foot like he had to go somewhere fast before his bladder burst.

'Forgive the interruption, sir,' he said, 'but I couldn't help overhearing.'

I stared at him. Bathyllus *never* overheard, on principle. By his reckoning it was on a par with embezzling the housekeeping and blowing the cash on booze and wild women.

'Is that so?' I said.

'Yes, sir. And I would like to come as well, please.'

'Gods!' First Perilla, now Bathyllus! Was I the only sane one around here? 'Great idea! Why don't we just all move on down to the Subura and be done with it? We can take turns breathing.'

Bathyllus didn't bat an eyelid. 'I don't think that will be necessary, sir. And I'd have to go somewhere.'

'I agree, Marcus,' Perilla said. 'Bathyllus can't stay here anyway. None of the household slaves can. It's far too dangerous.'

I sat down on the couch and put my head in my hands. That was something else I hadn't thought of: as soon as I disappeared my slaves would be seized with the rest of the property. And the first thing Sejanus would do – quite legitimately – was have them tortured for any information they might have as to the master's current whereabouts.

'Okay,' I said. 'So what do we do?'

'If I might suggest, sir,' Bathyllus said, 'Meton and I could go with you to the new property. With perhaps another slave for emergencies. The others could be distributed around your friends and relatives as appropriate. They would know nothing, and it would be in their interests to keep quiet.'

I almost laughed. I could just see Bathyllus sharing a cubbyhole with Meton. They'd be at each other's throats in five minutes. 'You think that'd work?'

He sniffed. 'It isn't really satisfactory, but it's the best I can offer.'

'Yeah. Yeah, I suppose so. We'll draw up a list.' There was a jug of wine on the table. I poured a cup and sank it. Life was getting complicated. 'Make your arrangements, Bathyllus. Oh, and Bathyllus?'

'Yes, sir?'

'Thanks.'

'Don't mention it, sir.'

He left.

Okay. So now we were committed.

26

The next day I played games. First I sent Bathyllus haring off down to Puteoli, to arrange passage on the first ship east: it was still fairly early in the season and most of the Piraeus traffic goes from Brindisi, but there would be something sailing from the west coast, and I wanted to show willing. More than willing: for this whole thing to work I had to persuade Sejanus that I was running scared. That shouldn't be all that difficult; being the cocky bastard he was he wouldn't expect me to do anything else, especially after the weak-livered impression I hoped I'd given him at Dad's funeral. After Bathyllus had gone I went down to the Market Square with the longest face I could manage and told anyone who asked that we were cutting the holiday short and heading back to Greece. Not that many people did ask, or even talk to me, come to that; the news had obviously spread that Corvinus was on the skids, and after the third so-called friend had cut me dead I felt like a leper with halitosis. Cotta was standing outside the entrance to the Senate House, talking to Trio. The consul smirked in my direction and threw me a wink, but Cotta didn't even look round. He'd seen me; sure he had. Up yours, pal, I thought. At least Trio made no secret about where his loyalties lay.

There was no sign of Lamia or Arruntius. I was glad of that. These two I couldn't've faced.

When I got back the messenger was in from the Alban Hills. Marcia Fulvina was more than willing to have Marilla for as long as she wanted to stay. Well, that was one load off my mind, anyway. I'd send a few more of my lads with them, as well as the coachman, for safety on the road and for their own good.

Two or three months away from the fleshpots of Rome would bring the roses back into their cheeks, anyway. And they could help out with the chickens.

We packed. That took Perilla and me about five minutes, but Meton agonised for three hours over his cooking equipment. I remembered what I'd said about lending the guy to Lippillus. Well, he'd be finding out what it was like to cook over a single charcoal brazier after all. Trouble was we'd have to eat the result. If I'd been on my own I'd've happily lived out of cookshops like tenement people usually do, but with Perilla tagging along things were different. Not to mention Bathyllus, who'd've burst his truss at the idea of us eating takeaway food.

The last thing I did was send a skivvy round to Lippillus's to check how he was getting along. I'd've gone myself, but I'd given my word to Marcina, and anyway I didn't trust myself not to tell him about the Subura bolthole. Sure, I considered it, but it wouldn't've been fair on him: he couldn't've done anything and the fewer people who knew where we were the better. Even Mother didn't know, and if push came to shove she could swear to it on the forehead of Jupiter Capitolinus himself. That was Dad's idea, too. I was beginning to have a healthy respect for Dad.

We left after midnight of the second day, through the garden gate at the back of the house. Everything had been carefully planned. The four of us – including the skivvy Alexis – would go on foot and meet up with Agron at the Sacred Way junction. Bathyllus would follow on, in his own time, when he got back from Puteoli. I just hoped I'd shown myself sufficiently spineless, and Sejanus wouldn't have us staked out, but that was a risk we had to take.

Marilla and Brito were leaving for Fulvina's at the same time, and the coach was parked in the alleyway round the side. Marilla came over to say goodbye. She looked very small in the darkness, and more like a dryad than ever.

'Thank you, Valerius Corvinus,' she said. 'For everything.'

I hugged her. 'Sure, princess. Look after yourself, now, okay? And give our regards to Fulvina.'

Then it was Perilla's turn. They were both sniffling by the time they broke up.

'Corvinus?' The kid turned back to me.

'Yeah?'

'I've remembered something else. About . . . what we talked about. The July business.'

'Uh-huh. Tell me.'

'Father had another visitor. He only came once, and he may not be important, but I thought I'd better mention him. A jowly-faced man with the top of his index finger missing.'

'*What?*'

'Mistress, come *on*!' Brito appeared out of the darkness beyond the gate and gripped her by the arm. 'We can't wait all night!'

Marilla let herself be pulled towards the waiting carriage. I stood staring after her, my brain numb.

Jupiter! Oh, sweet Jupiter best and greatest! A jowly-faced man with the top of his index finger missing! Marilla had kept the best for last, and she'd given me another name. I knew who that bastard was. Sure I did; we'd met before, ten years back, and we had unfinished business.

Publius Vitellius.

The Cyprian Street place wasn't nearly as bad as I'd expected. It was much bigger, for a start, and it took up a good half of the tenement's first floor.

'That was your father's idea.' Agron was showing us round. 'We knocked through the party walls into three other flats. He thought maybe you'd like some extra space to scratch yourself.'

'You sure they were party walls and not load-bearers, pal?' I said.

He grinned. 'Yeah. Don't worry, Corvinus, the building's safe. I had a friend of mine in the trade go over it thoroughly before I gave Messalinus the go-ahead. I haven't skimped on repairs, either.' That was a relief. Most tenements are built by speculators more interested in rents than bodies, and these guys cut their investment to the bone: property's a seller's market, and there're always more punters than rooms. I had enough problems with Sejanus without worrying about waking up under five tons of rubble and the guy upstairs's furniture. 'There're eight rooms altogether. Sextus says he got lost when he first moved in.'

'Sextus?'

'You remember. Little guy with a squint. He used to help me out in the metalsmith's shop. I brought him in as caretaker. Rent-free, too, so he's saved enough to buy a nice property near the Shrine of Libera.'

Uh-huh. That was another worry out of the way. Sextus was an old friend of Agron's, and he'd keep his mouth shut. Especially if he'd got no reason to grumble. Blacksmiths' assistants could work for a lifetime and still not be able to afford a place of their own.

'But Marcus! This is *lovely*!' Perilla was out on the tiny balcony. The view wasn't great, but at least it was a view because it looked out over a scrap of waste ground instead of into another flat across the alley the way most tenement balconies do. Someone was cooking meat on a stick in the street below, and the smells that drifted up were pretty appetising. 'It's like being on holiday.'

'Tell me that in two months' time, lady,' I said.

'Don't be jaundiced.' She came back inside and kissed me. 'Your father and Agron have done very well for us.'

'Yeah, I know.' They had; they'd performed miracles, in fact. It mightn't be what we were used to, but it was luxury compared with what I'd expected. And way beyond your average tenement dweller's wildest dreams. 'Thanks, pal.'

'No problem,' Agron said. 'Come and see the rest.'

The rooms were small, but like he'd said there were a lot of them. He'd even managed to fit up a small kitchen. Meton had taken up residence already, and he was looking almost perky. For Meton, that is, which isn't saying much.

'Everything fine?' I said.

'Fine?' He frowned. 'What with, sir?'

'With the kitchen, sunshine. Does it meet your exacting culinary standards or should we instal a couple more ovens for you?'

Sarcasm goes straight past Meton. He sniffed. '"Fine" isn't exactly the word I'd use, sir,' he said. '"Barely adequate", now . . .'

Jupiter in a basket! Chefs! I cut him short. 'That's good. Just forget the sucking-pig, okay? We won't be hosting any dinner parties.' Just then I noticed three large wine flasks propped up in the corner. I looked at the labels and whistled. 'Hey, now!'

The wine was Setinian. Life suddenly seemed a whole lot brighter.

Agron had come up behind me. 'So you've found the wine, Corvinus?' he said. 'Messalinus said you'd appreciate these. They're from his own cellar, eighteen years old now. I brought them round myself from home last night. I'd trust Sextus with my sister or my last copper penny, but three flasks of vintage Setinian might've been pushing things a bit.'

Too right! And I'd move them, too, first chance I got. Meton's kitchen was no place for this liquid gold, and we couldn't afford to risk any more unilateral binges. Meanwhile, though, they were just what I needed.

'Agron, scare up a mixing bowl and three cups, will you?' I looked at Meton and Alexis the skivvy, who'd been hard at work stashing away the stuff we'd brought with us. 'Ah, hell. House warming. Special occasion. Make it five.'

We left Meton and the skivvy with their own private party in the kitchen and took the opened flask and our cups into the living-room, the one with the balcony. You could've swung a cat in there, but only just, and there were chairs instead of couches, but at least it was homey. We sat down and I spilled some of the wine to Dad's ghost. I hoped the old guy could taste it, wherever he was. As a thank you it was little enough. For what he'd given me he deserved all three flasks.

'So.' I raised my own cup. 'Screw Sejanus.'

'You reckon this is going to work, then?' Agron said.

'Sure it is. I just wish I could see that bastard's face when he knows I've slipped off the hook.'

'You need anything else from my side?'

'You've done enough for me already.' I sipped the wine. It was good stuff, better than mine. 'But there is one more thing. You know where Publius Vitellius lives these days?'

Perilla glanced at me sharply: she hadn't heard Marilla give me that last bit of information.

'Vitellius?' Agron set his cup down. 'Germanicus's old pal?'

'Right. If you can call him that.'

'Somewhere on the Esquiline, isn't it? Near the Virbian Incline?'

'Could be. Wherever it is I'd like his house watched for visitors. I need faces, names if I can get them. Possible?'

'You think Vitellius is involved with this, Marcus?' Perilla said.

'I know so.' I told her what Marilla had told me. 'Maybe it's coincidence, but the description fits. And the guy's a prime possibility.'

Yeah, and I'd give my eye teeth to see him nailed, too. He'd been sitting on my conscience for ten years.

Agron had been thinking. Now he said, 'It's possible. Names, no, but faces I can manage, maybe. You ever meet Cass's nephew Paullus?'

'No.' Not surprising. Cass was Agron's wife Cassiopeia. She came from a big family, and she had more nephews and nieces than a dog's got fleas.

'Paullus is the artistic one, just turned ten. Give the kid a stick of charcoal and something to draw on and he's happy. Good at it, too. He did a sketch of Cass's father that had the ugly old bastard to the life. Took him about two minutes, and then three days before he could sit down again.'

Uh-huh. Paullus sounded perfect. 'This would be a long-term job, and it might be a waste of time. He'd need cover, too. Even a street kid hanging around day in day out is going to get himself noticed, especially in a high-class residential district like the Esquiline.'

Agron rubbed his jaw.

'We could give him a pastry-stand,' he said at last.

'A what?'

'A pastry-stand. Paullus's mother makes the best spiced sweet-cakes in Ostia, and the family's got three stalls there already. One more in Rome's not going to stretch them, if you can cover the pay-off to the syndicate that he'll need to get him a patch that far off his home ground.'

'Sure.' It was ideal. No one notices a corner pastry-seller. I might even be doing the family business a favour; the Esquiline's a rich area, and if the quality was good they'd coin money hand over fist. 'Can you fix it?'

'Leave it with me.' Agron drank the rest of his wine and stood up. 'Speaking of which, it's been a long evening, Corvinus. I'd better be getting back.'

'To Ostia? At this time of night? Come on, pal!'

'It's almost dawn. I can get a lift on a wagon from Cattlemarket Square. Besides' – he winked – 'Cass gets lonely when I'm away.'

'How is your family?' Perilla said. 'We should have asked.'

'Growing. There's another on the way. That'll make four.'

'Congratulations.' I glanced at Perilla, but she seemed okay. 'Which do you want this time? Boy or girl?'

'A boy would be handy in the business, but another girl would even things up. I'm not fussy.' He yawned and stretched. 'I'll leave you to settle in. Don't worry, I'll keep in touch.'

'Yeah. Yeah, thanks.' I saw him to the door. 'Look after yourself, pal.'

'You too. Work on your vowels. And remember: don't go out.'

Don't go out. Gods alive!

It was going to be a long two months.

27 ∫

It was. The longest I'd ever spent. Agron dropped by from time to time, but not often, and not for long: even that we couldn't risk.

The news he brought wasn't too good, either. I'd burned my bridges with a vengeance, seemingly. Marcus Valerius Corvinus had been condemned by the Senate in absentia, on a charge of treason backdating ten years: seditious activity in Italy and Syria compounded with bad-mouthing the emperor and spreading sedition in the provinces. Jupiter knew where Sejanus had got that last one from. I'd once at a party in Daphni described the governor as a stuck-up lardball with less brains than a hen, but that was it, and the Greeks had just smiled over their cold sardines with date sauce like they always did when some half-assed Roman stated the obvious. The prosecutors at the trial, I noticed, were Trio and Vitellius. There was no defence worth speaking of. So much for Cotta.

So the Palatine house was gone: not sold yet, but sequestrated, along with the rest of my property. Well, I hadn't expected anything else, but it meant that now I was really on my own, and it was a fight to the finish between me and Sejanus. Personally I wouldn't lay any bets on the outcome. I wasn't used to being cooped up, either, and my feet itched for the feel of a pavement under them. I even envied Meton, who had to get out if we wanted to keep eating. Sure, I'd had my doubts about letting him off the leash, but if I'd put my foot down and refused to let him do the shopping I'd've woken up one morning with a filleting knife between my ribs. As it was, I just warned him to forget his little gastronomic trips to the Velabrum and make do with second best from the local market. Spanish fish sauce and prawns from Minturnae we could live without, even if it did throw his menus out of kilter.

Meanwhile I let my hair and my beard grow, walked with a stoop and practised my Campanian accent. None of that would fool anyone I knew for a second, from close up at least, but it'd get me by with strangers if and when I had the chance to meet any.

By the time the Spring Festival came and went I was climbing walls. Perilla was lasting better: she didn't get out any more than I did, but she was filling in the time writing Greek poetry, working her way through the metres. Heavy stuff, and beyond me; her stepfather would've been proud of her. The only bit of light – and that was just a glimmer – was young Paullus. Every time he came Agron brought a fresh supply of the kid's sketches. Most of the faces didn't mean anything to me and the ones that did didn't strike any chords, but at least they made me feel I was doing something.

Spring passed into summer. We were halfway through June: two full months since we'd moved to the Subura, and slightly over one before Marilla's deadline. I was beginning to twitch seriously, but there was no point going anywhere until I had a lead. I'd thought about things, sure – the business with Titius Sabinus was still bugging me – but working on theories alone without being able to prove or disprove them is like trying to keep your eyes open when you sneeze.

Then one day Agron arrived, and everything changed.

'Corvinus. Perilla.' The big guy gave me a nod. 'How's it going?'

Bathyllus was already pouring the wine. Living in a tenement didn't seem to have fazed him any, and we must have had the cleanest flat in the whole Subura. Even the cockroaches shone.

'Perilla's on to augmented polyschematist dimeters with added adoneuses,' I said sourly: the sun was streaming through the balcony window, and he had that fresh-air look about him that I was beginning to hate. 'I'm scratching my armpits. So what else is new?'

'He doesn't mean it.' Perilla gave one of her tolerant smiles. 'He's being very patient.'

'Yeah, I'll bet.' Agron held up a sheaf of papers. 'I've brought some more of Paullus's sketches for you to have a look at.'

He handed them over. The face on the top one leaped out and hit me.

'Shit,' I said slowly.

'You know him?' Agron's interest sharpened.

'Sure I know him.' My brain was buzzing: maybe this time we were going to strike lucky. 'That's Caelius Crispus.' I turned the sketch over: Paullus would've written any information on the back. 'Three visits, all late, all lasting over an hour. So what would Crispus be doing visiting Vitellius?'

'Who's this Crispus?'

'A shady character with a boyfriend high up in the Treasury.' I caught myself, remembering our meeting just after Dad's funeral, when I'd first gone to check the Senate records. 'No. He's in the Treasury himself these days. Something to do with the military pay-chest.'

'Is he, now?' The corners of Agron's mouth turned down. 'You know Vitellius is the new Treasury Controller?'

'He's *what*?'

'Sure. As of four days ago.'

I was getting that prickly feeling at the back of my neck; the feeling I'd been missing for months.

'You happen to know how he got the appointment?' I said.

'Flamininus had to give it up. The guy's been ill recently.'

'What kind of ill?'

'That I don't know.' Agron was frowning. 'Hold on, Corvinus, you're building a case out of nothing here. Flamininus is sick, full stop, end of story. Vitellius has the seniority, and he has a sound financial background. He's a natural choice. Also, if Crispus is one of his juniors like you say then there's every reason for him to pay a call on his boss. Even three calls.'

'Outside office hours? When they work in the same building? And his *ultimate* boss?'

'Maybe it was an emergency.'

'You said it yourself. Three calls. One for an emergency I'd believe, but not three. In any case both guys are as crooked as an Ostian dice game. Come on, pal, you know I'm right!'

Agron rubbed his chin. 'Yeah, well. Maybe.'

'Maybe nothing. We're in business here.'

'Okay. So maybe we are. So what can you do about it?'

'I can talk to Crispus, of course.'

'Marcus, *no*!' Perilla said.

I shrugged. 'I've got to come out of hiding some time, lady. Otherwise I might as well not be here.'

'Perilla's right.' Agron was still frowning. 'You don't even know if there's anything in this. It's too risky, Marcus.'

'I told you. I know Vitellius, and I know Crispus. Put the two together and they stink worse than a bucketful of Tiber mud.' I stared at the sketch again. 'Besides, I can catch Crispus in the evening, on the way to his club.'

'Marcus.' Agron held up his hands. 'Be reasonable, pal! If you think it's important then I'll sweat the guy myself.'

'You wouldn't know what to ask.'

'So tell me, for Jupiter's sake!'

I shook my head. 'No.'

Agron sighed. 'Fine. Okay, fine. But we do it my way, once I've talked to a few friends of mine. And if you're only doing this to get a lungful of fresh air, Corvinus, I swear I'll kill you personally.'

'Yeah.' I grinned. 'Well, there is that too.'

It was good to be outside again, even at night. I'd arranged to meet Agron and his friends near the house on the Pincian where Crispus spent his evenings with other bachelors of a certain persuasion. The place lay beyond Lucullus Gardens, far out and isolated. Because of what went on there, intentionally so: the last time I'd been here with Perilla, Crispus had been wearing a napkin.

I'd brought Alexis with me to carry the torch. It would've looked suspicious otherwise, especially if I bumped into any of the Watch: no respectable citizen, even a plain-mantle, goes out at night without at least one slave to attract the mosquitoes and discourage more dangerous two-legged pests. I'd tucked a pair of party slippers under my arm, too, for appearances' sake.

I kept to the main drag, up Long Road to the Quirinal, then back the way along High Path to Flora's Gate and up to the Pincian itself. A long way round, sure, but I'd left myself plenty of time and like I say it was good to be walking again. It was a beautiful evening, too. Even from the road I could smell the cypresses in Lucullus Gardens. The dark scent reminded me of Dad's funeral.

I had Alexis douse the torch well short of Crispus's club and we cut across the waste ground towards the house itself. I'd almost reached it when someone stepped out in front of me. My knife was half out of its sheath before I recognised Agron.

'Corvinus?' he whispered: there wouldn't be anyone close enough to hear, or so I hoped, but he obviously wasn't taking any chances.

'Yeah.' I slipped the knife back into place.

'Everything's ready. Come and meet the boys.'

There were six of them, big Ostian bruisers who spent the day humping marble slabs on and off barges and the night doing Jupiter knew what.

'You'll recognise Crispus's litter?' I said.

'Sure.' Agron grinned in the darkness. 'I went round to his house this morning and checked it out. The litter slaves, too. No problem. We'll take them here where the path bends.' It was a good place, screened from the road behind and from the house in front, with plenty of cover; Agron had been a soldier once, and he still had a sharp eye for country. 'You sure about your timings?'

'I'm sure. The Happy Bachelors Club doesn't get going until midnight.'

'Okay. Leave the slaves to us. You take your pal yourself.'

'Fine.'

We moved back into the bushes and watched the track. Two litters passed: I recognised one of them as belonging to an ex-censor. The third was ours.

I had to admit it was slickly done: half a minute, max, from start to finish. Agron stepped out in front of the guy with the torch and had him by the throat before he knew what was happening. At the same time the Ostian bruisers slipped in behind and took out the others. Knives flashed, but there was no blood: we wanted silence, not killings.

Once the litter slaves were immobilised, I stepped forward and opened the curtains.

'Hi, Crispus,' I said. 'Surprise.'

He didn't recognise me at first. Then his eyes widened.

'*Corvinus!* What the hell . . . !'

I put my hand across his mouth and bundled him out while Agron's lads got the litter and its slaves off the track and into the shelter of the rocks in case any more punters came along while we were having our chat. Then I drew my own knife and set the point under his chin.

'Okay, pal,' I said. 'Take this easy and you won't get hurt.'

Crispus went limp as a rabbit. I half pulled, half carried him well away from the path to a hollow where the bushes grew thickly and shoved him in.

'I thought you'd left Rome, Corvinus.' He was grey with fear and trying not to show it. 'Everybody did. When Sejanus finds out—' His mouth shut like an iron trap.

'Yeah. Only Sejanus isn't going to find out, is he? Not from you, anyway.'

He must've read more into the words than I'd meant, because the grey colour went up a few notches and he passed his tongue across his lips.

'What do you want?' he whispered.

'What do I usually want from you? Information.'

'But I don't have—'

'Sure you do.' I crouched down beside him, still gripping his arm. He stank of fear and expensive aftershave. 'Let's take an easy question for starters. What sort of scam do you have cooking with Publius Vitellius? And don't bother to deny it, sunshine, because I just won't believe you.'

'Corvinus, for Jupiter's sake!'

He'd been shaking. Now I put the knife back under his jawbone and pressed. He stiffened and his eyes rolled until the whites showed.

'Listen, Crispus,' I said carefully. 'I'm running from a treason rap already. If they catch me I'm dead. So nailing your tongue to the top of your skull isn't going to make all that much difference to me, and I swear I'll do it with the greatest pleasure unless you tell me now what Vitellius is up to.'

'But I can't . . . !' he began. I moved my hand. The point of the knife broke through the skin and a drop of blood eased itself out. Crispus's head was as far back as it would go now, but his eyes were doing their best to see what my knife-hand was doing. 'Corvinus, *please*! I promise you . . .'

'Not this time, pal,' I said. 'No games. I haven't got the time or the inclination. Your choice, but you'll have to make it quick.'

I could feel him collapse. I took the knife away.

'Okay,' he said. 'Just give me a moment.' He rubbed his throat and gulped at the night air. 'Vitellius is dipping into the military pay-chest.'

Well, it had to be something like that, of course. Still . . .

'Uh-uh,' I said. 'That's impossible. Vitellius is no fool. There're regular checks, independent audits. He wouldn't get away with it for five minutes.'

'Maybe not five minutes. But two months is possible, and that's all he needs.'

'You mean until July 28th?'

He stared at me, and his jaw dropped. I swear his right hand was making the sign against witchcraft, and he even forgot to be frightened. If it hadn't been so serious I would've laughed.

'Corvinus, how the *hell* do you know about the 28th?' he said.

'Never mind.' Bang on the button! 'So Vitellius needs the cash to fund the assassination attempt on the emperor.' Crispus was still staring. 'And when Tiberius is dead and Sejanus is in control everything will be sweetness and light again.'

'Uh, yeah. Yeah.' He swallowed. 'More or less.'

'More or less?'

'If a few extra pennies are left unaccounted for at the end of the day, then no one's going to ask too many questions, are they?'

'Uh-huh.' That made sense. Crispus may've been a crook, but he left politics alone. They were too risky, and you might lose your head as well as your profit. 'So why should he involve you?'

'He had to,' Crispus said. 'I've got the other key to the strongroom door.'

Yeah. Well. The simple answers are the best. I straight-armed him upright and had the satisfaction of seeing the fear come back into his eyes. 'Now listen, sunshine. I'm going to ask you this next question once and once only, and you'd better be able to answer it or I'll break your arm. That's for starters. I should also remind you that I've nothing to lose and if I find later that you've lied or prevaricated I'll make a point of coming after you and breaking your neck as well. And if *that* doesn't persuade you to an answer, I give you my word that very soon now the emperor is going to know all about this business and who was involved in it, and he is not going to be a very happy little Caesar. Now. Do I make myself clear?'

He swallowed again and nodded.

'Good. The question is, what is the name of the assassin? You have a count of five. One.'

'Corvinus!'

'Two.'

He was sweating. 'Corvinus, please! It's more than my life's worth!'

'Three.'

'Sejanus will . . .'

'Four.' I shifted my grip so that my other hand was behind his elbow.

'*Okay!*' he screamed. 'The guy's name's Silanus! Appius Junius Silanus!'

I let him go. 'The Asian governor's son?'

He was breathing heavily and rubbing his arm. 'Yeah. Now just leave me alone, okay? I've told you all I know.'

'How's he getting into Capri?'

'He's carrying a message. From Sejanus. I don't know the details, I swear I don't know!'

His voice was sulky, but he was telling the truth. I got up.

'Okay, Crispus.' I jerked my head. 'Piss off. Have a nice evening.'

'You won't tell Silanus I gave him away?'

'No, I won't tell him.' Junius Silanus. The exiled Asian governor's son. Well, well. Junia Torquata would have another scapegrace relative to add to her list: *my nephew the assassin*. That was some family.

Crispus scuttled off with a nervous glance over his shoulder. Agron loomed out of the darkness ahead of him and he squeaked and dodged, but I gave a wave and the big guy let him pass.

A good night's work. Now I had to talk to Silanus.

28

That wasn't going to be so easy. Appius Junius Silanus was a top-notch noble, consul three years back and a relative of Tiberius's through his mother. I didn't know the guy personally, but I knew of him. He was the perfect example of the dangers of inbreeding: a vain, fluff-brained dandy who fancied himself a politician but whose grasp of life's realities would've disgraced an average twelve-year-old. In other words, a natural tool for Sejanus.

My hope was that guys like that make the worst traitors; they don't last the pace, and when things get rough they go to pieces. If I could get Silanus alone and off his home ground I might just be able to scare him into doing something Sejanus would live to regret. The only problem was how. Sure, I could break into his house and face him with what I knew, but I'd be a fool to try because one shout out of place and I'd be on my way to a rock in the Cyclades, at best. No, the meeting had to be on my terms, another dark alleyway tête-à-tête; and that was going to be difficult, because social butterflies like Silanus were never alone. They never willingly went down alleyways, either, dark or otherwise. It might mean getting mud on their Cordovan leather sandals.

We said goodbye to the Ostians and went back to the flat. We were both starving: I don't know about Agron, but with me it was the unaccustomed fresh air and exercise. Perilla had gone to bed and so, for a wonder, had Bathyllus, but I did a bit of foraging and rousted us out a jug of wine and a plateful of bread and cheese. We ate while we discussed what Crispus had told me and how best to handle Silanus.

'Corvinus, don't rush into this, okay?' Agron advised. 'You need a lot more information about the guy first. His movements, his daily routine. There'll be something. He has to be vulnerable somewhere.'

'I could go to the Wart now. I've got enough to make him listen.' Sure. Who was I kidding? I didn't even sound convincing to myself. 'At least . . .'

'Yeah, I wouldn't put any bets on it either.' Agron speared a bit of cheese with his knife. 'Anyway, how do you get into Capri to do it? Pretend to be a seagull? Apply for a pass to Sejanus?'

I grunted. That was another problem, and Agron had given me the only two viable options. If Capri was a fortress Sejanus held the keys. I could have the whole thing worked out six ways from nothing with proof oozing out of its ears and it still wouldn't do me any good. No one crossed the channel from Surrentum to Tiberius's private island without his deputy's leave. That went for letters, too. And if I was fool enough to try busting in without permission – by taking a fishing boat over, say, and climbing the cliffs – I'd leave in an urn. Unless the rocks got me first.

'Maybe the Wart'll come back for the Apollinarian Games this time,' I said. That would mean he'd be in Rome during the first part of July; and in comparison with sneaking into Capri even gatecrashing the Palatine was child's play.

'Yeah, and pigs might fly, too.' Agron frowned. 'Face it, Corvinus. If you want to stop the guy you'll have to do it from this end. And like I say to make that happen you'll need information.'

Yeah. True, all of it. I chewed sadly on a roll and took a swallow of wine. 'So. You got any clever ideas?'

'Sure.'

'Really?'

If he noticed the sarcasm it didn't show. 'You're forgetting. I used to be a client of the Quinctilii.'

'I'm not forgetting.' Agron had served under Quinctilius Varus, the old villain who'd got himself massacred along with three of our legions in the Teutoburg, and then been taken up by Varus's sister. It was how we'd met in the first place. 'So what? Quinctilia's been dead for years and we're talking about the Silani here.'

'Yeah. But Quinctilia was a close friend of your Silanus's mother, and the households met quite often. I know a couple of the guy's slaves from way back. Give me a few days. Let me see what I can dig out.'

This I didn't like the sound of. I was remembering what had happened to Lippillus, and one friend damaged on my account over this business was enough. Still, we had to have the angle. And it looked like the only game in town.

'Okay,' I said. 'But go easy. No risks, right?'

He impaled the last piece of cheese. 'Corvinus,' he said, 'that is something you do not have to tell me.'

It took Agron four days. When Bathyllus let him in to the flat on the fifth evening he was grinning all over his face.

'Got the bastard,' he said.

'Yeah?' I was feeling pretty chirpy myself. It was a lovely evening and I'd left Perilla scribbling in the study and slipped out for a cup of wine at the local wineshop. I'd got talking to a guy who half an hour into the conversation turned out to be from Calatia, which is just down the road from Capua, and who had a cousin in Pergamum. It ought to have been a recipe for disaster but it wasn't. We ended up slagging off the Romans and the Roman upper classes in particular, and parted the best of friends.

'Yeah.' Agron sat down. 'He's seeing the wife of a senator who lives on the Viminal near Patrician Street.'

'Seeing as in "seeing"?'

'Definitely. Every evening. The affair seems to be hotting up, and the senator concerned is busy with committee work.'

'Handy.'

'That's what I thought. Understandably, Silanus doesn't come calling with a fanfare of trumpets. Just him, on foot, with a single slave. Very untypical, very low-key.'

'Uh-huh.' It was perfect. 'How do we do it?'

Agron frowned. 'You sure you want this?'

'Sure I'm sure.'

'Okay. In that case we keep it nice and simple. Next time lover boy goes visiting I grab him and bring him here instead.'

I set down my wine cup. 'You do *what*?'

'Don't look at me like that, Corvinus.' He took one of the new season's grapes from the bowl in front of him and popped it into his mouth. 'It's the best way. I'll borrow two or three of the barge boys again and scare up a double litter with nice thick curtains. There'll be no hassle. None at all.'

'You want to bring Silanus *here*?' I was still staring at him.

'Why not? It's quiet, it's safe. What else do you want?'

Jupiter! And Perilla accused me of having crazy ideas!

'Safe, hell!' I said. 'If he traces me back then we're in real trouble!'

'Come on, Corvinus!' Agron popped another grape. 'We gag and blindfold him and run him around a bit before and after. By the time you're ready for him the guy won't know which way's up, let alone what part of Rome he's in. Besides, this is the best you'll get.'

Yeah, well. It might work after all. It was certainly better than taking him somewhere even semi-public and risking being interrupted. 'What about the slave?'

'The Ostians can handle that side of it, don't worry. If he doesn't co-operate we tap him on the head and bring him with us in the same litter.'

'Appius Silanus share his litter with a slave?' I grinned. 'He's going to love that part.'

'The last thing he'll have to worry about is compromising his aristocratic principles. Believe me.'

'Okay,' I said. 'So let's do it.'

'Tomorrow?'

'As ever is.'

I'd got everything set up for our guest's arrival. Perilla and Bathyllus had been warned to stay well away, and I'd closed the window shutters in case the view put any ideas into his head, immediate or retrospective. Plenty of lamps, though: I wanted to see how he looked when he answered my questions.

It was an hour before midnight when Agron brought him in. He steered the guy to a chair, sat him down firmly, and took off the gag and the mask. Silanus sat for a moment blinking in the lamplight like a parrot choosing between two swear words. Then he struggled to his feet.

Agron pushed him down. 'Easy,' he grunted.

'By the gods, I'll have you strangled for this, you wretches!' Well, he was gamer than I thought he'd be, even if he did sound like a character in a third-rate comedy. 'Let me go at once!'

'Sure,' Agron said. 'When we've finished.' He looked at me. 'You want to take over now?'

I'd been studying Silanus with interest. Late thirties, skinny, weak chin, watery eyes. He'd be short-sighted. I hadn't seen him around, and his face wasn't familiar from Paullus's drawings, either, so he hadn't been one of Vitellius's callers. I hoped we hadn't made a mistake. If Crispus had put one over on me after all I'd have the bastard's scrotum for a dice bag.

'Appius Junius Silanus?' I said. I didn't use my hick Campanian accent, and the patrician vowels came over loud and clear.

'Of course.' He was staring at my beard and long, bound hair. I could see him making a mental reassessment, wondering whether perhaps I might be worth his consideration after all. 'And who might you be?'

'The name's Marcus Corvinus.'

'Marcus *Valerius* Corvinus? Good grief, man, but you're supposed to be . . .' He half rose again, eyes wide, before Agron's hand stopped him.

'Yeah,' I said. 'Your pal Sejanus tried to set me up with a treason rap. Only I decided I wasn't going to play.'

'Sejanus is no friend of mine!'

I glanced sharply at Agron. Sure, it could've been bluster or an automatic denial, but he obviously didn't think so either; that had rung true. Shit. Maybe we had made a mistake after all.

'Is that so?' I said carefully.

'That is so. Sejanus was responsible, as you perhaps know, for my father's exile among many others. And if that is your reason for kidnapping me, Corvinus, then whatever you're planning you can forget it. I'm no friend of Sejanus's, I don't know anything about your little feud with him and he would certainly not care whether I went missing or not. Now get your fellows to take me back where they found me, please.'

'When we've had our talk.'

'Talk? What on earth do we have to talk about?'

Ah, well. In for a penny. 'Your plans to assassinate the emperor in forty days' time.'

I'd been watching his eyes, but I didn't need to look for any subtle signs of guilt this time. The guy went grey as an old wash-leather and collapsed into the chair like someone had sucked his bones out.

'What?' he said.

'You heard,' I said. 'You care to deny it, maybe?'

'Of course I deny it!' He licked his lips. 'The idea is preposterous! Why should I want to murder Tiberius?'

'I was hoping you'd tell me that yourself, sunshine.'

'You're mad.' He glanced back at Agron. 'Both of you.'

'Oh, we're not mad. We're not wrong, either. Sejanus is going to cash in his winnings on the 28th of next month, and you're going to help him do it.'

'I've told you, I have nothing to do with Sejanus!'

There was something screwy here. I'd got him cold and he knew it: the date had hit him hard, and he was frightened; but I had a gut feeling that he was also telling the truth.

'Okay,' I said. 'So if not Sejanus then who are you working for?'

'No one! I don't know what you mean!'

A lie. I looked up at Agron. 'You got your knife handy, pal?' I said.

Silanus shrieked; at least he started to, but Agron whipped the gag across his open mouth and pulled it tight. The shriek turned into a gurgle, and above the gag Silanus watched me with terrified eyes.

Agron handed me his knife. I held it against the guy's cheek.

'Okay, sunshine,' I said. 'We won't kill you. We'll just carve little bits off until you decide to talk. You can choose to co-operate or not, but you only get one chance. Understand?'

The eyes blinked rapidly. Then, slowly, Silanus nodded.

'Take the gag off,' I said. Agron did. Silanus never moved.

'Right. So I'll ask you again. If you're not working for Sejanus then who are you working for?'

He passed his tongue over his lips.

'The young prince, of course,' he said. 'Gaius Caesar.'

29

I sat back. This I hadn't expected. It didn't make sense, either. Why should Gaius want Tiberius dead? He hadn't a hope of taking power. He was only eighteen, hardly more than a kid. His mother and brothers were gone, the Julian party was smashed, he was living on sufferance already. And if he were stupid enough to put Tiberius in a hole then Sejanus would gulp him down like a shark swallowing a guppy.

Of course, there was the other obvious explanation . . .

'So tell me, sunshine,' I said. 'What is the plan exactly?'

'I'm going to stab him. With a dagger built into the spine of a letter-roll. Servaeus . . .' He stopped and put his hand to his mouth. It was almost comical.

'*Quintus* Servaeus?' Uh-huh. This was beginning to fit together. I remembered Servaeus, sure: one of the original Julians, a close friend of Germanicus and Agrippina, and the principal prosecutor in the Piso trial. The very *crooked* Piso trial. And Servaeus had been appointed to the College of Priests by the Wart shortly afterwards, together with his mate Vitellius. Oh, yes. I remembered Servaeus. 'Come on, Silanus! I knew you couldn't be in this on your own. So Quintus Servaeus is involved?'

'Yes. He's having the letter-roller specially made.' Now Silanus had been rumbled the poor sap was almost garrulous. 'And of course he's the one responsible for my inclusion in the senatorial party to Capri.'

'And how did he manage to do that, pray?'

'Oh, Quintus is a very astute man. Very aware. He pretends to be a friend of Sejanus's but of course that is a necessary and useful ploy. His loyalty is and always has been given, like mine, to the Julian family.'

Oh, sure, I thought. And I'm a blue-arsed Briton. 'So you go to Capri and stab Tiberius while he's reading his mail. This is fascinating. What happens next?'

'Tiberius's death is the signal for a general rising throughout the empire. The armies will give their oaths of allegiance to the Julians and to Gaius in particular.'

'Is that right now?' Jupiter! I couldn't believe this guy! He was so politically naïve it wasn't true. Even Agron was smiling. 'And what's Sejanus doing all this time? Playing marbles with the consuls?'

Silanus gave me a stare like he'd just found me in his salad.

'Sejanus will be gone,' he said. 'He won't last five minutes with the emperor dead, Corvinus. He derives his power from him, and the only reason he wields the influence he does is that Tiberius is a victim of delusions. You know that.'

'Do I?'

'Of course you do. You're no friend of Sejanus's yourself, either. No one can be who has Rome's best interests at heart, even if they're pretending otherwise at the moment. The Senate will have him arrested and executed as soon as the news breaks.'

'What about the Praetorians? Sejanus is their commander.'

'They won't support even him against a son of Germanicus, especially Gaius Caligula. And with Sejanus gone there'll be no one else left. We will have won, and Rome will have a Julian emperor at last.'

'Does he know about all this, by the way? Prince Gaius himself?'

Silanus hesitated. 'It was decided not to tell him,' he said. 'That way he couldn't be implicated if anything went wrong.'

Uh-huh. Surprise, surprise. Well, that about wrapped it up. I looked at Silanus consideringly. He was glowing with honest patriotic pride and self-satisfaction. I hated to spoil things for him, but it had to be done.

'Silanus,' I said, 'you've been had, pal.'

He stared at me. 'What?'

'Had. Swindled. Conned.' I was getting through at last. He was beginning to look less smug. 'Sold down the river. Screwed right, left and centre.'

'That's nonsense!'

'It isn't nonsense. Servaeus has been Sejanus's man for years, and Gaius hasn't a hope in hell of being acclaimed emperor. I've followed this up from the other end and believe me I know what I'm talking about. It stinks. Take it from me, sunshine, it's Sejanus's scam from start to finish.'

He looked shaken. 'That's not true! You're—'

'Look,' I interrupted. 'I won't confuse you by going into details. Just take my word for it. I've saved your life here, pal.'

'My *life*?'

'Sure. Use whatever serves you as a brain and you'll see I'm right. Do you honestly think that dagger-in-the-letter crap would fool the imperial guards for one second? There're these things called searches, Silanus, and on Capri they do them pretty well. You wouldn't get within a mile of Tiberius. Which was exactly what Sejanus intended.'

He goggled at me. I'd lost him. Jupiter! Scratch the twelve-year-old, I'd known more about political life in the raw when I was six. 'Silanus, watch my lips and try to follow, okay? Your so-called pal Servaeus was setting you up. The idea was that you'd get caught red-handed in an assassination attempt, and when they asked you cui bono you'd say Gaius.'

'I wouldn't! I swear!'

'Probably you wouldn't have to, not in words. The evidence would be there, neatly planted when you weren't looking. But a few touches of the red-hot iron would confirm it.' He winced. 'As a result Gaius would be chopped or exiled and the last obstacle between Sejanus and the succession removed.'

'But what about Servaeus? He'd be implicated too!' The poor guy was visibly struggling. Jupiter knew how he'd ever made consul, with his grasp of the realities. In families like his it was difficult to avoid, but in his case we'd've been better off with a tadpole.

'Servaeus would deny everything, naturally,' I said. 'And Sejanus would back him.'

'I don't believe it!'

I sighed. 'Silanus, have you got anything in writing? Anything confirming arrangements and so on? A letter? A note of some kind in Servaeus's handwriting or with his signature? So much as a laundry bill with the guy's name at the top?'

'Of course not! That would be . . .' He stopped. Clink. The penny had finally dropped.

'Stupid. Yeah. I agree.' I looked at Agron, who'd stood expressionless through this. 'Agron, I think you can take Appius Junius Silanus back to his girlfriend's house now. He won't be giving us any more trouble. Or the emperor.'

'Blindfolded?'

'Blindfolded. Brain-rot isn't endemic throughout the whole ruling class yet.'

Agron grinned and sketched a salute. I gave him the finger and reached for the wine.

They'd been gone exactly two minutes when my other visitors arrived.

They walked in without knocking. Felix and his big pal Lamprus. I wasn't really surprised because I'd been expecting them now I knew who they worked for and why they'd been tailing me.

'How are you, Valerius Corvinus?' Felix gave me his best smile. He was wearing a natty green tunic this time, with a yellow leather belt. 'Very nice to see you again.'

'Yeah.' I indicated the other chair and the stool. 'Sit down. Make yourselves comfortable. My home is yours.'

'Thank you.' Felix took the stool. The big guy just loomed.

We sat looking at each other for a couple of minutes like a Greek chorus that's strayed on to the wrong stage. Felix was still smiling and quite at ease.

'Okay,' I said at last. 'Do you want to start or shall I?'

'Oh, you first, sir. Please.'

'Right. A stupid question to begin with. How did you find me?'

He ducked his head. 'Actually, we've known you were here since the day after you moved. We followed your slave from Puteoli, and incidentally dealt with one of Sejanus's agents who tried to do the same. Since then you've been watched very carefully. Very carefully indeed.'

'Yeah? Is that right?' Galling, and probably true, especially the bit about the Sejanian tail. Thank Jupiter for minders.

'Yes, sir. In fact I'm told that you had a very pleasant conversation with one of my colleagues just the other day. He asked me to give you his regards and tell you how much he enjoyed your company.'

Shit. 'The Campanian in the wineshop. And I'd thought I was being clever.'

'Oh, but you were, sir!' The little guy looked pained. 'My colleague was most impressed. He told me particularly to be sure to compliment you on your Capuan accent.'

'Nice of him.' I poured a cup of wine and offered the jug to Felix. He shook his head. 'So. You work for Gaius Caesar and you've been tailing me in the hope that I'll uncover what sort of scam Sejanus has concocted to put the skids under your boss.'

'Oh, not the hope!' Felix smiled again. 'The confident expectation! We don't underestimate your skills, Valerius Corvinus. Isn't that right, Lamprus?' The thing grunted.

'By the way, you want to tell me your real names now that it doesn't matter?' I said.

'Oddly enough, sir, we really are Felix and Lamprus.' I stared at him. 'It's called a double bluff, sir. Of course, I only risked it as a tribute to your intelligence.'

Oh, shit. Outsmarted at every turn. Well, Bathyllus probably wouldn't've been able to trace them anyway. I sipped at my wine.

'Question number two, then,' I said. 'Festus, Rubrius Fabatus's gardener. How did you find out about him?'

'A rather lucky guess, I'm afraid, although one based on sound probabilities. We knew about Fabatus and Tubero already, and we were keeping them under observation. We also knew – having done our homework thoroughly, of course, via a kitchen slave planted in his household – about Fabatus's domestic arrangements, including Festus's little bolthole. When our kitchen colleague reported that the three men had had their discussion in the garden and that Festus had not been in evidence for some time we thought the line was worth pursuing. Fortunately we were correct.'

I whistled, impressed. 'Smart.'

'Thank you, sir.' The guy was almost blushing. 'Very good of you to say so. We do try. And of course we thought what Festus had to say would help your own investigation along.'

'You've got him safe?'

'Festus? Naturally. I won't tell you where – he's outside Rome in any case, and quite content – but he'll reappear at the proper time.'

'Good. One last question, if I may.'

'Certainly. As many as you like.'

'Just one'll do. You never did work for Titius Sabinus, did you?'

'No, sir.' He sighed. 'I'm sorry for the deception, but no. That was an untruth. Lamprus and I have always been Julian slaves.'

'So why mention him? It was intentional, wasn't it? To point me in a certain direction?'

'Oh, how very astute! Isn't he, Lamprus?' Felix looked positively delighted, and the man-mountain grunted again. 'I did wonder if you'd picked that up. Yes, it was intentional, Valerius Corvinus. It didn't achieve its purpose, of course, but since you approached the problem from a different direction and solved it in your own inimitable fashion that doesn't much matter.'

'You care to explain just exactly what that purpose was, then? Just for the record.'

He frowned. 'Oh, I don't think I could take that on myself, sir, could I, Lamprus?' Grunt. 'But then I'm sure the master will tell you in a moment if you ask him.'

Jupiter! 'Uh . . . the master? He's here?'

'Yes, sir.' He stood up and looked towards the living-room door which opened on to the empty lobby. What I'd assumed was the empty lobby. Then he said, in a louder voice, 'We're ready for you now, sire.'

30

I was standing myself as he came in. If I'd known I'd be entertaining royalty I would've put on a better mantle and got Meton to lay on cakes. Bathyllus would kick himself when he found he'd slept through this. A visit from a genuine Caesar would've satisfied the little snob's society cravings for the next five years.

'Valerius Corvinus!' The emperor's grandson strode across the room with his hand outstretched. 'How very lovely to meet you! I'm sorry about the unorthodox circumstances, but I thought I'd come and thank you personally.'

'Uh . . . sure,' I said. 'Don't mention it.' Not the most original of lines, but what can you expect under the circumstances?

Not a good-looking young man, Gaius Caesar. In fact he reminded me of a tall balding goat: hairy in all the wrong places with a face like he'd been sat on hard as a baby. He was beaming as he shook my hand.

'What a beautiful lobby you have,' he said. 'Most . . . ah . . . lobby-like.'

'Yeah. Yeah, it's okay.' I remembered, right at the last moment, to close my mouth when I'd finished using it. 'Would you care to sit down?'

'Thank you.' He threw himself into the other chair. 'Is that wine over there by any chance?'

'Sure.' I reached for the jug, but Felix beat me to it.

'Allow me, sir,' he said, and poured. The perfect butler. Eat your heart out, Bathyllus! I thought.

Gaius lifted the cup. 'Thanks, ah . . .'

'Felix, sire.'

'Of course. Felix.' He turned to me. 'What do you think of my two spies, by the way, Corvinus?'

'I'm impressed.' I looked at Felix. He smirked.

Gaius was nodding. 'They do a good job,' he said. 'Mind you, we had a terrible time dragging . . . Lamprus, isn't it?' He gave Felix an enquiring glance and got a nod in return. 'Dragging Lamprus away from his damned library and persuading him to help. These academics are such stick-in-the-muds, aren't they? And once they decide to write a treatise they simply will *not* take a holiday!'

'Uh . . . treatise?' I looked at the man-mountain in sudden horror.

'You mean you didn't know? He didn't tell you?' Gaius was grinning. 'Oh, how simply marvellous! What was its title again, Lamprus?'

'"On the Concept of Being and Non-Being as expressed by the Milesian Philosophers", sire,' Lamprus said. 'And I don't happen to like holidays all that much.'

I goggled at him. 'Being and Non-Being?' I said.

'*To on kai to mé on*, if you want the Greek, sir.' The mound of hair and muscle chuckled into its beard. 'I'm afraid I was playing a joke on you, even if it did serve as a little practical experiment as well. Very childish, of course, but I couldn't resist it. You have my apologies.'

'Uh, yeah. Yeah.' I sat down and poured myself a cup of wine. 'That's okay. Forget it.' Jupiter! They certainly made a pair, these two. Whoever the hell they really were.

Gaius was swinging his leg over the chair-arm, perfectly at ease. 'Now we've got that cleared up, Corvinus,' he said, 'perhaps we'd best get down to business. I really am grateful to you. Terribly grateful.'

'From the sound of it you were doing okay on your own, sir.' I took a deep swallow. Maybe things would seem more normal if I was drunk.

He smiled. 'Oh, we weren't doing too badly. We knew Sejanus was hatching a plot, of course, but we didn't know the precise details because we started at the other end and found ourselves up against a blank wall.' He took a swallow of his own wine.

'Mmm! This Setinian is rather good, by the way. Much better than Grandma Antonia's.'

'Help yourself.' I indicated the jug. 'A blank wall?'

'Our sources told us that Sejanus had co-opted a slimy little ex-city judge called Paconianus and his friend Latiaris to destroy me with Grampa Tiberius, but that was as far as we could get. The pair have been so careful over the arrangements you wouldn't *believe*! *Very* frustrating!'

Latiaris. Now that name rang a bell. Felix was looking at me, an expectant smile on his face. Who the hell was . . . ?

Of course! 'Latiaris was one of the four who set up Titius Sabinus!' I said.

'Quite right, sir!' Felix beamed at me like I was a performing monkey who'd finally managed to perform. 'Oh, well done! I knew you'd get there eventually. You see my reasons for mentioning the name now?'

'Sure.' Jupiter, what an idiot! I'd taken it from the wrong end myself. Felix hadn't been pointing me at Sabinus per se after all, he'd wanted me to think about the prosecutors. And I hadn't, because like the accusers in all the trials they'd simply been 'friends of Sejanus'. 'Next time just draw me a picture, pal. That way something might get through.'

'Actually, it was quite lucky you didn't solve Felix's little clue,' Gaius said. 'As I say, Paconianus and Latiaris were being terribly careful. You might have traced a link between them and Servaeus, but I doubt it. Instead, working from the other end you've given us all the information we didn't have. Not only about the precise nature of the plot but also the name of the assassin and the date. Personally I think that's first rate, my dear, and so much better than just finding mouldy old Paconianus.'

'There's more good news,' I said. 'You needn't worry about Silanus any longer. The guy's bowing out.'

Gaius's interest sharpened. 'You're sure about that?' he said.

'Yeah.' I told him about our interview.

'So Silanus thought he was doing it for me?' The prince frowned. 'A dreadfully stupid man, isn't he? And a positive danger.' He and Felix exchanged glances. Lamprus had glazed over; probably he'd decided the conversation wasn't stretching enough and had gone back to solving the problem of human existence.

Something touched the hairs on the back of my neck. 'Appius Silanus is no intellectual giant, sure,' I said carefully. 'But his heart is in the right place. And he knows better now.'

'Yes, that's true.' The smile was back. 'Perhaps you're right, Corvinus. I'll think about it. The date, by the way, is interesting.'

'Yeah?' I took a swallow of wine. 'How's that?'

'You know that I've been living in poor but honest obscurity with my grandmother since the old empress died?' I nodded. 'Well, Sejanus has been dropping hints that I might be invited to Capri shortly, and on a permanent basis.'

'Uh-huh.' He was right, that was interesting. 'Did he give a reason?'

'Oh, yes.' Gaius threw an arm over the back of his chair. 'He said that Grampa Tiberius felt he should have his beloved family around him in his declining years. Such of them as he'd left alive and at liberty, at least. And that I'd be much more . . . *comfortable* was the word he used, on Capri than at Rome. For which, of course, read isolated from my treasonous friends and wellwishers.'

'So the plan was that you arrive on Capri, closely followed by Silanus with his poison-pen letter. He tries to stab the Wart and then says he did it all for you.' I nodded. 'Yeah. That fits in nicely.'

'It does. Sejanus would have me bang to rights, as I believe they say. Caught' – Gaius gave a shudder – 'in flagrante delicto, and ripe for the plucking. Nasty but neat. Oh, dear, the man really is such a clever bastard, isn't he?'

'Yeah.' I was thinking hard. 'Yeah, he is. Still, it may solve one problem.'

'Oh? And what's that?'

'My ticket to Capri.'

'But why should you want to go to . . . ?' Gaius's brow cleared. 'Oh. Yes, but of course you would. I'm sorry, Corvinus. Now I'm the one who's being stupid.'

Uh-uh. That I wouldn't believe. Prince of the Blood or not, Gaius was a smart cookie. He just didn't look very far outside his own interests.

'I've got everything now,' I said. 'Or at least I think I have. In any case, it's all I'll get. My only problem is delivering it to the emperor, and I have to do that personally.'

'Part of your agreement with Great-Granny Livia, I suppose?' He smiled. 'Oh, Corvinus, *don't* look at me like that, my dear! Of course I know! The old harpy told me about it herself years ago.'

'She told you?'

'Oh, yes. We used to have such cosy chats about all sorts of things after Mother was exiled and she became my guardian. After all, if I was to be emperor one day I had to know what was going on, didn't I?'

'You . . . ah . . . you're going to be emperor,' I said as neutrally as I could manage.

'But naturally!' Gaius's eyes widened. 'At the very least! I've known *that* since I was a child.'

'"At the very least"?' I glanced at Felix, but he was carefully looking the other way. Lamprus was still communing with the celestial spheres. 'Uh . . . correct me if I'm wrong, sir, and no offence, but I sort of thought being emperor was top of the ladder.'

'Not in my case.'

'Ah.' Jupiter with little bells on! And Lippillus had said his brother Drusus was the crazy of the family! 'Fine, fine.'

'Besides,' Gaius went on, 'Thrasyllus said so. About the emperor part, anyway. And Thrasyllus isn't wrong, ever.'

Oh, yeah. The Wart's tame astrologer, the one Livia had been so impressed with. I edged my chair back a little. If the guy started talking about little green worms coming up through the floor I wanted room to move.

'Did Thrasyllus, uh, give you a date for this?' I said carefully.

'No, the old meanie. And he wouldn't say how long I'd last or who'd come after me, either. I told him I'd hand him over to the torturers and have them crack his crystal balls for him unless he made that my accession present, but he just said he'd be dead himself by then so I could do what I liked and sucks to me.' Gaius laughed. 'It's all silly. Don't let's talk about it. Now. How are we going to get you into Capri?'

My brain had gone numb. 'Capri?'

He sighed and held out his cup. Felix rushed over with the

wine. 'Corvinus, now don't *you* go stupid on me, dear! You were the one who mentioned the place, after all. You'll need a passport, of course, and you can't go as yourself, not with this treason thing. And an ordinary slave or freedman is really out, because you're so obviously Roman-stroke-Italian the guards wouldn't be fooled for a moment. Felix?'

The little guy was topping up my cup on the rebound.

'A consultant of some kind, sire?' he said. 'One of your personal retinue?'

'Mmm. That's a possibility.' Gaius took a reflective sip of his wine, 'A hairdresser, say. My professional hair stylist. Sejanus would love that, he's always getting nasty digs in with Grampa about me being too soft.'

'That would be admirable, sire,' Felix said.

They were both looking at me like I was the ape in Lucullus Gardens. I cleared my throat.

'Yeah,' I said. 'Okay. Whatever. So long as you don't expect me to do any barbering.'

'My dear man, I wouldn't let you anywhere near my hair!' Gaius chuckled. 'Very well. That's settled. I'll make the arrangements when necessary, and Felix will be in touch.' He stood up. 'Now we'd better be getting back, I suppose. Grandma Antonia will be worrying.'

'I'm sorry, sire,' Felix murmured. 'One more thing. You were going to tell Valerius Corvinus about . . .' He paused.

'What? Oh. Oh, yes. Silly of me. Our most recent acquisition.' Gaius set his cup down on the table. 'You said you had everything you were going to get for Grampa, Corvinus. Not so, my dear, not so at all, not by a long chalk. I really think you should talk to the cook at . . .' He turned to Felix. 'Where is the place?'

Felix smiled at me. 'The Plum Tree, sir. It's a cookshop off Cattlemarket Square, near the Temple of Fortune.'

'Yeah. I know the district,' I said. 'A talk about what?'

'The man's name is Lygdus,' Gaius said. 'And you'll come as a surprise to him, by the way, because he doesn't know we've dug him up, so do tread very carefully, won't you, love?'

'Sure.' The name didn't ring any bells at all, not even faint ones. 'You want to tell me who he is?'

'No.' Gaius smiled slightly. 'We'll leave that part as a surprise.

A sort of thank-you present for services rendered. Don't mention my name, or Felix's, just get him somewhere he can't run and whisper one word to him. I think you'll enjoy the result.'

'Yeah? And the word?'

The prince's smile broadened.

'Stibium,' he said.

I got him to repeat it, but I'd heard it clear enough the first time.

'And what the hell is stibium when it's at home?'

'You don't know, Corvinus? Then think of it as another surprise. Lygdus certainly will.'

31

I felt a bit chary about walking the streets during daylight hours, especially since to get to Cattlemarket Square I'd have to go past the centre of town, but I kept to the alleyways on the river side of Tuscan Street where you're about as likely to see a pig playing a tambourine as a striped mantle. The Plum Tree wasn't easy to spot, but I finally tracked it down: a scabby-looking cookshop squeezed between a pork butcher's that seemed to deal mostly in fly-covered tripe and a tenement I didn't dare lean against in case I knocked it over. There were no customers outside, which didn't say much for the culinary standards or the quality of the wine. I couldn't see any sign of the eponymous tree either, but there was a stump of wood sticking out of the pavement by the door so maybe they'd just kept the name for luck. It sounded better than the Wall-Eyed Sicilian, anyway, which from the look of the owner was another possibility.

The guy with the strabismus was shifting the grease on an outside table with a rag that might've started life as a breech-clout. When he saw me hovering he came over so fast that he blurred. Business must be bad right enough.

'You want to sit inside, sir?' he said. 'Pork liver rissoles, fresh today. Best Himeran wine, five years old.'

I took out my purse. 'Maybe later, friend,' I said. 'After I've seen your kitchen.'

He stared at the coin I held up – it would've paid for a meal three times over, easy – and his jaw dropped.

'You what?' he said.

I gave him my best smile. 'Call it a hobby. Some people look at statues, some people collect paintings. Me, I like looking round kitchens.'

The Sicilian gave me a hard stare, then shrugged, put the cloth down and held out his hand.

'Suit yourself,' he said. 'Follow me.'

'There's more.' I didn't move. 'I like to look at them alone, in private, and for an indefinite amount of time. Without interruptions.'

The wall-eye shifted. 'You serious?'

'Sure. I find it's much more satisfying that way. It conserves the ambience.'

His good eye was still on the coin. 'Shit!' he murmured. 'Capuans!' Then: 'Go ahead, pal, straight through the back. Don't mind me, I just own the place. Take as long as you like and enjoy.'

'Thanks.' I flipped him the silver piece and went inside.

There weren't any customers there, either, and from the looks of the room I wasn't surprised. Even the punters who hang around Cattlemarket Square have some standards, and they'd have to be drunk or desperate to patronise the Plum Tree. Cockroaches scuttled off the tables in dozens as I came in, but maybe they weren't so choosy. I followed my nose. Kitchen this way.

A tall thin guy was frying rissoles on a skillet. He turned round.

'Lygdus?' I said.

The skillet rang on the floor. He stared at me, his eyes wide.

'The name's Myron,' he said at last.

Too late, too nervous. 'Sure,' I said, 'and I'm Cleopatra's grandmother.' I'd already checked the place out. I was standing right across the only exit, and there was no one else here but us, the rissoles and the cockroaches. 'You and me are going to have a little talk, friend. About something called stibium.'

It must've meant more to him than it did to me, because his eyes went up under the lids and he crumpled. I stayed put in case it was a trick, but he was out for the count. I moved over to him, lugged him on to a stool, and slapped his cheek.

'Come on, pal,' I said. 'Wake up.' I noticed an old slave mark on his forearm: the initials DC.

His eyelids flickered open and he wet his lips with his tongue. 'How did you find me?' he whispered.

'Call it divine intervention. You okay now?'

'Yes.' He was shaking so hard his teeth were rattling. 'How did you *know*? It's been . . .' He swallowed, and the whites of his eyes showed again.

I had to go easy here. Damn Gaius, he could at least've given me some sort of a hint, but the name Lygdus and this whacky stibium stuff was it. If the word was Latin I'd never heard it, but probably it was one of the considerable number of Greek words that I still didn't know even after ten years of being bored to death by Perilla's philosopher pals. Sure, the guy was terrified and he had beans to spill. Trouble was, I hadn't the slightest idea what jar they came from.

'Never mind how,' I said. 'I know. And the emperor's going to find it pretty interesting too when I tell him.'

He gave me a look of pure horror. 'You'd tell Tiberius? Please, sir, it wasn't my idea, I only did what I was told. It was Eudemus and the mistress.'

Eudemus? Who the hell was Eudemus? A Greek, sure; but freedman? Slave? And the mistress . . . I tried not to let the puzzlement show in my face, but I needn't've worried: Lygdus was past playing games. The guy was in shock.

'Eudemus said there was no way of detecting it,' he said. 'None! He wasn't even suspected, none of us was, the death was put down to natural causes.' He was practically babbling. 'How can anyone know now, after eight years?'

I sat back, my brain numb. That made two of us in shock now. Oh, shit. Oh, Jupiter best and greatest. The mistress. Death by natural causes. Eight years. DC. All that could add up to just one thing.

He was talking about the Wart's son Drusus.

While he gibbered away I tried to remember what I knew already. Drusus had suffered from a chronic illness, something intestinal that had nearly carried him off ten years before. He'd survived that bout, only to succumb to a second attack two years later, and everyone had believed – still believed – that the death was natural. There was no question of poison at the time or subsequently, not so much as a hint or a wineshop rumour; I remembered Lippillus saying that when we'd first talked two months ago. Only now it transpired that the guy had been murdered after all. More: from Lygdus's mention of the mistress one of the murderers had been his wife Livilla. Who, much later and after a great deal of badgering on the Wart's new deputy's part, had finally been betrothed to Sejanus . . .

Gaius was right; this was major stuff. It put the lid on the case and screwed it down tight. When it got to Tiberius that Sejanus had rubbed out his only son and heir – and I'd wager a hatful of gold pieces to a bent cloak-pin that he'd been behind it – the Wart would cut the bastard's throat personally and whistle while he did it.

'Okay, pal,' I said. 'Let's have the whole story.'

Lygdus stared at me.

'But you said you *knew*!' he whispered.

'So I lied. You murdered Drusus, or helped murder him; that much I do know. And believe me it'll be enough for the emperor, too.'

'But I didn't!' He pulled his knees close in and hugged them. 'It was the mistress and Eudemus! I only . . .' He stopped.

'You only poisoned the guy's porridge. Sure.'

His eyes widened. 'You're playing with me, aren't you?' he said.

'I am?'

'You know about the porridge!'

Jupiter! 'You mean that was how it was done? Seriously?'

'Yes, of course. The master liked his porridge made with spelt. I put the stibium in that. A little every morning.'

'Uh-huh.' Yeah, well, we were getting somewhere, anyway. The stuff was some kind of poison right enough. 'Who's this Eudemus?'

'The master's doctor.'

That made sense. A doctor would know about poisons – who better? Also when Drusus did fall ill he'd be the one to advise what to eat and what not. For an invalid he'd recommend a bland, simple diet; more spelt porridge, for example . . .

'He's still in Rome?' I said.

'I don't know. Probably. With the mistress.'

'Who's now betrothed to Sejanus?'

A long pause. 'Yes.'

'And they fixed this up between them? Livilla, Sejanus and the doctor?'

'Yes.' It was a whisper.

Jupiter! It added up! The timing and everything! Sejanus had had to go carefully; sure, Drusus had to die, but he couldn't die quickly because that would've raised unwelcome suspicions and anyway Sejanus had needed the time to consolidate his own position. Livilla was an ambitious bitch, I'd known that for years, ever since I'd talked to Gaius Secundus, in fact: the guy with the shattered leg who'd served with Drusus in Pannonia. She'd thrown in with Sejanus because the Wart was grooming Agrippina's two eldest for eventual succession after Drusus, leaving her boy Gemellus out in the cold. And Sejanus, for all his faults, was a real tomcat . . .

'Sejanus and Livilla were having an affair,' I said. 'Before Drusus died.'

'Yes.' Lygdus had given up. He sat slumped on the stool like a bag of flour.

'So they murdered him together. And then they began working on Tiberius to allow them to marry. Sejanus would have the imperial connection he needed to legitimise his succession, Livilla would found a dynasty instead of simply being the wife of a caretaker emperor.'

'Maybe.' Lygdus shrugged. 'If you say so. The mistress wanted him for himself. That's all I know.'

'Yeah.' I looked at him. The poor guy was a weed, a long strip of dripping, and not the murderer type. He reminded me a lot of Celsus. 'So. How did you get out?'

'I ran. It was simple enough. I'm not a fool, I knew some day there'd be an accident. Suburinus, the man who owns this place, knew I was a runaway slave, but I'm cheap. I work for my keep and no more so he's happy. It's better than being dead, anyway.'

'Uh-huh. He know whose slave you are?'

'*No!*'

I nodded. No, he wouldn't, no way: you didn't mess with imperials. 'DC' could stand for anyone, and cheap labour didn't grow on trees.

Lygdus had been watching me.

'What are you going to do?' he said.

It was a question I'd been putting off asking myself. I couldn't leave the poor sod where he was, that was for sure. The minute my back was turned he'd head for the tall timber and I could whistle for my proof. At the same time, I wasn't under any illusions as to what Tiberius would do to a runaway slave who'd poisoned his son's breakfast; and I wouldn't wish that kind of death on anyone.

Hell. I had the details and I had the name of the doctor. That would have to be enough for the Wart. He could do his own dirty work.

'Can you write?' I said.

'No.'

'Yeah, I thought not.' I sighed. 'Just an idea. Okay, pal, what happens now is that I walk out of here and you rescue what's left of those rissoles from the cockroaches.'

He stared at me. 'You mean that?'

'Sure. They can't taste any worse than they probably would've anyway. Oh, by the way. What is stibium, exactly?'

'A kind of glittering metallic sand, Corvinus. It's mined in Asia Minor, among other places. Including Pannonia, incidentally.'

I whipped round. Felix was standing in the doorway. He wasn't smiling.

'The Greeks call it wide-eye,' he went on, 'because it's used to make eye-shadow paste; your wife probably has some in her cosmetic box. It's also, so I understand, employed medicinally as an astringent. For external application only, of course.'

No point asking the guy what he was doing here. I'd half expected he'd follow me anyway. Gaius was the type to keep a check on his investments.

'You're telling me Drusus was poisoned with make-up?' I said.

'More or less. Amazing, isn't it?' Felix came in and hoisted himself on to the kitchen table. He hadn't looked at Lygdus, who was staring at him open-mouthed. 'Actually, Eudemus was being extremely clever, and it explains why no one suspected poison at the time. A single large dose would've produced obvious symptoms, naturally, but the effect of many small doses was cumulative and gave the desired impression of chronic illness. Drusus died very slowly, Valerius Corvinus, over a period of months, if not years, and his murderers watched him die. That's not pleasant. Personally I wouldn't waste my sympathy on them.'

Uh-huh. 'Where's your friend Aristotle?' I said.

'Intimidating the owner. But he's within call, so I really wouldn't recommend any heroics.'

Yeah, well, it was worth a try. Unless he was lying again, but I wouldn't've liked to risk it. I turned back to Lygdus. The guy had gone as grey as his rissoles.

'I'm sorry, pal,' I said. 'It seems I've been overruled.'

'Indeed you have, sir.' Felix glanced at the slave. 'If you've finished your questioning we'll take over now. Don't worry, we'll keep him safe. Until he's wanted.'

I could've gone for him, sure, but it wouldn't've done any good, even without Lamprus waiting outside. Gaius would make a bad enemy, and I had more of these already than I could handle. Not that those excuses made me feel any better, mind.

I walked out without a word.

32 ∫

I spent an anxious month twiddling my thumbs. Here I was with all the proof I needed to grease Sejanus's wheels and I couldn't do a thing with it: now his spoof assassination had fallen through Sejanus had no reason to send Gaius to Capri, and if Gaius didn't go then I was screwed totally as far as seeing the Wart was concerned. Also there was Appius Silanus himself. The featherbrain might not blow the whistle on me of his own accord, but it didn't take much nous to see that five minutes after he'd told his ex-pal Servaeus where he could stick his special dagger Sejanus's frighteners would be round to ask why he'd changed what passed for his mind; and under that sort of pressure I reckoned our purple-striped Adonis would cave in faster than an egg under a marble cart. No, by this time Sejanus would know if he didn't already that Corvinus was alive and very definitely kicking. I just hoped he hadn't linked me with Gaius, because if so the pair of us were cooked.

It was a relief when halfway through July Felix brought word that Tiberius had insisted on having Gaius where he could keep an eye on him. The move was still on, and the passports had been approved. We left Rome before the month was out.

I hate travelling, especially slow travelling in convoy, and Jupiter! we were slow. Forget official messengers or two-horse chariots stripped for speed haring down the Appian Road with vital despatches; we had snails laughing themselves sick all the way to Capua. We'd left Lamprus behind solving the remaining mysteries of existence, but as Gaius's tonsorial consultant I shared the last coach with Felix, Gaius's head chef and the Master of the Wardrobe; both unselfconscious lardballs with a penchant for raw onions and cold boiled chickpeas. When the atmosphere got too thick – which was most of the time – I got out and walked. It was faster, anyway.

We took three days to reach Surrentum. I was blistered and footsore, but at least I could breathe. And by that time not even my own mother would've looked twice at me; which was just as well, because the next part was the tricky bit.

I had to hand it to Sejanus. Even with the local mayor escorting us personally security at the harbour was tighter than a constipated gnat's sphincter. The place was crawling with soldiers; not just marines, either, although I noticed a shit-hot little galley moored at the dock, but a detachment of hard-eyed Praetorians who looked like they'd run in their own grandmothers if they couldn't prove identity five ways from nothing. There were enough fishing boats around, sure, but I'd've bet a gold piece to an anchovy that anyone trying to bribe one of the local crab-catchers wouldn't even make it to the gangplank, let alone past the breakwater. As we climbed down from the carriages and Gaius's head slave handed the sheaf of passports to the guard commander I crossed my fingers and prayed to every god I could think of that nothing would go wrong.

I'd need all the divine help I could get, too. The guard commander was moving up the line, checking faces against descriptions. Not a cursory check, either, and he had a gorilla each side of him and two paces behind armed to the teeth and looking like they'd welcome the opportunity of terminating any poor bastard whose face didn't fit. I started to sweat. Maybe this wasn't such a hot idea after all. Maybe I hadn't been as smart as I thought. Maybe Sejanus had made the Gaius connection or traced me some other way and he'd simply given orders for me to be picked up at the boat. If so then I wouldn't even live long enough to wonder where I'd screwed up.

'Marcus Ufonius?' The guard commander's eyes were two chips of ice that flicked down to the passport and back to me.

'Yes, sir,' I said.

'You're a Capuan?'

'That's right.'

'You don't look it.'

I swallowed. Beside me I felt Felix stiffen.

'My father was Roman, sir. A senator, I understand. My mother was a laundress.'

'Uh-huh.' The eyes raked me again. 'So where's Harmodius's wineshop, then?'

'Off the main square, sir. By the Shrine of the Graces.'

He grunted. 'And the Statue of Pan?'

Oh, Jupiter! Dear, sweet Jupiter, do something! Capuan wineshops I could handle. Statues were another matter. I weighed up my chances of punching the guy in the throat and making a successful run for it. They were as close to zero as you can get. The silence lengthened . . .

At which point the chef – the only one of us left for vetting – belched and broke wind simultaneously, spilling a foetid smell of onions across the dock.

'Jupiter!' The guard commander fanned the air, scowled at the glassy-eyed chef, then snapped at the sniggering Praetorians behind him: 'All right. That's it. Let them board.'

I shuffled gratefully forwards. It's times like these when I feel that maybe there's something to religion after all. Sure, my flatulent pal's performance had probably been due to nerves, but it'd taken the soldier's attention off me when I least wanted it, and after all the fate of Rome had been in the balance there. For a manifestation of the divine it'd been unorthodox, but gods have their own way of doing things, and if I'd just witnessed a minor miracle then who was I to scoff. I offered up a quick but sincere thank you to Aeolus and boarded the ship.

Capri is something else. It rises blue-grey and sheer out of the sea three miles from the Italian coast, and there're cliffs everywhere except for the main harbour in the north and a cove on the south side where boats put in in bad weather. Both places are watched, seriously. Try landing anywhere else and even if you escape the patrol boats by the time the sea and the rocks have finished with you there'd be nothing to arrest. We were getting close. I could see a lighthouse at the point of the cape, and the sun glinting on white marble.

'That where we're headed?' I said to Felix.

'Yes, sir.' He motioned with his head: we were both talking in whispers. 'You can just see the road up from the harbour. That's the emperor's main villa. He has others, of course.'

'Is that right? How many?'

'Twelve, I believe.'

'*Twelve?*' Jupiter, I didn't think the Wart would stint himself, but twelve luxury villas on a piece of rock this size was pushing it. How did he fit them all in? 'Why the hell does he need twelve?'

'For guests. And, now, family. However, I suspect we'll be staying at the main one for the time being. You'll like it, sir. It really is very beautiful, by all accounts.'

'It'll make a change from the Subura flat, sure.' Well, I suppose he was trying to sound encouraging, but as far as I was concerned you could take the whole boiling and drop it down a very deep hole. I was wondering what Perilla was doing now. And whether I'd ever see her again.

We docked, and more sharp-eyed Praetorians double-checked the passports. I noticed that even Gaius was looking pale and preoccupied. I didn't blame him: Sejanus was the Praetorian commander, and these guys would be hand-picked for loyalty. Maybe we were on a hiding to nothing after all, and Tiberius was a prisoner of his own bodyguard; in which case Gaius was up shit creek without a paddle and I'd shoved my head into a noose and handed Sejanus both ends of the rope.

The trip up to the villa through two hundred vertical feet of formal gardens didn't offer any more encouragement. Once we were away from the quayside the only people we saw were slaves and soldiers, and there were more uniforms around than homespun tunics. Not friendly, either. From the way those bastards eyed you you knew they'd take you out just to break the endless monotony. Sure, the villa was beautiful, although not flashy – the Wart's dislike of flash was no pose – but I hated it like poison already. The whole thing was a gigantic trap, and you knew the further you went into it the more impossible it would be to get out again.

'Servants' quarters are in the south wing,' said the major-domo who met us in the colonnaded portico when we reached the top. 'You'll be escorted. Rooms have been assigned. Please keep to the designated areas unless you have specific duties elsewhere.' He didn't say what would happen if we were stupid enough to go walkabout, and no one asked. That was another thing that was understood. The sea was a long way down.

'The master has arranged for us to share, sir,' Felix murmured. 'We thought it safest. I hope you don't mind.'

'So long as you don't talk in your sleep, pal,' I said. Better than bunking down with the head chef, anyway. I may have owed the guy, but gratitude only goes so far.

'Of course not!' Felix looked like I'd impugned him professionally; but then again maybe I had. 'In any case it should only be for a few days. We'll be moving to one of the other villas shortly.'

I tagged along with the others to the servants' quarters. Being entourage rather than skivvies we shared cubicles rather than dormitories, opening on to a corridor that ran the length of the villa. They weren't so bad. You might not be able to swing even a short cat too confidently and finding space for a portable library might be tricky, but there was a truckle bed each and a shelf for your spare tunic. In Felix's case I'd make that six spare tunics, each one brighter than the last.

From a house on the Palatine to a tenement flat to this. And not a wine jug in sight. Ah, well, there was a moral here somewhere. And it was what I got for mixing with politics.

At least my time'd be my own. Before we left we'd agreed, Gaius and me, on how we were going to play this. No contact, absolutely none. He'd break the ground gradually with Tiberius and send for me when he reckoned the Wart was ready. There was sense in that: I'd only get one shot at it, and if I tried playing a lone game and walking off the boat straight into the old bugger's best sitting-room I'd be fish-food quicker than I could spit. So now it was up to goat-face. I didn't like that more than half, but so long as our interests coincided I thought he would play fair. My worry was that eventually they wouldn't.

Blowing the whistle on Sejanus, however, could wait. First things first. After three hours on a pitching ship my bladder was bursting.

'Hey, Felix,' I said. 'You happen to know where the lavatory is in this maze?'

The little guy was stowing his kit. Six tunics had been on the conservative side: I counted eight, with matching belts.

'No, sir,' he said. 'But I would try further along the corridor.'

'You plan on wearing all of these, by the way?' I said.

He frowned. 'All of what, sir?'

'The tunics.'

'Just because I'm a slave it doesn't mean I have to be scruffy.' He eyed my own tunic and sniffed.

'Uh, yeah,' I said. 'Yeah, I suppose not. Catch you later.'

He didn't answer. I went outside and turned left, looking for relief. Like I say, we'd got a string of cubicles together along the south wall of the wing. The lavatory would be at the end, where the drains could take the effluent straight over the cliff edge.

I found it, just beyond the baths: I could murder a bath, but it could wait. There was another guy on the beams, using the sponge: a broad-built guy with spiky straw-coloured hair and an unshaven chin. I nodded to him and undid my belt. His eyes widened, just for an instant. Then he nodded back, finished quickly and left without a word.

I stood staring after him, bladder forgotten and mind numb. Not for the reason you might think, especially in this den of depravity (if you believed half the rumours at Rome): he'd been looking at my face. I hadn't recognised him, but he'd known me. Sure he had, even under the beard and travel-stains. So much for subterfuge. Less than an hour on Capri and I'd been rumbled.

33

'He recognised you, sir?' Felix looked concerned when I told him, as well he might; personally I was worried as hell. 'You're sure about that? Absolutely sure?'

'Yeah.' I stretched out on my cot. 'It wasn't mutual, though. Maybe we have run across each other in the past, but not recently.'

'Perhaps he mistook you for someone else.'

'Come on, Felix!' I glanced sideways at him. 'Do you believe that? The guy shot off the beam so fast he took the sponge with him. And not in his hand, either. My explanation is that he'd just seen a disguised purple-striper named Marcus Valerius Corvinus relieving himself in a slaves' privy on the emperor's personal island and couldn't wait to pass the news on. What's yours?' I waited; no answer. 'Exactly.'

'I'll make enquiries,' Felix said.

'Screw your enquiries! I don't care who he is. The question is, who would he tell? Because if he goes to the officer commanding the guard then I might as well start running now.'

Felix sighed. 'You wouldn't get five yards, sir,' he said. 'And that would certainly give you away.'

'Congratulations. You've just won the prize for stating the obvious.' I sat up and hit the bed-frame so hard with my clenched fist that I heard the wood crack. 'Of all the things to go wrong! An accident! A pure fluke!'

'You don't know for certain yet that things have gone wrong,' Felix said calmly. 'If they have, they have, but acting on that assumption makes no sense at all, and it's the most dangerous course you could take. Sir.'

'And I thought your pal Lamprus was the philosopher of the bunch.' I stood up. 'Hell, I can't sleep, and I don't want to argue. I'm going outside for some fresh air.'

'It's forbidden.' His voice sharpened. 'There's a dusk-to-dawn curfew. You know that.'

'I'll risk it.' I turned to him. 'Or do you want to try stopping me?'

He sighed again and ducked his head. 'No, sir,' he said. 'Of course not. But if I may say so you're being very, very foolish.'

'Yeah, well. It's better than lying here waiting for the Praetorians. And if I'm going to die I'd rather it was in the open.'

'Now you're being melodramatic as well as foolish.'

I grinned. 'Yeah. I suppose you're right. About that and everything else. But I still need that fresh air. I'll see you later, okay?'

Felix snuffed the lamp. 'I hope so, sir,' he said. 'I really do hope so.'

I walked along the line of cubicles towards the lavatory: there'd been a door next to it, I'd noticed, leading outside.

I found it. The door was unlocked, and it gave out on to a strip of ground between the buildings and a low wall beyond; nothing special, no garden, not in this part of the villa, just plain tussocky grass and stones. It was a beautiful night, windless and almost clear as day with a full moon and stars. I could see the mainland in the distance, black on grey. Down below and to the left a fire burned: a beacon, probably, guiding ships bound for Puteoli away from the rocks and through the straits. A bird flew past, or maybe it was a bat, a fast black dot. Back in the Subura Perilla would be in bed by now and the carts would be starting up.

One difference between Rome and Capri at night was the quiet. You could just stand still and listen and be sure of hearing absolutely nothing moving for miles . . .

The footsteps were coming softly from behind. I turned, and the guy took the last few yards at a run. Instinctively my hand went for the knife I kept strapped to my forearm, but of course it wasn't there: get caught with a weapon, any weapon, on Tiberius's private island and you wouldn't have the chance to open your mouth, let alone use it, before someone shut it for good. Anyway, I was too late and his hands were already closing round my throat.

Jupiter, he was strong! From our short acquaintance in the privy I'd known he was heavily built. Now I could feel it was all hard muscle. I brought my own hands up to break his grip and tried to twist away, but I wasn't used to this rough stuff any more and his knee drove itself into my belly, leaving me gasping. Trying to gasp. I'd lost what air I'd had in my lungs within the first few seconds, and his thumbs pressed into my windpipe were making sure I didn't get a fresh supply. I felt myself lifted, pushed back against the rough masonry of the wall, and the stars began to flicker and go out . . .

Someone pulled me up and a hand slapped me hard across the mouth. I opened my eyes. A leather breastplate with bronze facings. Praetorian.

'Come on, you bastard, you're not dead!' The guardsman slapped me again, backhanded this time, and even harder. 'What the hell was going on here?'

'We were discussing Aristotle's Analytics,' I mumbled. 'What did it look like, chum?'

He dropped me like I was red hot. I stood. Just.

'You're no slave.' He was staring. Shit, I'd forgotten the accent. 'So who are you?'

'Where's the man who attacked me?' I wiped the blood from my split lip.

He jerked his thumb at the wall. 'He went that way. Five hundred feet, straight down. Pure accident. Now.' Slowly and deliberately, he drew his sword from its sheath. 'I asked you a question. Sir.'

I sighed. Well, it was done and there was no point flogging a dead horse. 'Would you believe a hairdresser? Tonsorial consultant, rather.'

He gave me a long, considering look and then spat carefully on to the grass.

'No way,' he said. 'You'd better come with me so we can clear this thing up.'

The cubicle he put me in was even smaller than the one I

shared with Felix. Had shared with Felix. It didn't even have a cot, just some mops and buckets and a foot-square window three-quarters of the way up the wall. I tried pushing at the door but there must've been a bar across the outside. Great. I'd got the only prison cell in the empire that doubled as a broom closet.

I had plenty of time to think. Maybe the guard commander responsible for dealing with purple-stripers who pretended to be hairdressers didn't come on duty until a reasonable hour. Maybe they were just waiting for it to be light enough to see the splash when they threw me off the cliff. It was pointless appealing to Gaius. He wouldn't help me, I knew that, not if he could wriggle out of it; in fact, if he knew I was here already then he was probably messing his privileged pants, because together we'd almost managed to duplicate Sejanus's plan with Appius Silanus. The lack of a dagger proved nothing. To a paranoid old bugger like the Wart that would be a side issue.

Nevertheless, I reckoned my best and only chance was a direct appeal to Tiberius in my own name. It might get me a hearing, at least, and if I could put a spoke or two in Sejanus's wheel before I was chopped then that was all I could expect. Of course, the chances were that whoever commanded the troops was Sejanus's man and knew damn well who I was already. Or could make an informed guess. In which case Tiberius would never even get to know I existed . . .

The sun was streaming in through the window when the door finally opened: the cubby must've faced almost due south, because it'd been light for hours. I stood up from where I'd been crouching on the floor, stretched the stiffness out of my bones and rubbed my swollen lip.

It was the same squaddie who'd arrested me the night before, plus two of his mates. All three had drawn swords and no smiles. This looked bad.

'Come out of there and follow me,' he said.

'You care to tell me where to?' No answer. I'd seen more animated expressions on a set of tree stumps. 'Listen, pal, my name's Marcus Valerius Messalla Corvinus. I'm a Roman knight and I demand . . .'

He reached over and, very carefully, put the point of his sword against my throat. I swallowed and shut up fast. Yeah, well, some you win, some you lose. You never know unless you try.

'Now listen to me,' he said. 'I don't want to hear any fancy lawyer's speeches, and I won't tell you to do something twice. You understand?'

'Yeah, sure.' My eyes were still on the sword. It hadn't moved an inch. 'Got you.'

'So let's go, then.' He took the sword away but didn't sheathe it. The other two squaddies fell in behind me.

We went along corridors, through peristyles and halls and up staircases, always climbing. So it was going to be the cliff for me after all. Well, at least it would be quick. I wished I could've got a message to Perilla, though. Maybe Felix would make one up that didn't sound too unconvincing. I had an idea that the smart little cookie would be good at something like that. All the way through the villa people we passed took one look at us and decided we didn't exist. It was like being a ghost. Well, I could use the practice.

We stopped outside an oak-panelled door at the top of a flight of stairs. My pal from the night before rapped smartly on it with his knuckles, then stepped aside as the door opened.

The walls of the room were made of translucent glass shutters, something I'd never met with before, even in Asia. Most of them were open, and we must've been high up because I could see not only Cape Minerva but all the way across the bay towards Naples. There was only one person present, apart from the slave who'd answered the door: an old man lying on a couch.

'Come in, Valerius Corvinus,' he said. 'I understand that my friend Sejanus is looking for you rather urgently. On a charge of treason.'

34 ∫

Tiberius had been a big man in his day. He was still a big man, even in his seventies, with huge bones, a strong face and massive hands that looked like they could crush marble. He must've given up on the boil plasters, though. Maybe he'd decided just to let his skin erupt and be damned. If so, it was doing a thorough job.

'On the other hand,' he went on, 'my grandson Gaius tells me you've proof that Sejanus is plotting treason himself, and has been for years. A paradox. Do you think we might resolve it together, perhaps?'

I stood gaping. The slave – he looked like a German – softly closed the door, led me to a chair and sat me down.

Tiberius watched, scowling. Neither of us moved. Finally, he said, 'Corvinus. I had you brought here to talk. Now I appreciate that you've gone to a great deal of trouble to reach me, and it would be a shame if I simply handed you back to my guards unheard.' His mouth lifted into something that wasn't qite a smile, showing a single yellowed incisor. 'Delighted although they'd be if I did. So talk, please. Now.'

He waited. I swallowed and opened my mouth, but no sound came out. Finally the emperor shifted irritably on his couch.

'Good Jupiter, man!' he snapped. 'I haven't got all day to waste! Sigmund, put some wine into him!'

The slave poured from a jug on the table and held the cup out to me. I drained it in two gulps and felt the warmth hit my stomach like a velvet club.

'I'm sorry, sir,' I said at last. 'I thought I was going to be executed.'

'What makes you think that you won't be?' The old mouth twisted again, like a pike's. 'In fact, I'd say it was almost a certainty.' He made a sign to the German. 'Pour me one too while you're about it, Sigmund, and damn the doctors.' He waited until the order had been carried out. 'So, then, Corvinus. How did my lads get you, exactly? A fight on the cliff edge, wasn't it?'

'I was attacked, sir. Attempted murder, by a slave. Or possibly a freedman.'

'Whose slave?' The question came fast and hard as a catapult bolt. 'Why?'

'I don't know.'

'You don't *know*?' Tiberius's boil-ridden face flushed and he made a *ttch!* of disgust in his throat. 'Sigmund! Talk to Macro.' The guard commander. 'Find out the truth.' Then, when the slave hesitated: 'Jupiter, go on, man, do as you're told! Valerius Corvinus isn't likely to murder me while you're away.' He turned back to me. 'Or are you, Corvinus?'

'Uh . . . no, sir,' I said. I wouldn't like to try it, either. I'd never experienced Tiberius at short range before, and now I could see how the leathery old bastard had managed to hold the empire together for seventeen years as emperor and almost twice that as Augustus's best general. The Wart would take some killing, and he wouldn't die easy.

The big German left, and Tiberius smiled his fanged not-quite-smile.

'Very well, Marcus Valerius Messalla Corvinus,' he said. 'You have the wine jug beside you and we're alone. So talk.'

Jupiter! Where did I start? 'I've no proof Sejanus is committing treason, sir,' I said. 'None. Apart from the testimony of a couple of slaves your grandson is holding.'

He raised a hand sharply. 'We'll leave Gaius out of this. We were discussing Sejanus. What about him?'

Okay, if he wanted candour he'd get it. Besides, it looked like I had nothing to lose.

'He's plotting to succeed you as emperor,' I said.

'Oh, is that all?' Tiberius grinned at me. I'd expected him to be practically toothless, but he wasn't, far from it: his teeth were strong and yellow, like an old dog's snarl. 'You thought

I didn't know? Corvinus, I may be many things but I'm not a dotard, I'm not a simpleton, and I'm not blind. If Sejanus wants this . . . apology for a life' – I don't think I'd ever heard such contempt in a voice before – 'then he's welcome to it. Only after I've done with it, naturally, and he isn't fool enough to think otherwise. And why shouldn't he be emperor? The man has most of the qualities needed, and at least he's no canting hypocrite like Augustus or a sour, twisted old society-hater like myself.'

I was staring at him. Jupiter! the guy didn't mince words, did he?

'He has his vices, naturally.' Tiberius was looking at me in a speculative way that I found unsettling as hell. 'However, his virtues more than balance them. Ordinary people may not see these virtues for what they are, they may even confuse them with the vices. But an emperor isn't deceived, Corvinus. He makes no mistakes because he has the virtues himself or can appreciate their occurrence in another man if he lacks them.' The upper lip lifted again. 'You'll note that modesty isn't included in the list. On the other hand, ruthlessness and perhaps the capacity for treachery are. Successful treachery, that is, rooted firmly in ambition. An emperor can't be weak, my friend. A weak ruler means a weak state.' He emptied his cup. 'My throat's dry. Pour me some more wine. And fill for yourself.'

I did both. I was feeling pretty fazed. 'Sir,' I said, 'I don't know what to say now. If you've decided, knowing that Sejanus is a traitor, that he'll make you a worthy successor and Rome a good emperor, then most of what I had to tell you isn't relevant. You may as well send me home or execute me now.'

'Don't you presume to advise me, young man!' He frowned and lay back on his couch. 'And don't be too hasty to condemn yourself, either. Haste isn't a virtue, in anyone's canon. Didn't your father teach you that?'

'He tried. Yeah.'

'Tried, did he? Well, that's something.' The frown deepened into a scowl. 'Messalinus wasn't much, but at least he was loyal to Rome. Loyal enough for me to owe his son a fair hearing. So present your case. In an orderly fashion, please.' Then, when I hesitated: 'Corvinus, listen to me. I'll only say this once. When I commanded armies – commanded them directly, I mean, not from a bloody couch – no one ever accused me of unfairness. Harshness, yes, but a general has to be harsh. He can't afford mercy, it's far too expensive in the long run. Nor can he afford to settle for a sanitised version of the truth, because that is even more dangerous. So traduce Sejanus to me as much as you please, so long as the traduction hangs together, and pity help you, young man, if it doesn't! I may interrupt, but it will be for reasons of argument, not of censure. And argument, by Hades, is what you will give me. Is that clear?'

'Clear, sir.' I swallowed. I was gambling with my life here, and I knew it. One false step and I was dead. 'Very well. You know that Sejanus destroyed your adopted son Germanicus? I mean for his own reasons?'

'Yes, I know that.'

'And that he systematically ruined the Julians? Again through his own ambitions?'

'Corvinus.' Tiberius sighed, as if I'd disappointed him. 'I don't share my late mother's personal dislike for Augustus's direct descendants, but I agree with her absolutely that the Julians had and have no divine mandate to rule. They're basically an unstable family and must be judged on their merits as individuals, taking the security of the empire as the one and only criterion. And once judged they must be dealt with accordingly, with no half measures or false sympathy. Now is *that* clear?'

'You include Gaius in that statement, sir?'

'Damn you, I've already said that we'll leave Gaius aside! My grandson is a special case, for reasons I don't wish to discuss with you.' He gulped down his wine and held out the cup. Trying to keep my hand steady, I leaned over and poured. 'Obviously it is *not* clear. Perhaps the fault lies in me, but I suspect the reason is your own stupidity.' I said nothing. 'Very well, I'll put it more plainly. To take the more recent examples. Germanicus was a shallow, idealistic fool. As emperor, he would have been disastrous for Rome, and Rome is well rid of him. Agrippina has far greater possibilities, but Agrippina is a woman, and she hates too openly and with her heart, not her brain. A fatal flaw. Her hatred would corrupt any weakling she married, and she could only bear to marry a weakling. You understand *that*?'

'Yes, sir. I understand.'

'Good. Of Agrippina's sons Nero was a milksop without a mind of his own and Drusus a potential madman who inherited the worst qualities of both his parents. I gave them their chance. They failed the test and were discarded.'

'And Drusus, sir? Your son?'

He was silent for a long moment, a purple flush spreading over his ruined cheeks. Finally he said, too quietly, 'Corvinus, freedom of speech is one thing, but you border on insolence. Drusus died. And he was not a Julian.'

'An assessment. Please.' This was no time for politeness. I might be out of order, but my neck was on the line here and I knew it. Tiberius gave me a long considering scowl.

'Very well,' he said at last. 'My son Drusus would have made an emperor. A good one. Knowing that, I treated him hard, as Augustus treated me. Used him, rather. He survived, as I survived. That is one thing kings and emperors must learn before they become kings and emperors, because once they have supreme power no one else can teach them it. They learn to use others but not to be used themselves, and that last is crucial because above them there is always the state. They may end up hating their teacher, as I hated Augustus, but that is unimportant. The lesson is too vital to be omitted, and far too vital for simple human considerations to affect.' He paused. 'Am I making myself clear now?'

'Yes. I understand.'

His mouth twisted. 'I doubt that, boy. I doubt it very much, but let it pass. None the less it explains why I couldn't care less what Sejanus's motives were in destroying the Julians. They were a needless complication; worse, a danger, because they blinded by their name. Nero and young Drusus served only to train my son for empire. If they had proved themselves, by themselves, one or both of them might have followed him in time. Neither did. Having failed, they had to be removed. Sejanus's methods may not have been my own and he might not have acted' – the top lip lifted – 'purely out of altruism, but in removing them and their supporters he did Rome a favour. Given the choice between a Julian as Rome's next emperor and Sejanus, and lacking a better alternative, I would choose him.'

'Even if you knew that he'd killed your son?' I said quietly.

Tiberius's eyes came up, and I read shock in them. So he hadn't known!

'It's true,' I said.

'Drusus died of a long-term illness aggravated by a fever and chronic fluxion of the bowels.' The Wart's face was impassive and his voice level. As a demonstration of self-control it was impressive as hell. 'My son's death was natural.'

'It was *not* natural! I've talked to the slave who administered the poison.'

'Which was?'

'A substance called stibium.'

He paused. 'Go on.'

'Sejanus seduced Drusus's wife Livilla. They poisoned him together, with the help of his doctor Eudemus. It was done gradually, over a period of years.'

'You can prove this?' His face was a wooden mask, and I could almost feel the effort he was putting in to keeping it that way. 'You had better answer Yes, Corvinus, because all the gods in the pantheon help you if you can't.'

Jupiter! 'I told you, sir. I've talked to the slave. His name is Lygdus and your grandson has him safe in Rome. Yes, I can prove it. No doubt you can question the doctor yourself.' The sweat was dripping from me now. I would've liked to wipe it off with the sleeve of my tunic, but I didn't dare risk it.

Tiberius lay absolutely still, his ice-grey eyes staring straight through me into nothing. Suddenly there was a sharp crack. I looked down at his hand, wrapped massively around his wine cup. Wine was spilling from the crushed silver and running down on to the couch. I doubt if he noticed. There was a long silence.

'Sir?' I said at last. 'Sir?'

The eyes came back into focus.

'Well, Corvinus,' he said. His voice now was dry and level, perfectly controlled. 'My congratulations. You've convinced me.' He picked up a handbell on the table beside him and rang it. The door opened at once and a guard stepped in and waited at attention. 'Publius. My compliments to Thrasyllus. Ask him to step along if he isn't too busy.' He turned back to me as the soldier saluted and left. 'I've changed my mind, young man. Perhaps I should discuss Gaius with you after all.'

35

I poured us some more wine while we waited. It was excellent stuff, Caecuban, from the same cellar as Livia's, but well watered: Tiberius might've been able to hold his own in the Rhine messes thirty years back, but he obviously had to go carefully now.

'You like the view, Corvinus?' he said. He might have been a dinner-party host showing his guest the property, instead of the most powerful man in the world interviewing a condemned traitor.

'Yeah,' I said. I hadn't really been looking after it had first registered. Now I did. The gods must have a view like that, from the top of Olympus. 'It's fantastic.'

'I had this loggia built specially. We're a thousand feet above the sea, and on a good day I can see almost to Naples. Birds fly level with the windows. I could reach out and touch them.' His lips twisted. 'Even wring their necks. Up here it's easy to think I'll live for ever, but of course I won't. In another six years I'll be dead. Or five years, eight months and sixteen days, rather.' I looked at him, but he wasn't joking. The hairs stirred on the back of my neck. 'Don't spread that around, by the way. It's a secret.'

'Uh, yeah,' I said. 'I mean no, I won't. I promise.'

He wasn't listening. He was still staring out over the sea. I didn't dare speak.

'I won't regret giving Capri my death,' he said at last. 'She's done me proud. You know the story of why Augustus bought her?'

I shook my head.

'He was visiting the town when a dying oak tree in the

market-place budded. The superstitious old beggar took it for an omen and exchanged the island with the Neapolitans for Ischia. They had much the better bargain, but they had the sense to keep their mouths shut.' Tiberius chuckled. 'Well, perhaps I shouldn't mock. Perhaps Augustus was right, superstition or not. He certainly lived far past his time. And in this air even the goats reach a ripe old age. If I'm to beat him – as I will – then I need all the help I can get. Perhaps even the Divine Augustus's.'

'What about Rome, sir?' Jupiter! This had to be the wine talking. Watered or not, Caecuban and raw nerves were a dangerous mixture.

Tiberius fixed me with an eye as cold and bleak as a boiled sturgeon's.

'What about Rome, Corvinus?' he said. 'I'll never see her again, nor do I have any desire to. Rome's a stinking sewer populated by sewer-rats. Or do you think I owe her any more blood and sweat than she's had from me already these sixty years past?' He paused. Then, when I didn't speak: 'Go on, man! I don't ask rhetorical questions and I expect straight answers. What about Rome?'

'There've been . . . uh . . . rumours.' Oh, Jupiter! 'About the way you spend your time here. Sir.'

'Oh, yes. The rumours.' The yellow teeth flashed in a snarl. 'That I indulge my depraved tastes with a constant round of perversions. That I live on aphrodisiacs and bugger painted children in the open air.' I said nothing: I hadn't known that he knew. 'Fools can believe what they like, Corvinus. I've never cared about their opinion. And so long as my writ runs and I hold the empire *here*' – he held out a clenched fist – 'I'll take Capri and slander over Rome and the petty squabbles of her fawning lickspittle Senate any day. In the end I'll be judged on my actions and not on wineshop rumours. And if I'm not then the future can go and fuck itself. Clear?'

'Clear, sir,' I said. I was still sweating.

'Good.' He raised his wine cup. 'Now. There must be more in that jug still, even though it is mostly water. We'll drink damnation to slanderers, timeservers and hypocrites. Well-intentioned meddlers, too.'

I poured. There was a knock on the door and an elderly man with a beard came in. He glanced at me, then away.

'You wanted to see me, lord,' he said. His Greek was quiet and sibilant.

'Valerius Corvinus.' Tiberius sipped his wine. 'Thrasyllus of Alexandria. The wisest man in the world.'

'Hardly that, lord.' Thrasyllus smiled and nodded to me.

'Rubbish. If you aren't then who is? You were right, my friend, and I apologise.'

'Right about what?' They were still speaking Greek.

'About Gaius.'

'Ah.' Thrasyllus sat down in a chair with his back to the Bay of Naples. 'Of course I was. I had to be. But apologies are unnecessary, especially from emperors.'

'I didn't bring you here just to apologise.' Tiberius motioned towards me with his wine cup. 'Go on. Tell him.'

Thrasyllus shot him a quick glance, then stroked his beard.

'Everything?' he said.

'Don't be a fool! No, not everything. Just the bare facts.'

The old Greek hesitated. 'If you think it's wise, lord,' he said, 'then certainly, but . . .'

'Do what you're bloody well told!' Tiberius snapped. 'I take full responsibility. Corvinus here has to know what he's asking of me.'

'Very well, lord.' Thrasyllus turned to me. 'Gaius will be the next emperor, Corvinus. Within the next six years. Not for long, fortunately. Four years after his accession the lord's nephew Cl—'

'Stop!' Tiberius held up a hand. 'That's enough. Well, Corvinus?'

I was staring at the two old men in shock.

'How do you know?' I whispered. 'Jupiter, how *can* you know?'

'Thrasyllus told me years ago. Before Drusus died, in fact.' Tiberius was watching me closely. 'He had it from his charts. I didn't believe him then, and later I didn't want to. Especially when he told me what kind of emperor my grandson would be, and how he would die. If allowing Sejanus to have his way would spare the empire *that*' – he spat the word – 'then I was ready to give him his chance. He could be no worse, and the end would've justified the means. However . . . unpleasant these might appear at the time.'

'Lord, you cannot cheat the stars,' Thrasyllus said softly. 'Sejanus has to fall. Has fallen already, in heaven's eyes.'

'I realise that.' Tiberius was still watching me. 'You think I don't? But I would still try, even now. Corvinus, if I'd known what you were going to tell me I would have ordered Macro to throw you over the cliff unheard. I still would, if I thought killing you would do me or the empire the barest scrap of good.'

I was shivering, and the hairs stood stiff on my neck.

'Lord, you cannot cheat the stars,' Thrasyllus repeated. 'Not even you can do that.'

'No.' Tiberius's eyes hadn't left my face, 'So now, my friend, you know just what you're asking of me. I'm going to do exactly what you want me to do; I'm going to destroy Sejanus, root and branch, and the responsibility for what follows will belong to you and to the people who sent you. I won't see the result personally of course, and nor will Thrasyllus, but I wish you and Rome joy of it.'

The soft tap on the door sounded as loud as a hand-clap. I jumped.

'Come in,' Tiberius said calmly. It was the German slave who'd been with the emperor when I arrived. 'Ah, Sigmund. You talked to Macro.'

'Yes, sire.' The German drew himself up. 'The attacker was a slave of Vescularius Flaccus.'

'Good. Thank you. Tell Macro to make sure Flaccus is confined to his rooms until further notice, with no visitors permitted. Then go and ask my grandson Gaius Caesar if he will favour us with an interview.' He turned back to me. 'Flaccus, by the way, is one of my oldest and closest friends. I love him dearly. If it interests you we are now at the start of a witch-hunt, here and at Rome. Several years ago I let Sejanus root out the Julian sympathisers, because there can be only one power in the state. Now I am going to smooth Gaius's path for the same reason by destroying Sejanus's party, completely and utterly. Flaccus is the first. I will be asking both you and my heir-presumptive to supply other names. Be thorough. I expect a full list, and if you're in any doubt then include.' I said nothing; I couldn't have spoken. 'You needn't be present at the family gathering, Corvinus. Your contribution is already made, and the rest is private business. Needless to say, however, I am grateful and I will give instructions for you to be properly accommodated.' His upper lip lifted. 'Not here, naturally, that wouldn't be wise. In one of the empty villas along the coast. In fact . . .' He paused. 'You're married, aren't you? To the Rufia girl, if I remember rightly?'

'Yes, sir.'

'Then give Sigmund her address. Only Sigmund, no one else.' It was an order. I swallowed. 'You'll be staying on Capri as my guest until this business is settled and she may as well join you.'

'For how long, sir?' I asked.

'Thrasyllus?'

'The calculations are already done, lord.'

'Really?' Tiberius smiled thinly. 'You surprise me. The date?'

'October 18th is the most propitious.'

'Two and a half months away.' Tiberius turned back to me. 'Plenty of time for a holiday. And you'll miss the summer heat of Rome, Corvinus. You really are a very lucky young man. Now go, please. Quickly, before I change my mind and have you killed.'

I went.

36

Perilla arrived ten days later, on a private boat sent specially to pick her up at Ostia. I met her at the landing-place, the smaller one on the south coast; Tiberius wasn't taking any chances. She looked thin and pinched, and the shadows under her eyes showed she hadn't slept all that much recently. That made two of us.

We hugged each other for a long time.

'You're all right?' she whispered finally.

'Yeah. I'm fine. You?'

'Happy to be here. Very happy.'

I kissed her and let her go. 'You should see the villa the Wart's given us, lady. I hope you like fancy marble and good bronzes.'

Her fingers were still touching my arm. They were trembling.

'Marcus, when the emperor's messengers came for me in Rome I thought you'd been executed,' she said. 'Even on the boat I wasn't sure.'

I stared at her. 'They didn't give you my letter?'

'Yes, of course. But I only half believed in it. Tiberius might have thought a forged letter would bring me more quietly.'

'Yeah.' I swallowed. Sure, and if things had worked out differently that was just what the Wart would have done. Still, I didn't want Perilla to know how close I'd come. 'That all the luggage you've brought?'

'Yes.'

'Ah, well.' I signalled to the waiting slaves to take up her single trunk. 'We won't be going to too many parties anyway. Jupiter!

I wish this was over and we were back home. I'm sick of hiding in corners.'

'How long will it be? Before . . .' She hesitated.

The litter slaves were waiting, but I waved them on out of earshot. The villa wasn't far, and it was a beautiful day. It was always a beautiful day here. I could see why the Wart preferred Capri to Rome. Not that I shared his opinion. Spectacular scenery's okay to look at, but it doesn't move about all that much, and it doesn't make a noise. 'Before Sejanus is chopped? Two months. That's if everything goes well, of course.'

'*Two months?*' Perilla stopped and stared at me. 'Why so long?'

I shrugged. 'Something to do with sidereal positions. If that's what you call them.'

'*Astrology?* Is the emperor mad?'

'Not so's you'd notice. And don't knock astrology.' It'd saved my life, for a start, although I wasn't going to tell her that. Not for a long time. 'If Tiberius takes his pal Thrasyllus's predictions seriously then I wouldn't lay any bets against them coming true. No bets at all.' The hairs on the back of my neck stirred at the memory. Jupiter! First Gaius, then Idiot Claudius! Maybe we should emigrate to Parthia. 'Besides, two months gives him time to plan.'

'Do you think the emperor has a chance? Really?' She was keeping her voice low. 'Marcus, you must have seen those soldiers on the quayside at Surrentum for yourself. They're Praetorians, Sejanus's men. And Sejanus's word is law in Rome.'

'You haven't met the Wart, lady.' I kissed her on the cheek. 'I'd back that grim old bugger against Sejanus any day, even with the whole Senate and all of the Praetorians in his pocket.' Yeah, well, but I'd keep my fingers crossed all the same. Perilla was right, the guy was dug in as deep as he could get, and if he even suspected that Tiberius was about to cancel his pension for him he wouldn't go without a fight. 'Let's get up to the villa. The holiday starts here.'

Holiday nothing. By the time October came I was twitching. It was like the Subura flat all over again, only what was driving me mad wasn't the confined space but the peace and quiet.

At least in the tenement I could watch what was happening outside the window, maybe broaden my vocabulary when two mule-drivers with full cargoes met head on in the street below. And latterly there'd been the wineshop. Sure, Tiberius's guest accommodation was impressive as hell – better even than I was used to back home – but the guy had us stitched up so tight I couldn't even swap visits with a goat without a passport. Perilla was okay. Half the trunk had been books, and she'd got her writing. Besides, the villa had a library. Me – well, reading isn't my bag, you can only soak up so much fresh air, and when I walk I like to feel limestone flags under my feet. This grass stuff is overrated.

I was getting quietly stewed on the terrace – Perilla was sipping a fruit juice and wrestling with a poem in Alcaean glyconics – when Felix walked in. I hadn't seen him since he'd put out the lamp in our cubby-hole, and I almost swallowed the cup.

'Good evening, sir,' he said. 'Madam. I hope I'm not disturbing you.'

'Uh, no.' I waved him towards a seat. No slaves; even the wine slave had made himself scarce at a nod from Felix. Uh-huh. So this was one of these unofficial visits that weren't actually happening. 'Not so's you'd notice. You know my wife? Perilla, this is Felix.'

'Rufia Perilla.' He ducked his head. 'A pleasure, madam.'

Perilla got up. 'Marcus, if this is business I'll go inside.'

'Really, madam, it's not necessary.' Felix sat down. 'In fact, the emperor told me specifically to make sure you were present.'

'Yeah?' I took a sip of wine. Perilla sat down again. 'So you're working for Tiberius now?'

'No, sir. Perhaps you had better see this as' – he hesitated – 'a joint communiqué. From the emperor and my master together.'

'How is Gaius? Got his first pair of winged sandals yet?'

Felix looked at me. He wasn't smiling now. Not a glimmer.

'Valerius Corvinus,' he said. 'I really would be very careful with the master, if I were you. I won't go into details, but some things you don't joke about, in his hearing or in the hearing of his servants. I say this to you as a friend.'

Jupiter! I remembered what Thrasyllus had told me, and a

cold finger touched my spine. Perilla gave me a sharp look, but I ignored her. 'Yeah. Okay. Forget I said it.'

'I will. Completely. Perhaps that's best for all concerned.'

There was an awkward silence. 'You, uh, want some wine?' I said eventually.

'No, thank you, sir.' The smile came back. 'I only came to tell you the news. The plans have been finalised and the emperor thought you'd like to know what they are.'

'Uh-huh.' I waited.

'You remember Sertorius Macro?'

'The guard commander? Sure.'

'Tiberius is giving him a letter to take to the Senate. A letter which ostensibly – and Macro will be careful to let our friend know this – grants Sejanus tribunician power equal to the emperor's own.'

That made sense. Ever since Augustus the ruling emperor's grant of the powers of a people's tribune had been used to mark the imperial succession. A tribune had the right to veto any motion passed by the Senate, absolutely and without giving a reason. Also he was personally sacrosanct. Offer violence to a tribune and you'd have several centuries' worth of divine law down on your neck before you could spit. There was no appeal, either. Sejanus had been angling for this for years.

'Ostensibly?' I said.

'The letter is Sejanus's death sentence.' That came out flat. 'The first he'll know of the contents is when the senior consul reads it out in plenary session.'

'Oh, Marcus!' Perilla murmured.

I picked up my wine cup then put it down untasted. My ears were buzzing, and the colours around us seemed somehow sharper. Yeah, sure, I'd expected this, but now it'd come it still knocked me for six. Sejanus had been a fixture for more years than I could count. The thought of Rome without him just didn't register. 'What will the Praetorians be doing meantime?' I said. 'Sejanus is their commander. These guys will be on duty inside the House and outside, and Tiberius can't be sure which way they'll jump. If they take Sejanus's part then we're talking trouble, maybe even civil war if he wins free.'

'Macro will carry another letter which he will show to the

Praetorians when Sejanus is safely in his seat. A commission appointing him as Sejanus's replacement. The guards will be told to return to camp with the promise of a cash bounty and their places taken by loyal men from the Urban Cohort.'

Neat. I sat back. It all fitted, and with luck it would work. Sure it would; it had to. And the promise of tribunician power would certainly hook Sejanus like nothing else could. The clever old bugger had done it again.

'There will be no mention of Sejanus's involvement in Drusus's death,' Felix went on. 'Not initially. That subject is . . . delicate.' Yeah. I'd bet, especially with the Wart's niece Livilla as co-conspirator. 'That will come out later. Perhaps a confession might be arranged. A posthumous one.' I felt Perilla shudder. 'Besides, the emperor is most concerned to use Sejanus's fall to strengthen my master's position. The charges against him will concentrate on his unjust persecutions of the Julians.'

'These being the persecutions that Tiberius knew about and encouraged? Including the plot against Gaius himself?'

Felix didn't answer; not that I'd expected him to. I took a swallow of wine, but it tasted sour. Sure, I knew the Wart's reasons and they made all sorts of sense, but the whole thing sickened me to the stomach. Even a quiet knife in the back would be cleaner than this travesty. 'So. When does all this happen?'

'I think Thrasyllus already mentioned the date to you, sir. The 18th.' Five days' time. 'We leave in two days. Perhaps you'd better start packing now.'

It didn't sink in. Not at first. 'You want me to go as well?'

'The emperor thought you would like to be in at the kill.' Felix's lips barely twitched. 'In fact, he insisted on it. He seems to think you deserve most of the credit, and I agree with him. Personally, I'd consider the invitation an honour.'

'Yeah.' I was staring out over the sea. There was nothing between us and Sicily, and the green of the submerged rocks off the coast contrasted sharply with the indigo of the deep sea beyond. 'Yeah. I expect you would at that.'

Perilla reached over and took my hand. She was trembling. 'I'm coming too, Marcus,' she said.

'The invitation was only for one, madam,' Felix said gently.

'I'm sorry, but that's final. You'll be brought back to Rome when it's all over and the city is safe.'

'How soon will we know?'

Felix hesitated. 'I understand the emperor has arranged a series of signal beacons. In the unlikely event that things go wrong. And, of course, a fast galley. The news should be in Capri within a few hours at most.'

'A fast galley,' I said sourly. 'Is that right?'

'So I believe.'

'Bully for Tiberius.' I tipped the cupful of wine on to the ground. 'Only question is, where could the bastard run to?'

37 ∫

We went by road, faster this time because we did the journey on horseback, not in coaches. The Wart wasn't taking any chances of a leak; on his instructions Macro stopped at the last posting-station before the city and sent a message ahead telling the senior consul Regulus to convene the Senate for the next day.

It was good to be back in Rome, but there was no time for walking around. We split up when we got to the Market Square. Macro had his own fish to fry; when Sejanus turned up he'd have to be on hand outside the Senate House to soothe any worries he might have and make sure the guy didn't bolt. Meanwhile I wasn't taking any chances either; I didn't want to be recognised at this late stage, because that would've tipped Sejanus off for sure. Luckily it was a cold day, with the wind blowing from the north, so I could wrap my face in my cloak without looking like a third-rate conspirator. That was even more necessary because I'd had my first shave and haircut for six months: a 'senator' with a curled beard and his hair in a queue would've stood out on the benches like a bull at a eunuch's party as much as one with his head swathed, and without Marcus Ufonius's protective covering it would've been evident to anyone who looked that Corvinus was back in town. I slipped in through a side entrance as unobtrusively as I could and waited in one of the privies until the tiers were full before shoving my nose above the marble barrier.

The consuls' chairs were still empty and there was no sign of Sejanus yet, but evidently news of the letter had spread because the House was stacked and buzzing. Well, mostly buzzing: I found a space on the topmost tier next to a couple of snoring broad-stripers who looked like they'd been there since before Actium. Perfect. A good view, and safe company: I'd bet the consuls could do a strip-tease up and down the gangways blowing army bugles and these two still wouldn't notice. Jupiter knows how they voted them. With pulleys, maybe.

I'd just got comfortable when there was a stir down below and the consuls Regulus and Trio came in, with Sejanus behind them. Macro had done his job well, and the guy looked solidly confident, grinning and shaking hands all round. While Regulus took the auspices and opened the meeting he sat in the centre of the front bench with a smile on his face that would've cracked marble.

Macro came forward with the Wart's letter, saluted sharply and went to deliver his own personal squib to the guard outside. Regulus broke the seal and began to read the contents aloud. Somewhere someone coughed, but it was the only sound in the place. Even my two bench-mates had stopped snoring. Instinct, maybe.

Ten minutes and two pages of undirected waffle later, there was still complete silence: understandable, because when a letter from the emperor is being read out even a cough in the wrong place can be misinterpreted, and broad-stripers learn early to yawn with their mouths closed. I had to hand it to Tiberius. He knew his audience, and he'd managed this brilliantly; the Praetorians would be halfway back to camp by now and their place taken by the troops from the Urban Cohort, while Sejanus still grinned on his bench like a happy tomcat. Even as the first jarring notes crept in no one looked especially concerned; it was only when they began to pile up one on another and squeeze out the waffle that the shuffling and throat-clearing started. Sejanus's smile began to slip, and it went on slipping.

He was grey as death when, a full half-hour into the session, Tiberius finally put the knife in.

'"I am informed, conscript fathers,"' Regulus read in his bland lawyer's voice, '"that without my knowledge acts have been performed in my name contrary to the laws and the well-being of the state. Innocent men have been falsely brought to trial and condemned, plots against my kindred fomented, and power devolved by me in all good faith grossly and callously abused. It is therefore my will and command that the instigator of these acts, my erstwhile representative Aelius Sejanus, be placed at once under restraint and confined to the Mamertine prison until his crimes can be properly investigated and punished."'

Regulus lowered the letter and turned to Sejanus. The coughing and shuffling had stopped, and the silence was absolute.

'Lucius Aelius Sejanus,' he said. 'You heard the emperor's instructions.'

Sejanus didn't move, except to run his tongue over his lips. His face was a mask. The main doors opened and Laco, the Urban Cohort commander, came in with four of his men. He stood silently by the door jamb, his hand on his sword-hilt and his eyes on the consul, waiting for further orders.

'Aelius Sejanus,' Regulus said again. 'You will come here, please.'

Sejanus was shaking his head slowly from side to side as if to clear it. The senators next to him were edging away.

'Sejanus.' Regulus raised his voice; not that it was necessary, you could've heard a pin drop. 'Did you hear what I said?'

The guy was on his own now, the bench he was sitting on empty for two clear yards either way.

'Me?' he whispered, and I could hear the incredulity in his voice even across twenty tiers. 'No, not me. It's a mistake, some mistake. You don't want *me*.'

Regulus made a sign, and Laco stepped forward.

'Take him,' the consul said.

The silence broke. As the soldiers gripped Sejanus's arms and pulled him to his feet the House erupted. Below me an elderly senator suddenly screamed, 'Give him the Hook! Give him the Hook!' Spittle flew from his mouth and hit the bald head of the man in front. Sejanus lifted his eyes, but he was beyond seeing, and if the two guards hadn't been holding him up I'd swear he would've fallen. Beside me, one of the oldsters stirred in his sleep and shouted, 'I agree!' Jupiter knew what he thought he was voting for, but it didn't matter anyway, and I'd had enough. The show was over, and Rome's august Senate could manage things by themselves now. I left before I threw up on the hallowed benches.

*   *   *

Later in the day the Senate reconvened and sentenced him formally to death. Against the Wart's own instructions, and his rule that stipulated a three-day interval between sentence and execution, Sejanus was strangled by the public executioner before sunset and his body dragged down the Gemonian Stairs with a hook in its gullet. I wasn't there, then or later when the celebrations started in earnest. I reckoned I'd played my part already.

38

I was lucky: the house in Poplicolan Street had been sequestrated when I'd been charged with treason, but it hadn't been sold or even had the contents auctioned, and with the Wart's formal pardon tucked into my mantle-fold I could move in straight away. Bathyllus and Meton, too. Maybe it would've been easier to have stayed in the Suburan flat for a few days, but I couldn't do that to the poor guy. He'd suffered enough, and he was pining for his set of matching skillets.

I spent the time catching up. Lippillus was back at work, and now his hair had grown to cover the scars he was ugly as ever. We split a jar of my best Falernian while I filled him in on what he'd missed, and I even got a smile from Marcina. Agron's wife had had a baby girl while I was on Capri, and the big guy was over the moon. When Perilla got back on the 23rd we went down to Ostia together and the kid was sick all over her best mantle. She didn't seem to mind. Yeah, well. At least Agron had the sense this time to keep his mouth shut. His wife had probably had a word with him before we arrived.

Otherwise I didn't go out much. They were pulling down Sejanus's statues and hacking his name off monuments all over Rome, and that I didn't want to see if I could avoid it. The bastard was dead and burned; killing him again in effigy just seemed pointless and spiteful. I thought a lot about Livia, too. Sure, she'd've been pleased we'd won in the end, but I wondered if she'd known about Gaius. Probably, almost certainly; but then the old girl was no Tiberius, she was more of an Agrippina. Livia was a cold bitch, but she also had the capacity for personal hate, whether she recognised it in herself or not. And what better way to destroy the reputation of the Julians for ever than to make their last representative emperor and have him do it for her?

I didn't want to think about Gaius. I didn't want to think about him at all, or about what the future held. I certainly didn't want to see him again. Maybe Thrasyllus was wrong, but the cold finger at the base of my skull told me otherwise. Six years from now Rome wasn't going to be a pleasant place to live.

We were just finishing lunch, Perilla and I, when Bathyllus came into the dining-room to say we had a visitor.

It was Lamia. I was surprised he was still alive, let alone mobile. The guy was a walking skeleton, and his hand when I shook it felt like a thin gloveful of bones. He had the look of his namesake, the witch who sucks children's blood in the stories.

'My congratulations, Corvinus,' he whispered: his voice was almost gone, now, too. 'Arruntius's also, although he's out of Rome at present. I'm sorry, I should have come before. Perilla, my dear. Delighted to see you again.'

I had Bathyllus manoeuvre him on to a couch and help him lie. Beside the dining table he looked like a full-sized version of these silver reminders of death that cheerier guests sometimes dangle at parties.

'Some wine for the governor, Bathyllus,' I said.

'No. No wine. The doctor forbids it. And soon no longer governor, either, even in absentia.' Lamia bared his teeth in a rictus grin. 'The emperor is doing me the honour of appointing me City Prefect. Although I doubt if I'll live to take up office.'

I didn't say anything, nor did Perilla. Even polite noises would've been out of place.

'Well. To the purpose of my visit.' Lamia coughed: the sound was hollow. 'Besides conveying the congratulations and thanks of my colleagues, naturally. I came to tell you the news, if you haven't heard it already.'

'What news?'

'Livilla is dead. Suicide.' He made a vague gesture with his hand. 'At least the official version is suicide. She poisoned herself, I understand, leaving a note for the emperor. An apology and – so it is said – a confession of some kind?' The question was in his voice and his eyes.

There was no reason not to tell him. He'd know soon enough, anyway.

'She and Sejanus murdered Tiberius's son,' I said.

'Ah.' He nodded. 'Yes, that would explain things.' He didn't sound too surprised, but then maybe nothing did surprise a man who was dying slowly himself. 'How was it done?'

I gave him the details, as far as I knew them. No doubt the Wart had already got Drusus's doctor Eudemus. And Lygdus; but I tried not to think about that.

'Then we've made a clean sweep.' He grinned again. 'Cleared the nest out. And the credit, my boy, is entirely yours.'

I shifted on my couch. 'A clean sweep?'

'You didn't know that either? About Sejanus's children?'

I felt Perilla stiffen. Oh, Jupiter! Jupiter, no! 'What about the children?' I said. There were three of them, two boys and a girl. The eldest was seventeen.

'They were executed,' Lamia said. 'Two days ago, by order of the Senate. The mother committed suicide.' He paused. 'A genuine suicide. We had no quarrel with her, and she and Sejanus had been divorced for years, of course; but she seemed to find it necessary.'

My brain had gone numb. I said, and heard my voice saying from very far away: 'The daughter couldn't've been more than twelve. A virgin. The law doesn't allow the execution of a virgin who's also a minor. Your bloody Senate knows that.'

Lamia had the grace to drop his eyes. 'The law was not broken, Valerius Corvinus. The executioner . . . remedied matters before he strangled her.'

Perilla gasped. I looked at her. Her whitened knuckles were pressed hard against her teeth, and I could see blood between them.

Jupiter. Oh sweet, suffering Jupiter. The bile rushed into my throat, and I forced it down.

'Get out,' I said softly. 'Get your stinking, fucking broad-striper carcass out of my house. Or I swear to you, Lamia, I'll kill you where you lie.'

He was staring at me, the eyes bright in his skull-like face. 'But we had to do it, my boy,' he said. 'We couldn't let them live. Not Sejanus's children.'

Bathyllus was standing frozen with the wine jug in his hand. I didn't dare speak, I only pointed. Bathyllus helped the old man off his couch and led him to the door. There, Lamia turned.

'It had to be done,' he said. 'For the good of Rome.'

When he'd gone I went over to Perilla's couch and lay down with her. We hugged each other for a long time, and I let her sob herself quiet against my shoulder while I stared into nothing.

The credit is entirely yours. We had to do it, for the good of Rome.

The good of Rome. Oh, Jupiter. The kid hadn't been Marilla's age, and she'd died for the good of Rome . . .

There was nothing I could do, not now. Tomorrow I'd get Bathyllus to check the sailings to Piraeus. It was nearly the end of the season, but there would be something. If necessary I'd get the Wart to lend me a fucking warship: he owed me that, at least, and he'd probably do it just to be rid of me. We could sell the house through an agent. Palatine properties sold easy, and I knew I'd never want to see Rome again. Not ever.

Marilla . . .

Her father would get the Rock, that was certain: even these days it was the statutory penalty for incest, unless the guy had clout, and Marius had no clout left with Sejanus gone. And now the god-rotting Senate had found a new taste for blood they'd vote him it *nem. con*. Sure, she still had family in Spain, but after what she'd said about her uncle I'd fight that to the death. Further.

'Hey, lady,' I said gently. Perilla stirred. She'd stopped crying now, but her face was still pressed hard into my tunic. 'How does Valeria Marillana sound for a name?'

There was no answer. I hadn't expected one; not yet, not this early. We'd have to give it time. Maybe lots of time.

It wouldn't lay all the ghosts, sure; but then I doubted if anything ever would.

AUTHOR'S NOTE

Sejanus follows on directly from *Ovid* and *Germanicus*, and uses many of the same characters. The historical details are (I hope!) accurate, although the interpretation of them, as in the earlier books, is my own. In this connection I ought to mention specifically the 'Julian scam' linking Asia, the Rhine, Spain and Gaul. I am quite proud of this, but although taken individually the details are correct the existence of the scam itself is pure conjecture. However, if anyone happens to be interested in the theory per se I would direct their attention to an additional oddity which Corvinus didn't unearth, the circumstances surrounding the Frisian revolt of AD28, described in *Annals* iv 72ff.

Like most of the characters in the book, Marcus Valerius Messalla Corvinus actually existed, although in his case (and in Perilla's) I have employed only the name and family connections. Thus having Sejanus accuse him of treason is a complete fiction, albeit not a historical impossibility, since Book Five of Tacitus's *Annals*, the main detailed textual source for this period, exists only in fragmentary form leaving the years AD30 and 31 (when the story is set) sparsely documented. Another slight abuse of names concerns the two Vibii Sereni. In reality both the Spanish governor and the son who brought the case against him in AD24 shared the same name: Gaius Vibius Serenus. Obviously this would have made for confusion in a novel, hence the change of the son's last name (quite arbitrarily) to Celsus.

I also feel a little guilty about my portrayal of the Watch (Vigiles or Cohors Vigilum in Latin). The Romans had a much narrower view of the state's responsibilities in the areas of crime prevention, detection and punishment than we have; there was, for example, no public prosecutor's office at Rome, and even prosecutions for crimes such as treason were initiated by private individuals. Although they did exercise certain policing duties, the Watch's primary concern was fire prevention, while the maintenance of public order was the province of the – purely military – Urban Cohort (Cohors Urbana). The Praetorian Guard was an elite body of troops recruited from the legions, whose prime function – as their name implies – was to guard the emperor.

My only other major assault on historical fact (intentional, at any rate) concerns the revelation of Drusus's murder and its contribution to Sejanus's downfall. The 'real' discovery of the murder actually postdated Sejanus's death, and came through his former wife Apicata's posthumous letter to Tiberius. It is strange but true that up to that time everyone, including the emperor, had believed that the death was natural, and there was no suspicion whatsoever of foul play. As to the poison itself, Tacitus says only that 'Sejanus chose a poison which counterfeited the gradual deterioration produced by natural ill-health' ('*Seianus ... deligit venenum quo paulatim inrepente fortuitus morbus adsimularetur*'), without going into further details. Consequently my suggestion of stibium – antimony, or one of its compounds – rests on no historical evidence whatsoever. I chose it after discussion with a doctor friend, Hamish Leslie, primarily because although the Romans knew of its medical uses – Pliny in his *Natural History* describes it as 'an astringent and coolant' – its long-term deleterious effects, and thus its candidature as a slow poison, seem to have slipped past them unnoticed; at least so far as I am aware. They, like the Greeks, Egyptians and Babylonians before them, used it widely in paste form as eyeshadow, and also in the manufacture of wine flasks.

The two years which followed the closing date of the story (late October AD31) were marked by a series of treason trials aimed at the destruction of Sejanus's partisans, and these I used as the 'quarry' for my villains. Those who died, committed suicide or were otherwise disposed of included Publius Vitellius (suicide), Sextius Paconianus (perpetual imprisonment), Latiaris (death), Quintus Servaeus (condemned but turned state's evidence, implicating Julius Africanus and Seius Quadratus), Appius Junius Silanus (pardoned), Vescularius Flaccus (executed or forced into suicide) and Rubrius Fabatus (perpetual imprisonment). Fulcinius Trio escaped immediate prosecution (although he had a rough ride) but succumbed in AD36, when he was forced into suicide.

Sextus Marius and Marilla require a note to themselves. Marius – who had indeed earlier been accused of involvement with Sacrovir – was thrown from the Tarpeian Rock in AD33 for incest with his daughter; Tacitus says that Tiberius had him killed for his money, but this is a typical Tacitean sideswipe at an emperor whom he disliked. The daughter is not named, but by Roman convention would be Maria. This I didn't want to use, since it would have given rise to too many unLatin overtones. Instead I used Marilla, an alternative Latin feminine form which was not directly derived from the father's *nomen*. Purists will have to forgive me.

One interesting non-victim of the Tacitean trials, from the point of view of my pseudo-history, is Corvinus's uncle Cotta. Not only did Tiberius himself intervene to quash charges against him (among others, casting aspersions on Gaius's manliness, a crime for committing which one of the emperor's oldest friends was later forced into suicide) but he took the almost unprecedented step of having his principal accuser investigated and subsequently put to death. Cotta seems to have wielded considerable influence with Tiberius (because the emperor was grateful to his nephew for services rendered?): in connection with the outcome of a financial dispute with Aemilius Lepidus and the 'real' Lucius Arruntius the same year, Tacitus reports him as saying: '"The senate will support them, but my little pal Tiberius will support me"' ('"*Illos quidem senatus, me autem tuebitur Tiberiolus meus*"'). The Wart did, too, against the justice of the case.

Finally, several thank yous: to Dr Hamish Leslie for keeping me right on the effects of antimony and head wounds; to Roy Pinkerton and Andrew Lang for fielding questions on subjects ranging from provincial governors' dates to the layout of the Villa Iovis in Capri; to my wife Rona for giving me access to books from her library; and finally to the shade of the late Professor Sir Ronald Syme, whose excellent *Augustan Aristocracy* is one of the most-thumbed books in my ongoing reference box.